"A bold new voice in high fantasy."
Lynn Flewelling, author of *The Hidden Warrior*

Resounding praise for

ODALISQUE
and
FIONA McINTOSH

"Fiona McIntosh keeps getting better and better.
Odalisque is fantastic—exotic, even barbaric at times.
The plot is fast-paced, introducing fabulous characters and
sensual settings."
The Advertiser (Australia)

"A magnificent setting. . . . Strong characters and an
enticing plot."
Publishers Weekly

"Fiona McIntosh's books move quickly and unpredictably;
if you are tired of plodding trilogies in which little seems to
happen, [her] books are definitely for you."
Robin Hobb

"McIntosh weaves an exciting, magical tale of forbidden
love, treachery, betrayal, and possession. Fast and furious.
A great read."
Sunday Herald Sun (Melbourne, Australia)

"Nothing short of astonishing. McIntosh weaves
a captivating web."
Bookreporter.com

By Fiona McIntosh

The Percheron Saga

ODALISQUE
EMISSARY
GODDESS
(forthcoming in trade paperback)

The Quickening Trilogy

MYRREN'S GIFT
BLOOD AND MEMORY
BRIDGE OF SOULS

ODALISQUE

*Book One
of The Percheron Saga*

FIONA MCINTOSH

An Imprint of HarperCollinsPublishers

This book was originally published in 2005 by Voyager, an Imprint of HarperCollins Australia.

EOS
An Imprint of HarperCollins*Publishers*
10 East 53rd Street
New York, New York 10022-5299

Copyright © 2005 by Fiona McIntosh
Excerpt from *Emissary* copyright © 2006 by Fiona McIntosh
Map by Matt Whitney
Cover art by Greg Bridges
ISBN: 978-0-06-089911-0
www.eosbooks.com

First Eos paperback printing: April 2008
First Eos trade paperback printing: March 2007

HarperCollins® and Eos® are registered trademarks of HarperCollins Publishers.

Printed in the U.S.A.

10 9 8 7 6 5 4 3 2 1

For Ian . . .
who gave me an old book one evening to browse through,
knowing the Topkapi Palace and its famous harem
would prove irresistible to this writer

N

PERCHERON

GREAT WASTE DESERT

WESTERN FOOTHILLS

WESTERN GATE

STONE PALACE

BARRACKS

ROYAL BOAT YARDS

LAZAR'S HOME

SLAVE MARKETS

PERCHERON BAY

EZRAM

STAR ISLAND

©MATT WHITNEY 2006

EASTERN FOOTHILLS

EASTERN GATE

EX

TAKER'S HOUSE

THE BAZAAR

WELCOME TABLE

SPICE MARKETS

CARAVAN STOP

OCH

SEA TEMPLE OF LYANA

THE
FARANEL SEA

LEGEND
STAIRWAY
MINARET
PALM GROVE
BEACH
ROCKS
BRIDGE

ACKNOWLEDGMENTS

This tale is the result of browsing through a centuries-old travel writer's account of his visit to Constantinople. He was particularly taken by the Topkapi Palace and the once-forbidden hallways of its harem. I followed in his footsteps in 2004 with a lively few days in Istanbul and experienced my own awe at this same palace and its historic city . . . a setting just begging to be absorbed into a fantasy tale.

As always, plenty of people support my efforts and must be thanked, including: Gary Havelberg, Sonya Caddy, Pip Klimentou, and Judy Downs. My thanks to Apolonia Niemirowski for her encouragement and international sleuthing skills in finding every kind of reference material this author could possibly need. Sincere thanks to Matt Whitney, who at short notice leaped at the opportunity to create a map of Percheron; and to Trent Hayes, who continues to keep my busy bulletin board and Web site running smoothly.

A nod to the booksellers around the United States for their boundless enthusiasm for the genre—particularly Steve Hubbard in Minnesota—and to all at HarperCollins—especially Kate Nintzel and Jennifer Brehl.

Special thanks to Chris Lotts in New York for helping to take my work to new markets around the globe . . . it is wonderfully rewarding to hear from readers all over the world.

Finally my love and heartfelt thanks to Ian, Will, and Jack, who keep me firmly in the real world despite my wanderings through make-believe ones.

ODALISQUE

The prisoners, chained together, shuffled awkwardly into the main square of the slave market of Percheron; six men, all strangers and all captives of a trader called Varanz, who had a reputation for securing the more intriguing product for sale. And this group on offer was no exception, although most on-lookers' attention was helplessly drawn to the tall man whose searing, pale-eyed stare, at odds with his long dark hair, seemed to challenge anyone brave enough to lock gazes with him.

Varanz knew it too; knew this one was special, and he sensed a good price coming for the handsome foreigner well worth the effort it had cost six of his henchmen first to bring the man down and then to rope him securely. It puzzled him why the man had been traveling across the desert, of all places—that in itself a perilous journey—but also moving alone, which meant almost certain trouble, particularly from slavers renowned in the region.

But Varanz had a policy of not inquiring into the background of his captives; perhaps to ease his conscience he didn't want to know anything about them, save what was obvious to his own eye. And this one, who refused to name himself, or indeed mutter much more than curses, was clearly in good health. That was enough for the merchant.

Trading for this cluster of slaves opened at the sound of the gong. The Master of the Market called the milling crowd of buyers to order: "Brothers, we have here Varanz Set Number Eight." His voice droned on, extolling the virtues of each on offer, but already the majority of potential buyers were in the thrall of the angry-eyed man, clearly the pick of the bunch and the only one of the six who held his head defiantly high. Sensing a lively auction, the Master of the Market decided to state more than the obvious healthy appearance, strong structure, and good teeth. "He was found emerging from the golden sands of our desert alone, not even a camel for company. Brothers, I'd hazard this one will make a fine bodyguard. If he's canny enough to travel our wasteland and remain as well as he looks, then I imagine he has excellent survival skills."

"Can he fight?" one buyer called out.

Varanz arched an eyebrow and looked toward the slave, wondering whether he'd finally get something out of the man. His instincts were right.

"I can fight," the man replied. "In fact," he challenged, "I demand to fight for my freedom."

A fresh murmuring rippled through the crowd. An oddity in Percheron's slave market was its ancient and somewhat quaint rule that a slave who was captured as a free person had one chance to buy his freedom—with a fight to the death. The Crown covered the cost of his loss, either way, to the trader. It was one of the market's oldest customs, set up by a Zar many centuries earlier who understood that such a contest from time to time would provide entertainment for the otherwise tedious business of trading in human cargo.

Such fights were rare, of course, as most prisoners took their chances with a new life as a slave. But now and then one would risk death in a bid to win back his independence.

Varanz strolled over to the man now that he knew his tongue was loosened. "You understand what you ask for?"

"I do. It was explained to us on the journey here by one of your aides. I wish to fight for my freedom. I also wish to speak with your Zar."

At this Varanz smirked. "I can't imagine he will want to speak with you."

"He might after he watches me best twelve of his strongest warriors."

Varanz was speechless at the man's arrogance. He shook his head and walked to the Master, briefly explaining in a quiet mutter what the slave was proposing. Now both of them returned to stand before the man.

"Don't try and talk me out of it. I want my freedom back. I will pay the price if I fail to win it," the slave warned them.

The Master had no intention of attempting to thwart the prospect of some sport after an already long and wearying day in the market. He could see that Varanz was unfazed, knowing that he would get a good price either way.

"What is your reserve, Varanz?" he asked.

"No less than two hundred karels for this one."

The Master nodded. "I will send a message to the palace for authorization," he said. Then, turning to the man, he insisted, "You must give us your name."

The slave knifed them with a cold gaze. "My name is Lazar."

THE PALACE DID MORE than give authorization. A runner returned swiftly with the news that Zar Joreb, his interest piqued, would be in attendance for the contest. "You understand how unusual it is for the Zar of Percheron to visit the slave traders," Varanz informed Lazar.

The foreigner was unmoved. "I wish to speak with him if I succeed."

Varanz nodded. "That is up to our Zar. We have told him you have offered to fight twelve of his men to the death. This is no doubt why he is coming to witness the contest."

"It is why I suggested so many."

Varanz shook his head, exasperated. "How can you best a dozen fighters, man? There's still time to change your mind and not waste your life. I will ensure a cozy position for you. A fellow like you will find himself in high demand by a rich man to escort his wives, families . . . take care of their security."

Lazar snorted. "I'm no nursery maid."

"All right." Varanz tried again. "I know I can sell you as a high-caliber bodyguard to a man who needs protection whilst he travels. I'll find you a good owner."

"I don't want to be owned," Lazar snarled. "I want my freedom."

The trader shrugged. "Well, you'll have it, my friend, but you'll be carried off in a sack."

"So be it. I slave for no one."

Their conversation was ended by the Master of the Market's hissing for silence—a troop of Percheron's guard had arrived, signifying that the Zar's karak was just moments away. Varanz nodded to one of his aides to escort the rest of the prisoners to the holding pen. Trading would resume once this piece of theater was done with.

"I wish you luck, brother," he said to Lazar, and moved away to stand with the Master, who was marshaling all the other traders into a formal line of welcome. The Zar finally arrived, flanked by several of the Percherese Guard, his karak carried by six of the red-shrouded Elim, the elite guardians of the Zar's harem who also performed bodyguard duties to royalty. The Zar's entry between the slave market's carved pillars of two griffins was heralded by the trumpeting of several of the curled Percherese horns, and everyone who was not attached to the royal retinue instantly humbled himself. No one dared raise his eyes to the Zar until given formal permission.

No one but Lazar, that is.

He was on his knees because he had been pushed down, but he brazenly watched the Zar being helped out of the karak; their gazes met and held momentarily across the dust of the slave market. Then Lazar dipped his head, just a fraction, but it was enough to tell the Zar that the brash young man had acknowledged the person who was the closest thing to the god Zarab that walked the earth.

The guard quickly set up the Zar's seat and the Elim unfurled a canopy over it. Zar Joreb settled himself. He had a wry smile as the Master of the Market made the official announcement that the prisoner, Lazar, captured by Trader Varanz, had opted to fight for his freedom against a dozen warriors from the Percherese Guard. No one watched the Master or even the Zar. All eyes were riveted on the dark foreigner, whose wrists and ankles were now unshackled and who was disrobing down to the once-white, now gray and dirty loose pants he wore. They watched his measured movements, but mostly they watched him study the twelve men taking practice swipes with their glinting swords, all bearing smirks, none prepared to take the ridiculously outnumbered contest seriously.

The gong sounded for silence and the Master outlined what was about to happen. It was a superfluous pronouncement but strict protocol was a way of life for Percheron's various markets, especially in the hallowed presence of the Zar.

". . . or to the prisoner's death," he finished somberly. He looked to Zar Joreb, who, with an almost imperceptible nod, gave the signal for combat to begin.

Those who were present at the slave market that day would talk about the fight for years to come. Lazar accepted the weapon thrown toward him and without so much as a hurried prayer to his god of choice strode out to meet the first of the warriors. To prolong the sport, the guard had decided to send out one man at a time—presumably they intended to keep wounding the arrogant prisoner until he begged for mercy and the deathblow. However, by the time the first three men were groaning and bleeding on the ground, their most senior man hurriedly sent in four at a once.

It didn't make much difference to Lazar, who appeared to the audience to be unintimidated by numbers. His face wore the grim countenance of utter focus; he made no sound, never once backed away, always threatening his enemy rather than the other way around. It was soon obvious that his sword skills could not be matched by any of the Percherese, not even fighting in tandem. His fighting arm became a blur of silver that weaved a path of wreckage through flesh, turning the dozen men, one after another, into writhing, crying heaps as they gripped torn shoulders, slashed legs, or profusely bleeding fighting arms. To their credit, the final two fought superbly, but neither could mark Lazar. He fought without fear, his speed only increasing as the battle wore on. Cutting one man down by the ankle, Lazar stomped on his sword wrist, breaking it, to ensure he did not return to the fray, and some moments later, fought the other into exhaustion until the man was on his knees. Lazar flicked the guard's sword away and gave a calculated slash across his chest. The man fell, almost grateful for the reprieve.

The slave market was uncharacteristically quiet, save for the cries of bleeding, paining men. Varanz looked around at the carnage, his nostrils flaring with the raw metallic smell of blood thick in the air, and he raised his eyebrows with surprise. No one was dead. Lazar had mercilessly and precisely disabled each of his rivals but claimed the life of none.

Throwing down his sword, Lazar stood in the circle of hurt warriors, a light sheen of perspiration on his body the only indication that he had exerted himself. His chest rose and sank steadily, calmly. He turned to the Zar and bowed long and deeply.

"Zar Joreb, will you now grant my freedom?" he said finally into the hush that had fallen.

"My men would surely rather seek death than live with the dishonor of losing this fight," was Joreb's response.

Varanz watched Lazar's curiously light eyes cloud with defiance. "They are innocent men. I will not take their lives for a piece of entertainment."

"They are soldiers! This was a fight to the death."

"Zar Joreb, this was a fight to *my* death, not theirs. It was made clear that I either win my freedom through death or through survival. I survived. No one impressed upon me the fact that anyone had to die as part of the rules of this custom."

"Arrogant pup," Joreb murmured into the silence. Then, impossibly, he laughed. "Stand before me, young man."

Lazar took two long strides and then went down on one knee, his head finally bowed.

"What is it you want, stranger?" the Zar demanded.

"I want to live in Percheron as a free man," Lazar replied, not lifting his head.

"Look at me." Lazar did so. "You've humiliated my guard. You will need to rectify that before I grant you anything."

"How can I do that, Zar Joreb?"

"By teaching them."

Lazar stared at the Zar, a quizzical look taking over his heretofore impassive face, but he said nothing.

"Become my Spur," Zar Joreb offered. "Our present Spur must retire soon. We need to inject a fresh approach. A young approach. You fight like you're chasing away demons, man. I want you to teach my army how to do that."

Lazar's gaze narrowed. His tone sounded guarded. "You're offering to pay me to live as a free man in Percheron?"

"Be my Spur," Zar Joreb urged. This time there was no humor in his voice, only passion.

The crowd collectively held its breath as Lazar paused. Finally, he nodded once, decisively. "I accept, but first you owe Varanz over there two hundred karels apparently."

Joreb laughed loudly in genuine amusement. "I like you, Lazar. Follow me back to the palace. We have much to speak of. I must say, I'm impressed by your audacity. You put your life in danger to get what you want."

"It was never in danger," Lazar replied, and the semblance of a smile twitched briefly at his mouth.

1

FIFTEEN YEARS LATER . . .

The Spur of Percheron was oblivious to the clandestine attention he was being paid from the city's favorite ratha emporium. Inside its kitchens a pair of women feasted their eyes on Percheron's most eligible bachelor while patrons took similar pleasure in the sisters' celebrated spicy pancakes.

The two women had been preparing since before sunrise for the busy morning trade. For years they had created what was considered by many to be Percheron's finest hot rathas, and as a result it was commonplace to see a long line patiently shuffling closer to the counter where the women's husbands took the orders. The wealthier patrons often sat at some of the small tables on offer and paid a premium for the privilege of being served their steaming rathas on warmed plates accompanied by mouth-watering sambas and chutneys.

Though the sisters never had any dealings with the customers, they seemed to know them as well as their husbands did.

This was because the open windows that allowed fresh air to blow through the busy kitchen also afforded a splendid close-up view of Percheron's city folk at work and play. With their hands lively about their work, so skilled in it now that their fingers required no thought or supervision, the sisters had become keen observers.

And no one gave them greater pleasure to watch than the revered Spur of Percheron, the long-legged, raven-haired former prisoner turned brother-friend of royalty, who was in their sights at this moment.

"Why do you think he looks at that stone carving each time he passes this way?" asked one woman, expertly kneading the dough into mounds between both hands.

"That carving is Iridor, isn't it, and the Spur's been doing that for years," came the reply over the sizzle of flattened rolls of dough frying in melted butter. "Keep fanning those flames now," the woman urged a young lad who sat between her legs, ensuring that the smoldering lumps of knotwood never lost their heat.

"I know that." The first sister raised her eyebrows in mock exasperation. "I'm asking you what you think he sees in it."

"Your guess is as good as mine, Mara. Perhaps he casts a silent prayer to it. Now that I come to think on it, I'm sure that owl has something to do with the old stories of the Goddess."

"Hoosh," said a man bustling in from behind. "You know not to speak her name."

"No one can hear us back here, Bal. And it's only an old myth. No one believes in all that Goddess stuff anymore. You go about your business, man, and let us get on with ours. There's a lot of customers queuing."

"And you stop flapping your gums, woman, and keep frying up those rathas."

"Oh, be gone," Mara said, shooing her husband back to the front of the shop. "You could be right, Hasha." She returned to her chore, the dough piling up in a neat, glistening pyramid. "The Spur's such a secretive sort, perhaps he's atoning for something."

"I'll show him atonement." Her sister rubbed her breasts and grinned wickedly. The look of disapproval on Mara's face made Hasha laugh out loud. "Don't tell me you haven't thought it at least once? Every woman in Percheron daydreams of a roll with the Spur." Though the child below remained silent, his soft smile of enjoyment at the women's banter suggested this was not the first time his mother and aunt had discussed this man and would surely not be the last. The Spur of Percheron prompted more conjecture than any other; the man with the curiously light-colored eyes was not just every woman's dream but was spoken of admiringly by the men too.

"I haven't," Mara lied, and stifled her laughter. "Oh, but if I were younger, I would."

Hasha flipped the four oiled pancakes currently in the pan and a delicious new aroma of cooked ratha spiced the air. "He always looks so serious, though. I don't think I've ever seen him laugh."

Mara stopped kneading the dough. "Oh, he's got secrets, that one, but he never seems to put a foot wrong. I'm told the Zar holds him in higher esteem than any of his council and his men in the protectorate would die for him. That sort of loyalty isn't won easily."

Her sister looked up and exclaimed, "Zarab save us, Mara, he's coming this way!"

Both sisters watched in genuine pleasure as the familiar long stride of the Spur brought him to the door of the shop and the chance to serve the highest-ranking soldier in the land became reality.

AS HE ENTERED the shop, Lazar was planning to order a dish known tantalizingly as the Feast of Seven Spices. Had he known what was to come that day, he might have found good reason to ignore the hunger pangs that made him so accessible to the Elim runner sent from the palace with such dire news.

As it was, ignorant of what was coming, Lazar sat down at a small table, smiling politely at the two middle-aged ladies who giggled coquettishly behind their veils from the kitchen, as if being visited by Zarab himself.

2

It was going to be unpleasant, she thought, tapping perfectly rouged lips with the tips of manicured nails that had been buffed by a slave until they shone. But it had to be done . . . and swiftly.

The First Wife and Absolute Favorite glanced down into the exquisite private garden where boys played among the cypresses with a ball made from an inflated pig's bladder. Their laughter prompted a smile, but anyone looking at this woman would have sensed no warmth. Herezah was already imagining how different those childish squeals would be when the order was given.

An agonized groan dragged her from her thoughts. Taking a moment to settle an appropriate look of sorrow on her face, Herezah turned from the beautifully sculpted window of the Stone Palace to the bed where Zar Joreb, Percheron's high ruler, King of the Seas, Ruler of the Deserts, Mightiest of the Mighty, lay dying. The man had been treated as a god these past thirty years. *But even gods have to die,* Herezah thought with fierce joy as she flicked a glance of summons to a slightly stooped man standing nearby.

Tariq spoke softly from behind the oiled beard carefully split into two narrow plaits and ostentatiously hung with a ruby at each end. These audacious accessories spoke much to Herezah about Tariq's designs for personal aggrandizement. She knew he wanted the title of Grand Vizier and she was sure he had never felt himself closer to his goal than now. That was good. He was well connected; she would feed his ambition, make him her puppet.

He kept his voice low enough for her ears only. "My lady Herezah?"

"Fetch Boaz," she whispered. The Vizier understood, bowing and withdrawing silently.

Herezah looked around the fabulously ornate chamber, gilded recklessly with gold at every turn. The room, already crowded, would get only more thick with people as the day drew on, for her husband would most likely die, if not this hour then within the next few.

Joreb had very particular tastes in art, which thankfully his Absolute Favorite shared, although in truth he had given her that appreciation, guiding her since childhood as to what constituted beauty. And it was certainly not this gold-laden room with its rich, gaudy colors. No, Joreb liked subtlety and understatement; his preference was for paler hues and simpler design. Herezah felt a fleeting pang that the man who had given her the opportunity to rise out of the slush of the harem would give up his soul in a room as vulgar as this. Her regret passed quickly, however, replaced by the thrill of knowing that her ultimate goal, the one she had been striving toward these past two decades, would be achieved in merely hours.

She calmed her racing pulse and tried to focus. Despite her anticipation at what her husband's death meant for her, Herezah had been shocked to learn that his injuries were, in fact, fatal, and she had made every effort to make him as comfortable as possible.

The large chamber they were in might be vulgar but it was cooled by a gentle breeze blowing from the massive, semicircular aquamarine harbor the famed city of Percheron overlooked. It was here that for thousands of years cultures had collided and mingled to yield the Percheron of today. Its strategic position and seemingly endless reserves of precious stones and metals gave the city riches beyond most realms' dreams.

But while those elements had once given Percheron such power, they were now its greatest threat. Herezah—keenly in tune with national security—was well aware that Joreb had begun fretting about Galinsea in particular. He had disclosed to her his concerns that their warlike neighbor to the west had designs on Percheron.

Herezah's wandering attention was arrested by the worried expressions of the court's two most senior physicians. The Zar would not see sunset, that much was obvious, and in turn their lives were forfeit for failing His Majesty. Understandably they continued to consult each other, desperately considering new, and hopeless, strategies.

At the foot of the Zar's bed cavorted a dwarf, sumptuously outfitted but looking ridiculous all the same. Herezah quelled a scowl. The fool was a constant annoyance in her life. He was "closed" too, which only served to irritate Herezah further. Not even a blood-telling by her crone, Yozem, had revealed anything about him. The Practitioner of the Blood Arts had termed him a blank, claiming the dwarf offered no clues about himself, thereby accounting for his madness. Herezah felt sickened to see the awkward antics he performed on his thick, short legs.

If Percheron was credited as being the most idyllic cove in the Faranel Sea, then its Stone Palace was the most breathtaking aspect of that cove. And within that Stone Palace its harem was the magnificent prize where beauty ruled supreme. It disturbed Herezah constantly that such vulgar deformity as this dwarf roamed among the beauty. He was the flaw in Percheron's jewel. Pez—she wasn't even sure whether this was his real name—had been a favorite clown of the Zar's for too many years for Herezah to get rid of him. She despaired that her son adored Pez in equal measure to her hatred.

She sighed; at least the palace buffoon, with his strange yellow eyes, would keep Boaz amused during the difficult times ahead. He might even prove a blessing, for there were occasions when time spent with Pez seemed to help her only child emotionally. Boaz was intense, often too serious, but the dwarf made him laugh with his ramblings. She couldn't imagine how. The dwarf could hardly string together a single sensible sentence without breaking into song, or acrobatics, or without his mind wandering elsewhere. How Boaz and Pez managed to hold even a simple conversation was a mystery to her.

A small movement at the corner of the room distracted her. She glanced over at the silent mountain of black flesh that went by the name of Salmeo. He put the fear of a thousand angry gods into most people around the palace, including herself. She had lost count of the times the giant man had reduced her to a shaking wreck. But never again, she promised, now that absolute power was within her grasp.

Salmeo was the cleverest, most sly man she had ever known—no doubt ever would know. He was as cunning as he was dangerous. He was also cruelty personified . . . but then you didn't become Grand Master of the Eunuchs without taking a perverse pleasure in punishment.

Salmeo embodied so many unpalatable characteristics, it was hard to imagine how they all came together in one person. For the umpteenth time her amazement was triggered by the sheer size of him beneath the richly patterned garments he draped over his folds of loose, flabby skin. Heavy folds, she knew all too well from her own experience, that had to be lifted away in order for him to be cleaned. He matched his revolting looks with a vicious demeanor more befitting a scorned woman than a grown man. Which wasn't far from the truth, perhaps. Salmeo had been cut at the age of seven, when his height and size fooled the Grand Master Eunuch of the day into believing he was older. He was an "almost complete": nothing much was left of his manhood save the painful yearning of desire. No toys, no tricks, no magicks helped ease Salmeo with his frustrations, so he took his pleasures in other ways.

Herezah's gaze was helplessly drawn toward the sinister, sharply pointed nail on the index finger of his right hand. He stained it red, so no woman could ever forget its purpose and no naive boy went beyond wondering at its use. She masked the shudder of the memory of that nail's cruel touch.

Salmeo must have sensed her attention and she just had time, before hurriedly looking away, to see the pale rope of the scar that ran the length of one of his fleshy cheeks pull as he raised an eyebrow at her interest.

As she turned away, Herezah's focus finally fell upon the Zar himself. He groaned and moved restlessly beneath silken sheets, fighting the unseen spirits who had come to claim him.

Death is ugly indeed, Herezah thought, watching the great one's lips draw back in a silent howl as a fresh wave of punishment rode his body. The door opened and to her relief she saw Vizier Tariq usher in her son.

"My lion," she said softly to the boy, reaching out her arms theatrically.

"Mother." He dutifully kissed her cheek but twisted away from the embrace.

Herezah did not outwardly react to his rejection but she promised herself that she would try harder with Boaz. After all, within hours she would be his regent, quietly ruling from behind the figurehead Zar of so few summers. She saw his intelligent dark eyes observing her and felt a momentary loss of composure, as if he understood precisely what she had been thinking. Before she could correct her expression, his gaze slid away to his father, moaning on the bed.

"You must be brave, Boaz," Herezah warned. "He will not last long."

"Can we not stop his pain?" he asked tersely, ignoring her concern.

"The physicians minimize it," Tariq offered, eager to include himself in the royal conversation.

Boaz ignored the sycophantic Vizier as well. It was shock enough for him to see his father in this state—especially as he had seemed to rally in the early days of the fall—but having his mother displaying her newfound devotion and feeling his emotions used as some sort of circus ground for everyone else's benefit was making him angry.

"Come, my son," Herezah said, taking his hand. "You are fifteen now and old enough to witness your father's final breaths."

Final breaths? Boaz scowled. He could hear the predatory tone in his mother's voice. He knew only too well what his father's death meant—his mother had comforted him to sleep when he was a young child with stories about how one day the two of them would rule Percheron. When he was small he had trusted and adored his mother, but for the past six or seven years she had essentially ignored him and he had been raised by royal servants, learning to live without the maternal love he craved. Now it amused him that both his parents doted on him: his mother because of the power he would bring her, and his father because he recognized in Boaz a future leader. Boaz knew the Zar loved his sharp mind, his scholarly pursuits and love of the arts, and it didn't hurt that he was described as handsome these days either—he could see how all of these attributes made him a most eligible heir. Nevertheless, it was sickening to watch his mother reveling in this same knowledge and using it to get precisely what she wanted, not for his benefit, but for hers.

Yet she was his only ally—not friend, not loved one, but someone he could count on to look after his interests because they served hers so well. It was a terrible thing to admit but he needed Herezah and her bright, agile mind, which could plot and plan faster and more skillfully than anyone's he knew.

Accepting this only made him angrier still, but these dark thoughts were put on hold as Pez scampered up. Boaz smiled inwardly at the dwarf's oversize pantaloons, which, because they had insufficient length to billow properly, pooled comically around his thick ankles. Nevertheless, the swath of fabric hid the savage bow of his legs that made Pez sway so oddly. He arrived pulling silk squares from his nose. It was a trick that had always amused Boaz, but not today.

"Hello, Pez," Boaz muttered.

"Master," Pez replied.

The boy looked sadly at the dwarf. "Is he truly dying?" he said, as if, by asking his friend rather than those he disliked, the reality might be different.

"We all die," Pez replied in a singsong voice. "You, birds, fish, me . . . your parents too." Herezah glared at the dwarf as Pez's gaze slid past her in a deliberate provocation. "You must carry yourself proudly now, young prince. Do you know why?"

Boaz looked at his friend—the only one he trusted in this room—and nodded. "Because I'm to be Zar."

"That's right, my darling," Herezah gushed, clearly surprised that the dwarf was making sense. "Your father awaits," she urged, pulling Boaz away from the jester.

The young man glanced at Pez, who blinked slowly in that curious manner of his. Then the dwarf bowed theatrically, the bells on his velvet cap tinkling into strained silence, for the groaning had just subsided.

Aware that all eyes in the room were trained upon him, Boaz took his father's hand. It felt dry, too cold, as if death had indeed arrived, although a sudden rasping groan put an end to that fright. Through puffy eyes, the King of Kings tried to focus.

"My lord." Herezah spoke lovingly near the Zar's ear. "Our son, Boaz."

The man rallied ever so slightly, a brief smile immediately replaced by another grimace. "Boaz."

"Father, I—"

"Hush. Listen now," the Zar growled, though it took all his effort to endow his weak voice with the tone needed to make the youngster pay attention. "You are the Chosen One. No one else! You alone. Never forget it!" He gasped desperately, tried to take one last struggling breath, and failed. The stricken physicians watched as the head of the Zar lolled to one side; a trail of spittle escaped, running down his chin. Herezah looked away in feigned despair, the action hiding her triumph. The men of medicine hung their heads, imagining what their own last words would be that evening when their throats were cut. No point in fighting it now. Their wills were written and they knew their families would be well looked after. They had enjoyed position and wealth for many years and had always understood that when Joreb died, they would too.

They went about their final duty now, one checking that no pulse was present while the other held a small mirror against the Zar's mouth and nose. As a final precaution, the first man drew a long pin from a pouch and pricked the Zar's body repeatedly. Herezah was busy removing the large ring from her husband's finger. Boaz, his eyes stinging with tears, turned his head away.

Pez, sensing the boy's distress, suddenly sank to his knees before him. As if the dwarf's sudden movement was a signal, everyone in the chamber also dropped. They bent to touch their heads on the floor before Boaz, the son of their Zar's Absolute Favorite and his chosen successor. Salmeo took longer than anyone to kneel, but after much grunting he too paid the new Zar appropriate homage.

Boaz froze, stunned; he wasn't ready to accept this new role, even though he had been groomed for many years to take his father's crown. If not for the sly wink that Pez gave him from under a short arm, he might have fled the chamber.

"Your Majesty," Herezah cried, and Salmeo, Tariq, the physicians, and even the servants attending took up the chant. "Hail the Zar!" They repeated this several times until the new King of Kings commanded them to stop.

Into the instant silence that followed, Pez broke wind, his rear pointing suspiciously toward the new Valide Zara and her bejeweled Vizier. Boaz knew this sort of lewd behavior should have made his father sit up from death and roar with laughter. Joreb had so loved Pez's wickedness. Boaz felt a nervous flutter of amusement threaten to explode from his own throat but he controlled it with effort and focused on his scowling, clearly offended parent. He ignored the mortified Vizier, who, in his opinion, deserved all the bad smells that came his way.

"Mother," he said. "Rise."

And she did, first crawling forward—as one should before the Zar—and then straightening on her knees to place the diamond-encrusted emerald ring onto her son's finger. She nodded reassurance before bowing her head over her son's hand and kissing the ring fervently.

"My lord Zar," she said, pride catching in her throat. "How may I serve?"

"Hail, Valide Zara," Boaz said, and Herezah basked in the words she had longed to hear for so many years. Now, as the Zar's mother, her very name would strike fear into the hearts of those around her.

She accepted their obeisance, noticed the wry smile on Salmeo's normally unreadable face, and gave her first order as the most powerful woman in the land.

"Rise, all," she said, turning to Tariq. "Where is Lazar?"

"Waiting, Valide Zara," the Vizier replied, fully recovered from the dwarf's insult and barely able to contain his glee at the thought of the potential riches and power spreading out before him. Hail the Valide! He had aligned himself well.

"Admit him alone," she ordered, resisting smiling at the notion that Lazar would share this moment of high joy with her. "The passing of the old Zar is a secret until I say differently."

The physicians were smoothing the formerly rumpled sheets neatly over the corpse as the tall, sun-browned Spur entered the chamber.

"Lazar," Boaz said, his expression lightening. The formidable warrior was the only person who walked the palace corridors whom he truly considered a friend, aside from Pez.

The Spur spared only a fleeting glance toward the prone figure on the bed. His shock at the news of the Zar's imminent death had already been suffered at the ratha emporium; he had concealed it with effort as he strode in disbelieving stony silence ahead of the runner who had brought the dire message. He would reflect on his grief later, in private. Right now his focus was firmly on the new Zar and on ignoring Herezah, who stared at him with the hungry gaze of a hunter.

Lazar dropped to his knees, reaching to the huge ring that was barely able to sit straight on the slender fingers of the young man's hand. "Zar Boaz, Your High One, I offer my services and my life to you."

In a show of affection, Boaz covered Lazar's hand with his own, pale and unblemished against the tanned, strong fingers of the bowed man. "I hope we never claim it, Spur."

The Spur of Percheron stood and nodded at Boaz, proud of the boy's composure. The light gray eyes that marked Lazar as a curiosity looked now to Herezah before he bowed low. "Valide Zara."

The Valide stifled her pleasure, hiding it behind the grave

expression she had contrived; there would be plenty of time to enjoy Lazar's new fealty to her. Right now there were urgent arrangements to make and she reveled in the thrill of finally being able to give him a direct order.

"Take the physicians away and do what you must," she said coldly, glad that protocol did not insist she be veiled within the palace confines so long as the Zar was present. It pleased her hugely that the Spur could see her beauty and know what he was missing.

If he could sense her pleasure, he did not show it. "May I pay my respects?" he asked, looking toward the body draped in silken sheets.

The new Valide inclined her head and watched the Spur cross the room in four strides, kneeling to kiss the hand of the dead Zar. He took a moment in silence before he stood and soberly turned toward the men who had tried to prevent death. "Physicians" was all he said.

"You must be gentle with the gentlemen's throats," Pez began to sing. He cartwheeled once before an exasperated look from Herezah told Lazar that it was in the dwarf's interest to be removed as well.

"Come, Pez. You can keep us company," the soldier suggested.

The dwarf agreed but not before a loud and long farewell belch to those gathered.

Annoyed at being so insultingly upstaged, Herezah made her voice chilly. "Do it immediately, Spur, but no word of Zar Joreb's death is to get out until I sanction it."

Lazar noted Herezah's lack of deference to her son, but said merely, "As you wish, Valide," and bowed. The Faranel Sea below blew a sweet wind into the room that was nevertheless unable to cover the stench of ambition. It revolted him and he was grateful to escape, even if it were only to carry out the unpalatable task of having the physicians executed.

After the door had closed on the five men, Herezah turned and said, "Tariq, Salmeo."

"Valide?"

"You understand what needs to be done." It was not a question.

"I do," the avaricious Vizier replied.

"Salmeo?"

The huge black man sighed. "Enemies will be made, Valide Zara."

She could smell on his breath the violet-fragranced tablets that he habitually sucked. "The enemies of Boaz will be dead. The other kind will be helpless."

"Mother? What's going on?" Boaz, lost in his grieving thoughts, was unable to follow the conversation.

"Come with me, Boaz. I want to explain something to you." The Valide took his hand, looking pointedly at the two men who had been charged with the ugly task.

She did not need to say any more. The darkly ambitious eyes of the woman who now essentially ruled Percheron said it all.

B oaz was deeply disturbed. The morning had begun like
any other in the palace and then, during a language lesson,
Vizier Tariq had arrived looking grave. Initially the son of the
Zar's First Wife and Absolute Favorite had leaped at the interruption; any distraction that released him from Galinsean verbs
and tenses was a blessing. It was a language that tested even the
most accomplished linguists in Percheron. His mother had told
him that very few could master the strange tongue and she had
explained that she had also tried to learn the tiresome language
for many years but failed. Boaz couldn't imagine his mother
failing at anything and he'd initially thought she was just saying as much to flatter him, but others who had tried to learn the
language had confirmed its immense difficulty. The tongue of
the people from the west was seemingly impossible for a
Percherese to speak fluently. His mother jested that should a
Galinsean suddenly arrive in the city, not a soul in Percheron

would be able to conduct a worthwhile conversation with the visitor. Boaz had laughed and returned that any Galinsean landing in Percheron meant trouble, not conversation.

The golden-haired race allegedly wanted Percheron so badly that Lazar had set up a special spy network throughout the city just to keep the Zar constantly updated on every item of news that could be gleaned from the trading ships. It had gotten to the point where no ship with Galinsean registration, or on which even a single Galinsean was aboard, was permitted to pass between the stone giants, Beloch and Ezram, who guarded the bay of Percheron, let alone dock in the harbor.

Lazar seemed to know something about Galinsea, having apparently roamed around it for a number of years and he agreed that its King would certainly have designs on beautiful Percheron. Boaz remembered how the Spur had scowled when he spoke.

". . . not that the Galinsean royals would know art from their arses," he had warned. "They want one thing only and that's the harbor. They'd sack the city and then raze it without so much as a look backward."

Boaz didn't believe this but grasped the sentiment behind it.

"They may be good sailors but we can protect our waters. Our good fortune is the desert to our back. No Galinsean would know how to survive in that unforgiving terrain."

At the Vizier's interruption Boaz had briefly entertained the thought that he might be allowed to play pigball with his brothers. But his anticipation of a fun afternoon was immediately dampened by the Vizier's solemn request for Boaz to accompany him.

The day had turned much worse, however, than discovering that pigball was not on the agenda. Having witnessed his father take his last breath, Boaz had not only had to deal with everyone suddenly on their knees to him but he had learned something so terrible he had fled his father's chamber. The new Valide's whispered words had set off such a panic within him that he had to run to the only person he knew might soothe his mind, assure him it was some horrible game his power-obsessed mother had dreamed up to frighten him. This was why he now found himself in the private chamber of the court jester, the one other person he could genuinely call friend.

Pez sat cross-legged and cross-eyed, but he was not winning any smiles from the new Zar.

"I thought my fart well timed," the dwarf offered into the silence.

"My mother didn't."

The dwarf sighed and for a rare moment became serious. "You cannot escape this, Boaz."

"It's barbaric!"

Pez nodded his oversize head.

"There must be another way." Boaz begged.

"Well, certainly not one your mother would entertain. You know this is her way of protecting you."

"My father would never have condoned this."

"Boaz," Pez said mildly. "This is precisely how your father's throne was won and held."

The Zar had not expected this and gave a soft sound of surprise. "I never knew that."

Pez shrugged. "It's hardly something he was proud of and it was something he deliberately asked that his own sons be shielded from until his death came about. You are Zar now and your mother can't keep the harsh realities of life from touching you."

"You sound as if you support her," Boaz replied sourly. Pez said nothing and the Zar looked appalled. "They're my brothers," he appealed.

"And would be your murderers if the shoe were on the other foot. Boaz, don't be naive. Every wife in the harem thinks the same way as your mother. The Valide is doing what she must to protect you and Percheron's throne."

"She is doing this for her own chance at power!"

The dwarf shook his head sadly. "Your father chose you for succession. She only dreamed it. He made it so."

"Why can't I rewrite the history books and magnanimously send them away?"

"And watch your back forevermore? No, child, they each have a rightful claim to the throne—the older ones every bit as eligible as you—and you might not think so now, but each of those boys is your enemy. Their mothers would see to it."

The new Zar made a sound of anguished disgust. "I cannot be there. I will not witness it!"

"You must!" Pez countered equally firmly. "Or you will be viewed as weak."

"So be it!" Boaz shouted, slamming his hand onto the table. He regretted the raised voice and his tone softened to a plea. "Save me, Pez—don't force me to bear witness. I cannot."

The dwarf was torn. He understood the young man's fear and felt sorry for him, but conspiring against the Valide Zara would be tantamount to treason and he had no desire to have that charge leveled at him, especially with Herezah searching for any excuse to have him killed, or at the very least banished from the palace. He began to shake his head when an idea struck him. It was unpleasant but effective, and hopefully without repercussions.

"Hold out your arm."

"What?"

"Do it."

Boaz obeyed, nervously. "Only Lazar and I know the real you, Pez. Everyone else thinks you're demented."

"And you've never told the truth. Why not?"

"Because you're my secret. The only thing truly mine that my mother can't spoil or interfere with. I don't share it because you're true; there is no one else I trust in the way that I trust you."

Pez smiled and his collection of odd features seemed to blend and become . . . not handsome—not by any stretch—but suddenly right. The warmth and beauty in his smile revealed his heart.

"There will be, son."

Boaz frowned, confused. "Who?"

Pez burped theatrically for his answer and Boaz had experienced the dwarf's evasive tactics enough times to know he would get nothing more from his friend on the subject.

"This is going to hurt, Zar Boaz, but not nearly as much as watching your brothers die."

The new Zar instinctively closed his eyes.

"HOW DID THIS HAPPEN?" Herezah growled at Tariq. "Today of all days!"

She'd donned an exquisite black tunic over matching silk trousers, presumably her mourning garb, but no one could miss how the cut of the outfit showed off her sensuous figure. Even in grief Herezah intended to take everyone's breath away.

To the Vizier's credit, his somber expression did not falter at the outburst. "Pez found him, Valide Zara. Apparently Boaz had been running to find the jester when he fell and sustained the injury."

Herezah made a sound of disgust at the Vizier's pointless explanation. "I worked that out for myself, Tariq." Her eyes blazed anger as she turned toward the Spur. "Spur Lazar, what do you have to say about this . . . situation?"

"Pez fetched me when it happened. I could see that Boaz's arm was broken and I sent for one of the city physicians immediately. I didn't have much choice, Valide," Lazar said. He did not wish to anger her further by reminding her that it was she who had called for the palace physicians' deaths to be carried out immediately.

The men had died bravely. They had said their prayers and written notes to their families before kneeling calmly in the execution courtyard and together chanting the mantra to send their souls safely to the Garden of Zarab.

Lazar would not permit the palace soldiers to handle this sort of killing. He had assembled a small team of executioners to carry out any deaths ordered by the royals or their agents. In this instance two experienced men had arrived quietly to stand behind the physicians. A third, the most senior man, gave the signal when the mantra had been cast. The executioners had reached a blade around each victim's throat and expertly slashed the jugular. It was not pretty but it was swift and it was honorable. The heads were later fully severed but would not be pushed onto spikes until the Valide gave permission for the city to learn of the Zar's passing.

"Well, I've sent the city physician away," Herezah said, exasperated. "Yozem will take care of Boaz. We shall need to hire a new team of physicians for the Zar."

"As you wish," Lazar murmured, still wondering at the senseless waste of life. The dead doctors would have made fine physicians for Boaz.

"Nothing is as I wish," she replied acidly. It was galling to know that Boaz would not be present, but having seen the gray-faced Zar sweating from the pain of his damaged arm, she knew it was impossible. Yozem had already mixed the pain-relieving opium paste, including the crushed dust of diamonds, emeralds, and rubies accorded royalty, although, from now on, Boaz would take his opiate in the gilded tablets prepared for the Zar alone.

"If not for Pez—" Lazar began, but the Valide cut across his words angrily.

"Yes, yes, if not for Pez! If I didn't know he was so feeble-minded, I could almost believe he works against me." Both men made noises of gentle admonishment, which she ignored. "What have people been told?"

Lazar answered. "They know only that the Zar is injured and that he is with his physicians. No one knows of Joreb's death yet."

Herezah nodded, seemingly no longer interested. "So is everything ready, Tariq?"

"As ordered, Valide. Salmeo is with them."

Herezah knew Lazar would find her latest scheme heinous but he would hide his disgust behind that irritating mask of his face. Hoping this man would ever show any emotion seemed a lost cause. The gods knew she had been trying long enough. Why he intrigued her so much she couldn't say; perhaps it was his very remoteness that made her yearn to be able to reach him. All her life men had looked at her with lust, but this man hardly looked at her at all. And when he did, she felt as if he were looking through her. She hated him for that; it was a worse kind of humiliation, insulting her far more cruelly than being wanted purely to satisfy fleshly desires. Even a kind word beyond the courtesies he was bound to show would be something to cling to. Still, she thought, with no small measure of satisfaction, everything had changed as of this morning. It was obvious Lazar knew it too, which would explain his reluctant manner. Good. It was high time he had his feathers ruffled.

"Your men will secure the area, Spur Lazar. I trust I can count on them to be discreet?"

He bowed his head in acknowledgment but not before she saw the unhappiness flit across his face, so briefly that anyone else might believe they had imagined it. But not Herezah. She knew the planes and nuances of that face as well as she knew her own; had imagined herself touching it often enough, kissing those angry lips, staring into those furious silver-gray eyes.

"Valide—" Lazar started.

"Don't," she warned. "I will not be swayed. It is the only way to protect Boaz. You know that as well as anyone. Now, where are the women?"

"At the pools, Valide," the Vizier answered.

She turned away from Lazar to make sure he understood who was controlling the reins of power now. Boaz might be Zar but his mother was the ruler. She allowed herself to watch the Spur from the corner of her eye, though. No need to waste any opportunity to feast on the looks of a man who genuinely fueled her own desire. Zarab knew there was no other man around her who could. Too long had she had been forced to serve the whims of Joreb: old, fleshy Joreb and his strange sexual habits. And then of course there were the half men, the eunuchs, with their soft tongues, who illegally satisfied many in the harem, but not her. She found them repulsive. As for finding solace in another woman—she felt her stomach twist at the thought, although she knew that a number of the odalisques and wives took their pleasures in one another. She scowled to push the notion away. Lazar alone made her heart pound.

"Good. And the wives?" she asked her Vizier.

"Salmeo arranged for them also to go swimming this afternoon, Valide. It is such a warm day. Everyone but Ameera took advantage of his opening up a long-unused gate to the Sapphire Pools."

She raised an eyebrow in response. "He *is* spoiling them," she said, pretending not to notice Lazar's grimace at her condescension. "And Ameera?"

"Unwell. Confined to her quarters."

"Set a guard upon her." The Vizier nodded. Herezah continued: "So to the boys."

"At the Lion Fountain," Tariq confirmed. "Salmeo is meeting them."

"We're ready, then." She turned to the Spur and leveled a flinty gaze at him. "Wipe that scowl from your face, Lazar. You take your commands from me now, and as distasteful as you find this, your men will see it done properly."

"Yes, Valide Zara." The words were dutiful but she heard the contempt; saw it flash angrily in his eyes. Still her cold heart leaped, enjoying that ferocity in him, and yes, the defiance. He was the only man in Percheron who wore his face clean-shaven, save the youngsters waiting desperately for stubble to show as their voices deepened. But Lazar was no adolescent and he deliberately wore no beard with pride. The nakedness showed his firm jaw; he wore his dark hair loose and longer than any

Percherese dared, and that, she knew, was another refusal to relinquish his independence. No jewels or adornments for Lazar either. No, she admitted, he was dazzling enough.

Too many of the harem's women committed hours of conversation to what it might be like to bed Lazar. Not once had he shown the usual foibles of men, and fallen for their charms, though. To do so was an offense of the highest order, of course, and would have meant instant execution.

Love it was not; Herezah would be the first to admit it, but she desired him with an irresistible passion, and she was the only woman of the harem who could now compel him to do her bidding. It would make for interesting times ahead.

"Good," she said, hoping her cheeks were not as flushed as they suddenly felt. "Let's finish it."

THE PRINCES of the harem wives, ranging in age from fifteen to just seven moons, were rounded up after midday, the baby seized from his wet nurse. It was she who set off the alarm with her terrible wails. She couldn't guess what might be occurring but she instinctively went running for the Sapphire Pools and the child's mother. The news of the snatching set the wives screaming as the reality of their fragile existence became clear. The Zar must have succumbed to his injuries, and that could mean only one thing. Why else would the baby be taken so carelessly? Clambering out of the pools, they ran wildly in the direction of where they had last seen their sons, their eunuch servants throwing cloaks over bared flesh in a desperate attempt to protect the modesty of these women who were not permitted to show their faces, let alone their naked bodies.

But it was already too late for the mothers. Their lions were gone, vanished away to a secret place from where they would not return . . . not alive, anyway.

THE GRAND MASTER EUNUCH had quickly overcome any reservations he harbored at the Valide Zara's orders. He should not have been surprised at her choice of action and regretted his subtle warning of earlier. Never again would he underestimate Herezah, certainly not now that she held his future in the palm of her hand. Oh, how the tables had turned!

Life had been near perfect for him with the old Zar. No one, not even calculating Salmeo, could have foreseen the accident that had ended the Zar's life. A fall from a horse, of all things! And Joreb such an accomplished horseman. He had been showing off for his sons; two men on horses charging toward the same flag stuck in the ground. Joreb had run the same race countless times, had gleefully wagered five of his prettiest odalisques against that crimson flag. And he had won this time, but paid handsomely with his life. Who could have known he would slip off his saddle as he reached down to grab the prize? Or that the other horse would arrive not even a full second later, without any opportunity to avoid trampling the Zar's body so viciously that he would never recover from the massive internal bleeding?

Salmeo sighed. All was not lost. He was still the most powerful man within the palace next to Boaz, despite what that ambitious Vizier might believe. His wealth was so vast and his influence so far-reaching that Salmeo feared no one. No one that is, except Herezah.

He must ingratiate himself swiftly. They'd had their differences but Herezah was not a foolish woman. Better the devil you know, as the old adage said. He could count on her knowing how to play the game; it was why today she was Valide Zara. He admired her in spite of their mutual distrust. They were similar creatures: both prisoners, both wildly ambitious, both with sufficient survival instincts to beat their rivals.

Perhaps they could start again and she might let the past remain just that? He had hurt her physically and emotionally, but that was life in the harem, she knew that, all the women did. If she would permit him to work with her, together they would be a formidable pair supporting the Zar. Boaz was still so young, it would be up to Herezah to run the realm for him. Oh yes, initially she would rely on Tariq, but soon she would need Salmeo's influence and he would ply it gladly.

He would start by pleasing her with today's event. It was regrettable but necessary. No one appreciated the need for absolute supremacy more than Salmeo. He thought about the harem and the great pity that it would be dismantled. It was one of the finest selections of women in several centuries, and he had had each woman in it in her place.

The sound of approaching children pulled Salmeo from his thoughts. It was time. He hoped Herezah would appreciate the symmetry between the old Zar's injuries and the spectacle he had hastily planned for the execution.

Salmeo met the youngsters in a long-unused pavilion. The slaves, who had been given their sorrowful orders, herded the boys toward the huge Grand Master Eunuch. Salmeo took the baby into his own arms and placed the infant in a crimson velvet sack.

"Is this a game?" one boy asked eagerly.

Salmeo's scar twisted as his mouth widened into a grin, revealing his massive pearly teeth. There was a gap—as wide as a child's finger—between his front teeth that never failed to fascinate in a macabre way, for his tongue would flick in and out of the hole and cause a lisp to his speech. "That's right, my prince. It's a new game we've devised just for this afternoon."

"What's it called?" another boy yelled, cheerfully climbing into his own velvet bag.

"It's called Trample," Salmeo replied in his effeminate, lisping way. "Now hurry, boys."

Giggling and pushing at one another, the boys—even the eldest—managed to wriggle into their sacks.

"Now we're going to tie you in," Salmeo warned, keeping his voice light. "Just loosely," he lied.

He nodded and the slaves obliged, securing the children tightly into the velvet pouches.

"Everyone be still now," the fat eunuch warned. "The Zar will be present," he added untruthfully, as an unnecessary threat.

Each velvet bag with its precious cargo was picked up by a eunuch slave and carried to a large pond that had been drained of water. Within moments, however, the baby began to cry and this set off some of the smaller boys, who had tired of the heat and the dark of the bags. The game wasn't fun anymore.

4

Herezah did not need to be veiled within the privacy of the harem courtyards or, indeed, anywhere that was considered the realm of the harem proper. Nonetheless, she wore a piece of silken gauze draped over her head. She knew those present would think it was a sign of respect but her intention was to hide her expression. It was precaution only; Herezah had little doubt that she would handle the spectacle with grace, unpleasant though it was bound to be.

Salmeo had sent a unit of his eunuchs to carry a silken canopy to shade her from the sun, a special honor that symbolized the new royal she had become today.

Striding unhappily behind her was the Spur. She felt sure Lazar was angry by nature. He was abrupt and distant with everyone except Boaz and the hated dwarf. Those two alone won amusement, even the spark of friendship. She knew Lazar had liked Joreb and there had been a closeness between them, but

they had not had much to do with each other in recent years as
the Zar had slumped into a lazier lifestyle. His slide into more
carnal activity had disappointed the Spur, or so she guessed. It
was just another reason, she was sure, for Lazar's fury at the
world.

He was young to be head of Percheron's security. Joreb had
admitted as much one night after she had satisfied his latest in a
line of curious fetishes.

The Zar had been relaxing in the pleasant stupor that usually
followed a long session of sexual release. Her work was not
done, though. Herezah, then just an odalisque, had offered to
massage the Zar's spent body into sleep. She always preferred
him in this mood, when his mouth was as relaxed as the rest
of him.

Herezah took her chance. "Tell me about the Spur."

"Lazar?" Joreb asked in a lazy voice. "What a find he is for
us. He was a prisoner, actually."

Herezah knew from Lazar's looks that he was a foreigner.
No Percherese had such light eyes or that aquiline nose, the
sharp angles to their face.

"Where is he from?" she asked, intrigued.

"Guess," the Zar suggested playfully.

"I cannot, High One. I am not experienced in lands beyond
our shores . . . I know only life in the palace."

Joreb reached under his silk pillow and slowly withdrew the
lightest of sapphires. A smile stretched across his mouth. "If
you guess right, this is yours."

She paused in her massage and looked at her Zar somberly.
"I don't want jewels, High One."

"What is it you want, then, Herezah, my ambitious slave?"

She hated that word. *Odalisque* was bad enough but at least it sounded pretty. Nevertheless her expression did not betray her feelings. "I want the status of Zaradine."

And he had laughed with genuine pleasure. "I knew it. Wife you shall be, then, if you guess correctly."

"And the sapphire?"

"Is yours anyway for amusing me."

"Tell me about him first and let me guess after." Her hands were working slowly, rhythmically once again.

"You know that a captured prisoner can fight his way to freedom?" She nodded. "Although most don't take that option, for the fights are to the death."

"Among how many, my Zar?"

"Six is usual. As you can gather, not much chance for the prisoner." He rested his chin on his fists as he recalled the incident. "Ha!" He laughed. "Lazar demanded twelve and the chance to speak with me. It was his audacity that won my interest. I asked the man who was Spur then to choose a dozen of his best swordsmen and pit them against the prisoner."

Herezah's dark eyes glowed as she pictured the scene. "He obviously won, Great One," she said, reaching to pour the Zar a goblet of sweet wine.

Joreb turned, sat up, and sipped. "He barely broke a sweat, leaving each with broken limbs or groaning from some gash or injury, all disabling but none life-threatening, which was the amazing part. He told me later, when I fulfilled his wish for an audience, that he thought it a waste of good men to kill for exhibition purposes only. And when I asked him whether he thought it a waste to risk his own life, do you know what he answered?"

Herezah shook her head; she hardly knew Lazar even though they were of similar age.

Joreb grinned. "He said his life was never at risk! The cheek of it."

"And what did he want with you, my Zar?"

"He wanted the freedom to live in Percheron. I offered him more—he accepted the position of Spur."

"Why did he choose Percheron?"

"He told me that the city was a thing of such beauty it lifted his spirits. Our language, culture, people, art, architecture—he wanted to be a part of it."

"He must have come from a place sorely lacking in all the loveliness we take for granted."

Joreb had swallowed the goblet's contents and laid back again on his pillows. "You are crafty, Herezah," he said, and moved her hands to his sex. "Massage me there, but guess quickly, or I'll forget our bargain."

Herezah remembered how her mind had raced that evening to seek the right answer. The prize was the first major step toward her goal. As Zaradine, wife to the Zar, she could bear him a son, a prince, and that meant a chance to become Valide Zara. She knew she would seal her fate with her answer and that the Zar would never enter into such a curious bargain again.

"Well?" he asked. "My mind is drifting, pretty one. It is heading south to where your fingers are calling me."

She took a deep breath, remembering something she had overheard horrid Salmeo once airing about getting his greatest pleasure from making a Galinsean a eunuch. *I've only experienced such a joy once and the wretch died anyway but it was wonderful to watch a Galinsean's manhood removed,* he had explained. *They are the most arrogant of races and the hardest to tame.*

She risked it. "You know, my lord, if I didn't know better I would think your Spur was Galinsean."

"You know that cannot be, Herezah." Joreb yawned. "True Galinseans are golden of hair and curiously light of eye, and he is dark. Besides, Lazar has no animosity toward Percheron—he begged to be allowed to remain here."

"May I have one more try, my Zar?" She did not like to beg but she had to win this contest.

"Why not? But I warn you, Herezah, although you arouse me, I tire of conversation and should I fall asleep before I can take my pleasure, your guess will not count, so be swift." He yawned to make his point.

"Zar Joreb, I would hazard that Lazar hails from somewhere near to Galinsea, then. I would guess at Merlinea." She knew her geography of the region well and held her breath after giving her answer.

Joreb had moved fast, twisting her over onto her back, amusement twinkling in his no-longer-tired dark eyes. "I shall give you a son tonight, wife," he had proclaimed, and Herezah had arched her back with unrestrained joy as the Zar kept his promise.

Later still, as the Zar curled himself around her to sleep, she suggested he call another exhibition so the women could appreciate Lazar's fighting prowess. Joreb refused.

"Not even for your favorite?" she begged, relishing the thought of seeing a half-naked Lazar oiled and made to do combat.

Joreb shook his head sleepily. "A bond between two men."

"He hardly counts, my Zar, he's only a Merlinean, barely one step better, in my opinion, than a Galinsean barbarian."

Her new husband was wide-awake then. "We should never underestimate them, my beautiful, ambitious one. We must teach our son the same. Yes, we are a cultivated nation with art and language to impress. Galinseans may seem vulgar in comparison. But, Herezah, you should fear them, not poke fun at them."

She listened and nodded, knowing she had pleased the Zar tonight. The jewels that would be left for her tomorrow would be enough to send the other wives into a frenzy of jealousy. But Herezah wanted only one jewel now. She wanted a son and for him alone to take the title of Zar. The rest meant little to her. Power was everything—riches could follow.

She had pleased Joreb enough that night almost sixteen years ago not only to be showered with jewels but to be called back for the next four nights. This was unheard of for Joreb and this was the moment Herezah signaled her intention to take the title of Absolute Favorite. It was during these torrid nights of sexual play and favor that she had become pregnant with Boaz. She had not reached fourteen and the Zar had been an old man by her standards, but that had not mattered. She had given him a prince nine months later and he had given her the ultimate reward, calling her Absolute Favorite.

Someone cleared their throat and interrupted her private musings. She spun around to see Tariq.

"We're here, Valide," the Vizier said.

Herezah bit her tongue on the retort that the unhappy moans of children had told her as much. "Remove the canopy," she ordered, and it was done.

Salmeo bowed his enormous bulk before her. She noticed he was wearing all black silks in honor of the soon-to-be-dead. His painted nail was the only patch of color amid the dark of his skin and robes. She glanced briefly to her left and saw Lazar, grinding his teeth. He had already given his orders to his men and did not need to remain. She knew that a reluctant sense of honor and respect for the young princes would keep him there.

"Shall we call for the creatures, Valide?" It was Tariq again, determined to take charge of proceedings.

She saw Salmeo scowl. "Grand Master of the Eunuchs," she called. Much as she detested Salmeo, she knew he was vital to her success. Despite her new status, Herezah did not relish him as an enemy; besides, he would be a powerful ally. "Please take charge." She refused to look at the Vizier, who she was sure was visibly fuming at being overlooked.

Again the huge man bowed, and as he straightened, the look that passed between him and the Valide Zara spoke much of what never needed to be said out loud. An understanding had been reached. They were now a partnership, the past set aside.

"Bring the elephants," he bellowed in a voice the harem rarely heard. Salmeo preferred to intimidate with his gentle, lisping lilt.

At the order fresh screams erupted from the imprisoned children. Suddenly none of them felt comforted by the notion of a game. Elephants were neither cuddly nor playful. Why were they being called? All of the children had marveled at them in their father's magnificent private zoo, but the lumbering giants were dangerous, especially the four males, which were now led by their keepers to the pit. The noise of the children's terror increased as the large animals trumpeted loudly.

At Salmeo's signal the huge animals were run into the pit and encouraged to raise themselves on their hind legs and stomp down, a trick they had been taught to entertain the children.

The first bag to stop moving was the smallest. Herezah winced. Ayeesha's baby. Her thoughts went to the mother for a moment of pity; then she promised she would wince no more. All these children were potential murderers of her son. Even the other wives, demented by grief as they were, would ultimately understand, as she too would have had to do had she not been the mother of Joreb's Chosen One.

Soon enough all the bags stopped their writhing and pitiful screams. Odd moans were quickly dealt with by an elephant's strategically placed foot. The Vizier, Herezah noticed, did look away when one sack broke and bright blood splashed the dazzling white cotton robes of one of the handlers. She recognized the face of that child, but only just—he was Boaz's closest half brother; they had been born just weeks apart. The back of the boy's head was smashed, its wet contents leaking out. She did not look away but cast quiet thanks to the gods for saving Boaz this trial.

Lazar, beside her, had not spoken or moved, but she was sure if it were quieter she would be able to hear his teeth grinding, for his jaw was working furiously. However, her stolen glance from beneath the gauze told her he did not cower but stared straight ahead at the grisly scene until Salmeo called a halt to proceedings. The Grand Master Eunuch had decided that the bags contained little more than pulp now. No bodies would be handed back to grieving mothers. They would be burned immediately, following the Valide Zara's instructions.

Herezah sighed, relieved that it was done. The throne was safe.

As if reading her thoughts, Lazar turned slowly, deliberately, and looked straight into her eyes as though he could see through the veil and deep into her soul. "Satisfied, Valide?"

She would not be baited. "Careful, Lazar. A new Spur can be appointed as easily as I blink."

"As you see fit, Valide Zara," he said, not intimidated at all. "Excuse me, duty calls," he added before she could return his brittle reply.

Herezah reined in her natural reaction. She might suddenly be the most powerful woman in Percheron, but she was far too mindful of the Zar's warning when he had called for her earlier that day.

"Keep Lazar close to our son. He alone understands the Galinsean mind."

No, she would not be replacing this Spur when he might be all that stood between Percheron and a Galinsean uprising, especially now that a boy sat the throne. She would let him have his anger for now. Herezah was clever enough to work out more subtle ways to have her revenge and she would exercise these as soon as the old Zar was cremated.

In fact, a wonderful notion was already taking shape in her mind.

5

Lazar shaded his eyes and squinted into the shimmering scene below. He and his longtime companion, Jumo, had been directed here by scouts. Out to the west the sun was already past its high point, and the fiercest heat of the day was scorching. He wrapped the tail of the white turban around his face, a gesture born purely of habit; in the foothills, sand was not a problem unless the feared Samazen whipped up, and that was a month away at least. Though it would get hotter still today before it cooled, time was against them. Night fell fast across the desert plains, and although these were only the western foothills, barely fifteen miles from Percheron, the darkness would race to claim them faster than they could ride home. Not that being away bothered Lazar. They had been out on the ridges for days and he was happiest when he was away from people.

Home! He scorned himself for thinking of it that way.

Percheron had, however, become a sanctuary. It still had its distasteful elements, and immediately Herezah came to mind, but surely there could be no realm more beautiful. Percheron had seduced him and he had become her willing lover. He wondered, as he gazed down at a tiny dwelling that clung to the steppes, whether he could ever leave the stone city. Until recently he would have answered no. Now he wasn't so sure. Herezah's influence was already being felt and he sensed her bite was only going to get worse.

She had disbanded the harem the same day as Joreb's funeral procession. Once more he had been forced to grind his teeth and sit out an entirely unpleasant spectacle. The Valide Zara had masterminded the event down to the tiniest detail, to the point of ordering that the horses that pulled the open-topped carriage and the old Zar's corpse have the underneath of their eyelids smeared with pepper paste, to make it appear that even dumb beasts had shed tears for the Great One's passing.

Lazar had never heard of anything quite so ridiculous, but there was plenty more to come. Four virgins, holy women chosen for their beauty, had been drugged and thrown into the flames of the pyre. This was supposedly to symbolize each season of the old Zar's life, from birth through childhood, to adolescence and manhood. It was also a sly reminder that Joreb was the god Zarab's appointed representative on the land. Burning the holy women reinforced the destruction of the Goddess Lyana and the pointlessness of those who still privately worshipped her.

Herezah's third and final spectacle was to have the women of the harem unveiled, which was the most painful humiliation she could impose. It was more grievous than death for most of these women, who were put into ordinary clothes before being paraded on foot and forced out of the palace and into the streets. Each one was given a pouch of gold and cut loose from the protection of the harem and the lavish, lazy world she had known. These women could sew, make fine quishtar, and gossip: that was the sum total of their accomplishments . . . unless, of course, one counted their ability to pleasure men to heights of ecstasy. If they looked after their money, hopefully that talent would not need to be promoted in the outside world that these confused wretches now inhabited.

Where they went, how they lived, or even if they survived, Herezah could not have cared less about. They were no longer required. Their role as servants of the Zar died with him. As for those who claimed the title of wife, they no longer had status. That had died with the Zar and his eleven precious offspring.

Her next step was to assemble a new harem. Displaying her dark sense of humor, she had ordered the Spur of Percheron to join the hunt for suitable young girls. Fuming at his orders, personally delivered by the Valide, Lazar had considered riding out of the city gates and never returning.

To calm himself he had strode in the direction of the harbor, knowing he would pass some of the city's inexplicably beautiful sculpted beasts on his way. Despite their implacable silence and stone flesh, the creatures of myth had a warm, lifelike quality to them. The only humanlike sculptures were the twin giants, Beloch and Ezram, who presided over the city's busy harbor, a massive horseshoe-shaped sparkling bay.

No, despite Herezah's presence, Percheron's enchantment for him had not waned over the years. In fact, he felt more connected to this city than to his own.

His own. The thought made him sigh inwardly; it was his homeland across the ocean he had been thinking about as he had reached to touch his favorite creature—Iridor, the owl . . . the messenger of the Goddess Lyana.

Iridor had always attracted him and he could rarely pass any of the bird's images dotted around the city without pausing momentarily to admire the owl or share a thought. Though Lazar would never admit it to anyone, Iridor felt like an old friend. He was the first of the stone sculptures Lazar had seen when brought through the vast Golden Gates of Percheron, and the knowing expression on the owl's face had left a lasting impression. Lazar had often thought somewhat whimsically that it was the secretive bird who had urged him to put forward the reckless challenge to the Zar that had won him favor.

No one else, or so it appeared, bothered with the owl or any of the other magnificent engravings or sculptures. Some argued that Percheron was spoiled for art treasures and that the Percherese, who grew up surrounded by such beauty, took it for granted. But there was more to it than that. Lazar knew that the people had been taught from childhood that the ornate statues of the beasts and giants were linked to the Goddess, and Lyana had no place in Percheron. Her followers had long ago been dismissed as cranks, and although some women still continued to worship at her shrine, they were few and far between.

Percheron's spiritual well-being had been cared for by the priesthood for many centuries now and Lyana had faded to myth. It was thought that the statues themselves dated back to the last occasion when the cyclical battle of the gods had erupted, but no one knew for sure.

Nevertheless, whether it was truth or folklore, Lazar loved the story. He thought about it again as he stared at Iridor, sworn enemy of Lyana's nemesis, Maliz, the demon warlock granted eternal life by the jealous god Zarab. Hating Lyana's popularity,

Zarab had offered Maliz the ultimate prize if he would rid the world of the Goddess and give men ultimate ruling over the matriarchal society in which form Percheron had thrived.

Lazar gave a rare smile as he thought about the rising of Iridor, which signified the return of Lyana and triggered the reincarnation of Maliz. They would do battle every four or five centuries, or so the story went. But too many battles had been fought since Lyana had prevailed, her memory all but wiped out as a result of constant defeat; the statues were the only testament to her once powerful hold over Percheron. According to the myth, these beasts had been part of her army, supposedly turned to stone by Maliz in the last great battle.

The few true believers swore Lyana would rise again to fight another battle. Lazar liked this notion.

He had left behind the city proper to stroll down to the harbor, into the more seedy area of Percheron, always a hive of activity and somewhere to lose oneself. Here, in the mass of twisting lanes that had sprung up haphazardly around the eastern rim of the harbor, he could be anonymous. This was not a place where the wealthy or famous went. It was the haunt of the peasant Percherese and thieves, sailors, low-class merchants, and prostitutes. Lazar, wearing the common robes of the streets, had moved swiftly through the market area and beyond to an open road that led to a lonely temple, a tiny one that sat on a narrow strip of a peninsula jutting a mile into the bay. Not as far out as Beloch, of course, but only people on boats could get close to the brothers. Lazar looked out to where the enormous stone giant stood proudly guarding his city. Opposite him, flanking the other tip of the harbor's horseshoe shape, was Beloch's twin, Ezram.

Arriving at the tiny place of worship, Lazar had climbed the

short flight of stairs into the small vaulted space of simple design. This was a temple that harkened back to the old ways, to a
time when goddesses were worshipped and priestesses led
prayers. Although he had never been inside it before, Lazar
liked its remoteness, and as Lyana had been in his mind, it
seemed a good enough place to go for some quiet. He lit a small
candle and knelt at the altar below a sculpture of a serene
woman who looked down upon him. He should have bowed his
head in prayer but he could not take his eyes from the statue.
Her soft smile was so tranquil, her eyes so sad, reflecting his
mood. He fancied that her expression had been carved just for
him, for this very day when he entered her temple with a heavy
heart and a question on his mind. On her right shoulder sat an
owl—Iridor—and amid the folds of her dress flitted an assort-
ment of birds and strange symbols. Just looking at her soothed
his anger.

"She's beautiful, isn't she?" a voice had said, and when he
turned a tiny hunched woman emerged from the shadows. She
was dressed in aquamarine robes the color of the sea her tiny
temple overlooked.

"I am Lazar, Spur of Percheron, Priestess," he had said,
standing and bowing.

When he straightened she was smiling. "We have been expecting you."

He had been taken aback. "We?"

In answer she had looked toward the sculpture. "This is
Lyana. She especially welcomes you."

"She is the loveliest of all the stone sculptures in Percheron,"
he had replied.

"Has she helped?"

"Pardon?"

"Did she answer your question?"

He had frowned. "I haven't asked anything of her."

Again the soft knowing smile. "Not yet, perhaps. Forgive my disturbance, son. Please continue." The old woman had made as if to leave.

"Wait." When she had turned to look at him, he had hesitated. "What did you mean, you were expecting me?"

"We have been waiting many years to meet you, Lazar. You have a reason for being in Percheron. You are welcome here always."

He had had no idea what she was talking about but her soft voice had been mesmerizing, as soothing as her sculpture's smile. "I don't know your name."

"I am Zafira. We shall meet another time soon." Once more she had turned to leave and again he had stopped her.

"What can she tell me?" he had asked.

She hadn't turned that time. "Please stay—you are needed here," she had said as the shadows swallowed her.

Lazar had puzzled over that brief conversation for many days now. How could the old priestess have known he was thinking of leaving the city? In fact, it had been her words that had convinced him not to ride out of the city in anger but to remain in Percheron—for now anyway. There was something about the certainty of the way she spoke to him that made him obey.

Jumo disturbed Lazar's thoughts. "Is all well, Master?" he asked, guiding his horse to stand alongside Lazar's.

Lazar smiled. He and Jumo had long ago ceased being master and slave, ever since Lazar had granted the reed-thin man his freedom. But Jumo had neither refrained from using the title nor from serving Lazar. They were now the closest of friends, their deep bond an unspoken commitment between them. Lazar had once described to Pez that losing Jumo would be like losing his limbs or his sight.

"All is well," he answered, looking into his friend's swarthy face, the color of molasses and creased in bemusement. Jumo came from an exotic land far to the north that Lazar had never seen and was unlikely to see. "Am I making you nervous?" he asked, knowing full well that very little, least of all silence, unsettled Jumo.

They had been a party of twelve, but as each girl had been found, she had been sent off with two escorts to the city. Herezah had demanded six girls from Lazar's foray into the foothills. He had sent five safely on their way.

Jumo's face broke into the smile he reserved for very few. "No, your quiet manner is not making me nervous. What is troubling you, Master?"

Lazar sighed. "Nothing, my friend. I'm fine. Just still questioning this unpleasant task of ours."

"They will fill a harem with or without your help," Jumo offered. "We need only one more girl to fill our quota. Her family will be happy, the Valide will be happy, surely the Zar will be happy, and you, Master, you will be happy to be returning to your proper duties. Everyone will be happy."

"Typical Jumo reasoning," Lazar replied drily. "You're right, although I don't know why I feel so reluctant to disturb that gentle scene down there."

They both looked at the hut, its chimney smoking cheerfully. Outside two young girls, presumably sisters, sat, their backs to the men. They were as different as two sisters could be; the elder was dark, the younger one lighter; the sunlight picked up fiery glints in her hair as her sister brushed it. A much smaller child, a boy, buzzed around them like a fly. Nearby another female squatted, sorting rice in a large basin, her repetitive action one Lazar had often seen in the neighborhoods of Percheron. Lazar and Jumo watched her drag her hand flat across the surface of the grains, spreading them, then begin sorting grit and stones from the rice.

"Do you think that is the mother, Master?"

"Looks rather young," Lazar replied, slightly mesmerized by the simple toil that the woman somehow managed to make elegant with her slim arms and long fingers. "No, this would be the mother," he added as a broader, clearly older woman emerged from the hut. He watched her squint as her eyes adjusted to the brightness.

"The father is a goatherd, I gather," Jumo said, nodding toward the small pens beside the dwelling.

Lazar nodded. "The scouts warned he would probably be away."

"Does that bother you?"

"To take one of his children in his absence? It is up to the mother, I suppose."

"You will offer a high sum for the lighter-colored child, of course," Jumo said, referring to the youngest girl.

"We need to see her face first," Lazar answered, his tone dark with gathering anger. "Herezah might blame me for not selecting suitably but I know how her mind works—she'd punish the child to get to me. No, we've done well so far, even the Valide could not complain, but I'll be damned if I'll give her anything to gripe about. I've seen what she's capable of and age is of no relevance to her."

"Let us see for ourselves, then. Come," Jumo replied. "It is getting late."

Lazar sighed. He looked out from the foothills. Through the hazy heat he could just see the whitish sprawl that was Percheron, but the sea and the sky blended into a mass of bright blue. He wondered briefly whether he should take a voyage. It had been a long time since he'd seen his parents and siblings. His mother might even have forgiven him by now, although he doubted it. She was carved from the same block as Herezah—neither of them would ever forgive.

"You love the desert too much to leave it, Master," Jumo said softly beside him, and their eyes met.

"You frighten me the way you can read my mind."

Jumo grinned. "I've just known you long enough to guess."

Lazar thought otherwise. It was uncanny how often Jumo seemed to know his private thoughts. But he left it alone, as he always did. "Lead the way," he said, and as he did so the younger of the two girls turned and looked directly at them. She did not seem troubled by their presence, but the others were when she pointed, the mother gathering up her family around her and watching their approach wide-eyed, ready to flee like a startled animal.

Lazar pressed on doggedly down the incline, for even from this distance he could see the child was pleasant enough to look upon. Herezah would certainly have nothing to complain about.

"Don't be frightened, woman," Lazar assured the mother as the land flattened out and he was able to dismount. "I am the Spur of Percheron. This," he said, nodding behind him, "is Jumo."

The mother nodded at both of them. "What do you want?"

Lazar had done this five times in the last few days but it never got easier. It was unlikely that anyone had brought these people news of the Zar's death, so it was not as though they could even guess at his purpose. How he hated this task.

"May I know your name?" he asked the mother.

"Felluj," she said abruptly.

"Well, I bring a proposal from the palace, Felluj."

Felluj looked momentarily startled. "No one in the palace knows us."

Lazar cleared his throat. "That's probably true. But I have offered this same proposal successfully to several families in the foothills in the last few days."

"You come for my girls, don't you? My brother-in-law warned you might."

There was no point in denying it or hedging around it. He nodded. "Not all of them."

Her solemn expression did not change but he saw something flash in the dark eyes. "You can have only Ana."

"No, Mother!" the daughter who had been brushing her young sister's hair cried, and Lazar turned to her, despising himself for the pain he had caused to cross her features. His gaze shifted to the small child whose hand she clutched.

"Ana," he began, talking to the youngest girl.

"That is not her," the mother interrupted, before turning to the daughter who held the rice bowl. "Fetch her."

"Uncle Horz said—"

"Hush!"

"But Father won't—"

"Do it!" the mother ordered. The girl disappeared into the hut. "How much?"

Lazar was taken aback by the harsh exchange between mother and daughter and unsettled by Felluj's cold attitude. "Er, we need to see her first."

"Oh, she'll suit your purposes. But I won't let her go cheaply."

To add to Lazar's discomfort, the two younger girls were weeping now. At least the young boy continued to run in small circles, chasing insects and wholly oblivious to the transaction that was occurring.

The mother must have heard some movement because she called into the silence: "Don't hide, Ana! Come here, girl."

The elder sister who had been sent to fetch Ana appeared first, scowling, reluctantly pulling another girl who seemed unaffected by all the attention.

She looked like a young colt, with long legs and square shoulders tapering through a slender body beneath the loose-fitting sheath that clothed her. Despite the roomy garment, the definite swell of a woman's body was visible beneath. In truth, only Jumo noticed the rest of the child; all Lazar could focus on was her face, which was oval and framed by darkly golden hair that fell carelessly to her shoulders and seemed to absorb the very sunlight. But it was her eyes, shadowed by long dark lashes, that dragged him completely into her spell. Lazar could not register their color even though he was staring right into them, for they seemed to dominate him, to own him. There was a sense of drowning in those dreamy pools.

"Master?" Jumo urged quietly.

Lazar pulled himself free of his suddenly muddled thoughts and saw that the girl's eyes were a sea green and that her mother was mocking him with a sly smile.

"Good enough?" she asked, unable to hide her sarcasm.

The Spur's mouth felt so dry that he could not trust himself to speak. His gaze was drawn back to the girl who stared unerringly at him.

"How old is she?" he finally asked.

"I'm nearly fourteen summers," the Ana replied.

"She's ripe for your purposes," the mother said matter-of-factly.

Lazar watched the eldest girl scowl again. "What is your name?" he asked.

"I am Amys," she answered sullenly. "And my father will not agree to this."

"Hush!" Felluj admonished. "I will make the decision. Come, Masters, let us talk in private over kerrosh."

Lazar could not refuse. Hospitality was the way of the desert people; even the poorest family would slaughter its last goat to entertain a visitor. The brewing of the bitter kerrosh was high tradition in Percheron, and among the harem women it was nothing short of an art form.

"Where is your husband?" he asked the woman when they were seated in the hut.

"He is moving some of the goats. He has been away for several days."

"Why is your older daughter worried about her uncle? She's also adamant that her father will object—is this true?" It seemed a stupid question even to him. Which father wouldn't object to losing his daughter to a stranger?

Before the woman could answer, Jumo spoke up. "The harem will take care of your daughter and raise her in unrivaled splendor," he assured the mother. His eyes met Lazar's, and Lazar realized the words were meant for him as well.

"She will be taught skills and she will read, write, dance. She will be given wealth and even status if she pleases her elders."

"How much are you prepared to pay for her?" the mother demanded, ending Jumo's gracious explanation.

"You seem quite keen to be rid of the girl," Lazar commented.

Felluj shrugged. "She's not my child." As Lazar's eyebrow rose in query, the woman explained. "She belongs to my husband."

"She's his daughter?"

The woman laid three glasses on the scrubbed table.

"She's not his either. He found her."

"Pardon?"

The woman poured a steaming glass of kerrosh before him. "I've put in one ball," she said, referring to the sticky mass of sugar favored by most in the beverage.

"Thank you. Please continue." Lazar sipped his drink. It was good, strong and sweet.

The mother passed Jumo his glass. "My husband found Ana as a newborn on the northern ridges. It had been a wild night, the Samazen had blown through, and the next morning he went in search of the goats that had been pastured up there. He'd lost his animals but found her instead. A useless exchange as far as I'm concerned. At least goats keep us fed, give us milk, provide yarn and skins."

"A baby survived the storm?" Jumo voiced Lazar's silent incredulity.

Again the woman shrugged. "I'm telling you what happened. You can believe me or not. He brought her home and raised her as his own. In truth, one more mouth didn't matter so much then, but we've had two more children since. I've never felt about Ana the way my husband does."

"Your daughters show a concern you don't," Lazar commented.

"Pah! They're just worried about their father's feelings but I worry about how we will feed and clothe ourselves. She's another woman's daughter! I'm glad to see the back of her."

"Clearly," Lazar muttered, as if he were tasting something bad. "This must be done properly, Felluj. I won't be accused of stealing a child." There was derision in her laughter at these words and Lazar understood. Girls were often stolen from these tiny foothill families by bandits and sold into slavery. "I am a royal representative of the highest law in the land," he qualified. "Your husband must—"

She interrupted him. "He will understand when he sees your coin."

Lazar felt suddenly sickened by her attitude; it reminded him of Herezah. Two mothers, both using children to elevate their status. He knew what it was to live without a mother's love. Perhaps a life of luxurious imprisonment was better for Ana than what was on offer here.

"What price freedom?" Jumo said, as though responding to Lazar's silent thought.

"You tell me," Felluj said, "and then I'll tell you whether it's enough to appease my husband."

"Twenty-five karels," Lazar offered, which was low. He hated Felluj's greed.

She laughed. "Fifty and you can have her."

He drained his glass. "Fifty?" He raised an eyebrow, waiting for her to capitulate and decrease her price.

"She's worth twice as much," Felluj said, not at all intimidated.

"Not to us," Lazar said, and stood. "Thank you for the kerrosh."

She said nothing but he saw a slight hesitancy in her expression.

The children watched them wide-eyed as they emerged from the hut, squinting from the bright sun, and only Ana smiled, a bright, spontaneous gesture. Lazar felt the jolt of it catch in his throat; the warmth in her innocent expression reached into his chest and touched a cold heart. How long had it been since he had felt anything for anyone? Oh, the friendship between himself and Jumo was indestructible, as was the curious affinity he felt for the strange dwarf, Pez; and he liked Boaz well enough. But love? Love had visited briefly in his youth and then been torn away; since that time he had let no one into his heart. Something about Ana's simple smile stirred thoughts long buried and wounds he had healed through detachment and determination. He felt suddenly weakened.

"Farewell, sister," he said deliberately—the words were meant for Felluj but he spoke toward Ana's soft green gaze.

No one responded as the two men silently climbed onto their horses. Lazar gave one last look at Ana, who was now expressionless, and at her stepmother, in whom he sensed growing disbelief. He turned his horse back toward the steep path and began counting. He would give it to fifty.

He had passed the count and was resigning himself to having read the situation wrongly when he heard a voice. It was Felluj; she had run swiftly up the incline at a sharper angle than they were traversing and was waiting for them at the top of the ridge. She was breathing hard and still looked defiant. There was no preamble or pretense at dealing with honored guests now; there was a bargain to be made and goods to be negotiated. He had seen it often enough in the slave markets—this was no different. "How much, then?" she demanded.

"I told you before," he said coldly. "Twenty-five."

"That is too low, sir," she pleaded, her first display of courtesy since they had arrived, save the kerrosh.

"It is fair," he replied feeling rather than seeing Jumo's unease. They both knew Ana was worth three, maybe four times as much, and even Lazar couldn't understand his reluctance to pay a premium for the stunning girl.

"My husband will grieve for her. She is his favorite and she's not even of his own flesh." Felluj spat into the sandy soil of the ridge.

Ana appeared behind her stepmother, clambering up the ridge. Lazar could see in those long-lashed eyes that this girl knew no affection existed for her in Felluj's heart. And it was this notion alone, this sense of pain on behalf of the girl—a pain he understood—that forced Lazar to relent.

"I shall give you forty karels. Ask no more, woman, for you shall get not a zeraf extra from me."

"I shall take it," she replied instantly, "if you take her now. She has no possessions."

"Will she not want to wish her family farewell?" Jumo asked.

"Take her, I say!" Felluj urged, pushing Ana toward them.

"Give her to Jumo," Lazar ordered, reaching for a pouch at his side. He counted out the karels and said: "Hold out your apron."

She did so and he dropped the silver from a height, not even bothering to reach down. One karel bounced out and Felluj went scrabbling after it.

"I don't want to leave my father or my brother and sisters," Ana said into the awkward silence.

"Hush, child," Jumo murmured. "You must come with us now."

She did not struggle but began to weep softly, looking behind to wave pitifully to her brother and sisters below.

"Fret not, Ana," Jumo soothed. "In the palace you will have fine gowns and beautiful jewels, all the food you can eat, and lots of friends."

"But I have no desire for fine gowns and I have never wished for a jewel. We eat well here—simply but well, and I have all the company I could ever want." Her tears continued to fall down her cheeks as she fell quiet.

All the purchases of young girls had been hard on Lazar but this one touched his heart, for in truth the other girls had been seduced by the idea of wealth and luxury. Ana was by far the most beautiful, but by her own admission, neither riches nor pampering held any appeal for her.

They departed with the sound of forty pieces of silver jangling in Felluj's apron as she stomped back down the ridge to her family, and soon Ana's home and even the ridge she lived below was out of sight.

"What do you want me for, sir?" she asked, reaching from Jumo's horse to tug at Lazar's sleeve.

"I do not want you for anything, Ana," he said, more sorrowfully than he intended. "You belong to the Zar now, his odalisque."

6

Zafira lived in a tiny dwelling in the attic of the temple, reached by narrow stone stairs and with a breathtaking view across the harbor. She shared it with doves mainly, who liked the high vantage point of the eaves to roost amid, but she made welcome the many small birds that came daily to her window for scraps and fresh water.

She had her back to that window and its sprawling vista at this moment and wondered again, as she stared into the steamy swirls rising from her cinnamon tea, about her recent visitor and his importance. The voices that haunted her dreams had told her to wait for him and to welcome him when he finally came. She had waited in vain for several years, almost forgetting about it, and then suddenly, two days ago, the man they had spoken of had wandered into the temple. They had given her no description of him and yet she knew instinctively that the Spur was the one. She had seen this man from a distance ranging around the city, but now that she could see him from such a close perspective, he was younger than she had expected, with rugged looks and a remote disposition. Everything about him was hard: the angular planes to his face, the way he carried himself with such bristling strength beneath the loose robes, the determined stride, the glower he regarded her with, even the anger she sensed he repressed. His words, his attitude—all of him seemed hardened. But not cruel. No; secretive perhaps, determined, bitter even, but not cruel, for all that hard exterior.

Why was he important? Important to what? She could not guess.

Her present visitor interrupted her musings. "I'll pay you for them," he said.

She smiled. "Mindless stuff, Pez, I promise," she said, sipping her tea. "Is your quishtar all right?"

"Delicious and you know it," he replied. "No one brews better than you, Zafira."

"Perhaps that's what I'll be remembered for," she said, amused.

"More, I imagine," Pez answered, something cryptic in his glance.

She left it alone. Pez was mysterious enough without reading into his words or second-guessing the strange machinations of his mind.

"How did you come to be here, Pez?" she asked suddenly, glad to move away from her confused thoughts.

"Like most of the foreigners here, I was captured and sold as a slave. Except I was such an oddity there was really only one place for me."

"How convenient, then, that you have such an amusing way."

Pez eyed the priestess in a serious manner very few were permitted to see. "You know better than to goad me, Zafira."

She took his admonishment in the gentle manner it was given. "You're such an enigma, Pez. Why is everyone around me so mysterious?"

"Oh? Who else has you so baffled?"

"The Spur paid the temple a visit."

Pez nodded. "Yes, well, he left the palace seething. I'm not surprised he needed somewhere to calm himself. And where better than here?"

Noting Zafira's expression of query, Pez explained about Lazar's special duties.

"Oh, I see," the priestess said. "He did seem troubled."

Pez's odd collection of features rearranged themselves into a smile. "Troubled is an understatement. I think it was very good that he left the city for a while."

"Why to the temple first, though?" she wondered aloud, adding unexpectedly: "I've been having dreams, Pez."

"Oh?" he said, unfazed by the sudden switch in topic. "Can I help?"

"I don't think so. I don't even know why I'm telling you this."

"Because we're friends, Zafira, and heaven knows there are few enough of those in this place."

She nodded, understanding only too well. "But why are we friends? Why have we chosen each other? How is it that I know you are perfectly sane whilst the palace believes you are the opposite?"

"You question life too much, old woman," he replied gently, cupping his deformed hands around the cooling bowl of half-drunk tea. "You and I are both seeking the same thing—we recognize it in each other; it's why we are friends."

"What is it we search for?" Zafira heard the plea in her voice and wondered at it. Why did she think Pez would have an answer for her?

The jester shrugged. "We shall know it when it presents itself. And to answer your other question, I keep my sanity a secret because the semblance of madness protects me. It is my only defense in a highly dangerous place."

"I'm sorry, Pez. I don't know what's come over me today. I have this sense of . . ." She trailed off, shaking her head.

"A sense of what?"

The priestess turned her hands palms up in bafflement. "That something is in motion and it somehow involves me."

"What do you mean?"

"Something important."

"Go on."

She gave a look of exasperation. "I don't know, Pez. That's just it."

"Is it connected with your dreams?"

She nodded. "I'm sure of it but I can't really remember anything specific. I was told to expect a man and that he was important."

"The voices you spoke of told you this?"

"Whispers, really. But I can't tell you precisely what they said."

"How do you know they meant Lazar?"

"I don't but I feel very sure it's him. Why I was told to expect this person I have no idea. Oh, Pez, I'm sorry to sound so vague."

"Don't upset yourself, my friend. I myself feel I'm here for a reason but can't tell you why." He smiled sadly.

"How long have you been in Percheron, Pez?"

He looked around and scratched his chin. In profile, his hooked nose looked even more prominent. "It must be past two decades now," he answered.

"That long!"

"Must be. Boaz is fifteen and I was the Zar's jester for at least six summers before our new ruler was born."

She smiled. "And you've frustrated, exasperated, and deliberately irritated Herezah for all that time, I'm sure."

"Oh, that's the least I can do," he replied, sharing her amusement. "I hope you have no spies here, my friend, or our new Valide will have our heads on spikes before we pour another glass of tea."

She stood to heat fresh water. "Fret not, Pez. My doves here would warn me if anyone is around . . . they coo at the slightest thing. I gather the changes have already begun at the palace. You'll have to watch yourself."

"She hates me, that's clear, but mainly for the reason you speak of—that I frustrate her. I know she's using magical means to dig into my past, my mind."

"What kind of magic?"

"Yozem."

The priestess made a sound of disgust. "Evil woman, a curse to her kind."

"She can find nothing on me," he said softly.

"Why not? Aren't people terrified of her because she can read anyone?"

Pez pulled an expression to suggest he was not bothered by it. "Most don't even know whether or not she exists. She does, of course, holed up in the horrid cryptlike chambers beneath the palace. Either I'm impervious to her dark magicks or they don't exist and she's a fake. Whichever way it is, Herezah has nothing she can lay at my feet, and besides, Boaz loves me to bits. She will not win an argument for my death with the new Zar—trust me."

"You're very confident, Pez," Zafira said warily.

"I am also very careful, my friend. Don't worry about me."

"What about Tariq and that vile head eunuch?"

Pez nodded. "With Herezah's influence and the power she will extend to them, I think we have a right to be worried. It's why Lazar's presence around the palace is important. He brings balance. Boaz worships Lazar, which is good fortune for us, for he listens to what the Spur advises. I don't think our new Zar has much time for Tariq but he's still young. We cannot expect too much of Boaz too soon—he still has a very young man's notions and urges. In all truth, I'm sure that he would rather ride and shoot, fish and play, than think about political matters. This is what Herezah is counting on, of course. She'll fuel his pleasures, all the time usurping more and more power for herself and her sycophants."

"It's a grim picture you paint," Zafira said.

"Well, the assembling of a harem will keep all three of them busy for a while."

Zafira nodded and they sat in comfortable silence for several moments as she poured fresh bowls of tea and moved to the window. She sighed. "So, I wonder what it is that we're both waiting for." She stared out to sea and, as always, marveled at the grandeur of the twins in the harbor. "I feel like we're Beloch and Ezram out there, waiting for something to happen."

"You might be right, old friend," Pez answered.

LAZAR SEEMED TO BE in no urgency to return to the city. They had made camp on a rocky outcrop and could now clearly see the sparkling waters of the Faranel and the glittering city spreading down to her edge. It was as if pastel lava had erupted from the hilltop where the palace stood and slid down to the natural harbor, hardening on its slow journey to form the superb architecture of Percheron.

It was Ana who made this observation, much to the silent delight of Lazar, who was quiet at the best of times but downright sullen this evening. "And you've seen a mountain erupt and spill the earth's hot contents, have you?"

"In my dreams I have," she said, frowning. "I think they must exist somewhere across the lands—though when I saw it, it was frightening, whereas Percheron lifts my heart."

Lazar said nothing but was secretly pleased by Ana's description of Percheron. Since first seeing the city, he too had always felt . . . what was it? Restored?

"Well, I think it's a beautiful notion, Ana," Jumo said, filling the silence, "and shall always think of the city that way from now on."

"Do you not like me, sir?" Ana asked, turning her direct gaze on Lazar.

"What makes you say that?" he growled, busying himself with stirring the glowing coals of their small fire.

"You glare a lot at me, sir. I don't know what I've done wrong."

"You've done nothing wrong, Ana," he answered.

"That's his happy face," Jumo chimed in, and Ana giggled with him, which won a fresh scowl from Lazar.

"What are you sad about, then?" she persisted.

"I don't know," Lazar answered, a sudden wistfulness in his tone that puzzled Jumo. "Here, eat," he added, handing Ana a piece of the poultry they had cooked.

"I don't eat birds," she said apologetically.

"This is chicken. Not a real bird," Jumo put in.

"Because it doesn't fly, you mean?" she said. At his nod, she shook her head. "It has wings, Jumo. I think a chicken would fly if it could, which makes it a bird for me."

"We'd all fly if we could," Lazar grumbled.

Ana seemed to find this amusing and laughed again at the Spur. Jumo thought about the last person who laughed at Lazar and wondered where his head had ended up. And yet here he was allowing a young slip of a thing tease him. Would wonders never cease?

"Well, I think you'd better change your attitude and at least pretend to be gracious about any food put before you. The palace will indulge its girls but not necessarily their personal whims. As it's your final night of freedom, I will respect your aversion to eating bird, but if you're not going to eat, let me suggest you sleep," Lazar said to Ana. "Tomorrow we'll ride all day and reach the city late. There won't even be time to catch your breath. Valide Zara will be keen to see you."

"Who's Valide Zara?"

Lazar frowned at the thought. "She's your new mistress."

"Is that who you're selling me to?"

"She has already bought you, Ana, not me. Your mother sold you to the harem."

"Felluj is not my mother. I should prefer to stay with you and Jumo."

The men glanced at each other. "You will be all right in the harem, Ana," Lazar assured her. "You'll make friends quickly, I promise."

"Are you my friend, Lazar? Promise me you'll always be my friend."

Jumo grinned privately. He had never seen his master so disconcerted.

"You have my word," Lazar promised awkwardly.

7

They arrived before sunset, a couple of hours earlier than Lazar had anticipated, so he decided to give Ana a brief tour of Percheron, knowing she might never be permitted to see the beautiful city again. By tomorrow morning Ana would know she was a prisoner, with all those qualities that made her such an intriguing free spirit stamped out of her until she performed in the remote, rehearsed manner of all the harem women. He had heard tales of their personalities surfacing in the bathing rooms and behind closed doors, and he could believe it. Wanted to believe it. But for all intents and purposes, the women of the harem lost their right to free expression. Perhaps even Herezah had been a carefree young thing once.

Herezah! The very thought of the woman made him want to linger as long as possible outside the palace itself.

"Jumo, perhaps you could take the horses and our things back to the palace barracks?"

"Are you not coming, Master?"

"I thought I'd show our guest a little of Percheron's sights before I deliver her to Salmeo."

"Very good," Jumo replied, but his warning glance said far more. "Good-bye, Ana." He helped the youngster from the horse they had shared.

She surprised him with a hug. "Good-bye, friend Jumo. You won't forget me, will you?"

"Never. You will make us proud. One day I suspect Spur Lazar and I will have to bow before you."

"I would never make you do that." She smiled softly.

Jumo straightened and took the reins of Lazar's horse. "Be careful, Master" was all he would risk.

"I shall be back within a couple of hours at the most," Lazar assured him. "Come, Ana, let me show you some of this beautiful city." He turned his back on both of them and strode off.

"You'd better hurry, child," Jumo urged. "He waits for no one."

Ana spared a final glance for the tawny man and then she was lost amid the crowd of people pushing toward the main gates. It was not hard to spot Lazar towering over the shorter Percherese population. He had taken off his head covering and his dark hair had fallen loose to just above his shoulders. It could do with a good wash and brushing. Ana imagined how it might feel if she was attending to it, and a warmth passed through her body. It felt good to be near Lazar, yet, if asked to explain why, she was not sure she could do so, particularly as he was so distant and grumpy. Her young mind could not wrap itself fully around it but she wondered if he was someone who could be badly hurt. A person who covered his weakness with his gruff manner. Despite that vulnerability, Ana sensed only intense power in the man. Although he might follow orders, she guessed that no one told Lazar what to do; she knew in her heart that she had a similar trait. Life was obviously going to be difficult for her now that she had an "owner" to answer to. Ana decided that she and Lazar were souls who were destined to meet, and as this notion gelled in her mind, she realized she had caught up with the man who claimed her thoughts. Startling both herself and him, Ana reached for his hand.

"I might lose you," she said in answer to his surprised glare.

He frowned but let his hand remain in hers. "Look at these creatures, will you?" He marveled as they approached the city walls. "Aren't they spectacular sculptures?"

"They are beautiful," she agreed, her eyes sparkling with equal wonder. "But they are not sculptures, Lazar."

"Oh?"

"They look alive because they were alive a long time ago."

He snorted. "They lived? What, that gryphon over there?"

She nodded seriously.

"How do you know? Are you so old that you have seen them?" he challenged, with amusement in his tone.

"I think perhaps I am what they call an old soul."

The huge gates of Percheron were supported by two monstrously large lions with jagged manes and huge wings that folded down their strong backs.

"Aren't they magnificent?" Lazar said, pausing and bending to touch one. He felt compelled to do so every time he passed.

"They are Crendel and Darso."

"Oh, they have names too?" he said, disbelief lacing his tone now.

"Just like you and me," she said, unaffected by the jest in his voice.

"I'm not even going to ask how you know," he said, "because I too can make up things, Ana, and I'm glad of your imagination." He surprised himself by bending to pull her close and stare at her. "Because it's your imagination that will save you. You will always have it to escape to."

"Don't be sad, Lazar," she said, impulsively stroking his dark hair.

Her touch was so innocent and yet so intimate it took his breath away. As he stared at her large trusting eyes, he considered her bleak future as a plaything to a man, and for a fleeting moment considered running away with her, taking her back to the foothills, or better, trying to find her true mother. Or he could just take her into his own home; he didn't actually live at the palace or in its barracks, so it could be done discreetly. Perhaps he could say he bought her at the slave market to help keep house for him. Then she would be safe. He would see to her education and he would help her make a good marriage. But even as his mind raged, Lazar knew in his heart he could do nothing of the sort. Herezah had demanded six girls of him. The men he had sent ahead already knew he and Jumo were last seen heading toward one of the families in the western foothills. The Valide was too cunning—she would learn of his new housekeeper. And Ana was far too beautiful to escape notice.

He looked away, resigned to her fate and hating that he had personally chosen her destiny. "Let me show you some more," he said, hoping his voice did not reflect the anguish within. Silently he berated himself for his strange attitude these past couple of days. Suddenly he was an emotional liability: eyes misting without warning, feeling introspective, questioning his life and its meaning. And worst of all, allowing a young girl to add fuel to the fire of those insecurities.

Once again holding Ana's hand, he weaved her through the streets of Percheron as dusk descended, lamps were lit, and the city clothed itself in its more sensual mantle.

"You must be hungry?" he asked. She nodded. "How about a sharva?"

"What's that?"

"I'll show you," he said, his own mouth watering at the thought. "I trust you eat meat?"

"I do. Just not birds," and she smiled her apology. They wended a slow path into the markets, a warren of alleyways. People meandered around them, going about their business of buying everything from fresh meat to silver bracelets.

"I love it here," Lazar admitted. "Each narrow lane is known for a specific craft. Now this one that we're in specializes in the flat triangular sort of hats that the ordinary Percherese favor. The hats for our esteemed citizens are made in another street. See that woman over there?" Ana nodded. "She uses twelve needles to knit the yarn."

"Ah yes, they do this in the foothills too."

"Of course, you would have seen it."

Ana smiled. "It's knitted very wide and then they dye the hats and shrink them in the huge boiling bowls."

"That's right. They call them the cauldrons. After drying them, they use a dry thistle to tease up the fibers, like this." He pointed to another woman hard at her toil. "And you end up with one of these beauties." He put a red coriz, as it was known, on his head, its tassel dangling in his face.

She laughed. "Another street?"

The next alleyway was devoted to rugs, and the one after that to fabulous cushions fashioned in velvet and silk, wool and skins, in every size and shape imaginable. They made their way through the torch-lit alleys past shops selling fabrics and beautiful hanging lanterns, then exquisitely painted tiles, and finally into the maze of lanes given over to the art of cooking.

Ana was drawn to the spice sellers, whose sacks of brightly colored powders and seeds, beans and pods, were displayed. She stood quietly and watched as women pointed to what they wanted and paid for their purchases. A man who sat cross-legged near a set of scales called to his helper—a tiny boy—who scampered around scooping up the wares and placing them in squares of fabric. The man would weigh them; almost always the boy's estimate was right, and he rarely had to return to the designated sack to fetch more of the spice or return some. Satisfied, man and customer would exchange money while the child expertly tied the bought produce into the square of fabric with a piece of silk.

"Tamara, caracan, alpse, vergun, zarakor," Lazar listed, pointing to the various sacks. "Smell this," he said, picking up a small pod and crushing it in his palm.

"Gezil?" she asked.

Lazar grinned. "You're very clever, Ana. Do you know what it is used for?"

Ana shook her head. "I know its fragrance because my father showed it to me once, growing on the long-leafed trees in the foothills. As the berry hardens, it turns from red to this shiny black."

Lazar nodded. "They flavor custards with it, but if it is crushed before it hardens and rubbed on raw, I'm told it's very good for toe sores," and he pulled a face, making her laugh.

A man roasting nuts over a small open fire beckoned to them. Ana looked up at Lazar hopefully, but he was looking away. She followed his gaze and saw another man in a tiny hole in the wall, slicing roasted meat from a spit.

"Sharva," Lazar said theatrically, leading Ana to the tiny booth. He put two fingers in the air and dug into his pockets for coins.

The man handed them each a folded flat bread, from which emanated a heavenly smell. Inside the folded bread Ana could see thin slivers of the flame-cooked meat, green leaves she had never seen before, rounds of something else green that looked like a fruit but not one she knew. She did recognize the fat chickpeas and translucent slices of onion, though. Everything was drenched with a thick, tangy white sauce that was soon running down their chins and her slim arms.

They sat down around a central stone fountain.

"Good?" he asked in between bites.

Ana's muffled response through her bulging mouthful made him laugh—it was obvious she was enjoying her meal. When they had finished, he bought her a small sherbet made from pulped fruit.

"This finishes it perfectly. It takes away the spiciness from your tongue and adds a cleansing tang. This sherbet is not as scrumptious as you'll eat in the palace, of course, and I'll let you discover why," he said with a wink, handing her one half of a purple berren fruit, whose flesh had been scooped out and replaced with the cool sherbet.

She used the wafer he gave her to ladle the fruit pulp into her mouth and groaned her pleasure. "I've never tasted anything like this before. I shall never forget it," she said, laying a small hand on his wrist. Again she felt a pulse of warmth move through her as their skin touched. Lazar didn't say anything but she knew she had pleased him, adding, "And I don't think even the palace sherbet could taste this good."

"Why do you say that?" he asked.

"Because right now I'm free as I eat this. The next time I taste anything as good I shall be a slave—I'm sure that will make it taste very different."

Lazar nodded seriously. There was something unsettling about Ana's insights and yet, at the same time, they gave him a rush of pleasure. As though he'd finally found a haven in someone else's mind. They washed their hands and mouths in the small fountain.

"What's through there?" she asked, flicking water from her fingers.

"Aha, well now, beyond that bend are the lanes of gold. Would you like to see them?"

"Oh yes, I would."

He guided her through. The sky overhead had deepened to black and the stars were bright and shiny like tiny jewels flickering amid the inky cloak of night. Lazar realized he was having fun. He could not remember when he had last felt so carefree. Many people had recognized him, of course—the Spur was a distinctive man in Percheron—but it didn't matter tonight. Normally he hated the intrusion on his thoughts but tonight he nodded at the passersby, accepting their acknowledgment and salutations, even smiling once—much to the surprise of the courteous person hurrying past.

In Gold Alley, as it was known, Ana watched the shopkeepers haggle over prices with their customers. It was a hive of activity and yet it seemed unhurried as people were absorbed in their transactions. Her gaze was drawn to one dark corner where she saw a tiny old woman, her face veiled, pulling what looked like a gold chain from beneath her robes. She cupped the piece in her hand so quickly Ana couldn't be sure what the jewelry actually was. The man she spoke with loomed above her, dirty, unshaven, clearly a street seller rather than a registered shopkeeper.

Ana mentioned it to Lazar, pointing to the large man.

Lazar nodded. "Yes, they're called alley cats here. They have no set spot; you'll see them roaming all the laneways, looking for people to buy from and sell to. The shopkeepers hate them but it's not against the law, so they continue, though I imagine it will be outlawed soon as there are just too many of them suddenly. They ask no questions, need no proof that the item you're selling is yours, give you no guarantee that the coin they pay or the gold they sell is genuine."

"Then why does anyone do business with them? Surely it would make more sense to deal with someone who must trade honestly?"

"Because the alley cats ask no questions. That woman probably needs the money so badly that she will deal with this person, even though she would prefer not to."

"Can we not help her?"

"Why?"

"Because it's a good thing to do."

He smiled at the earnestness in her expression. "How, Ana?"

"You buy her gold."

"What?" He laughed. "I don't think so."

"Please, Lazar. That man will try to steal it from her. She looks desperate, so he'll not pay a fair price."

"You're perceptive, Ana. That's surely what will happen but it's not for us to interfere."

Her expression clouded, grew grave, determined. "How much did you pay for me?"

"Pardon?" he said, taken aback by her directness.

"What was I worth to my stepmother?"

Lazar could see it was pointless trying to skirt this issue. "Forty karels."

"Offer the old woman the difference. I have no sense of value, Lazar, but I think you probably took advantage of Felluj's desperation to be rid of me—just as the alley cat is taking advantage of the old woman. You could see that our family was penniless and so you could offer what you wanted. What am I truly worth to the palace . . . twice as much?"

"Probably," he admitted, compelled to be honest. Ana's harsh words hurt deeply as she held him seriously in her gaze. He felt the ache all the way to his heart.

"Then offer her the other forty—you can tell the Valide that I cost that much," she begged.

Without giving Lazar another moment to consider, Ana rushed over to the old woman who was about to hand over her jewelry.

"Wait!" Ana cried. "How much are you selling your gold for?"

The old woman—far older than he had first thought, Lazar noted—turned and smiled gently at Ana. "Twenty karels, my girl."

"I will give you forty for it!" Ana exclaimed.

"Hey!" the alley cat said angrily. "Stay out of it, stupid girl. You don't look as though you have a zeraf to your name!"

Ana ignored him. "Please?" she asked the old woman. "Let me buy it."

"Go!" the man yelled, shoving Ana hard. Within a blink he felt his arm enclosed in a grip so hard he squealed.

"Don't touch her, scum," Lazar said, squeezing harder, watching the man double over slowly. "You're lucky I don't throw your kind into the pit, or worse." He let go of the man.

"Spur," the merchant bowed. "Forgive me, sir. But I was doing an honest trade with a customer."

"Honest, my arse." Lazar sneered. "Go on, be glad I don't take it further."

The man glared at Ana and the old woman but turned furiously and left without another word.

"It was honest by his standards anyway," the old woman said generously from beneath her hood. Her voice was kind, with a soothing singsong quality to it.

Lazar retrieved his money pouch from his belt. "Here, forty karels is the agreed price, is that right?"

"It is, I thank you, Spur Lazar," the woman said. Rather than holding out a hand, she opened a pocket, encouraging him to drop the coin into it, which he duly did.

The woman turned to the girl. "And this is for you, Ana." She handed the youngster an exquisitely sculpted gold owl.

Lazar took a sharp intake of breath. It was a tiny statue of Iridor. He could have sworn she had been selling a plain gold chain. Even to his untrained eye the statue looked as if it was worth more than forty karels. Something about her manner, however, prevented him from saying so.

"Are you sure you can bear to part with this sculpture of Iridor?" Ana asked, stunned by the bird's beauty.

"Oh yes, and particularly to you."

Ana smiled and the old woman reached out to hug her. Then

she turned and tottered off. Lazar was still frowning, not only baffled by the gift itself, which had seemed to change shape before his eyes, but by Ana's knowledge of who it represented.

"I could have sworn she was selling a bracelet or necklace, not an ornament," he said.

"I agree." She hesitated briefly. "And I never gave her my name and yet she knew it."

Lazar swung around but the old woman had disappeared into the darkness of the alleys. "She knew my name too, although I suppose I'm known in the city." He frowned again. "Ana, how do you know the name of the bird that sculpture represents?"

"Everyone knows Iridor," she said casually.

"Not everyone. Certainly not people your age."

She shrugged as if to assure him it was of no importance, then added, "I've always known him."

He wanted to press further but Ana pushed the gold bird into his hand, taking him by surprise.

"It's yours," she said. "You paid for it."

"Keep it, Ana. It was you who paid for it. You are worth ten times as much."

She looked up at him, a tinge of regret in her soft smile. "They will not permit me to keep it, will they?"

Lazar shook his head. She was right, of course. "I suspect not. It will go into the palace coffers and probably never be seen again or, worse, melted down. Iridor isn't exactly a friend to our people."

"Pity he's seen that way," she said sadly. "He's always been our friend."

Lazar, taken aback by her words, couldn't respond. How could she know what he had always felt?

Ana filled the awkward pause. "No, you keep the statue for me. Let it remind you of me and of our friendship."

Lazar pushed the bird into his pocket and took her hand. "I shall keep it safe for you" was all he would risk saying. "Now, it's time I took you to your new home."

"Lazar, don't just keep it safe. Keep it near." She searched his face intently for confirmation. He nodded gravely and that seemed to satisfy her.

He hated every moment of the journey that brought them closer to the palace. With each step he felt that former sense of freedom, that release from the weight of his world, dissipate. With each stride he felt his shoulders hunch closer and his insides harden.

They arrived at the palace gates. He announced himself and his charge at the Moon Courtyard and it was made official. Ana had arrived and been registered by name at the palace. There was no turning away now.

She was palace property.

8

Pez found Boaz alone in his chambers. Joreb had long ago given permission for the dwarf to have access to all areas of the palace—he was the only person in the entire retinue who had absolute freedom. Thus the guards were used to seeing him come and go as he pleased, whether it be to the Zar's rooms or even to the harem. He was the only intact male permitted to visit the prized, most viciously protected place in the palace without forewarning, or any threat to his well-being.

"I thought I'd find you here," the jester said. "Would you prefer to be alone with your sorrow?"

"Do you know," Boaz said, "you're the only one who has even considered that I might be grieving for my father. Everyone else is treating me as though I should get over it and get on with taking on my new role. My mother's the worst. For her my grief is akin to a headache: something to sleep off with a mild soporific." The last few words were uttered with such disgust that Pez remained quiet. The boy was angry and entitled to be. "Don't they understand? My father has died! I loved him as any child loves his father."

Pez moved deeper into the room. "So how can we help you?"

"I just want to be left alone," Boaz replied, sullen now. He had seated himself at a window and was gazing out across the harbor.

Pez looked at the Zar and realized suddenly how tall his young friend was, and lean—as his father had been. But that was where the physical similarities ended. In looks, Boaz was all Herezah: dark hair and eyes, smooth olive skin. He possessed her strong, beautiful bone structure, and Pez imagined how hearts must already be fluttering in girls' breasts at the thought of their new Zar.

"You know that cannot happen, Boaz," Pez said gently. "One of the major attributes that everyone will be looking for in you is strength of character—" He held his hand up to stop the Zar. "I know you possess this but you need to show it to those who are waiting to pounce on your weaknesses and prey on them."

"I don't want to be happy yet," Boaz replied. His tone was haughty now. "It's obscene to think I should sing and dance with my father's body barely cold."

"I understand, truly I do, but you must demonstrate that you are strong. I don't suggest you make merry, Boaz, but you must participate in palace life. Don't withdraw. Be seen, be noticed. You don't have to smile or give pretense at happiness. In fact it will be all the more powerful if you are grave. It means you're taking your father's death seriously and that you're anything but a throne-hungry son. But let the palace see you around its halls and let the people know you are going about your duties stoically."

There was silence for a minute.

"You're right, as usual," Boaz said eventually. "I'll make an effort."

"I'm proud of you. Let your mother know you are equal to the task, and that this is your throne."

"And not hers?" Boaz finished, turning around to regard the dwarf.

"I didn't say that."

"You didn't have to."

"I have no doubt that she can assist you immensely. But she can also undermine you." Pez changed the subject, his voice turning bright. "So, what have you been thinking about all alone in this grand new chamber?"

There was a silence and then Boaz sighed heavily. "I've been staring out to sea all evening, watching Beloch and Ezram."

"Oh yes?"

"Do you know, Pez, it's the first time I've ever really paid attention to them. They've always been there, so I suppose I didn't take much notice as I was growing up."

"I think most of the city folk suffer the same disease. One of Lazar's great gripes is that none of us appreciate the fine art all around us. Do you know their story?"

"Of the giants? No, I've never been taught the old legends—they think it's sacrilegious! Me, I want to learn the stories."

"Of course they would think this! The priests fear a return to the old ways of worshipping the Mother."

"You'll have to explain that, Pez," the boy said, crossing his legs, knowing he was about to be told a story.

"How about I pour some wine first?" Pez filled two cups with watered-down sweet wine and waddled over to the window seat, where he made himself comfortable and then cleared his throat.

Boaz gave a small grin, his first in days, and raised his glass. "To a lighter heart," he said. The two of them drank.

"Now, where to begin?"

"Tell me about the priestesses," the young Zar suggested as he settled back into cushions.

"All right. Centuries ago, Percheron followed the ways of the Great Goddess whom we know simply as Mother, and worshipped female deities. The temples were inhabited by holy women. They were silent places, which is why you'll see so many of the sculptures in our temples with fingers to their lips."

"What does it mean?"

"Silence represents the soundless womb that gave birth to the first gods. Some of the oldest writings teach that Silence was the mother to the Great Goddess herself."

"But now they're noisy places. I don't often enjoy a visit to the temple."

Pez nodded. "The priests changed everything. Now the temple is a gathering place. Prayer blends with socializing. Moneylenders, as you know, now set up their stalls outside the temples because these are places where lots of people meet."

"So temples were once quiet places of prayer and overseen by women?"

"Yes, indeed. The holiest of our people were women. Lots of the symbols you see around you, Boaz, have female connotations."

"Oh?"

"Over here." Pez pointed to a recurring motif on a painted frieze on one wall of the chamber. "You see this. What do we call it?"

"Wait," Boaz said, screwing his eyes tight and concentrating. "It's known as the universal life charm."

"Good, your scholars teach you well, even though they don't explain much. Did they teach you that it's also known as the Cross of Life and that it represents the union of the female and male?" Boaz shook his head. "The oval shape on the top of the cross is female. The cross itself is male. And there's more if you look for them." The dwarf paused and took a sip of wine. "Think of the decoration of the great feasting hall in the palace. What symbol comes to mind first?"

"Er, the one that looks like the shell you can hear the sea in."

Pez smiled. "Right again. That shell is called a cowrie."

"I know that."

"Do you know what it symbolizes, though?"

"No. Tell me."

"It's the female sex and was often used to represent the Goddess."

Boaz opened his mouth in wonder and Pez grinned. "But the cowrie symbol is everywhere in Percheron—in our homes, our paintings, on our porcelain . . ."

"Everywhere," Pez echoed. "This land celebrated women once; it prayed to the Mother Goddess and it revered its holy priestesses."

"But . . ."

"But now they are nothing," Pez finished for him. "Yes, people have forgotten and your generation isn't even taught

Percheron's spiritual history. It's the smug priests who run the temples, and the few remaining holy women are ridiculed."

Boaz looked out to sea and digested what he had heard. Minutes passed and Pez sat comfortably in the silence. Finally Boaz turned back to his friend. "So, in truth, the Zar's harem is a mockery of what we formerly worshipped and held dear. Women are no longer revered in the same way; they are slaves to men's needs and whims."

Pez had not expected the youngster to make this connection so swiftly. Perhaps there was hope for Percheron with this intelligent, perceptive young man so quickly growing into his throne.

"One might look at it that way, Boaz, yes. The women of the harem are powerless, and the luxury and decadence in their lives all but makes them useless. They have no role to play other than to serve men. The priests of yesteryear encouraged it for that reason and now in a twisted way the palace harem is all but sacred."

"When did this happen?" Boaz asked.

"Oh, a very long time ago. At some point the holy men became jealous of the power of their female counterparts and decided to do something about it. I simplify it, of course, but only to make it easier to understand. I hadn't planned on giving you a lecture in history tonight." He smiled crookedly.

"But it's all so fascinating. My father's women were happy, of course," the boy said. "Well, until the harem was disbanded."

"Were they happy, Boaz? Do you think they would choose their bored, decadent, sometimes debauched existence over freedom, the right to choose their mate and have children who wouldn't be slaughtered simply because they might threaten a throne?"

"I did not order that murder." The boy bristled.

"Nor did I say you did. We come full circle. Your mother did what was right for today's times. She did the only thing she could to protect the security of the Chosen's throne. Every one of the other women would have done the same and yet that doesn't make it sit any easier in the mind, does it?"

Boaz shook his head. "I have nightmares about it. I'm not just grieving for my father, Pez, I'm trying to come to terms with the loss of my brothers . . . my friends."

"I know, child, and we must respect that."

"Isn't the position of Valide Zara a contradiction, then, to the way you say we now live? Surely my mother's power harks back to the days of the Goddess when a woman was powerful?"

"Not really. You see, your mother is powerless without you, Boaz. Never overlook that. You are her power; your position nourishes her influence. She has none in her own right. If something were to happen to you she would be stripped of her title and cast onto the streets as she cast her rivals not so long ago."

Boaz frowned. "I've never looked at it like that."

Pez said no more. Enough seeds had been planted in the boy's mind tonight. "So now, Beloch and Ezram, our magnificent giants you asked me about."

"Oh yes, I'd forgotten."

"Some people believe, myself included, that giants once roamed the land and that these two were the most powerful warriors amongst their race."

"This is a myth, surely?"

"No myth," Pez said gravely. "Beloch and Ezram worshipped the Goddess and it is said that the warlock Maliz—aided by the god Zarab—founded the new movement to dislodge holy women from their pedestal. Through Maliz, Zarab fueled the jealousies, weaved magicks upon his followers to overthrow the priestesses and install the new era of the priest."

"The giants?"

"They were a threat to Maliz. Not only them but the rest of their kind. Also all the strange statues you see around the city. They were once beasts who revered the Goddess, who gave her power."

"So?"

"Maliz made a bargain with the god Zarab and turned them to stone."

Boaz clapped his hands, enjoying the tale. "What happened to Maliz?"

"No one knows. His is a murky history. The old stories say he was turned into a demon. Some believe he still works through others."

"What, today?" the Zar asked, incredulous.

The dwarf nodded. "They say he never died, that his spirit lives on. He just moves from one body to another."

Boaz grinned, impressed. "That sounds rather terrifying."

"Believe me, it is."

"How could he do that?"

"Maliz practiced the Art Noir—have you heard of this?" Boaz shook his head. "Well, suffice to say it is an unpleasant pastime. His bargain gave him everlasting life."

"And Zarab? What did he get out of the pact?"

"The destruction of the religion of the Mother Goddess. Now Percheron prays to Zarab."

"Oh, I see. How very neat."

Pez ignored the flippant remark. "There's a catch, though. Zarab knew the Goddess would rise again, so Maliz's everlasting life was inextricably linked to her."

Boaz frowned. "I don't understand."

"Well, it is because of this link that Maliz can continue to live. It is said that he moves through bodies awaiting the coming of the Goddess, watching and studying who it might be. There will be signs of course—Iridor, for instance—and then once again they will battle it out."

"Iridor?"

"Surely you've seen all the images of the owl around our city?"

"Of course. That's Iridor from the old stories?"

"From Percheron's history," Pez corrected, wondering if his tale was falling on deaf ears.

Boaz's eyes shone. "A brilliant story."

"It's so many centuries old, it feels like folklore," Pez cautioned.

"We still have priestesses, though."

"Indeed they exist, but very few. They remain powerless, though always believing that the Mother will rise again. They are tolerated because most in Percheron hardly know the history and don't care about the women who keep to themselves and keep the ancient unused temples in good order . . . for posterity."

"So do you believe Maliz exists, Pez?"

The dwarf hesitated. "Yes," he answered truthfully. "I think he is always watching, waiting."

"You believe he continues to reincarnate himself so that he can watch for the Goddess?"

"He doesn't reincarnate himself, Boaz. He simply claims a

fresh body as his old one begins to perish or become too frail for his needs. He is unnecessary as long as she is powerless. As her power increases, so does his."

"So how can either win if each one's power is balanced by the other?"

"They are not equal. At present the balance of power is with Zarab, but that might change as each of the two rivals—Lyana and Maliz—has helpers of a sort to assist them to outwit the other."

"Oh?"

"The Goddess, for example, has Iridor. He too only comes into fleshly being as a herald of her arrival. He is her messenger, and as Iridor gets closer to incarnation, Maliz gains strength and goes looking for his new body, new victims to pull into his web."

The mention of claiming bodies had pricked Boaz's interest further. "Could Maliz be anyone, then?"

"Presumably," Pez said carefully.

"Me?"

The dwarf frowned uncomfortably. "I would know if you were," he finally replied.

"Why?"

Pez shook his head. He began to hum to himself. "I just would," he said in a singsong voice.

Boaz ignored Pez's antics. "So he's always alive, then. Always looking for the next victim?"

"You could say that."

Boaz didn't mean to tease but it was rare for Pez to seem in the slightest ruffled, and he pushed his advantage. "Could he be you?"

Boaz had meant it playfully, to loosen Pez's lips again, but the dwarf looked up, alarmed, the mask momentarily gone. Then, within a blink, the vulnerability was gone and Pez was laughing. "No, child. I am too stupid-looking for Maliz to want this body." Pez suddenly became conspiratorial and surprised his companion by radically changing the subject. "Boaz, do you know your mother is welcoming forty-two of the girls from which she hopes one day you'll select your wives?"

Boaz scowled. "I'm not ready to, er . . . you know."

Pez laid a reassuring squat hand on the boy's good arm. "I know. But she must prepare them for the day when you are ready, so they're brought in very young and taught everything they need to know about palace etiquette and you. Some girls will be marked as special and they will learn their letters and language, dance and poetry."

"I'm not sure I'm interested in girls," Boaz replied glumly.

"I suspect you will be soon. Shall we spy on them?" Pez asked, a glint of wickedness in his yellow eyes.

"What?"

"I know a hiding place. We can watch the girls being presented to your mother. No one need know. Perhaps we can pick out a couple of beauties for you." Pez nudged the Zar, who laughed unconvincingly

"You're mad, Pez."

"Apparently I am," and the jester pasted his face with the grin of a lunatic.

EACH MAN WHO HAD secured his quota of girls was required to present them to the Valide. Lazar stomped gloomily through the corridors lined with marble sculpture. Snatches of torch-lit gardens and tiny, exquisite courtyards could be glimpsed through the latticed walkways; the sounds of cicadas singing and fountains gently gurgling permeated the heavy evening air scented with jasmine and honeysuckle. But the Spur was blind to the beauty of the palace tonight.

His mind was filled with worry for Ana, wondering how he might help ease her into palace life, the prison to which he had sentenced her.

There was no way out for her now. Ana had been whisked away by guards before Lazar could say good-bye. The young woman had turned solemnly as she was led away and her sad gaze had held him as though she could actually touch the deep pool of sorrow he thought he hid so well.

Bah! he said to himself. *What you need, Lazar, is a soft bed, a good woman for the night, and several carafes of wine. No better way to drown your sorrows.* But the words sounded as hollow in his mind as the click of his boots on the marble floor.

He was the first to arrive at the Choosing Room because he was the only man sent out to find suitable girls who had the run of the palace. Like Pez, Zar Joreb had granted Lazar access to the entire palace—except, unlike Pez, Lazar was forbidden to enter the harem. The others would probably be gathered in the Moon Courtyard, the first entry point into the palace proper, awaiting their escort of eunuch guards.

The Choosing Room was the chamber where the new odalisques were brought to be looked upon and judged. The chamber had been opened only once in the last few decades and Lazar could tell that a veritable army of slaves had been sent in to air, clean, and freshen the room. Now all the shutters were open and the glass lanterns were clean and lit; formal seating had been arranged, including a thronelike setup, presumably so Herezah could play at being a queen and forget that she too had once been brought here as a young slave.

He could feel the bitterness welling up again, knew he must get a grip on it before proceedings began. He emptied his mind—something Jumo had taught him to do—and focused on the ancient, intricately painted friezes around the walls. He had never visited this room before, and although he recognized the pattern as being common enough in Percheron, now that he was concentrating on it, he realized it wasn't just an abstract shape but in fact was the curve of a cowrie shell. Painted in soft hues, the design rolled elegantly around the walls, framing arches and windows, small recesses and the great doors that had guided him into the chamber. And now that he studied them he noticed that the doors themselves had the same sweeping curves of the shell hammered out of the bronze they were fashioned from. The walls were washed in shell pink and the floors were a pinkish marble—all in all a thoroughly feminine hall, Lazar decided, impressed.

His pleasure was interrupted by the swish of silks and a voice he knew and despised. "Ah, Spur Lazar," Salmeo lisped. "I hope you've found our boy some beauties to bed."

"Not so fast, Grand Master Eunuch. Boaz will choose his time."

The eunuch licked his lips and Lazar hated the way his pink tongue flicked through the gap in his teeth. There was something quietly obscene in the gesture. "I noticed you admiring the decor," the eunuch said. "It signifies the female form—did you know that, Spur?"

Lazar shook his head and strolled away as if his interest had been caught by something on the other side of the chamber.

"Ah yes," the huge man continued, following him, "this chamber is dedicated to women. It is where they are formally given into the care of the harem; their last contact with men." He giggled and covered his grin with his huge hand. "But of course they've known no men," he added as if in self-admonishment.

Lazar made a soft growling sound of disgust at this sudden affectation. He'd heard enough stories to know the chief eunuch took his own cruel form of pleasure at the expense of the harem women. Except there were no longer any women in the harem; they were still essentially children, who needed protecting and nurturing. He wanted to laugh at himself for his own ridiculous sentiment—it was so ironic, since he was one of the perpetrators who had brought children to the palace—and moved farther away, not wanting to smell the fragrance of violets that Salmeo habitually blew over all those he spoke with.

"Spur, Salmeo."

Lazar turned to find Tariq bubbling over with self-importance.

"Are you required here, Vizier?" Lazar asked, his tone as casual as he could achieve. "Surely your expertise is needed elsewhere?"

The man swelled with pride. "You're right, of course, Spur. But the Valide is keen for me to see all aspects of the palace workings. Establishing a harem is fundamental to the smooth running of the new Zar's reign. She believed it worthwhile that I be present." He shrugged, feigning gentle modesty at her order.

The jewels on his split beard were now accompanied by tiny bells that tinkled as he moved and Lazar was reminded of another reason why he wanted to be gone from the palace. What would happen to Percheron in the hands of Herezah and this supercilious fool? He forced a smile to cover his disgust and breathed a sigh of relief as a gong sounded somewhere close, distracting his companions' attention.

"The Elim come," Salmeo said.

Footsteps sounded louder, and low murmuring voices of men could be heard. Six spotters, as Herezah called them, were led in, blindfolded, flanked by twelve guards, all distinctive by their loose, pristine red uniforms. Each guard had his head shaved—there was no mistaking the Elim. The spotters themselves were mainly merchants, and among them was a man Lazar was acquainted with. Bosh could supply almost anything anyone could ever want, legal or illegal. Finding young girls for a harem would have been easy for him. Lazar had had his run-ins with him over the years, thanks to the man's natural tendency toward breaking laws, but Bosh was good-natured enough and Lazar would rather deal with ten or even twenty of his kind than one of Salmeo's or Tariq's.

"Why the blindfolds?" Tariq asked.

Lazar refused to answer the mindless question but Salmeo was more enlightening. "Although the Choosing Room is not technically within the borders of the harem, it remains close enough that traditional precautions are still taken. These men have no idea where they are right now and they will never find out. The blindfolds will be removed once the great doors are shut and returned just before they open and the six are escorted back out." Salmeo's smile was predatory. "You are most fortunate that we did not provide similar treatment for you, Vizier." Though the words were delivered lightly, the undercurrent in Salmeo's tone was all too clear.

Salmeo gave a sign and the great doors were closed with a deep clang. The blindfolds were removed and the spotters blinked, got their bearings; Bosh saw Lazar immediately and nodded.

"Welcome, brothers," the Grand Master Eunuch said. "May we offer you some refreshment?"

Curtains at the back of the room were pulled apart and a small stream of servants—all male—flowed smoothly into the room and around the newcomers. Each held a golden tray upon which sat great goblets, dewy on their sides from the iciness of the beverage they contained.

Bosh stepped over to Lazar. "Do you know they lug blocks of ice and sometimes snow from the Azareems, across thousands of leagues, just to chill the palace beverages?" he declared in wonder.

"So I've heard," Lazar replied in a voice to deaden all awe.

The wealthy trader raised his goblet. "To the new harem, then. Zorash!"

Lazar couldn't bring himself to toast the very thing that was making him feel so disturbed. "To beautiful women," he offered instead, and Bosh drank with him, winking as he did so.

"I'm surprised you were asked to get involved in this task, Spur," the man commented.

"So was I. Excuse me." Lazar nodded and moved away.

Bosh was not upset by the Spur's abrupt manner. Everyone in Percheron knew him to be a difficult man who rarely involved himself in anything deeper than cursory conversation. The man shrugged, approached another of the merchants, and was soon comparing notes on the quality of the girls.

Lazar wondered where Ana was, wished again he could

change everything that had happened since he'd arrived on that ridge in the foothills. He should have left the tranquil scene as he'd found it; listened to his heart and turned for home.

He had a vague feeling of impending danger. A sense of something dark building, gathering, forming itself. And he was afraid that he was at its center.

9

Pez led Boaz through a maze of corridors the boy was sure he had not traveled before. Now that he thought about it, his world was so small. Life in the palace might well be grand but everything about his existence was controlled by his mother. Herezah authorized everyone who was responsible for his getting up and going to bed, being bathed, fed, educated, even choosing where and with whom he played, when younger.

He and Pez were thumbing their nose at traditional rules and Boaz knew he had agreed to this lunacy only because he was angry with his mother. It felt satisfying to act independently without worrying about the consequences. *I am the Zar after all,* he told himself.

Mind you, now that they were here—in what was the most dangerous part of the whole of Percheron if you were an intact male—he didn't feel quite so keen to snub authority or risk the certain wrath should anyone, not just his mother, find out. He wanted to say as much, but as he opened his mouth to speak, his friend hissed a warning.

"Now silence, Boaz," Pez urged. "We're about to enter the realm of the harem."

Boaz took a sudden fearful breath. "It's forbidden, Pez."

"Not forbidden to me," the little man said, grinning wickedly. "And let's not forget who you are."

"Nevertheless," Boaz protested, grabbing his friend's short arm, "I cannot. My mother would—"

"What? Kill you? I think not. Not when you are the source of her status."

"Well, she'd never forgive me."

"What if I told you I could ensure that you were never seen?"

"I should not believe you." Boaz laughed.

"Then you must trust me. I will not lead you into trouble, Boaz. I am leading you toward enlightenment."

Before the Zar could reply, a boy of about his age rounded the corner.

"Zar!" he exclaimed, cringing instantly into a bow.

Pez sighed. That was that, then. Lucky they hadn't actually crossed the official, invisible line that separated the harem from the general palace.

"Hello, Kett," Boaz said good-naturedly, recovering with effort from the shock of discovery. "I'm escaping my tutors and keepers, guardians and mother. Everyone, in fact. Do you know Pez, my jester?"

Pez began to pick his nose, rendering a small jig.

Kett, a servant to the eunuchs, shook his head dumbly, looking from the Zar to the clown, who was now examining the contents from his nostrils.

Boaz winced. "He has some awful habits. Don't mind him. I haven't seen you in ages."

"Forgive me, High One. Since turning fourteen, they think I'm ready to take on more duties. They keep me busy, Majesty." The boy bobbed another bow. "But I miss our fun."

"Kett was a playmate of mine for a while," the Zar explained to Pez, who pretended to pay no attention to anything but digging at his ear. "His mother served my mother when she first came to the palace. Kett was allowed to join in some of my games until my mother felt we were becoming too close. She separated us." He looked back to the boy, whose dark face had not lost its expressiveness with the added years. "How many years ago was that, Kett?"

"Four, Majesty. My humble prayers for your father but I admit I rejoiced to hear that you were to be our next Zar."

"Thanks, Kett. So . . . what are you doing?" Boaz was keen to lose the royal tag for just one evening. He pulled the dwarf's hand away from his nose. Pez began to sing, loudly.

"Is he always like this, High One?" Kett asked.

"I'm afraid so. He can be very amusing, though."

Kett looked dubious but remembered his manners. "I've finished for the night, Majesty. I was on my way back to my quarters. I'm not allowed anywhere near the harem, of course, but some of us use this corridor as a shortcut to our dormitories."

"Oh, of course. I guess you would get into trouble if you were seen in the harem."

Kett grinned. "I don't want to follow in my superiors' footsteps and be a eunuch—I think I like girls too much. I want to be one of the Spur's men if they'll let me. My mother's connection to yours might help, now that your mother is Valide Zara."

"Good for you, Kett. I hope you get what you want."

The boy nodded. "Is there anything I can do for you, High One?" he asked. "I hope you don't mind me mentioning that you shouldn't be here either."

"No, you're right. We were just larking around. Pez's silly singing and dancing led us here."

"Let me guide you from here, Majesty," Kett offered.

"Do you like to see naked girls?" Pez asked, a question that brought polite conversation to a halt. The two boys stared at each other, both stifling embarrassed laughter. "Because I know a hiding spot where we can see them, tra-la-la." He began to dance again, a dullard's grin on his face.

"Is he mad?" Kett asked.

"Completely," Boaz confirmed.

The dwarf slid through a doorway hung with black velvet.

"What's he doing?" Kett asked, alarmed. "That's forbidden!"

"Not to him. Pez has royal permission to go wherever he likes, including the harem's hallways and chambers."

Pez stuck his head out of the curtains. "And so do you, Zar Boaz. You *are* the royal authority. There is no higher authority in the land than yours."

"What's he talking about?"

Boaz sighed. "He's daring me to go into the forbidden halls of the harem."

"No, High One. You cannot," Kett begged. "Come, I shall take you from here."

Boaz looked between the two, but the challenge in Pez's expression won out. This was the way of the Zars of Percheron—strength and discipline were the foundation of the rule. He must dig deep and turn quickly into the man his father had chosen him to be—firm, decisive, ruthless . . . and not afraid of breaking a few rules.

"Come, Boaz," Pez urged in a whisper. "You must see what your mother is planning for you."

"Come with us, Kett," Boaz offered, on a whim.

"Cannot protect the servant boy," Pez muttered in a sing-song voice, but Boaz ignored him.

"You said you liked girls," he challenged.

"I do. But not enough to be beheaded for them."

"I won't allow that. You forget that I am Zar," Boaz answered haughtily. Surprised at his own courage, he grabbed Kett's arm and dragged him between the curtains.

Kett yelled but Boaz pushed a hand across the boy's mouth. "Hush now!"

"Can't protect him," Pez sang softly as he waddled deeper into the dark corridor.

"You hush too," Boaz growled to Pez. "This is your fault. Now lead on!"

The three adventurers moved in silence. This particular passageway remained black, draped with fabric. Finally they emerged into a dimly lit opening from which several corridors led.

Pez put his finger to his lips and Boaz felt a tingling fear crawl up his spine. Zar or not, this act they were committing was fraught with a danger he didn't want to meet.

"Where we need to be is still on the fringe of the harem," Pez whispered. "Follow me," and the boys dutifully followed the little man, hoping to the gods that no one was coming the other way.

Pez appeared to read their thoughts. "Everyone will have been banished from these hallways for the duration of the

Choosing Ceremony. Fret not, we are alone. But from now on we must remain silent as mice."

They nodded, spectral in the murkiness of the corridor, where tiny flames in hanging lanterns cast a thin, ghostly light.

They twisted and turned down various other corridors until finally Pez slowed and gave them a look of dire warning. Boaz could see a new intensity of light ahead and nodded to his friend. They had arrived.

Moving forward tentatively, they held their collective breath until they reached some latticework, which offered thin protection between themselves and a gathering of men in a decorative chamber. They were drinking, socializing—their noise drowned out any noise from the three interlopers.

"This is called the Choosing Room. It's where a selection of girls will be presented to the Valide Zara. It is from this range of lovelies that you will eventually choose your wives, Boaz," Pez whispered.

"Do I get any say in the matter?" the young Zar asked.

Pez grinned. "Of course. But your mother makes the initial selection. She is seeing forty-two girls today."

"Where is she?"

"Arriving any moment now, I'd suggest." Pez glanced at Kett, could see the strain of terror on his face, wished deeply that Boaz had not invited this boy along. He was a danger to all of them and yet, that thought aside, there was something else about Kett that nagged at Pez. Something important. He didn't know the boy but he felt as if he should—felt, in fact, a sudden sorrow for the child.

But it was too late to turn back. Guards would have been posted now that the Valide Zara was on her way. They were trapped and would have to remain here, silent, until Herezah had left the chamber and returned to her own rooms.

This was madness—for all he had urged Boaz on, Pez knew that himself. And yet he had felt compelled to see the Choosing. He came out of his worried thoughts to concentrate on peering through the latticework, feeling his heart hammering with anticipation.

A HERALD SOUNDED LOUDLY from the surrounding balustrade, calling everyone to order. The men hushed. The Valide Zara was announced and Herezah swept into the chamber from a secret entrance that connected to the harem proper. Lazar noted she was following strict protocol in being covered head to foot but there was nothing modest about the way she presented herself. Dressed as she was in brilliant emerald silks, only her eyes showed, and they were dark and dangerous. She had expressive eyes and even from this distance Lazar could read the excitement in them.

She shimmered as she moved, the lantern light catching the tones woven into the silk, one moment violet, the next deep emerald. Even veiled, she commanded attention.

Everyone bowed low to acknowledge the Valide's arrival. Then Tariq and Salmeo moved forward to join her on the special plinth erected for this evening's proceedings. Both seemed to be basking in her bright glory. Oh yes, Lazar thought, Herezah would find willing servants in these two. And again a gloom settled about him as he considered just how Ana would fare among these cruel, ambitious people who would be controlling her life.

"Hail, Valide Zara," Salmeo called, and everyone responded.

"Thank you, brothers, for your rousing welcome." There was a playfulness in Herezah's tone tonight. She was enjoying herself; had surely dreamed about this moment.

Herezah continued. "We are gathered this night for you to present suitable girls for inclusion in Zar Boaz's harem. I thank you for helping us to find the raw material from which he will select his wives and thus the future heirs for Percheron, and we will be glad to pay handsomely for each of the girls deemed suitable." She nodded toward Salmeo, who beamed in response and stepped forward as she moved to sit on her throne.

The chief eunuch cleared his throat. "I would like to clarify on behalf of the palace how the choosing of the Zar's harem works. Firstly, you have brought among you forty or so girls aged between ten and fifteen. We thank you for this. As agreed, we will pay twenty-five karels per child, no matter whether they are chosen or not. The girls we accept will attract a further fifty karels paid to you as your finding fee. Those we do not select you may sell in the market for your personal gain or keep to do with as you wish." His tongue flicked between his teeth and his lips shone with the moistening. All but Lazar laughed at his innuendo.

Salmeo was still speaking. ". . . Vizier Tariq will see to payment, yes," he answered in response to a question. "Which brings me to the point that the entire fee will not be settled for the girls chosen this evening until they have completed the Test of Virtue." He allowed this seemingly innocuous statement to hang for a moment. "I'm sure you understand, brothers," he added lasciviously.

If he had not heard his name called first, Lazar was sure he would have found a reason to leave the chamber.

"Spur Lazar kindly agreed to help us fill the quota of girls and I'm sure none of you will mind if he presents his selection first. He's a busy man, as you know, and no doubt is eager to return to his duties, having been away. Spur?"

Lazar ignored Salmeo and cleared his throat. "Valide Zara, please forgive my dusty appearance. I have not had time since returning from the foothills to change into something more appropriate for your company," he said as he approached the plinth. In truth he could not have cared less about his appearance, especially where she was concerned, but he knew he must play to her vanity.

Herezah nodded. "Worry not, Spur. I'm sure most men would give an eye to look as good as you do even in dirty garments."

The men around him sniggered, mostly out of jealousy, but Lazar deliberately kept his expression blank, his eyes firmly fixed on the Valide. Herezah always tried to provoke a reaction from him. So far she'd never provoked the anger she so craved. He would not give it now even though it simmered inside.

"Thank you, Valide, for your generosity." Lazar moved quickly to business. He wanted to be gone as soon as possible. "I present six applicants for your consideration."

A bell sounded, another set of curtains was pulled back, and a line of girls was led in, all naked but for a gauzy sheath that gave them a sense of modesty although it hid nothing. Lazar ignored all the others and looked only at Ana. He hated that the other men in the room were enjoying the sight of her body, just ripening into womanhood.

"Come, girls." Salmeo shooed them into position in front of Herezah and began the introductions. "This is Fajel, she is ten, and as you can see is straight-limbed with a tendency toward being tall, I would suggest . . ." Lazar forced his mind to drift. He did not want to listen to this.

He fixed his own stare on Herezah to give the impression that he was paying close attention. He knew she watched him more closely than she watched the child and he deliberately blanked his face, knowing how much it irritated her. She soon grew bored with trying to win any flicker of interest from him and returned to the job at hand.

"Can you sing something for us, Fajel?" she asked, and the girl nodded. "Go ahead, then."

A sweet sound broke across the mainly silent room, interrupted only by shuffles or coughs. There was no more socializing now. Each man wanted his six chosen above all the others.

The girl finished her song. "That was very nice," Herezah said condescendingly. "Turn around for me, child."

Salmeo aided the girl as she slowly spun around so the Valide could see her from all angles. "This one will stay slim, Valide Zara," he hazarded.

"Yes, we'll take her," Herezah said, sounding slightly bored. "Next."

It continued. Lazar was not involved in any of the choosing but he was required to stand alongside the line of girls and he was pleased that Ana was last and he was able to be next to her as the line dwindled. He could feel the heat from her body radiating to the back of his hand, which barely touched the thin gauze that separated his skin from hers. He wished he could offer reassurance. It would be hollow, though—it would be a lie and Ana would know it.

Finally it was her turn and he took a deep, steadying breath, hoping nothing of the turmoil he was feeling would be given away on his face.

Salmeo continued. "Valide Zara, this is Ana, found in Shanar. She is almost fourteen and already a dazzling beauty, if I might say so. I would urge that this girl is the pick of the forty-two on offer this evening. I understand the Spur paid a premium for her."

"Indeed, Salmeo, and rightly so." Herezah stood. Lazar knew her interest had been piqued. It was everything he had hoped would not happen. "She's from the foothills, you say?"

Lazar took a moment to realize Herezah was addressing him. "Er, yes, Valide, from the west. She belongs to a goatherd's family, but she was originally an orphan, adopted by them."

"That hair!" Herezah said, unable to hide her excitement. "Where does one find a child of this coloring in the foothills?"

Lazar shrugged, feigning boredom. "I'm told by the step-mother that she was found as a newborn after the Samazen had passed through. Presumably her family perished. As for the color, I suspect she is from the far, far west, probably merchants."

"Oh yes, yes." Herezah smiled, pleased. "Spin, child, let me feast my eyes upon you."

Ana obeyed and for the first time Lazar looked too. She was perfect. He had been wrong to think her coltish; he had been fooled by the baggy clothing her stepmother had forced on her and by her square shoulders. Beneath Ana's transparent shift was a nubile body rounding into the fullness of womanhood. Her belly was taut, flat; her curves still gentle but filled with promise. Her breasts were already full and high.

Herezah stepped down from the plinth and shocked everyone by reaching out and pinching one of Ana's nipples. To her credit, Ana did not flinch.

Herezah laughed with pleasure. "Oh yes, watch them rise strong and ready to the touch. This one is more than wanted; this one is desired. Boaz will love her. Congratulations, Lazar." Herezah looked directly at Ana now. "You're very beautiful, my dear. Do you know it? Will you use it in the right way, I wonder?"

"I am how I am, Valide," Ana said levelly, taking everyone by surprise. Herezah's question had been rhetorical and no one had anticipated a response. When it came, it silenced those gathered, including the Valide. Salmeo glared at the child.

"And headstrong too, I see," Herezah continued. "That we shall need to work upon." She looked toward the chief eunuch. "Salmeo."

"Yes, Valide," he lisped enthusiastically.

"I may even take this one on myself."

Lazar's heart sank.

"Who better to prepare her for Boaz than the person who knows him best?" the Valide asked, laughing beneath her veils.

"That is a high compliment to the girl, Valide," Salmeo admitted. "You are fortunate, child," he said to Ana, though he still glowered from the audacity of her earlier comment.

"Ana, you are now odalisque of the harem of Zar Boaz, King of Kings, Mightiest of the Mighties." Then Herezah smiled. "And I am your mistress."

Ana said nothing, though everyone was anticipating some response.

Lazar felt frantic. He had to do something. "Valide?"

"Oh yes, Spur, you will be paid handsomely for this find."

"That is not my query, Valide Zara. Ana's purchase came with certain conditions." He wondered whether he could pull this off.

"Conditions?" she said in the quiet voice he knew well. Herezah had learned long ago not to fall into the trap of screeching as other women might do, or raising her voice when she disagreed. She had taught herself to harness the emotion into a deadly calm.

Lazar, however, was ready for her. "Yes, that's right. It's unusual, I agree." He contrived a tone of embarrassment. "Valide, this girl was too special to pass up. I thought you might be prepared to make an exception. But I understand if you'd take umbrage at being dictated to by a mere peasant." He did his best to insult her politely, hoping against hope that she'd rise to his bait and banish both him and the girl. "In fact, if you are offended—and I would not blame you if you were—I shall stand by the rules you have made."

"Which are?" she asked.

"That the money I spent on her is my loss and I must make it up as best I can."

"I see," Herezah said, and he knew he had not won the gamble. Her interest in the girl was too strong, and he knew how she loved to trade words with him.

"So what are these 'conditions'?" She laced the final word with grim humor and Lazar could hear the men muttering behind him, could imagine the wry smiles on their faces.

"The mother insisted that Ana be permitted freedom one day each month."

"Preposterous!" Tariq cried on behalf of the Valide, his beard jewels flashing as he shook his head in anger.

Herezah raised a hand. She looked toward Salmeo, a question in her eyes.

"Never previously permitted, Valide Zara," the eunuch replied, equally outraged.

She nodded and returned her dark gaze to Lazar, who refused to squirm beneath it.

"I understand," he said, beginning to bow, hoping to remove himself.

"Not so fast, Spur," she said softly. "The girl is young. What sort of freedom did her mother have in mind for her daughter? Perhaps we could send Salmeo to escort her. She would be veiled completely, of course, at all times."

Now he did squirm. "Er, well, Valide, I think she rather had in mind something less constricting."

"Oh?"

"Her mother impressed upon me that Ana is startlingly intelligent. She had hopes that we might be able to encourage learning language, culture—"

"Yes, of course," Herezah interrupted, "she will get all of that and more if she shows talent."

"I'm not explaining myself well, Valide. Perhaps it's because I feel extremely awkward about the full extent of the mother's conditions."

Herezah's patience was wearing thin now. "Why don't you lay out the full extent of the conditions, Spur, so I can make a firm decision."

Lazar paused. "She required me to be her escort," he said firmly.

"You!" Her voice was soft but her fury was unmistakable.

He nodded. "My apologies, Valide. Felluj entrusted this most precious child of hers to me personally. She charged me with Ana's safety and education. She understood me to be a soldier and decided that I was the most appropriate . . . um . . . guardian, for want of a better word."

The pause—and what wasn't being said in the dread silence that followed his words—was so palpable and heavy, Lazar felt quite sure it could be cut up, served on a platter, and forced down his gullet. He had played his hand.

"And if I did not choose Ana, Spur, what would you do with her? Make her your own?"

"I would sell her, Valide," he said, adding an undertone of insult to his voice. "I have no need for a child."

Herezah's eyes sparkled in between the slit of the veil. She was loving watching him bristle.

"But you want to be her guardian, is that right?"

He deliberately took a controlled but audible breath to suggest that he was getting tired of this line of questioning. "The promise under which she was sold demanded that I agree to this condition on your behalf. I knew I had no right to do this, Valide Zara, but I believed the girl was worth it. She is special, as I'm sure we all agree, and someone to match minds with Boaz, who is something of a scholar. Ana has the potential to be a fulfilling mate for him, rather than just a plaything. I'm sure you above most would understand such a thing." His words couched insult with compliment, deliberately. Certainly his final line was meant to remind her that Joreb had chosen her for Absolute Favorite not only because of her beauty and prowess as a lover but because she had a bright, quick mind to match his own.

"One day a month, you say?"

"That's right. She would be in my care for that full day."

"She would be fully veiled. No one may look upon her."

"Of course," he said indignantly.

"Let me think on this, Spur. Ana must pass her Test of Virtue. Present yourself at the palace for my answer in the late evening tomorrow. We shall take supper together and discuss it. Until then, you are dismissed."

He bristled silently, hating the position he found himself in, being ordered around by this woman. Supper! Allad save him, he thought, calling upon his homeland god. "Thank you, Valide Zara." He bowed, and as he did so a loud sneeze exploded from nearby—from behind the walls.

Salmeo looked thunderstruck, and with his single signal, men began to swarm.

"YOU FOOL, KETT," Boaz rasped, terrified.

"I . . . I couldn't help it, Zar. I will not let them know you were here," the youngster beseeched, scared that he might bring down the wrath of the harem on the Zar. "Run!"

Pez had to admire the young servant's courage. "No use running. There have been guards at every point since Herezah left her chambers."

"What can we do?" Boaz asked, his head swiveling from side to side as he looked for an escape.

"There is no escape. We must wait." They could hear men's voices, footsteps.

"Wait?" Boaz whispered frantically.

Pez noted how calm Kett appeared, his only show of anxiety the way he shifted his weight from foot to foot. The dwarf spoke in a voice Boaz had never heard before. "Boaz, stand close to me." The Zar spluttered a noise of hesitation but Pez ignored him. "Do it now! We have no more time."

"What can this possibly do?" Boaz asked, putting his arms

around the shoulders of the dwarf, who in turn leaned back against the Zar.

"Hush, Boaz, not a sound!" Pez commanded. "Forgive me, Kett," he added. "I cannot protect you, as I warned, but you and I will see each other again."

"Who are you?" Kett asked, his voice trembling but his expression stoic. The voices of the guards grew louder.

"Wait for me," Pez said. "Betray me not."

It was all he had time to say before the guards were upon them.

They descended on Kett; the boy made no protest. Boaz couldn't understand it; they were standing so close to him, it was obvious—surely—that he and Pez would be seen as well. Yet the guards' gazes appeared to slide past them. The Zar wanted to shout orders at them, demand to be heard, even though they seemed not to see him. His mouth was too dry to utter a sound. Boaz felt as though the glow from the main chamber through the latticework had lit them up like the trees they decorated for the Festival of Light, but the guards ignored the Zar and Pez and simply manhandled Kett away down the corridor. Zar and the dwarf were left alone, the voices and footsteps dissipating as the confusion in the Choosing Room increased.

"Pez," Boaz whispered, quite sure his bowels had turned to water, "what just happened?"

The dwarf sighed. Boaz was too intelligent to trick. "I told you I could protect us, not him."

Boaz broke away from his friend, spinning the small man around. "What do you mean by that? The guards were as close as I am to you and they didn't see us!"

"Hush, High One, or they'll be back."

"Tell me how it can be that they saw Kett but not us!"

"Another one of my tricks, Your Majesty" was all Pez would answer.

"No!" the boy growled low. "That was nothing like pulling kerchiefs from your nose or doves from your hat. That was much, much more."

"Boaz, I have asked you to trust me and I'm going to ask you to indulge me a little longer."

"What just occurred is impossible," the Zar moaned, but he was prevented from saying more by Kett's arrival in the Choosing Room. The boy was hanging limply between the grip of two guards. The Zar's attention was diverted but he gave Pez a warning glare, their conversation was not done with yet.

"IS THIS WHO was snooping?" Herezah demanded.

"We caught him in one of the corridors behind this chamber, Valide Zara," one of the Elim answered. As he bowed, the two soldiers dropped Kett between them. The slave kept his head lowered.

Herezah looked to Salmeo, who moved, his huge bulk surprisingly light of tread, to the cringing boy.

"Look at me," he commanded. "What were you doing in the corridor in a restricted area?"

"Grand Master Eunuch, I was lost," Kett said, his voice pitiful. "I was hurrying about my duties, I took the wrong entrance—I'm so sorry, sir—I found myself on the other side of the room and knew I shouldn't be there and I became too frightened to move or make a sound."

"You weren't very successful, were you?" Tariq piped up. He looked around, waiting for someone to snicker at his sarcastic jest.

"Forgive me, Grand Master. I tried so hard to stifle my sneeze but that only made it worse."

Lazar grimaced. He sensed it would get ugly for this child. Salmeo was too cruel to let pass an insult to his authority, particularly such a public one. Glancing behind to Ana, Lazar realized that she was still in the chamber; her minders had not had the opportunity to leave since the interruption.

Ana returned his concerned look, her own expression fearful.

"What is your name, boy?"

"I am Kett, Grand Master Eunuch. I run errands for some of your men, although I hope to join the palace guard when I reach a suitable age. I am the son of Shelah Mohab." Kett struggled to keep his voice steady. He hoped that mentioning his mother's name would help his perilous situation.

"Shelah?" Herezah inquired. "My old servant?" She moved to stand beside Salmeo in front of the boy.

Kett bowed low again on his knees, his head touching the pale marble floor. "Valide," he whispered. "Yes, you were her mistress."

"I see." Herezah glanced at Salmeo.

Not to be outdone, the Vizier sidled up beside the Valide and the Grand Master Eunuch. "The penalty is death, surely?"

Salmeo turned to address Herezah, although everyone could hear him. "The Vizier speaks true. Death is the punishment to any unauthorized person who sees the girls of the harem. Guards!"

Lazar, horrified, stepped forward. This boy was clearly an innocent. His life must not be taken. "Valide, if I may be permitted?" Hoping to flatter Herezah, he bowed.

"What is it, Spur?" Herezah asked, pleased by the attention but feigning irritation.

"Thank you, Valide Zara. I don't believe this boy's life should be forfeit."

"How dare you!" Tariq began.

Herezah held up a hand, silencing the Vizier. "Why do you say that, Lazar?" She spoke from behind her veil; he could not see her face but there was laziness to the tone that he knew well—it was seductive and dangerous.

"This boy—and let's not forget he *is* only a boy—is innocent of anything sinister, Valide. He has told you that he was lost and it would be generous of you to spare his life."

Lazar could see the Vizier fuming; Salmeo, though equally angry, was not nearly so obvious. The lids of his eyes had closed slightly, shading the windows into his thoughts.

"He must be punished," the eunuch said softly.

"And I agree," Herezah added. "Innocent of intent or otherwise, this boy was where he knew he must not be. It is forbidden."

"But, Valide, he did not realize until it was too late that he was somewhere he shouldn't be. He is a child. If he were a man, I would agree he should know better. If he must be punished, so be it, but not death. If I may be so bold, perhaps you might start your son's reign with a show of mercy, Valide. The palace will learn soon enough of your magnanimous gesture."

He was daring her into doing something generous, he was counting on her vanity to win through all the obstructions. He held his breath as she watched him intently.

It was at this moment that someone else joined the debate, someone so unexpected that it made Lazar draw in his breath sharply. The situation suddenly turned exquisitely dangerous.

"Valide, High One," Ana said, sliding in on her knees next

to Kett, head bowed to the ground, her creamy back exposed through the transparent sheath.

Salmeo signaled angrily to two eunuchs. "Girl, this is not permitted. You may never address the Valide first! You may never speak in fact unless addressed."

Herezah smiled slyly. "No, wait. Let's hear what this girl has to say. Ana?"

"Spare him his life, High One," Ana said, using all the wrong terminology to address Herezah, not that it offended the woman who gloated above her to be addressed in the manner reserved only for the Zar. She was not looking at Ana, of course, but watching the Spur of Percheron, who stared at the prone figure beneath him, aghast.

"Why should I, Ana?" she continued.

"Because you can. You are all-powerful, Valide. If that is not reason enough, High One, I will exchange something precious for Kett's life."

At this Herezah gave a tinkling, affected laugh. "My dear, what can you possibly have that I would want?"

"My freedom, Valide Zara. I relinquish all of it. If I pass the Test of Virtue, I will give up the condition my mother placed upon the Spur. I will remain in the palace for—"

"No!" Lazar interrupted, unable to help himself. It had taken all of his wits to negotiate the release—however limited—of Ana into his care and now she was casting that freedom to the wind. He admired her courage in placing herself at the mercy of such people as Herezah and Salmeo. But his despair was selfish. He wanted to see Ana again, not see her so fully absorbed into the harem that he might never again hear the musical lilt in her voice or watch her beauty settle into full womanhood. "This cannot be permitted, Valide."

"Why not?" Herezah was relishing every moment of his discomfort. "Ana makes a gracious plea for Kett. Surely you admire it?"

There was little he could say to that. "I made a promise," he said helplessly.

"And you saw it through to its conclusion. I had already decided to grant Ana the condition you argued for so eloquently. It is Ana's freedom and so it is hers to give back to me if she so wishes."

He had not hated Herezah so much in all the time he'd known her as he did at this moment. Clever Herezah had seen through his ploy; she knew how to read men and she had read him like an open book. She could tell that he wanted Ana, and no matter how noble his intentions were, she intended to deny him. And why? he asked himself. Because he would not give himself willingly to her? Because he would give his time and affection to a girl, but not to her, Herezah had found a new way to punish him.

Young Ana could not understand all these undercurrents swirling around her. Innocently she asked, "Will you spare his life, then, Valide Zara?"

"Yes. I will take the precious exchange you offer, Ana," the Valide said, loading the word *precious* with sarcasm. "This boy will not be executed," she added, to the audible disappointment of the Vizier and the relief of the others who were audience to this surprising piece of theater. Salmeo remained unreadable.

"He will, of course, be punished," Herezah added, and Lazar heard viciousness in her voice.

She addressed the boy now, still bent in obeisance. "Kett."

"Yes, Valide Zara?"

"Ana here has bought your life with her own freedom. You

will not be executed as protocol calls, but I fear you must now join the very place you have trespassed upon."

Kett looked at her, his bewilderment clear in his expression. "Valide?"

Salmeo however understood. "Call the priests," he said to his guard.

"Valide," Lazar began.

"Enough, Spur!" Herezah snapped. "We have indulged you. Please step back." At her dismissal, the Vizier gave a triumphant glare at Lazar, who had no choice but to do as he was ordered.

"This will not take long, brothers," Salmeo assured.

"I am going to ask you to step outside for a short while," Herezah warned those gathered. She glanced Lazar's way and he knew that beneath the veil, she was smiling.

10

Pez and his Zar were still trapped in the corridor running alongside the Choosing Room. Like Salmeo and Lazar, Pez had understood the Valide's words almost immediately. He knew precisely what was about to transpire and he did not want Boaz present for it. "Quick, we must leave now," Pez urged.

"What will happen to Kett?" Boaz demanded.

"You heard. He is to be punished. Let's go."

"Shouldn't we stay?"

"It won't be pretty," Pez said. "Trust me, you don't want to witness it."

Boaz followed his friend out from behind the curtain, his mind racing. "Where are the guards?"

"They've gone to fetch the priests. I know a way we can get out. Hold my hand."

"Why?"

"Do it!"

Boaz assumed that they were fortunate and that the excitement of the proceedings had made some of the guards sloppy enough not to notice them. Pez knew otherwise. He guided them expertly through the various twisting walkways until Boaz found himself arriving by the Lion Fountain.

"Here? How?"

"I told you, I know my way around. Now come, we are still in danger."

They arrived breathlessly back at the Zar's quarters, Pez affecting a wild laugh and somersaulting down the main hallway to Boaz's huge doors. The two Elim bowed to their Zar and then laughed. They knew the lad well enough to share a joke with him.

"Where does he get the energy?" one asked.

Boaz shrugged and pushed the dwarf into the main chamber.

Inside, the Zar ignored protocol and, with difficulty due to his injured arm, poured two goblets of wine. He handed one to his friend with a shaking hand. "Now, tell me what happened back there." Boaz sipped his wine, attempting to calm his frayed nerves and rising temper.

The little man sighed and all amusement died in his eyes. "It's called shepherding."

"What does that mean?"

"I can—temporarily at least—block people."

"Block them?" Boaz frowned.

"You know," Pez said awkwardly, "steer them away—you could say—as a shepherd steers his sheep."

"You mean, prevent their seeing you?"

The dwarf nodded. "But not for long."

"Actually invisible?"

"No. How can I put this? I force their gazes to slide past me, you could say."

Boaz suddenly understood. "You have the Lore?" His tone was leaden with fright.

Again Pez nodded, his expression grave. He had hoped to avoid revealing all this to Boaz.

"And do you use it often?"

"No. I have little need for it."

"So what are you? Some sort of sorcerer?" Boaz asked, aghast.

"No. I possess such a tiny sense, I wield no real power." Pez crafted a necessary lie. "A throwback to my great-grandmother, who was sentient. For the most part she kept her power a secret." He watched Boaz's eyes widen. "It's nothing, Boaz. I have only a touch. Something only slightly more impressive than my silly tricks."

"Why have you not mentioned it to me before?"

Pez shrugged. "It didn't seem important—as I said, I haven't used it since I came to the palace." In this, he told the truth. "I'm the Zar's idiot. It wouldn't do to be casting spells."

"What is the extent of your magic?" the boy persisted.

"That's it," Pez replied diffidently. "I can shepherd and that takes so much out of me I usually need to sleep for a whole day afterward. In fact I feel quite ill now." He blinked slowly. "I would never have used it but I couldn't risk you being found there."

The boy continued to watch him, curiosity in his eyes. "I shall have to think about what you've told me."

"You'll keep it our secret, won't you?" Pez hoped that the words *our secret* might prompt Boaz to feel he held yet more information from his mother.

"I have no reason to betray you, Pez. You're my friend, aren't you?"

"I am. More than you can know."

The Zar nodded thoughtfully; then his expression turned suddenly apprehensive. "Why did they call for the priests back there?"

"There is to be a ceremony."

"Oh? I didn't understand what my mother meant by 'welcoming Kett to the place he had trespassed upon.'"

"She is formally making him a member of the harem, Boaz," Pez replied.

Boaz considered this. "But how can she when he's . . ." His face drained of color. "He's to become a eunuch?"

Pez nodded. "She will be taking his manhood as we speak."

KETT, IN HIS FEAR and confusion, seemed to be the last person in the chamber to understand what was about to happen. Even Ana had grasped what was unfolding and had tried to squirm away through the legs of her captors.

Herezah was having none of it. "She must bear witness. It was she whose body he watched. She who has caused his downfall, you could say."

"Valide, I really must object," Lazar began, but he was cut off again, this time aggressively.

"Don't ever object to me, Spur. Remember your place. The girl will bear witness, as will you."

Salmeo whispered something to her and she nodded.

"Guards, please show our guests into the courtyard across the hall. You can take some fresh air and we shall serve refreshments. We shall not keep you long."

Muttered whispers of concern, confusion, and relief broke out among the guests.

Salmeo's voice rose in command. "Elim, Spur Lazar and the girl, Ana, are to remain. Vizier, my humblest apologies, but I must ask you to leave also."

The Vizier swelled like a rooster about to unleash a tirade of protestations when Herezah used her quiet voice to still him. "Thank you, Tariq. I know how careful you are to observe the traditions of the harem. Perhaps you can keep our guests entertained on my behalf. We shan't be long."

The stooped thin man pursed his lips and had no choice but to take what was clearly an order in the same gracious manner in which she had delivered it.

The priest, another eunuch, arrived with a trio of helpers in tow. He'd obviously been informed of the nature of his visit for he carried a small velvet roll and his aides carried towels, pails of steaming water, and various other instruments.

They bowed to Herezah. "Valide Zara," the priest said. She nodded in response and he turned immediately to Salmeo. "Grand Master Eunuch, this is most unusual." There was a slight quaver of worry in his voice.

Salmeo gave a gesture of helplessness. "These are unusual circumstances." They both looked down at the trembling Kett. An assistant, known as a knifer, began lighting small wax candles, placing them in a crescent around the boy; another doused some of the lanterns around the chamber, throwing Kett into a small pool of light as the rest of the people around him were cast into shadows.

Herezah, who had never witnessed the making of a eunuch, felt a thrill of excitement. "How long will this take?" she asked.

"We shall be swift, Valide" was all the priest could offer. He wasted no further time, giving whispered orders to his assistants.

Lazar moved back, leaning against the wall. He knew its solidity would be a welcome friend within a few minutes. The Spur was hardly a squeamish man but this was one ceremony he was glad was a secret ritual. He cast a careful glance toward Ana; she looked desperately pale and frightened. Ana turned as if hearing his thoughts and met his gaze. The depth of sorrow in her eyes awakened a fierce yearning in him. She was so young, so innocent—he wanted to protect her but now she was lost to him. Kett would hardly thank her for her sacrifice, Lazar thought grimly; he himself would rather die than go through this barbaric procedure and, worse, live with its results for the rest of his life.

Salmeo began to speak quietly as the preparations continued. Catching sight of a small curved blade now being studiously sharpened by the priest, Kett began to whimper.

"What you are about to witness is one of the most secret of rituals preserved in the harem. It is not to be spoken about outside the harem walls. In this rare instance it is being used as punishment, but Kett will appreciate in time to come that he is privileged. It is a high honor to serve in this way." Salmeo stopped abruptly and turned to the priest. No doubt both men were remembering their own rite of passage. Lazar held his breath and prayed the next few minutes would pass quickly.

"Ready?" Salmeo asked.

The priest glanced at his helpers, each of whom nodded solemnly. "We are."

"Kett," Salmeo began. "Be brave now. Your blood has been spared and you are entering a new way of life. A new form of service. The most secret and privileged of slaves." His voice was so cloyingly gentle that Lazar had to look away from Kett's trusting face. The boy knew something terrifying was about to occur, and Lazar could see that he also grasped that he had no power to prevent it. It was easier to cooperate and, like Lazar, pray to the gods that it end quickly.

The assistants undressed Kett and laid him down on his back, his head and shoulders framed by the flickering candles. The priest threw a powder into the flames, which sparkled and crackled, signifying the commencement of the ritual. Two of the assistants flanked Kett to hold the boy down. The third man used long strips of white linen to bind the area tightly beneath Kett's navel. They did the same to the high part of his thighs. Kett began to moan. Curiously, he turned his head and searched for Ana, who locked her gaze with his. Lazar watched the two youngsters share something. Sympathy? Fright? He didn't know, but with the adults in the chamber perpetrating this horror, it was little wonder that they sought solace in each other.

"The bandages prevent excessive bleeding," Salmeo explained softly to Herezah.

"Can he die from this?" she whispered.

"Oh yes. Many do, in fact. Zarab will choose."

"Drink this," the priest said, handing Kett a small cup and helping him to sit up.

Herezah was intrigued. "Is that for pain?"

"A dulling concoction to prevent panic," Salmeo answered.

A prayer was murmured over Kett as the boy was laid back down, the priest and his assistants holding hands above the child. An assistant reached for a bowl and the priest cast another prayer before dipping a sponge into the bowl and squeezing it out.

"What's that gray liquid they're smearing on him?"

"That's boiled water-of-pepper and juniper. It is made by the priest, who casts prayers to purify it and to purify the boy. He must do this three times in between praying for Kett's life to be preserved and for his own hand to be guided for the cut."

Kett squirmed under the heat of the liquid around such a tender area. Lazar could see steam rising from the boy's body, wanted to close his eyes, but kept them open to honor the slave who was showing such courage—more than Lazar felt he would have shown under the same circumstances. The boy was moaning, yes, but no words, no pitiful cries, no begging for mercy. Why? And all the time his head was turned toward Ana, watching her whisper her prayers.

"What is it supposed to do?" Herezah asked as they watched the priest complete the third bathing. Salmeo kept his voice low but Lazar could hear the words plainly enough, which meant they were sparing Kett none of the grisly details. "It simply bathes the area. Makes it as sterile as possible, Valide."

"I see. And you, Salmeo, went through this precise procedure?"

"Yes, Valide, to a point." His timing was perfect, for the priest had just positioned himself between Kett's legs. As the other man reached for the sickle-shaped knife, Salmeo raised his voice. "And now we must choose."

"Choose what?"

"Which type of emasculation you wish for Kett."

Lazar fancied that he saw Herezah tremble at the eunuch's words. "Choose?" she repeated in a smoky voice. "Explain the options to me again."

"Yes, Valide." Salmeo had known she would ask this of him, understood her need for theater and the cruel streak that demanded she make the boy suffer a little longer. "Three methods are used. There is the clean-shaven, or the Varen, in which all of the sexual organs are removed in a single cut. There is the Yerzah—this fellow loses only the shaft. Perhaps the worst of the three, Valide."

"Oh? Why do you say that?"

Salmeo shrugged. "Well"—and somehow everyone in the room knew the Grand Master Eunuch was Yerzah—"though he will have the ability to procreate, he won't have the . . . tools."

"Why is that hardest of all?" Herezah persisted.

Salmeo's lids lowered slightly and Lazar noticed the rope scar twitch. "Because he doesn't lose the desire to copulate, Valide. He cannot satisfy a woman by traditional means and he cannot satisfy himself by any means."

"I see," the Valide said, smiling beneath the veil, storing away another treasured item of information about the Grand Master. "And the third method?"

"Is called Xarob. This eunuch is rendered sexless by the damage, often removal, of the testicles."

"How do you damage them?"

Salmeo looked at Kett; the boy needed to be cut before all blood was strangled by the tight bandaging. "We must hurry now," he said softly, adding: "Damage can be achieved by twisting the testicles, searing them, bruising them, or bandaging very tightly as one might an animal who is to be castrated."

"Thank you, Salmeo. I think Kett is best served by becoming Varen."

"Clean-shaven?" the priest repeated.

"Yes," Herezah affirmed. "Proceed."

The priest nodded at the assistants who flanked Kett and they immediately held down his arms. He did not struggle; he was frozen in fear, refusing to look at anyone but Ana. Two of the assistants placed a knee across his bandaged thighs. They could not risk him jerking when the blade was doing its work.

When both were satisfied they had the boy effectively pinned, they nodded. The priest carefully grasped Kett's genitals, ensuring he had them in a firm grip before he pulled them away from the boy's body, and in a single motion cut through skin and tissue until everything formerly attached came away in his hand.

Kett screamed and mercifully blanked out, as did Ana, who hung limply between the arms of her guards. Lazar, helpless to aid her, was working hard at damping down his own bile.

The priest reverently placed the bloody mass in a white porcelain bowl. "They will preserve that for him. Most of us like to keep the removed flesh," Salmeo explained.

Herezah had not so much as blinked at the ghoulish procedure. "How generous," she commented. "Actually, I should like them."

Salmeo looked at her sharply. "That is not traditional, Valide."

"Nevertheless," she said, offering no further explanation.

The priest and his assistants worked fast now, taking advantage of Kett's swoon.

"They are placing a wide needle into the tube at the root of the shaft," Salmeo said. "It is made of pewter and will keep that tube of flesh open but plugged until Kett heals."

Lazar watched as the wound was dressed with papers saturated in chilled water. Then it was bandaged. The priest sighed and nodded. "It is done," he said.

"And?" Salmeo asked.

The priest stood, wincing as he straightened. "He will live.

He's young, he'll heal fast. It is a clean wound. Now he must be walked."

Salmeo looked at the Valide. "Kett will be kept conscious now and mobile for the next four hours. Only then will he be permitted to rest."

"Can you do the walking somewhere else? We need to continue with our Choosing Ceremony," Herezah replied.

The priest nodded. "Who will be looking after him?"

"I shall arrange for helpers," Salmeo said.

"Thank you. You know the routine, Grand Master, nothing—absolutely nothing, not even a sip of water—must pass his lips for three days."

"I remember," Salmeo said, and Lazar heard the anger—or was it pain?—in his tone.

"He will be in agony, of course, and he will beg for relief from feeling parched. He will want to pass water but he must not, under any circumstances." Salmeo nodded. "I will return in three days to remove the spigot."

"What happens when that occurs?" Herezah asked, clearly fascinated.

The priest answered: "When the needle that has plugged the hole is removed, a fountain of bodily fluid should spurt from the opening. Kett will feel immense relief, and it will signal that he is out of danger and can begin his healing."

"And if not?" Herezah asked.

"If he cannot pass water, then he is doomed to a slow, agonizing death. I would suggest it would be easier to put him out of his misery in this instance."

Kett groaned. He was coming back to consciousness. Tears leaked out of his closed eyes and his body trembled. Ana was still slumped between her captors.

Lazar could no longer bear it. "Valide," he began.

"Yes, you are dismissed, Spur. Don't forget our appointment tomorrow—I do not like to be kept waiting." She turned to Salmeo. "Let's get this all cleared up. The merchants will be eager to complete their business."

It was all Lazar could do to affect a terse bow before he stormed from the chamber.

Ranging swiftly through the palace, he finally emerged into the Moon Courtyard and the balmy evening. He dragged in a lungful of air to quell his mounting rage.

Furious with himself for having shown his feelings to Herezah, he was also torn apart by the loss of Ana. Thinking about Kett made him value his own body and the fact that it was whole. Perhaps what he needed was a jug of wine and a willing woman to ease his despair. But without him realizing it, he was drawn elsewhere for solace, to where a woman who could not speak might offer some comfort.

11

Tariq sat alone on the balcony of his home and seethed. Not even the soft moonlight glinting off the calm harbor could ease his anger—not that anyone would know he was in this mood. Vizier Tariq was a master of hiding his thoughts, although he deliberately played a dangerous game within the palace. He knew they all thought he was both a shallow fool and desperately ambitious. He permitted the Valide—and to some extent the fat black eunuch—to trample him because for now it suited his purposes. Unlike the old Zar, who, although he had disliked Tariq, had sought his assistance, neither the Valide nor Salmeo took him seriously, even though his position required them to make pretense of doing so. And no doubt the Valide could see the value of being seen to have the Vizier on her side. He hoped she might consider him even more valuable in time to come.

Oh yes, he could see all of this. But they could not see him.

And they did not know him or what he might have the power to do.

The harsh voice invaded his thoughts. *All alone, Tariq?* When it spoke it sounded like boulders chafing against one another.

As you find me, he answered carefully. Although the shock of its invasion had dissipated, its intimidation had not. He felt intensely frightened by it and hoped the voice—whomever it belonged to—could not see into his thoughts as easily as it seemed to enter his mind.

Your jewels glitter in the moonlight. When they do that it means your beard is trembling. And when your beard trembles, Vizier Tariq, I know you are angry and no doubt plotting.

Is that so? Tariq was impressed and terrified. He closed his eyes to steady himself, for there was no way to rid himself of the voice. It came as it chose and he had no control, no power to block it. Something in that deep, almost ancient tone suggested he not attempt to banish it. *Am I that easy to gauge? Perhaps I should rid myself of the beard if it so easily reveals me.* Tariq was proud of himself for feigning such a relaxed approach.

Perhaps you should. It's an affectation only. The time is drawing close when you will need none of those things.

You speak as if you know me, yet this is only the third time we have spoken.

I do know you, Tariq. I know you better than anyone.

May I ask some questions?

Why not?

Do you talk with others?

Few.

Do you visit other people as you visit me?

Now?

Yes.

No.

But you have?

Over time.

The Vizier repeated that cryptic answer in his mind. What could it mean? *Where are you?*

Close.

In Percheron?

Yes. But time, usually my friend, is now my enemy.

Tariq found some spine. *Do not push me.* He held his breath, then added: *What you ask is complicated.* He heard the plea in his own voice—and was ashamed of it.

There was a silence in his mind. He waited.

What is the basis of your reluctance? the voice asked.

Tariq sensed it was less sure of itself than before and was pleased. It felt good to sow some doubt in its arrogant mind. *I'm just not sure, that's all.*

I have watched you for years. I have smelled your ambition, tasted your desires, felt your anguish at those who think you stupid. I admire your resolve and the way you have disguised your true self, beguiled the new Valide, tricked the black eunuch. The cunning in the voice was back.

The compliments worked; Tariq couldn't help but swell with pride. He was secretly pleased that his intruder knew how crafty he was. *Why do you know all this?*

Because I have chosen you.

Chosen me? Tariq took a risk despite his fear. *What if I don't care to be chosen? What if I am happy as I am?*

Now the sinister voice boomed laughter in his head. It sounded like mountains of granite shifting. *Content? I think not, Vizier. Consider that I bring all my knowledge to you. Imagine it!*

Centuries of information. I can tell you anything you want to know about our history—even where the Zar Fasha's famed treasures are buried. Tariq's beard quivered and the thing laughed again in his head. *You thought it was only legend, didn't you? It is truth. He buried it with all of his wives and his heirs. He was quite mad.*

The Vizier shrouded his thoughts as best he could, uncertain of how successful his attempt was. *So, you can offer me riches, what else?*

Isn't that enough? Isn't that what you want, Tariq? To be wealthy beyond imagination?

Oh, I have a vast imagination.

Again amusement rumbled through his mind. *What else can I tempt you with?*

What else can you offer? Tariq tried to sound casual.

He had heard the voice for the first time the evening before the Zar had died. It had come to him as he was relaxing on his balcony, as he was doing now, taking the night air. He had been startled, had dropped his wine. The voice calmed him, told him Joreb would be dead before noon the following day and that he, Tariq, was in a perfect position to stamp his claim as premier counsel to the new power entering the palace, the Valide Zara. The Vizier had woken before dawn the following day thinking he had simply dreamed the episode. But as his mind cleared, so did his memory, and by the time the sunlight had shyly stolen across the sky, Tariq knew he had experienced some sort of premonition and had hurriedly made his way to the palace to tell Herezah. It was only his insistence that this was an emergency that had persuaded the First Wife and Absolute Favorite of Zar Joreb to agree, irritated, to meet with him before her grooming was done. Heavily veiled, she had greeted the news with disdain, particularly as the physicians had tentatively hazarded that Joreb could recover and be back on his horse by the next moon.

When the news of the Zar's decline through the night was delivered to Herezah, she had instantly resummoned the Vizier. His confidence restored, he had smiled at her, throwing caution to the wind and his fate in with hers.

"If he dies, I shall need the right men in the right places, Vizier Tariq," she had said, a new level of respect in her tone.

"*When* he dies, Favorite Herezah, you will need me alone."

He had noted the flash of contempt that sparked in her eyes and imagined the scowl behind the veil at his audacious claim, but then Herezah did not know about his visitor. Tariq had realized with the news of the Zar's worsening health that the voice had spoken truth.

It interrupted his thoughts now. *I offer you power.*

I am already Vizier.

You are nothing, Tariq. You have a title but no real power.

Then you must explain this power. What you want of me is significant. The return for my generosity must be equal in measure. The voice had a way of firing his imagination and greed. He wanted power. That was his true desire. He wanted Herezah and that fat slave to know the truth. They would no longer dismiss him from the chambers where they whispered. He wanted to be Grand Vizier, to see fear in their eyes, to have the pair defer to him. *Now who is reluctant?* he gibed.

Anger this time. Controlled but certainly there. *I will bring you real power, Vizier, of the sort you cannot attain alone.*

Tariq persisted. *As Vizier, I have authority over the whole of Percheron.*

This time the voice sounded more like a growl. *Pitiful! That is not the sort of power I speak about, you fool. I'm talking about sentience and sorcery . . . the power of the gods!*

Tariq felt his skin prickle with excitement and fear. This claim was far darker, far more frightening, than the Vizier could possibly have dreamed. Sorcery . . . power of the gods. What could the voice mean? Who was it? The intruder had so disturbed him that he had not once had the presence of mind to ask for a name. Surely it, or he had one?

Tariq felt his heartbeat accelerate. With magic he truly would have power of the sort he could only dream of. Old Yozem and her blood-tellings would be cast into the streets. Herezah would have no need for the crone. She would have him, Tariq, and need no one else. *Tell me how,* he asked, glad he did not have to use his voice to speak, or the visitor would surely know how nervous he was and how dry his throat had suddenly become.

I have said enough. I offer power of a nature you have never known and can never know without me.

And all I must do is temporarily surrender my body to you?

Yes, the voice answered. *A small gift in comparison.*

What will you do with it?

I need a body, Tariq. That is all.

In order to do what?

Nothing that will affect your lifestyle or pleasures. You will be rich, you will be empowered, and you will be indispensable to the ambitious Valide Zara. How much more could you want?

What more indeed, Tariq privately reasoned. The bargain was more than tempting. *Can you give me youth again?*

You'd look rather obvious as a young man, the voice baited. *Don't you think someone might notice?*

Tariq gritted his teeth. *Can you make me feel younger, appear less aged?*

Like the Spur? The voice knew his weaknesses too well.

How did you— Tariq blustered.

I told you; I know you, Tariq. I know your desires as well as I know my own and I feel your envy for the man Lazar. He is the most handsome man in Percheron. Every woman's heart flutters when his glance meets theirs. Is this what you want?

I hate him!

I know. If I gave you such a dashing appearance, you would suffer a notoriety that your more secretive side would not appreciate. I imagine the Spur does not care much for the attention he wins from the fair sex.

He's a fool!

Because he doesn't lie with every woman who throws herself at him?

Tariq chose not to answer.

Yes, I can make you appear younger, more charismatic, and thus attractive to women. Would that satisfy you?

I shall give you my answer tomorrow.

I want it now.

I need to think it through. You are not in a position to demand anything.

You are right. The voice's amusement was back. *Tomorrow, then.*

What is your name?

What does it matter?

I must know who you are, what you are. Silence made Tariq's head feel suddenly hollow. He tried to be patient, but he could not wait. "I must know," he whispered in a croaky voice.

I am called Maliz.

12

As Tariq was haggling over the darkest of bargains that night, Lazar strode—he believed aimlessly—with only his deeply disturbed thoughts for company. He felt numb. The evening's events had unfolded so rapidly and turned into such an ugly scenario that he could hardly believe he had participated in it.

One minute he had negotiated the monthly release of Ana into his care and the next she was a prisoner for life. He knew he would never see the girl again and the thought of it made him sick. He was convinced that his heart had taken too many years to recover from the adolescent sickness of being in love and having it ripped away; it had healed over the years but badly, and it remained fragile. He had never allowed himself to open up to any woman again. Oh, he enjoyed them well enough, and he knew they responded with great fondness to his temporary affections, but that was all it was. Affection. He rarely permitted himself to see a woman more than a few times. Lazar wanted no attachments, no heartbreak for her or for himself. But Ana! How could he have let down his guard so recklessly and allowed her in?

He could hardly be in love with Ana, he reasoned through his distress, and yet he felt deeply attached to her. Was that love? He was fifteen summers her senior, almost old enough to be her father. Talking of love sounded somehow obscene even when it was safely hidden among his private thoughts. But he wanted her close—and it had been permitted. Royal sanction. But Ana had given it up for the life of a stranger—a slave. A child. And she was all the more precious for her sacrifice. He felt nothing but admiration that she would act so selflessly while he could not.

As he acknowledged this, he looked up, expecting to find himself entering the Carafar neighborhood, and realized that he was standing once again on the steps of the tiny temple. He shook his head in wonder, with no idea what he was doing here and the realization that he had been walking with no purpose. It was late.

He ran up the stairs, two at a time, and bent to pass through the entrance into the serene peace. The temple was illuminated softly by a tiny rose-colored bowl of oil that hung from the ceiling. It threw long shadows across the altar and lit a glow around the statue of the beautiful woman with birds flitting around her skirts. The owl regarded him. He felt sure there was a hint of amusement in its gaze—as if it knew some great secret. He looked at the woman and again her soft smile seemed as though it was meant just for him. He approached and stood before her, staring. Something compelled him to touch her and he reached for her smile, expecting to feel the cool lips of the marble she was sculpted from. Except they weren't chill to the touch. Lazar could have sworn that the woman's lips were warm beneath his fingertips. He started, and looked more closely at the statue. Now he was convinced there was a blush to her face, the lips flooding with life.

"Welcome back, Spur."

Lazar stepped back, startled, only then realizing that the voice had come from behind him.

"You have superb hearing, Zafira." He bowed courteously.

"Once again I interrupt you. Forgive me."

Lazar glanced at the statue again. It was ghostly white in the soft glow. "No, I had nowhere better to go on this eve. I took a walk to clear my head and found myself here."

"As good a reason as any. Come, will you take some quishtar with me?"

"It is near midnight."

"No matter."

"I would be delighted."

He followed the tiny priestess to the back of the temple and up some stairs, finding himself in the small but airy space where she lived.

"It's adequate," she said, noting how his eyes moved swiftly around the room.

"The view is worth the climb," he said, and she smiled at his compliment.

"Make yourself comfortable, Spur."

"Call me Lazar, please."

"Thank you."

He looked at her living space: the tiny cot neatly made; a shelf with a few items, hardly valuable but no doubt precious to her—an old vase, a tiny painted tile, some delicate glass. The furniture was sparse and battered and yet it looked lived in, appreciated. The single cushioned chair was threadbare but it too appeared comfortable, molded to her shape. A few scattered cushions looked as though they had been embroidered by her own hand.

Zafira spoke as she worked. "I prefer the dried husk of the wilder desert cherry myself. Makes for a more delicate infusion than its city or foothill cousins."

"Can you tell the difference?"

"Oh yes, Lazar, you should pay more attention. Quishtar has many flavors, depending on the region where it is made. It's part of our life's fabric—far more than a mere beverage. It promotes fellowship, it calms, it loosens the tongue," and she smiled knowingly at him.

After the water had boiled, he watched her pour the delicately golden infusion from a spouted metal jug, deftly lengthening the stream between the spout and the bowl-like porcelain cups she aimed for. He had seen this done in the marketplace but it was a pleasure to watch it being effected with such care for his benefit alone.

"Is that just for theater?" he asked. "Where I come from, we just pour our drinks."

"And where is home for you, Lazar?"

His answer was terse. "Merlinea."

Zafira must have guessed he did not enjoy speaking of his background, for she deftly returned to their original subject of conversation. "Everything in the making of quishtar has a purpose. Quishtar needs to breathe as it arrives into the drinking bowl. I always like to think that it's sampling the air it is being exposed to. Then it knows what to reveal when it's drunk."

He laughed. "You make it sound alive."

Zafira tapped the large cup three times with a single finger before pushing it toward him. "An old custom. Seals friendship," she added, and there was the soft amusement on her lips again.

Although he hardly knew the woman, Lazar already liked her very much. There was something about her; he was surprised he had told her as much as he had. For now he was glad of her uncomplicated company and the diversion of her chatter about the customs of Percheron.

". . . or you'll burn yourself," she finished.

"Forgive me," he said. "My mind was wandering. What did you say?"

"Pay attention, Lazar," she warned gently. "I said use the linen or you'll burn yourself."

He nodded. "You know I've lived here for almost as many years as I did in Merlinea, and yet I tend to take kerrosh rather than quishtar."

"Then you are in for a treat." She chuckled. "Enjoy its fragrance first. What can you smell?"

"Spice, although I can't say which one."

"Good."

He smelled again. "Um, faint citrus?"

"Yes."

"The roasted aroma is not there as I'd expected."

"Excellent, Lazar. It is not meant to be in the higher-quality infusions. Anything else?"

"Yes, but I don't know how to describe it. Vaguely floral, somehow earthy."

She smiled. "You have a good nose. This means you have keen taste."

"Explain it to me."

"Well, quishtar has no taste as such. It is not bitter. It has no sweetness, no sourness. Obviously nothing salty about it. It is not savory. It has no flavor at all."

"I don't understand."

"Quishtar is all about fragrance. Your nose does the tasting for you, which is why you were able to pick out the flavors from the fragrance. So drink, my friend, and tell me what you taste."

He sipped and instinctively closed his eyes. "All that we listed before. Spicy, citrus, something vaguely floral and earthy."

Zafira enjoyed regarding him while his eyes were shut. He was, by nature, a watchful man and having him so relaxed changed his whole demeanor. Gone was the caution and tension. She noticed the gentle lines that ran along either side of his aquiline nose to his mouth. When he smiled, they deepened, only adding to the handsomeness of his face. "You see?" she said. "You are tasting what you smell. But this only happens with the best infusion."

He opened his eyes. "How intriguing."

"Life can be like this drink, Lazar," she said, eyeing him closely over the rim of her bowl.

"How so?" He felt himself relaxing.

"It can fool you." His glance flicked away from the freshly scented steaming vapors and into her rheumy gaze. "Not everything is as it seems," she added.

He sensed she was trying to tell him something, but the message was too subtle. He groaned slightly as he finished the warm drink and she smiled. "Let me pour another bowl for you." When he didn't decline she took his cup and went through the same motions as before—in comfortable silence this time—and set it down before him.

"Aren't you going to tap the bowl three times?"

"No, we are friends now."

There was something final about that comment. As though something secret had passed between them.

"Why do I feel like talking," he wondered aloud, "when I should be going?"

"Are you in a hurry?"

"Only to escape."

"What are you running from?"

He sighed. "My life." And then, for no reason he could explain, Lazar began to tell her about Ana. It seemed to pour out of him, as the quishtar had poured out of Zafira's spouted jug. He spoke at length, running his fingers through his long dark hair as he concluded, ". . . they made her watch it all."

The priestess took an audible breath, hissing it through her aged teeth. "Cruel," she whispered. "And so your bargain is nullified?"

He nodded, feeling intense sorrow at admitting it openly.

"The child has a curious background," Zafira mused.

"She has no background that I know of."

"The fact that any baby can survive the Samazen, when goats could not, makes her special in my eyes."

He shrugged. "She was fortunate . . . born lucky, perhaps." The old woman said nothing, allowed him to continue. "She is special, though, for many reasons."

"Be careful, Lazar. She belongs to the harem now."

"Yes," he said, hearing the hateful resignation in his voice. "Untouchable."

"Of course, Pez is in the palace," she said, the merest hint of cunning in her tone.

"You know him?" Lazar looked up in surprise.

"I do."

"How?"

"Why should I not? Because he's considered a half-wit, you mean?" Lazar nodded. "Oh, come now, Lazar, we both know he is no such thing."

The Spur suddenly found himself on unsteady territory. Pez's sanity was unknown to almost everyone. Only he and Boaz knew the truth, and Pez had sworn both independently to secrecy. Lazar had shared that knowledge with no one, not even Jumo, and he never discussed it with Boaz, for they were rarely alone to talk about anything so private.

"Relax, my friend. He has revealed himself to me," Zafira assured him, although she could see that the Spur was not prepared to confirm or deny her words. Good. He was true, then.

"You have not answered my question," he began. "How do you know Pez?"

"He visits now and then."

"Here?"

"Where else?"

"When was the last time?"

"Yesterday. We shared quishtar."

"And what else?"

"If I'm being truthful, I'd say we also shared confusion." Now she looked hard at him.

"Over what?"

"Why we both feel that we have been brought together. That there is some purpose to our existence in Percheron."

Lazar snorted. It was an attempt at derision he wasn't truly feeling. "Everyone has purpose."

"Do they? What's yours? Why are you here and not in Merlinea? What keeps you here? There is anger in you tonight, and rightfully so, but nothing prevents you from walking away. Yet you stay. No one invited you to the temple, yet you came. Not once in all the years you've lived here . . . and now twice in a few days."

Her observations prompted a strange new sense of disturbance in his world. The world he thought was so straight, so balanced, so controlled, suddenly felt out of kilter.

"I think I'm the one now confused."

"Don't be. Just don't shut possibility out."

"What possibility?"

"That there is a reason for Pez revealing himself to you and me; that you have felt compelled over the last few days to visit the temple; that a baby survives the Samazen and you find her some fourteen or fifteen years later."

Lazar frowned. "You think there is a link between us all?"

"Who's to say?" Zafira answered, irritating him slightly by the sudden sidestep. She had deliberately led him through this conversation and now she seemed to be pulling away. He wanted answers.

"Why won't you be frank with me?"

She put her bowl down, taking a few moments to fold the linen napkin. "You think I am evasive?"

"There's something you're either frightened of or not prepared to share."

Now it was the priestess's turn to shrug. "Forgive me. I don't mean to make you feel uncomfortable."

"You don't," he replied.

A silence stretched between them, each measuring the other, knowing that whatever was said next would likely change what had begun as a casual acquaintance.

It was Zafira who began. "I have had the feeling for a long time now that there is a force at work. I cannot explain it; it is just something my instinct tells me. Recently it has become more insistent. It speaks of danger and yet it also speaks of deliverance. I don't understand it myself."

"And this feeling relates to you?"

"Yes, but to others too."

"Who?" She didn't answer. "Am I now making you feel uncomfortable?" he asked.

She laughed quietly. "Yes, as a matter of fact. I feel as though I'm talking nonsense, and to a very new friend."

"You've called me friend twice now."

"Aren't we?"

"We hardly know each other."

"We've shared quishtar. It's enough." And her words felt true to him. "But what binds us, Lazar?" she suddenly asked. "What compels you to come here? What makes me know that it is you who approaches even when I can't see you? What do we have in common?"

He hesitated, then offered, "I can tell you what attracts me, Zafira, if that would help."

"Please," she replied, "go on."

"I think I came to see the statue again. The one in the temple."

"Lyana."

He nodded. "I have never seen anything so beautiful, and Percheron is filled with beautiful art."

"And you like beautiful things, Lazar. It is why you like this odalisque so much, perhaps?"

"How odd that you mention her in the same breath as Lyana. At times I do feel about Ana the same way I do about the statue. Yes, I want to gaze at them for their arresting beauty, but I also want to protect them from those who would do them harm. I want to communicate with them. I think I came here tonight looking for an answer."

"And have you found it?"

"I don't know. But I also wanted my mind to be eased and that has certainly been done in talking to you."

The edges of Zafira's eyes crinkled as a smile lit her face. "That is a high compliment, Spur."

"Isn't that what friends do for each other? They comfort."

"Indeed they do."

"And does Pez come for comfort?"

"No. He comes and stirs me up." They shared a moment's amusement. "It's a strange thing, Lazar, but there are times when I feel that Pez knows much more than he lets on. There is wisdom in that curiously deformed face of his. Does he stir you up too?"

"No!" He laughed. "But he certainly knows how to frustrate people when he wants to—people like the Valide and our Vizier, draped in all his trinkets and gold. Oh," he said, reaching into his pocket, "that reminds me. The most curious thing happened around sunset. Ana spotted an old woman in the bazaar—you know, in Gold Alley?"

Zafira nodded absently. She began clearing away the bowls. "Go on, I'm listening."

"Well, the woman was bargaining, selling some gold. I could have sworn it was a chain . . ." He frowned to himself as he recalled the scene. "Anyway, she was negotiating with an alley cat."

Zafira, her back to him, made a sound of disgust. "At her age she should know better."

"Yes, that's what I thought too. But before the alley cat could close the deal, Ana leaped in and begged the old woman to let her buy the piece instead."

"Why?" the priestess asked, retrieving the jug and emptying its contents into a pot plant outside one of the small windows.

"You know, I'm not sure. She said it was because she felt the bargain would not be fair. But there was more to it than that."

He heard Zafira chuckle quietly by the sink of water where she cleaned the bowls. "I suppose you bought it, Lazar?"

"I did," he admitted, sheepish.

She turned with a look of soft admonishment, as though he should not have spoiled the child so. That expression froze when she looked at what he held out in his hand.

"Where did you get that?" she asked in a harsh whisper, dropping the bowl she held. It shattered on the floor at her feet.

Lazar was taken aback by her reaction. The small gold owl sat small but heavy on his palm, warming against his skin. It was only now as he scrutinized it that he could swear the jewels in its eyes glinted with a light of their own. "This is what Ana bought."

"Hide it!" Zafira's tone was filled with fear.

"What?"

"Put it away—now!"

Alarmed, he slipped the owl back into his pocket. "What's wrong?" Zafira was breathing heavily and she suddenly groaned, leaning against the sideboard. "Do you need a healer?" Lazar asked uncertainly.

"No," she assured him. She took several deep breaths. "That's Iridor you hold in your hand . . . or at least his image."

"Yes, I know. So?"

Zafira sighed and turned to extinguish two of the three

lamps, the shattered bowl forgotten. She took a taper and lit it from the remaining lamp, then sat down at the table and lit a half-burned candle. The flame instantly threw a glow onto their faces. "How much do you know about the owl?"

Lazar shrugged. "As much as the next person, although I should admit I'm rather fond of him. He was the first of the graven images I saw upon entering the city . . . I regard him as . . . well, as an old friend."

"I see." Zafira nodded gently. "Another coincidence or is it part of the web that binds us?"

He looked at her quizzically.

"Let me tell you what I know. Iridor," the priestess began, "is as old as time itself. He is a demigod who takes the shape of an owl. The owl works for the Goddess. He is her messenger."

"And why are you scared by him?"

"Not by *him*, Lazar. By those who would see him dead."

Lazar leaned back and regarded her. Battling with his curiosity was skepticism; she could see that.

"Come with me," she said.

Downstairs, she led him again to the statue. "Do you see now, Lazar?"

"Iridor," he murmured, looking at the sculpted owl on the statue's shoulder, with its enigmatic expression.

"What does he say to you?"

"I don't understand."

"He is a messenger. What does this sculpture of him say to you?"

Lazar took a long look, then said as honestly as he could, "He has a secret."

"Ah," the priestess replied. "Does he wish to share it with you?"

He looked again at the owl. "Yes, I believe he does. He seems faintly amused. Isn't that how he strikes you?"

She shook her head slightly. "He looks extremely somber to me."

"No smirk?"

"Not at all. He has only grave tidings to give to me."

"Surely not?" the Spur said, disbelieving. "We are both looking at the same image."

"That's the way of Iridor. He brings different tidings to each; he is one thing to one person and something else to another."

"And he belongs to her." Lazar reached again to lift the golden statue from his pocket. The eyes no longer glowed, although curiously the gold felt warm. He felt Zafira flinch as it emerged. "I haven't told you the whole story yet."

"I would hear it—but first put that owl away, Lazar, and promise me this: that you will never tell anyone of this possession."

He regarded her intently, baffled by the fright he read in her eyes. "Ana knows of it. It is hers. She asked me to keep it for her."

"Then she is supposed to know of him and she was right to ask this of you. The statue would have been confiscated at the palace anyway."

"Yes, that's what she believed. She . . ." Lazar hesitated. "When I said I would look after it for her, she insisted that I not just keep it but that I keep it close. I have no idea why."

Just for an instant, in the priestess's eyes, Lazar thought he saw a brief flare of knowledge. A moment later it was gone, and Lazar convinced himself that he had imagined it. "Zafira," he said, "there is another confusing aspect to our meeting with the hooded old woman."

The priestess looked again at the statue of Iridor and Lazar obediently secreted it away. "Tell me," she said.

"She was a stranger to me, and as Ana had only entered the city an hour or so eartlier, it was impossible that the woman could know her. The girl has never been beyond her dwelling in the foothills."

"So?"

"So how come this woman called Ana by name?"

They stared at each other, said nothing for a moment. The wick sputtered in the oil lamp and the harbor water sloshed gently outside. The silence thickened around them.

"Are you sure Ana did not introduce herself at any time?"

"Quite sure."

"Would you recognize this woman again?"

He shook his head, not releasing her gaze. He was certain she knew something, or at least suspected something, but he could not read her. "She was hooded."

Her lips thinned and her hands trembled slightly. They had been sure and steady when pouring the quishtar—Zafira was now nervous . . . or was she scared?

"Describe what you remember," she asked in a choked whisper.

"Tiny figure, hooded, dressed in dark clothes—black, I think. Gentle of voice—a beautiful voice, in fact, and if not for that recognizable quality, she could have been any frail old woman of Percheron."

"Not any. Not carrying a statue of Iridor," Zafira assured.

Lazar lost his patience. "What are you not telling me, Priestess? What is scaring you? What does your life have to do with mine or Ana's or Pez's? You are hiding something."

She shook her head sadly. "I hide nothing. I am as confused as you, Spur. But I have knowledge and that can be frightening."

"What do you know, then?"

She raised her eyes once again and regarded him fiercely. Her voice was hard when she finally replied. "I know only this. With the coming of Iridor, the cycle will turn. The demon is remaking himself."

Lazar felt his blood chill at her words even though he didn't understand what she meant. "So what now?" he asked.

"We wait."

"For what?"

"The rising of Iridor."

13

Pez, feeling unsettled, had left a perplexed young Zar on the pretext that he was fatigued and feeling ill. He roamed the palace, imagining he was on some sort of slippery slope, grabbing for purchase but failing, falling fast into an abyss. He couldn't pinpoint what it was that was disturbing him, and he needed quiet to think it through. People were used to seeing the dwarf moving through the hallways at all hours, often giggling to himself or sliding down the banister of a staircase. He almost always appeared distracted, but tonight he needed no artfulness; his mind was working overtime. What was giving him this premonition? Was it Kett? The young black slave had been the first surprise, he had to admit, and the girl had been the second.

But even though he had been surprised by both Kett's behavior, and Ana's impulsive reaction, Pez realized he had not been surprised by the disturbance. The sense of destiny had been niggling at him for a while now. The first inclination that danger was headed his way had been the arrival of the old woman. He frowned. Was that it? Yes, it had all begun there.

Pushing aside heavy curtains, Pez entered a darkened room. Moonlight filtered through the shutters, and as his eyes adjusted to the depths, he could see that he was in a reception chamber. It looked as though it hadn't been used in an age. No one would come in here tonight. Still, he took the precaution of hiding in the inky shadows before he allowed his memories of that strange event to filter back into his consciousness.

It had been almost four moons ago, when Joreb was still healthy on his throne and the harem had been bustling with the activities of women and their idle chatter. It had been an ordinary day, nothing different about it; no omens or warnings. He had been in the harem at the time, awaiting the Bundle Women who brought goods into the protected place. Each had been handpicked by Salmeo and was required to show proof of his authority—his seal on a small parchment—permitting each to trade within the harem. The Bundle Women's arrival always caused a stir; anything to break the tedium of another day of bathing, dressing, resting, and eating. The women of the harem wanted for nothing—except freedom—but still they bartered furiously for the cheap, gaudy fabrics and silly trinkets these purveyors brought to them. Serious purchases of silks and jewelry were all handled by Salmeo. The Bundle Women were a diversion, nothing more.

One particular woman, younger and sweeter than most, had arrived to peddle ribbons. No one had seemed at all interested in her goods that morning. And so she had turned to Pez, a simple bystander—there for amusement and not much else—and offered him a red ribbon. He had looped it around his ear and danced energetically, weaving among the wives and odalisques who were rummaging through the displayed goods, making a few laugh, and then, shaking his head sadly, had returned the ribbon to the woman.

As their fingers touched, she had grabbed his hand. "I must speak with you, Pez," she had whispered.

Pez had been taken aback, not just by the nature of her message but by the fact that she had named him—and spoken to him as though he were of sound mind.

"Come" was all he had said, leading her to the back of the room. No one paid any attention but he had been glad that Salmeo was not present, for the Grand Master Eunuch missed very little.

The young woman had followed, bringing with her several ribbons. "Look as though you're considering them," she had suggested, although it had sounded to him more of a command.

And when he looked up in response he saw before him not a young woman but a crone. This use of magic terrified him. He remembered now, as he sat in the dark, how some of the women had glanced over and he had seen their gazes slide back to their own negotiations. No one else could see the truth. The crone had looked young and desperate to them, trying to get a fool to buy her wares. He saw differently; could see skin stretched as thin as a veil across her skull. He could see the marks of age on it and the tiny veins beneath. Although he had stared at her features, he could not readily bring her face to mind now. Her coloring had been ghostly pale and he recalled how he had found himself breathing shallowly from the fright of discovery.

"Don't be frightened of me, Pez," she had said kindly, handing him a green ribbon. "Forgive my guile. I am your friend. We have always been friends."

"Who are you?"

"That is not important. What is important is who you are."

His expression had turned to one of confused query. Had she not just named him, known who he was?

She had seemed to read his thoughts. "You are Pez for this battle, yes. But you must know who you truly are. There is so little time. We must gather ourselves. It begins. He is remaking himself."

"What begins?"

"Listen to me," she had said, her urgency infectious. She had looked over and seen that the Bundle Women were packing up their wares. "They are leaving and I with them. You must discover yourself."

She had turned to leave but he had grabbed her arm, confusion warring with irritation. "Who is remaking himself?"

The crone had said only one word but it had been enough to freeze him to the spot.

He had still not moved even minutes after the departure of the Bundle Women and the harem atmosphere had died back to one of bored quiet. Some of the girls had called for their pipes. Soon they would be in an opium haze of oblivion. No one had taken any took notice of Pez, probably thinking he was off on one of his fanciful voyages in his head.

Finally he had found the courage to repeat in his mind the word she had spoken.

Maliz.

Since that day Pez had committed himself to learning all that he could of the demon, once a warlock, who had given Percheron its famous stone creatures. And he had learned much.

He had learned nothing about himself, though, and that

bothered him. Why had the crone told him to go in search of himself? Kett's appearance and the beautiful girl presented before Herezah had for some strange reason prompted him to recall the old woman's warning. But why?

He sat in the dark and teased at his problem. What did he know? He had spent many hours in secret wandering through the great library of the palace, which had some of the oldest tomes in Percheron. No one else seemed to visit the library, although an old fellow by the name of Habib seemed to know his way around and didn't appear to mind that the Zar's jester was wandering through the silent rows of books.

And so over the past months he had learned that Maliz, originally a mortal and a warlock, had supposedly begun the campaign to topple the might of the Goddess to ensure that the priestesses of Percheron—who had held such quiet power— were reduced to nothing more than a memory. His jealousy regarding the power of the priestesses over their male counterparts had known no bounds and his efforts were noticed by the god Zarab, who also wanted to see his nemesis, Lyana, fall from grace. Zarab offered Maliz a reward in exchange for his continuing enmity against all who supported Lyana, not just the female spiritualists. Maliz had agreed to the dark bargain, for his reward was immortality as a demon—perhaps the most powerful demon. Now the priestesses, like Zafira, practiced their faith very privately and humbly. Today they were no longer persecuted, for it had all happened so many centuries ago that those who pursued the faith of the Mother Goddess were so few and scattered they were considered harmless, reclusive. The Goddess's followers had been rendered so impotent that most of today's parents, ignorant of the history, believed the Sisterhood of Lyana was only a good place to send wayward girls and unencumber themselves of ugly daughters who might never make a good marriage. More as a place to rid themselves of these children than as one to offer them to a goddess and a faith they believed in.

Pez had been surprised to learn that Maliz was inextricably linked with the Goddess. His antipathy to her was not just a passing whim. She was his nemesis. And, so the writing told, he remade himself—whatever that meant—when all the signs were right for her to rise again.

It was written in the tales of legend that Maliz had beaten back the Goddess thrice, but on each occasion, over many centuries, she rose stronger. It was predicted privately by those in the faith that her next return would be her final one and that Percheron would once again worship Lyana.

Pez thought about that now. The crone's visit suggested that he was being somehow drawn into that struggle. Why? Why was he important? So far nothing had surfaced to give him a clue. It was intriguing but unsettling. Perhaps the crone had sensed his magicks? But until this evening with Boaz he had not wielded them. Nor would he again, he hoped. Once was dangerous enough and now Boaz appeared mistrustful and even hurt that his friend had kept this secret from him.

Thinking of Boaz gave Pez a prick of regret for the young black boy.

He had felt an instant connection to Kett but no inclination as to why. He did not know the family; had never come across the child before. Perhaps that was a good place to start. Pez stirred from his shadowy spot, fixed a vacant expression on his face, and emerged into the corridor of the harem. He knew they would still be walking Kett, keeping him conscious, and he went in search of the knifers who he hoped would save the boy's life.

FOLLOWING THE SPUR'S DISMISSAL by Herezah, Ana had been removed to a waiting chamber. She had had to be carried from the Choosing Room after witnessing Kett's savaging but she had noticed the Valide's intent gaze following her and she had intuitively sensed the despair raging within Lazar, even though his stony-faced expression betrayed nothing. She wondered if he would ever forgive her.

As she sat, feeling guilty and saddened, Salmeo had entered the chamber. The Choosing Ceremony had obviously concluded. "Are you recovered, child?"

She nodded. "I am well but not recovered. Never will I recover from what I witnessed."

His scar moved in tandem with his knowledgeable smile. "Come, my dear," he said, taking her hand, his voice gentle. "There is something we must do together."

Ana instantly recoiled. The huge eunuch was frightening, but not because of his appearance. It was his manner; her instincts suggested that intimidation was always his intention despite his avuncular tone. She had seen enough in the Choosing Room to know that within this man lay power, driven by a hunger she was not mature enough to understand but could certainly detect.

"Ana, you must do as we say now," he continued, more firmly, not perturbed by her reluctance. He had seen it many times, knew the reaction he could provoke simply by his presence. He loved the reaction he could inspire and it mattered not to him that his victim was so young. Fear was power.

"I don't want to," she answered.

Brave, he thought. *Most would not challenge me again.* No doubt that courage would manifest itself as feistiness in future years. She was just another in an endless line of rebellious youngsters who believed they could fight the system in the harem. Herezah had been one herself. But soon enough they learned the way. There could be no resistance. His word was law.

"Must I have you carried?" He spoke in a patrician tone but his words were all threat.

"No," she fired back, "I shall walk."

He smiled at her. Yes, indeed, this one would be a challenge. "Good. Walking will help you orient yourself inside the harem. It is important that you become familiar with your new home."

"This is not my home. This is my prison."

He made a soft sound of admonishment. "That attitude will not help you, child. You must work hard and learn your duties and then perhaps you will come to the notice of the right people."

"I already have," she said.

He knew she was right and felt a brief flicker of annoyance. But her arrogance meant that this one's spirit would be fun to break. The feisty ones always were. For now he would be content to continue with the charade of kindness. By tomorrow she would understand that he was never to be challenged again.

"You are now in a part of the harem where no man may trespass, Ana. Eunuch slaves alone are permitted to walk these hallways amongst the women." He watched as she touched a painted frieze. "Beautiful, isn't it?"

"It is the mark of the Goddess."

"Hush, we do not speak of that here," Salmeo chided, though he wondered how a peasant girl might know of such ancient stories. He had no idea whether or not it was the mark of the Goddess she had touched but it irritated him that she sounded so confident of the fact.

"Why? Does it frighten you?"

"No. It is irrelevant, that's all."

"Not at all, Grand Master Eunuch. It is extremely relevant, considering that you only move amongst women and men who are more feminine than male."

He recognized the direct insult, quietly again admired such composure in one so young. It would desert her shortly, of course, when she understood what was about to occur. He had the patience of a crocodile, and he would punish her in oh so many ways for her provocation.

They moved in silence through a series of dim hallways, Salmeo relishing the knowledge that the silent walk would aid in building tension in this youngster. He would teach her a second lesson tonight. Her first had been visceral and collective, but she had been an observer. Tonight's would be far more personal.

They reached an arched opening, and as they stepped through, two eunuchs straightened at the sight of their chief. Both reached to push open the double doors that led Salmeo and Ana into a sparsely furnished room warmed gently by a small brazier. Arched windows were latticed and only two candles burned, flickering in a soft draft.

"This room is very private, Ana. It is attached to my suite." The girl did not respond. "We are surrounded by a walled garden; all eyes are turned away, child. It is just us now."

She found her voice. "I thought I was being taken to my sleeping quarters."

"No."

"But it is so late."

"This will not take long."

"You have told me where I am. Why am I here?"

"You have been chosen by the Valide Zara as a suitable mate for her son, Zar Boaz." He watched carefully as her gaze darkened slightly. Good, she was nervous. He waited, and when she said no more but instead fixed him with a stare, he continued, "I must check that you are a virgin, Ana."

"Reminding you of my young age is not enough, presumably."

He almost clapped at that. He did appreciate her spirit. Most of the girls usually broke down at this point.

"No," he answered. "It is not enough. I must personally verify it."

"Or what?"

"Or you cannot join the harem."

"That's perfectly acceptable to me."

Now Salmeo did allow the broad smile to break across his wide face, revealing the cavernous gap in his front teeth. His tongue flicked into and out of the hole like a snake tasting vibrations in the air. He saw the girl's flinch of disgust, fed on it. "Ana, pay attention," he warned softly. "You cannot break the promise that has been made to the Valide. Money has exchanged hands, agreements have been reached, and you yourself have made a bargain with the Zar's mother. There is no higher commitment you could make."

"Other than with the Zar himself," she qualified.

He nodded, continually impressed by her steadfast manner. "Yes," he agreed. "But this means you cannot leave the harem—"

"You just said that unless you affirm my virginity I cannot

join the harem, which suggests there is a lawful way to leave it," she interrupted.

He put his meaty hand to his lips to stifle the chuckle. "You did not let me finish, child. There is most certainly a legitimate way—as you describe—to leave the harem before you join it." He paused before saying quietly: "You may leave it dead. Your throat slit or your head severed, or perhaps you prefer drowning, which is certainly the least messy but presumably a more uncomfortable method than the others, available for our use on the women. You may most definitely leave the harem in a velvet death sack."

"I see," she answered, holding his gaze. "Then proceed."

"Good." He clapped his hands and seated himself behind an ornate desk. A side door opened and a small man entered, carrying a salver of water. Another followed, bearing a tiny jar of oil, a pot of soap paste, and linens. In silence the Grand Master Eunuch allowed his hands to be washed by the first slave after the second had tipped some oil into the water. His hands were then lathered with the soap paste and rinsed before Salmeo held them out to be meticulously dried.

The slaves bowed and departed, having not uttered a word. To their backs the chief said, "Send in the ferris."

Now Ana watched a third person enter, a tall slave bearing a tray set with a small clay bowl.

"Undress now, Ana," Salmeo began, saw her open her mouth to contradict, and added, nodding at the slave, "or he will do it for you."

She didn't look at the man but regarded Salmeo instead, their glares locking. "Assist her!" the Grand Master Eunuch barked, feeling disquieted that it was he who had capitulated first.

"Don't touch me," Ana snapped. "I shall do it."

She lifted the sheath over her head and stood naked before Salmeo, defiance in her eyes, hate in her heart, and fear tingling through her body as she watched him dig into the pot. When he withdrew his finger she noticed that it contained a thick, sticky substance.

"This sap of ferris will make it easier on you," he said, taking his time smearing the gluey white paste over two of his pudgy fingers.

Fright took hold within Ana. She could guess where those hideous fingers would probe. She glanced at the hand with the long nail painted red and wondered what it signified.

The Grand Master Eunuch sighed and slowly lifted himself to his full, intimidating height.

"Ana," he began, noting by her scowl how she despised hearing him utter her name. "I know this sounds difficult but you will make it far easier on yourself if you can relax."

She could not. Her body began to shiver as he approached.

At last he could see her fear, and although it made him gloat inside, he masked his expression into one of concern, ignoring the pulsating sensation that rushed through his body to his groin and lay there an angry, bitter, unanswered need. "You must trust me. It will be over quickly if you do not struggle."

Ana backed away, only to feel the unyielding body of the slave behind her. There was nowhere to flee.

The Grand Master Eunuch often had the girls held down by another but he wanted Ana all to himself. Wanted to feel the heat of her through his silks, experience her fear as her trembling body touched his, see the anger in those clear, bright eyes.

He wanted her humiliation to be complete and provoked by his touch alone.

He arranged himself opposite her on a cushioned bench, his glistening fingers held in the air. "Lay her across me," he ordered the slave, who effortlessly liften the frozen girl.

Salmeo expected the usual screams and pleas, wanted them, but all he got was a groan, deep and angry but resigned. He smiled inwardly. This girl would be a match for Herezah. He couldn't wait for the sparks that would fly when these two spirited personalities clashed.

The long-limbed girl was laid across his expansive lap. "Go now." He dismissed the slave and turned his attention back to the girl. "Now remember what I said. This goes much easier if you find a way to loosen all the tension in your body, especially here." He touched the rise of her pubis. "Open your legs, child," he added firmly.

"I hate you, Salmeo."

"Everyone does," he said, grinning as he pushed his finger into Ana, feeling for the hymen that he already knew would be intact.

PEZ FOUND THE KNIFERS with Kett's seemingly limp body hung between them. The boy's toes trailed now and then, but with their whispered encouragement he found the wherewithal to stagger in a slow circle.

Pez skipped into the room and circled the strange trio. He cackled, pointing toward the bulk of bandage between the boy's legs, and then held his own crotch in mock sympathy. Continuing his merry way around the perimeter of the room, he burst suddenly into song and turned a somersault before arriving to stare deeply into Kett's stricken, exhausted face. As Kett and his handlers moved rhythmically forward, Pez skipped back, keeping pace.

"Will he die?" he chirped in a singsong voice.

One of the men shook his head. "Now that he's endured this long, he will survive, I'm sure."

"Hsst!" the other warned. "We must not assume anything until he makes water."

"Kett, Kett, Kett," the dwarf sang into the boy's face, working the name into a strange playful rhyme. All the time he stared hard, waiting for the slave to register his presence.

Finally, painfully, Kett opened his bloodshot eyes to slits. The red of his eyes matched his lips, which were bloody from from being bitten hard when the cut had been made.

"The drug is wearing off," one of the knifers whispered. "He'll start to cry out soon."

The other nodded. "How long to go?"

"Another fifty revolutions of the chamber at least, or until we hear the third bell."

"Leave us, Pez, you're not helping him."

"But I like him," Pez replied. The handlers both looked at the dwarf, baffled, and then ignored him again, vaguely irritated by his presence as he waddled backward in time with their steps. "We are friends aren't we, Kett?"

The boy winced, raised his head, and for a moment appeared conscious. "I am the raven," Kett slurred.

As Pez felt his blood turn to ice, the slave's eyes closed and he returned to his dazed stumble.

14

Jumo was relieved to see the familiar figure and distinctive lope of Lazar arrive at the Spur's house in the early hours of the morning. The man he had waited for all night had arrived tired and distracted.

There was no greeting. "You shouldn't have waited up, Jumo. You know you don't have to wait on me."

"I have left a carafe of wine on the veranda."

Jumo left the Spur to brood alone, staring out to the Faranel, and presumed he would remain there for what was left of the night. He was right; the next morning he found the chair empty but a discarded blanket lying across it and a second carafe of undiluted wine nearby.

Lazar emerged minutes later looking freshened and clean-shaven but drawn, as if sleep had eluded him. His eyes possessed a haunted quality that Jumo had not seen before. Something was brewing; he had known this man too long not to be able to read the signs. It would be best, then, to give him the news now.

"A messenger arrived not long ago, Master."

"New orders?"

Jumo heard hope in his friend's voice and he knew how much Lazar must want to escape Percheron. "He was sent from the palace . . . from the Grand Master Eunuch's office." He watched Lazar's temple pulse. Knew that sign well.

"And?"

Nothing to be gained by hedging. "It's Ana. She has gone."

"Gone?"

Jumo nodded. "Escaped in the night."

Lazar looked at him, pain fleeting across his face. It was impossible. No one escaped the harem. The palace would expect him to find her, of course, not just because he had brought her to the harem but because he was the Spur and in charge of all security. "Any clues?"

"They think she slipped away disguised as a black eunuch."

Lazar, turning to move away, swung around and regarded Jumo with a hint of amusement. "They jest!"

"Apparently not," and Jumo couldn't help a small smirk himself. "They believe she wore a black jamoosh and blacked the area around her eyes with ash from a brazier."

Lazar couldn't help but admire Ana all the more for her defiance, but his pleasure in her act died quickly when he grasped the import of her rash actions. "They'll punish her, of course."

Jumo nodded. "I would say so. The Valide will want to do so for the spectacle of it and Salmeo will have to comply in order to reinforce his authority."

"We must find her first."

THE VALIDE HAD SPENT a restless night, her slumber disturbed by memories of Spur Lazar arguing—no, pleading—for the monthly freedom of the golden girl from the western foothills. Oh, he had disguised his anxiety with his usual confidence but she had seen through it on this occasion; something about the way Lazar avoided looking at Ana. The rest of the men in the room could hardly keep their gazes from the youngster and yet Lazar had all but ignored her while requesting her release so eloquently . . . so insistently. Herezah had slipped between her silken sheets with a sense of triumph the previous evening. Nevertheless, a poor night's sleep and her suspicions being piqued aside, everything, she decided, was coming together nicely. She had both the fat eunuch and the fool Vizier eating out of her hands. She was confident that Boaz's harem would be one of the finest ever assembled and the goatherd's adopted daughter was a prize jewel among a veritable collection of precious gems. All the girls were stunning but it was true that there was something extraordinary about that one. She felt sure Ana would be one of those who would produce an heir; Boaz would pick her as soon as he was ready to lie with a woman, for Ana's looks were too startling to ignore. However, Herezah would have to be careful that the girl did not steal her son's heart entirely. Herezah wasn't ready for a power struggle.

Boaz was going to need careful handling. She needed to find challenging diversions for him so he would feel important and useful while not meddling in the day-to-day running of what was clearly now her realm.

"I've waited too long for this," she had muttered as she

sipped on the citrus infusion she insisted on taking every morning. A lot of the other women had allowed themselves to run to fat in the harem, especially those who had never caught the attention of Joreb. Joreb quickly sorted out his favorites from those he was not interested in, and although these estranged women remained pampered and primped, they were largely ignored. With no future other than slothfulness available to them, it wasn't long before their lives diminished into a continuing indulgence of food and mind-altering confections to dull their frustrations.

Herezah had not had cause for the same frustrations and thus she took great care with her body's appearance—no, her frustrations were born of ambition and impatience. Now that she had in her grasp what she had dreamed of for so long, she was not going to let it go—not even to the son who had made it all possible. Boaz was young; he had plenty of wild oats to sow and energy to burn in playful pursuits. He did not need the serious burden of running a realm she could so easily handle for him. She was going to make everything as easy as possible for him, and she reasoned that this new era in their lives was going to give them a wonderfully new and close relationship.

After her tea she rose, her mind still battling with the question of Ana and what to do with her. She decided that the best way to handle the child was to put her own claim on her. Mark her as the Valide's own slave. Then she could break and control the girl before she became available for the Zar's needs. Herezah smiled, pleased with herself. How clever that she might turn the new odalisque into one of her own agents, use her to plant ideas into Boaz's mind, control him fully. Especially if he chose Ana to be one of his wives.

Before she could take her morning exercise, the news had come, delivered personally by Salmeo. When he was announced she knew it had to be something of importance. She had him admitted but did not offer him a seat—he was interrupting her morning routine, after all.

"Speak," she commanded, more than enjoying her new authority over the one who had inflicted humiliation upon her in years gone by.

"Valide," he began as she reached for her steaming cup of kerrosh, which she took in its most bitter form. "One of the new acquisitions has escaped the harem during the night."

If he thought the Zar's mother might overreact, he was very wrong. In wonder, he watched Herezah's unveiled face display no outward signs of anger. She paused in her sipping of the kerrosh and then delicately reached her long arm to place the porcelain cup back on the tray. Herezah, for all her failings, was a naturally elegant woman. It was little wonder that Joreb, a lover of the finer things in life, had fallen for her dark beauty and exceptional grace.

"Ana?" she asked, almost as though she were expecting the news.

He nodded. His scar appeared all the more livid for the shame he was obviously feeling.

She spoke with chilling softness. "How did this happen, Salmeo? I belong to the harem, I have been one of its odalisques, and I know that what you're suggesting is impossible."

"Nothing's impossible, Valide," he tried, but at her instantly furious glare changed his mind, nodded, and sighed. "Normally, yes. We are, however, not dealing with a normal child, if you'll permit my saying so, Valide."

"How so?"

"She has intelligence and defiance enough for ten odalisques."

Herezah smirked. "I think you're right. How did she escape?" She was intrigued that any girl could find a way out of the harem; almost jealous, in fact.

This was not difficult to answer but it was horribly embarrassing for Salmeo. He tried to hold the Valide's keen gaze but soon found himself looking elsewhere. "After completing her Test of Virtue, she was left alone momentarily to gather her composure and reclothe herself. She took that opportunity to steal some garments and blacken her face. We discovered that a jamoosh was missing and the grate of the brazier had fallen to the ground. She used ash on herself, apparently." He shrugged. "There were black smudges on my walls and she had thrown . . ." He hesitated.

"Thrown what?"

"She had smashed the clay pot of ferris and thrown it into the burning embers."

Herezah gave a gurgle of laughter. "Oh, such spirit. She hates you early, Salmeo."

"I am used to it, Valide," he said softly, and this time successfully fought the urge to look away from her sardonic smile. "She loosened some fretwork and escaped through my courtyard."

"Why wasn't I informed immediately?"

Again he hesitated. "I thought she would be found more swiftly, Valide."

"It looks like you thought wrong, Grand Master Eunuch. So what do we do now?"

"I sent a message to the Spur at dawn."

Her eyes flashed at his name, "Why, because she was his bargain?"

"Because he argued for her release. I think the Spur is fond of the child. He looked upset when she relinquished her freedom for the slave's life." Salmeo watched with pleasure as Herezah's lips thinned. *Oh yes,* he thought, *you don't like the idea that Spur Lazar may feel affection for someone else.*

But the Valide did not rise to the bait. "I saw it too. What does it mean, Salmeo?"

The large man moved his huge shoulders in a shrug. "I cannot tell," he lied. "The Spur has always been one so devoid of connection to others that I can't reason this link."

"Can you not?" He shook his great head. "I would say that our young odalisque has touched the man of ice, warmed his frozen heart."

His tongue flicked out to moisten his lips. He'd suspected as much but considered it politic, at this point, to let the Valide feel as though she might know more than he did. "I thought it to be simply a brotherly fondness. Are you suggesting it's more serious?"

"Call it female intuition. He argued too passionately not to be involved with the girl somehow."

Salmeo was impressed with Herezah's composure, for it obviously grieved her to admit this. "You are perceptive, Valide."

She dismissed the compliment with a wave of her hand. "So what of the child?"

"She will be found within the hour, I promise. She could not get far at night—and she was barefoot, I believe. She is too recognizable and, I suspect, tired, hungry, and already regretting her wild adventure."

Herezah didn't necessarily agree with his summary but she understood that he needed to save face. "You must ensure word of this does not get about. We must not allow our girls to have any notion that escape will be tolerated. It was not even dared in my time," she said, quietly irritated that she had not thought to try.

"No one will know, Valide."

"She must be punished, of course."

"I agree," he said, again relieved. "May I make a suggestion?"

"Go ahead," Herezah said, knowing how his cruel mind worked. She stood and took her half-finished cup of kerrosh to the window.

"She should be flogged."

Herezah did not turn from the idyllic view of gardens stretching before her. "And break that beautiful skin?"

"It will heal. She's young enough that it won't scar if we use an expert. Anything less would be a compromise, I fear, Valide."

Now she laughed, deep and sly. "A compromise to your position, you mean. I understand, Salmeo, better than you know. But it's fine with me. I want a physician's opinion before it's done, though. She must not mark." She turned now to emphasize her instructions and fixed him with a stare.

He nodded. "As you command, Valide."

"And her virginity?"

"Intact."

"As we knew. Did she weep when you did it?"

"Not even a tear," he confirmed, recalling only too well how Herezah had cried hysterically when it had been her turn many years before. He watched disappointment dance briefly across her face but she masked her expression in a moment. *Good*, he thought, *I can still hurt you.*

"Find her!" she ordered.

LAZAR AND JUMO had started from the palace and agreed to work out in a broad sweeping arc—Jumo heading away from the city and Lazar moving deeper into it, toward the bazaar.

"We were there together, she might head for the familiar spots I showed her."

Jumo had nodded agreement. "I shall meet you by the People's Fountain by fourth bell."

They now stood worriedly side by side, having met as planned but with no good news.

"Where would a child go?" Jumo wondered aloud. "With her looks she would be an instant target."

This comment served only to frustrate Lazar further and he punched the marble of the fountain. It hurt, but rather than showing it, he plunged his aching fist into the pocket of the long white formal jamoosh he wore.

And felt the warmth of gold. "Iridor," he muttered.

Jumo turned in query. "Master?"

"Iridor! Of course." Lazar began hurrying away. "Keep looking through the bazaar," he called back. "I have a hunch where she might be."

Lazar suddenly felt sure he knew where Ana would have ended up. He arrived at the tiny temple, out of breath, having woven his way at full tilt through the harbor streets and out onto the peninsula. To compose himself, he leaned against the white wall of the holy building and sucked in several long, deep breaths before he bent and entered the hallowed space.

It was cool and dark as usual. But this time Zafira did not pray alone. Kneeling next to her was another, engulfed in a black jamoosh that was far too big for her slender frame.

"Ana," he said, his voice sounding loud and coarse in the silence.

Zafira opened her eyes from prayer and turned, putting a finger to her lips. Then she stood, awkwardly, grimacing from old aches in her back and knees before she approached Lazar, a look of understanding on her kindly face. "As you see, another visitor," she whispered. "Troubled, like you."

"They'll be turning Percheron upside down for her, Zafira."

The priestess nodded. "Give her a few more moments. She is as taken by the sculpture of Lyana as you are."

Lazar grimaced at the delay, but nodded.

"How did you know to find her here?" Zafira asked softly.

He shrugged. "I didn't. I've just looked everywhere else." His stomach turned at the lie, but he did not want to bring Iridor into the conversation again, knowing how it had affected the priestess the last time he had done so.

"She's been here since the early hours."

"How did she find it?"

"I thought you might have told her about the temple." At Lazar's negative head shake, the priestess smiled. "Well, she told me all about you and how kind you've been."

"Kind?" he mocked. "I sold her to the harem."

"For which she forgives you, Lazar."

He grunted. He did not want forgiveness; he wanted to feel a sense of control again. "I have to return her."

"Will they punish her?"

Though Lazar could not bring himself to reply, his silence told the priestess what she needed to know.

"You must protect her from this," she urged, clasping the hard muscle of his arm.

"I have done all I can," he replied, his anguish obvious.

"There must be still more you can do."

He shook his head. Everything was spiraling out of control. "I am honor-bound to the Zar and by my position in Percheron. I must take her back to the palace," he replied, his voice hard. "I'm sorry, Zafira."

"So am I," she said, her voice just as cold.

And it was with those words that Lazar decided he would follow through on his formerly vague plans—plans he had made only during this last restless night. He would leave Percheron. He walked over to Ana, lifting her into his arms. She permitted him to do so without a struggle but her eyes were filled with a sorrow that broke his heart.

"I'm sorry," she whispered.

"I know." He wanted to kiss her golden hair and tell her he would make everything right again. Instead he stalked out of the temple with her. He did not look back at Zafira.

The priestess's words rang in his ears. She had insisted he could do more. Could he? *What?*

"Take me away, Lazar," Ana moaned as he set her down.

His jaw ached from the way he was grinding it. "Ana, my duty is to the Crown of Percheron." For lack of anything remotely comforting to say, he quoted an old Percherese military saying: "A man without honor is a man lost."

Ana gave a wan smile. "My uncle said that once."

"Ana, I—"

"Please. I know I have to go back, Lazar. It's all right. Ah, here comes Jumo," she said, effectively ending their awkward conversation.

"Ana." Jumo moved quickly to hug her, relief in his eyes when he stepped back. "You frightened us."

"I knew you would come and that Spur Lazar would find me," she answered. "Thank you, friend Jumo, it is precious that I can see you again." She kissed both of his weathered cheeks.

Jumo glanced at Lazar. "Do we have to take her back immediately?"

The Spur sighed. Wretched Jumo could always read his thoughts, and worse, Jumo got to hug Ana and be kissed by her. It annoyed him that he was himself so reluctant to show her even the slightest amount of the affection he felt. "No," he said, running a hand through his unkempt hair. "We can at least share a kerrosh together."

They walked with Ana between them to a shop they knew sold the best morning kerrosh in the bazaar.

"Find a spot," Lazar suggested to Jumo, having noticed the long line. "I'll get them," he added, knowing one of the advantages of being Spur was that a small crowd such as this would simply part at the sight of him. "Thank you," he uttered to those who bowed and moved aside to allow him through to the counter.

"Spur Lazar," the owner acknowledged, grinning to show the few teeth in his head. He expertly poured hot frothing milk from one long-handled jug into another. Years of practice meant he didn't even have to look at the motion—it all happened through sense, touch, and skill. The milk turned a burned golden color once it was combined with the hot kerrosh, and the smell of it made Lazar's belly grumble. "Three, and give me that plate of skazza."

"Hungry today?" the shopkeeper said, still grinning as he reached to fill the heated glasses.

Soon Lazar was shouldering his way back with a tray of steaming kerrosh and pastries oozing with honey.

Ana's eyes lit. "Our mother never offered it with milk!"

"Paradise in a glass," Lazar said, trying hard to lighten the gloom that had settled around their tiny table.

Jumo raised his glass. "Recovery for the troubled soul." He looked hard at his friend.

"Ana," Lazar began gently, pushing the plate toward her. "Eat." She took one of the sticky pastries. "Did you run away because of Kett or because they scared you afterward?"

"Doesn't Salmeo deliberately scare everyone?" she asked.

Lazar felt her quip bite where he was hurting the most. What could he have been thinking to have given her over to that evil man? He watched her chew on the pastry, the syrup oozing over her lips, glazing them to a high shine.

She pulled a strand of hair from her face with sticky fingers. "Salmeo did an inspection of my body," Ana said matter-of-factly. "Inside my body."

Lazar slammed his cup down onto the table. He didn't flinch at the scald of the hot milky drink that spilled over his sunburned hand.

"I gave him no satisfaction. That eunuch will never break me, although I can tell that's his intention."

Lazar had no chance to reply, for a group of Salmeo's Elim pushed their way through the bazaar, their distinctive red jamooshes giving them away instantly.

"You have found her, my lord Spur," their leader said as all in the group bowed low.

"Only moments ago," Lazar answered.

"My lord Spur," the first repeated, "we have orders to—"

Lazar held up a hand. "Yes, I imagine you do . . . er?"

"Farz," the man answered.

"Thank you, Farz. I found the child cold and hungry. I am seeing to her well-being immediately and then, as requested by your master, I shall return her to the palace."

"May we not relieve you of this burden, Lord Spur?"

The man was persistent. Jumo could see the pulse at his master's temple throb again, a sure indication that the Spur had run out of patience. It never took very long.

Jumo spoke quickly into the thick silence. "No, Farz. You go on. Return to the palace and inform your master that Ana has been located. The Spur will bring the girl as soon as she has been nourished. You can see for yourself that she is appropriately covered. There is no insult to the harem."

The men looked among themselves, clearly concerned. They did not want to act without courtesy to the Spur and yet each knew Salmeo would cut his throat just as soon as reward him, depending on how each pleased him. It would not please him if they returned empty-handed.

Lazar understood. "Take a kerrosh—put it on my slate. Then you can escort us back to the palace if that is easier."

The men still looked uncertain.

"Come, let me order with you, I need another." Jumo stood, shooing the men deeper into the shop. He shot a wink at Lazar as he herded them toward the counter and saw his friend give a sad smile of thanks. Both knew Jumo had bought Lazar and Ana a few precious private minutes together.

Lazar turned back to Ana, who was staring solemnly into the dregs of her glass. "You must promise me that you'll never attempt anything like an escape again."

"I cannot promise you that, Lazar."

"Ana, I will not always be around to save you."

"You do not need to save me. Your responsibility ended when you presented me to the Valide and collected your gold."

He flinched; her words hurt. She shook her head, frowning to herself. "I'm sorry, Lazar," she said, contrite. "Zafira told you I'd forgiven you for selling me to the harem. And I have. Please ignore my accusations. I am tired."

"You've made me extend my commitment to you," he said carefully.

She eyed him gravely. "I don't recall how."

"By insisting I keep the owl statue close."

Recognition dawned. "And have you kept him close?" A soft smile played at her lips as he lifted the gold statue out of his pocket. "As beautiful as I remember him. Lovely Iridor."

Lazar sat back in his chair, once again astonished. How was it possible that a young goatherd's daughter of today would know about a long forgotten, ancient demigod? "Ana, I must know, where did you hear that name? Is your father religious? Is your family followers of Lyana?"

She shook her head gently. "Iridor is my friend," she said, a faraway look in her eye. "Take me back now, Lazar. I don't want anyone to get into further trouble on my account. It was wrong of me to leave as I did. I knew I could never escape, in truth. I was upset over Kett and then the Test of Virtue. I wasn't thinking clearly, and once I was out I felt compelled to find the temple . . ." Her voice trailed off.

He had no time to ask how she knew the temple existed because he could see Jumo approaching, an expression of help-lessness on his face. The Elim seemed to have knocked back their kerrosh so fast it had hardly touched the sides of their throats. They were taking no chances with their own lives. Though Lazar was frustrated, he understood. Salmeo could be hideously cruel. "Come then, Ana" was all he said, hating himself for not having an answer to this dilemma. She rose soundlessly as he pocketed the owl.

It was a silent troupe wending its way back to the palace and certain punishment.

15

"How is your arm this morning, my lion?" Herezah asked, reaching to run her hand through Boaz's hair, relieved when he didn't pull away from her touch. She had made a silent promise that she was going to find again that affection they had shared in his early childhood—and Herezah knew it was up to her. Boaz would not give it willingly; he felt he had been deserted by her. He had learned to live without her and now she was going to have to turn that all around. She had begun this morning, coming to her son directly after her meeting with Salmeo.

"It hurts still but the new physician says I will heal fast because I am young and it was a clean break."

"I never quite understood the gibberish explanation that was passed from Pez. How did it happen again?"

Boaz shrugged, pretending to put a book back on the shelf so she would not see the lie in his eyes. "I fell awkwardly."

"Because I frightened you, my darling?"

"Yes. But I am stronger now."

"I know you are," Herezah cooed, "and I'm impressed." He was taller than her now. One more summer perhaps and he would be a man. "Boaz, it is vital that you show that same strength now to those around you."

"It's a little early to impress myself on the people, Mother. Father's only been dead a short while."

She heard the bitterness in his tone. "Nevertheless," she persisted, following him to the window. "Here, sit with me a moment." She took his hand and pulled him down beside her. "Precious Light, I don't mean the people of Percheron as such—not yet anyway. I mean that the people in this palace need to know you as a strong leader. It's their idle chatter that will pass through the city like wildfire. What they see they won't hesitate to gossip about, whether good or bad. But you must always remember, no one is your friend, Boaz, except me. I'm the only person who has your absolute best interests at heart."

Boaz tried not to show his disdain at her claim. "Pez is my friend."

"He's a fool and you would do well to be rid of him," she replied briskly. She softened her tone again. "I know you like the dwarf but you don't want people thinking your only companion is an idiot."

Boaz sighed. She was right, of course, but then she didn't know the truth about Pez. "I have many friends in the palace," he said.

"Oh? Name one for me."

"My tutor—"

"Whom I've specifically appointed. No, Boaz, name me

someone who is a true friend to you, who is not paid to attend you and owes you nothing."

He hated the way she always needed to be right, never allowed him credit or even the room to make the simplest of decisions. Here she was again all but humiliating him in trying to make her point. There was only one other true friend and it was a name he knew would stick in her craw, for even Boaz could see how his mother craved the attention of the Spur. "Lazar is my friend." He watched her pause, take a slow breath.

"How true." She forced a smile and took his hand between hers. "But apart from the Spur, who is not in the palace often enough to be relied upon, you have no real friends."

"What is your point, Mother? Does any Zar have any real friends? He is the ruler and by his very position is envied or despised or feared." Boaz removed his hand.

"That is my very point, son, which is why you must count on me and trust me. I am your flesh. I want what is best for you."

He sighed. "What is it you want of me, Mother?"

Herezah smiled, pleased. At last they could get down to business. "I want you to be more visible."

"To whom?"

"To those who count, those in authority who influence others."

He smirked. "The Vizier and the eunuch, you mean."

She ignored his barb. "You're going to have to attend dinners, meetings, a lot of tedious gatherings." She paused. "Some of these events are going to be harder than others."

"What do you mean?"

"Well," she said, playing with the sash of her gown. "Your brothers—"

"Mother! We have been through this. I was injured!"

"I know, my lion. I know. But you were not present for Joreb's funeral or the festival to commemorate his life, and your absence was noticed."

"I was still very upset by his death."

"And I wasn't?" Herezah challenged. Her son's defiant gaze faltered. "No matter what's happening in here"—she pointed to his heart and then to his head—"you must always do your duty and appear strong."

They were interrupted by a knock at the door. Though Herezah looked to her son to give permission, she knew she had won today's battle.

"Enter," Boaz said, distracted.

His private servant, a young man called Bin, stepped in and bowed. "Your High One, Valide Zara." As both royals nodded, he continued: "I'm sorry to disturb you, Zar Boaz, but the Grand Master Eunuch wishes to speak with the Valide. He says it is urgent."

"Show him in," Boaz ordered. After the servant had disappeared again he looked quizzically at his mother. "Trouble?"

She had no time to answer, for Salmeo entered immediately. He too bowed and acknowledged both his superiors. "Forgive my interruption, High One. The Valide Zara asked for this news as soon as it was available."

"Ah, the girl," Herezah said. "She's been found?"

"Yes, Valide. At the bazaar."

"By the Spur?"

"Yes. They were sharing a kerrosh."

"Oh?" she replied, stung. "How cozy."

"She was cold, we were told, and the Spur felt it was neces-

. sary to offer some nourishment. They shared pastries too."
Nothing in Salmeo's bland expression suggested that he was
enjoying baiting Herezah.

"So thoughtful of him," she said in a contrived tone of
boredom. "Where are they now?"

"Awaiting you, Valide Zara."

"Dismiss the Spur. Leave Ana in the harem. She can suffer
the wait a little longer at my pleasure."

"As you command, Valide." Salmeo bowed and departed,
relishing the chance to send the arrogant Spur packing.

"Mother, what is this about?"

"Nothing I can't handle, dearest one," Herezah assured her
son breezily.

Boaz recalled Pez's warning. It was vital that he begin to
impress upon his mother whose throne she served. His tone
bristled. "If you want me to be more visible, Mother, then I demand to be included in all matters relating to the palace. Is that
clear?"

Herezah turned, surprised by his sharp tone. This she had
not anticipated. "Why, yes, of course." She felt her own anger
stoke but pulled it back just in time. "Forgive me, my son. I just
didn't think it was of importance."

"I will be the judge of what is important. Tell me what this is
about."

"There is a girl—"

"That much I gathered."

For the first time Herezah saw Boaz clearly, and as a rival.
This journey back into his affections might take longer than
she'd thought. She tempered her tone. "I'm sorry, darling. Let
me start from the beginning. Last night we made the selection

of young women who will form the new harem." She could not know how he held his breath, relieved beyond belief that she would never know he had been present. "And there was one particular girl called Ana—quite a remarkable child in looks and composure—who obviously hasn't taken to our hospitality." She chuckled.

"She ran away?" he asked, incredulous.

"Yes, silly girl. Disguised herself with a eunuch jamoosh, blacked up her face with ash, and somehow sneaked out of the palace." Though Herezah feigned nonchalance, she noticed how her tale fired her son's imagination—how his dark, intelligent eyes lit up with interest.

"How ingenious," he said. "I should like to meet this Ana."

Time to get her own back. She knew how squeamish Boaz could be. "Well, now, that's a fine idea, Boaz. I shall include you in her interview."

"For what?"

"For punishment later today," she said, and smiled demurely at her son as she took her leave.

LAZAR SEETHED SILENTLY, glowering at the all-too-polite Elim guard who reassured him that the Grand Master Eunuch would not keep him long. Jumo, of course, had not been invited into the waiting chamber, and Ana had been whisked away by the red-draped guards who insisted it was their role to escort her into the harem. His only consolation was that Herezah was not there to gloat.

Salmeo must have dropped in on his thoughts, for the Grand Master Eunuch entered at that moment and smiled condescendingly, the smell of violets wafting about him. "Sorry to keep you, Spur." It had already been two bells since they had arrived. Lazar glared at him.

"This is a delicate matter for the harem, Spur. You must show patience."

"I think I have."

"Indeed," Salmeo replied dismissively. "We have kept you from your duty long enough, which is why we no longer require your presence."

Lazar could hardly believe what he'd heard. "What sort of jest is this, eunuch?"

"Grand Master Eunuch, if you please," the huge man corrected, which only served to infuriate Lazar further. "No jest, Spur. The Valide's orders."

"Orders? I wish to see her."

Salmeo closed his eyes and shook his head. "Impossible. She is not seeing anyone today."

"Then I shall speak with the Zar."

"He is unavailable," Salmeo replied curtly.

Lazar forced back his wrath. "This will not do."

"Spur, if you please, this is no longer a matter for your consideration. The girl is returned—we thank you for aiding in that but she is the property of the Zar. She belongs to the harem and the harem alone will decide her fate."

"Fate? What are you talking about?" Lazar demanded, hoping to buy some time.

"She is to be punished. It will be private. Look, Spur, you have exchanged the girl for gold; your business here on this matter is concluded. We shall look forward to welcoming you to the palace on your other official duties, but now I must ask you to leave. My men of the Elim will—"

"Don't bother." Herezah had put Salmeo up to this, Lazar

was sure. He could see her delight flashing in the man's triumphant gaze. "You may tell the Valide, when she is available, that I wish to speak with her about my position as Spur."

"I shall do that," Salmeo promised as Lazar stalked away.

Lazar found Jumo waiting in an open-air walkway that led out to the Moon Courtyard.

"I see it went badly," Jumo said, hurrying to keep up with the Spur's long, angry strides.

"That fat lump of dung!" Lazar muttered.

"Where are you going?" Jumo asked as his companion swung down a hallway.

"To find Pez," was the gruff reply.

THE DWARF WAS SINGING to himself in the library, turning pages of books far too quickly to be reading them. Lazar noticed, however, that Pez was not looking at the books he held and discarded but one volume that lay open on the floor.

"Pez!" he hissed.

The little man looked at him with a mixture of surprise and amusement. "Yellow?"

"Don't play with me. This is important."

"Well, keep your voice lower, then."

Lazar crouched by Pez on the floor between dusty books and two vast rows of tomes rearing up toward the ceiling. "I need your help."

"What can I do?" the dwarf whispered, eyes watchful for Habib, the library caretaker.

Lazar understood his worry. "Don't worry, Jumo's keeping watch."

Pez nodded. "Let us speak plainly then. What's wrong?"

"There's a girl called Ana who joined the harem last night."

"Yes, a very special child."

"You know her?"

"Only by what I gleaned from eavesdropping."

"Where?"

"Hidden in the corridor during the presentation ceremony."

"You were there!"

Pez nodded. "So was Boaz."

"What?"

"They caught the slave . . . Kett. We escaped."

It occurred to Lazar to ask how the guards had missed the peeping Zar and his jester, but he had more pressing things on his mind. "That savory episode aside, Ana took fright and escaped last night." He was pleased that the dwarf didn't bother with asking how she had done such a thing.

"And Salmeo wants blood?"

"Herezah, of course, is pulling his strings."

"Of course. How can I help?"

"Just speak to Ana if you can. I don't think they'll hurt her. They'll try to frighten her more than anything. But let her know she has a friend in you. I've been banished. They want me nowhere near her."

"Until you sleep with Herezah, this persecution will continue."

"In that case, let it continue!" Lazar scorned. "I must go."

"I shall see if I can find Ana now," Pez assured. "Boaz is smitten, I'm sure. He hasn't said much but he'll get around to talking about it soon enough."

Lazar didn't know if this pleased him or not, but at least it protected Ana. "Good, perhaps he can offer her the sanctuary I couldn't. Thank you, Pez."

"Don't mention it. I've needed an excuse to meet this fascinating creature. Now go, or you'll get us both into trouble. I'll send word, I promise."

"I shall be leaving the city in a few days," Lazar warned as he left.

Pez adopted his vacant expression and went in search of the child who was at the center of the harem's controversy. He found a group of girls crying as they were led out of one of the main chambers behind two eunuchs. Another pair of the men brought up the rear. Pez deliberately skipped past the line, twirling and whistling. It didn't do much to improve the girls' mood but it cracked a smile on the faces of the lead eunuchs.

"Where do you go?" Pez sang, although he could not see the child he sought among them.

"Even you won't cheer this lot, Pez," one man answered. "This is the second group headed for their Test of Virtue."

Pez reeled away, making odd and senseless rhymes with the word virtue. The girls did not laugh and he couldn't blame them. He weaved his way among the halls of the harem hoping the girl wasn't bathing, the water pavilion being the one place from which he was excluded. It seemed strange to be roaming this area, normally full of whispering or excited giggling, plotting or sighing, now so devoid of noise. He found Ana alone in a room of divans, curled up in a window seat and staring out through the lattices.

He sang her name into the silence, and when she turned he saw that she had been weeping.

"Who are you?" she asked, not at all discomfited by his appearance.

He skipped up to join her, hefting his short body onto the seat. "I'm the court idiot. Are we completely alone?" She nodded. "I belong to the Zar. Do you know his name?"

"Boaz?"

"Good girl. Well, I am a friend of Boaz but I am also a friend of yours."

"Why are we whispering?"

"Because I cannot risk anyone knowing that I am not a fool."

"Oh." Her eyes shone. "No one knows?"

He put fingers in the air as he whispered the names of those who shared the knowledge, pasting a manic grin onto his face in case anyone should walk in on them. "The Spur, his shadow Jumo, the Zar, and a priestess called Zafira. No one else except you now."

"Why can't people know?"

"Too dangerous," he mouthed, suddenly leaping up to spin around the room.

She couldn't help but grin at him. "And you trust me with such a secret. Why is that? You don't know me. I don't even know your name."

"I am Pez. I trust you because of Lazar. He trusts no one, of course, but he seems to care about you."

She looked suddenly awkward, shy. "Did he send you?"

"Yes."

"Why is it dangerous for anyone to know about you, Pez?"

"Because it is. You have to trust me but you must trust no one else in the harem. None of its odalisques, none of the eunuchs or other slaves. Do you understand?"

She nodded, wide-eyed. "You'd better do another twirl around the room."

"Has anyone said anything to you since you were returned to the harem?" he asked as he returned to her.

Ana sighed. "They've told me nothing. The eunuchs who wear red asked me to wait here. Where are the other girls?"

"I met some of them in the halls. They were facing their Test of Virtue." He watched her defiant expression falter and understood she must have already undergone the humiliating ritual.

"The Grand Master Eunuch is detestable."

"That's his intention. He wants you to loathe him. It makes him more powerful."

"He wants to frighten me."

"And did he, Ana?"

She shook her head, defiant once again. "No, I just hate him, that's all."

"In truth, you would all have had to face the unpleasant test anyway."

"Except outside the harem, it would be done by a trusted woman, and only when I was facing marriage. Not done by some fat, sweaty eunuch who has the desire but nothing save his groping finger to satisfy it."

Pez remained silent, sympathizing with the horror of Ana's memories.

"I don't like men," she suddenly said.

"Don't you like me?"

"Except you," and as she touched his arm, Pez felt a thrill of something pass through him, something that made him feel suddenly safe.

"And Jumo. Surely you liked him?" he continued.

"Oh, I do. Jumo is lovely."

"Lazar? I admit he's hard to like. In fact——"

"Yes," she cut across his words. "I do like Lazar . . . very much. I'm just not sure if he likes me."

"Take no notice of his brooding silences. If Lazar speaks to you, he likes you. He usually kills those he doesn't like and those he can't kill he simply ignores."

She exploded into laughter and Pez smiled at the sweet sound.

"You have a wonderful laugh, Ana. It's like birdsong and sunshine, a sea breeze and the scent of peryse, all thrown into one delicious sound."

"How can a laugh have a smell, Pez?" she said, smiling, liking his imagery. She loved the delicate peryse blooms that only flowered briefly in spring for a short burst of spectacular color and their soft yet somehow intense fragrance.

"Well, your laugh conjures an image of a field of peryse flowers."

"Everyone else is right, you know; you're definitely mad."

He leaped from the seat and began to dance again.

"Do you know what they're going to do with me, Pez?" Ana asked, suddenly sounding nervous.

And he too became serious. "They will need to punish you, Ana, as a warning to the other girls. To my knowledge no one has ever escaped the harem before, so they'll use you as an example."

"They'll hurt me, then?"

Pez looked into her trusting face and knew he couldn't lie to her. "Not to the point of marking you. Something brief and scary for the others but transient, I imagine. Lazar asked me to tell you to be of stout heart. He will see what can be done."

"He can't save me this."

"From what I hear he's already stuck his neck out for you, child. He won't stop now. Lazar is one of the most intense people I know and the most driven. I imagine when he loves, he loves hard and in a single-minded fashion."

Ana dropped her gaze, blushing. "Are you saying he loves me?"

"I'm saying he will never allow someone he considers a friend to suffer if he can help it. Not very much stands in his way if he wants something."

"Except Herezah," she said, remembering the previous night and the way the Valide's eyes had so often glanced toward him.

"Be careful, Ana. The Valide is more dangerous than you can imagine. You must ingratiate yourself with her—far more than with Salmeo even."

She didn't reply but nodded her understanding.

"And now I must go," he said.

"Must you? Can't you keep me company?"

"I want to check on Kett."

"The slave boy?"

"Yes."

"Can I come?"

"No, you must—" Pez heard footsteps and he immediately began cartwheeling, just as three Elim arrived.

"Miss Ana?" one said politely, bowing slightly.

"Yes?"

"We have come to fetch you."

"Anything to save me from this fool," Ana replied haughtily, pointing to the spinning dwarf.

Pez felt his heart lurch for the girl. She sounded so brave and yet he knew she must be terrified. "Where does little Ana go?"

he sang at the men, darting in front of them and pulling their sashes.

"Not now, Pez," the leader said.

"I must know or I shall start to screech." He'd done this once before; the man must have remembered, because he instantly capitulated. "She is to be flogged. Valide's orders."

Flogged? In her shock Ana could only repeat the word soundlessly.

"Then take her away," Pez managed to sing, though his heart was racing with fear, before he twirled out of the room and hit the hallway running at full tilt.

He had to find Lazar.

"IT'S PEZ, MASTER. He says it's urgent."

"Bring him in." Lazar turned to step inside from the balcony and saw that Pez was already present. The dwarf offered no salutation. "What?" Lazar asked, his gut twisting with worry.

"They're going to flog her," Pez said, still breathing deeply from his run.

Lazar looked to his manservant. "A horse, Jumo." The dark man turned and hurried from the room. "How much time have I got?"

"Little. The Elim fetched her whilst she and I were talking."

"Knowing Herezah, she'll want to turn it into a spectacle."

"In which case you can still make it before they begin."

Lazar crossed the vast chamber in six strong strides. "Will you be all right?" he asked, looking over his shoulder to his friend.

"Don't worry about me. Just get to Ana and think of something quickly, Lazar."

Pain mingled with frustration on the Spur's face. "That's just it, I have no idea how to save her. I've been racking my mind all morning." His voice sounded hollow.

"Get a message to Boaz," Pez said. "You could claim the Right of Protectorship!"

His words turned the agony on the Spur's hardened features to dawning realization and relief. "Thank you, Pez," he said simply.

Pez suspected that the Spur felt more for this young woman than he cared to admit, probably even to himself. The Right of Protectorship claimed no small sacrifice. The dwarf shook his head, for if he was truthful, there was something about Ana that compelled him too.

Jumo returned, disrupting his thoughts. "What's he planning? He wouldn't say."

"Right of Protectorship for Ana."

"May Zarab save us," Jumo said, touching hand to lip in a calling to the great god. He looked so fearful it sent a fresh wave of guilt through Pez for having even suggested the idea. "Herezah will love it."

Pez nodded in agreement.

"Come, let me take you back in the cart," Jumo offered. "Lazar's going to need all the help we can give."

LAZAR REACHED THE PALACE in minutes, leaping from his horse and throwing the reins at his men. Patrolling soldiers saluted, fist on head then heart, but he didn't acknowledge any of them.

Once inside, he ran directly to the office of the Vizier. Tariq kept a suite of rooms at the palace for official duties. It was a stroke of luck that the bejeweled peacock of a man happened to step out of his chamber the moment Lazar barged into the suite.

"Tariq, I must speak with you urgently," he bellowed.

"My, my, Spur. This is most unusual. Can we not set an appointment?" The Vizier's oily manner never failed to stoke the embers of anger that always glowed within Lazar.

"Do you think I would come to you like this if the matter could wait?" With effort, Lazar controlled his wrath—it would get him nowhere. "I would appreciate your help, Vizier," he added contritely.

"I see. Come in." Tariq's tone was bland and disinterested but he was clearly relishing this show of unnatural humility in the Spur.

Lazar stalked past him and closed the door of the ostentatiously appointed chamber he rarely found himself in. He remembered now why he hated to speak with the Vizier in his rooms. The man's choice in furnishings and decor was incredibly vulgar. Everything about him was contrived. And besides, he knew how much Tariq disliked him. It had never bothered him but it made their dealings tense. When Joreb was in power, it had been easier for Lazar to work with virtual autonomy, but with Herezah now pulling Boaz's strings, that would be impossible. Lazar suddenly felt revolted by the notion that he was now somehow beholden to this fool of a Vizier who had the ear of the Valide and thus of the Zar. He forced himself to be polite. "I must speak with the Zar."

Tariq made an irritating noise of condescension, as if scolding a child. "That won't be possible, Spur. He is taking some quiet time for reflection and study."

"I wouldn't make such a request if it were not important."

"So you say. But so is the enrichment of the Zar's knowledge. Could anything be more important in fact, hmm?" the Vizier asked, jewels twinkling in the shaft of sunlight in which he had deliberately chosen to position himself.

Lazar knew it was pointless to argue. "Then will you get a note to him on my behalf?" he said, adding: "Please, Tariq."

The man quivered slightly at the humble tone in Lazar's voice. "I shall do my best." He pointed to a small table in the corner. "There is a tablet of paper; use what you will and ink is in that pot—I shall order a runner."

"Thank you." Lazar wasted not another moment in scribbling out a rushed message, folding it, and placing it into the small silken purse the Vizier indicated. "One more thing. I now need to speak with the Valide Zara." He saw the Vizier open his mouth to say the obvious but Lazar cut him off. "Don't tell me this is impossible. I am the Spur of Percheron and require access to the most senior person in the palace. If I am not able to speak with the Zar personally, my rank demands I be given an audience with the Valide." And then he added: "I would not ask if it was not critical."

"Spur, this is not the way we—" Interrupted by a soft knock at the door, the Vizier snapped, "Enter."

A servant stepped into the room, bowing deeply. Lazar was relieved to see the silken purse put into the man's hands. Now that the message was on its way, he could be more forceful.

"Hurry please," he added to Tariq's instructions, and the servant nodded and left promptly. Turning back to the Vizier, who was no longer in sunlight, Lazar realized the man looked decidedly gaunt and old. It was hard to tell his age because he hid behind so much decoration, but perhaps for the first time,

Lazar realized that this was Tariq's last chance to stamp his mark on Percheron; he would not survive another shift in power. This was the moment to play on the man's fears. "I know this is not usual. But the circumstances are not usual either. I've told you it's important, and if you ignore this request, Tariq, then I will be forced to use all my status to make this go badly for you."

"How dare you threaten me!" The Vizier fairly shook with indignation.

"That is not my intention. I'm trying to impress upon you how important it is that I see the Valide."

"And you will not share this important matter with me?"

"Tariq, you are more than welcome to join the meeting, but if you don't organize an immediate audience, I will make my own way to the Valide's suite right now."

It was an audacious threat; Lazar had no permission to enter the harem. The Vizier looked horrified by the suggestion but he knew that challenging the Spur to defy palace rules would only ensure that they were broken. The man was a law unto himself. May Zarab rot his soul! And what if his news really was important? The Valide would be furious if she found out he hadn't allowed it to be passed on. Thinking of the Valide made Tariq frown. Unless he ingratiated himself fully with her, he would remain her puppet. Or she might choose to crush him and leave him nothing, perhaps not even his life. And she a slave! He himself came from a fine family with a proud lineage. This woman had been bought in a slave market where a representative of the harem had dug his finger into her mouth and checked her teeth while she stood naked and humiliated. Now she ruled the country!

Wasn't getting rid of powerful women the way of Maliz? Tariq's frown turned into a smile as he thought of the demon, not even realizing how easily its name slipped into his mind. Oh yes, Maliz's mission had been to undermine and destroy the power of the priestesses, to prevent Percheron from worshipping the Goddess, and to replace her with gods, like Maliz's own master, Zarab, upon whom everyone now called.

Maliz's whispered promises made Tariq feel as though he too could be like Lazar, showing disdain for rules, always assuming he knew best. And what if he could look younger and more handsome too? Perhaps Maliz could help rid Tariq of Herezah as well and he could take her role as chief adviser to the Zar. The demon was still waiting for his answer. In truth, Tariq was terrified. If he was honest with himself, he admitted that he still had not come to terms with the fact that the demon had sought him out, that something he had always considered only folklore was suddenly so real.

Suddenly he realized that the Spur was glaring at him, still waiting for an answer. The arrogance of the man—oh, how he longed to make him suffer!

And you will if you say yes, the familiar voice whispered, obviously eavesdropping on his thoughts. *I will help you to do just that . . . but not yet. Give him what he seeks. I promise you will have the last laugh.*

I must capitulate? Tariq answered, aghast. *What good is that to me?*

Wait and see, Maliz promised, laughing deeply and darkly in his mind.

"I'm waiting, Tariq," Lazar reminded him, tiring of the long time the Vizier was taking to consider his request.

The Spur's voice jolted Tariq from his thoughts. He was torn. Follow his own instincts or follow Maliz's? The demon seemed to know something he did not. If he took Maliz's advice, it would be a signal that he was ready to take the next step. Was he ready to give Maliz what he wanted?

Lazar made a sound of impatience.

"All right, Spur!" Tariq replied, angered. "I shall organize your visit. Wait outside, if you please."

"I don't have time to——"

Perhaps it was Maliz's laugh that gave him spine. "Do as I say. Sit outside and wait until I can contact the Valide Zara and get permission. That is the best I can do." Tariq was even able to hold the Spur's steely gaze without flinching or backing down.

Lazar sighed. "Thank you. You might as well call the Grand Master Eunuch into the meeting. It concerns him too." And he turned away.

TARIQ STOOD BEFORE HEREZAH in one of the palace salons, quietly fuming that Salmeo, who had been summoned by the Vizier's staff, had somehow sidled his huge bulk to stand beside the Valide Zara, giving the impression that they were both in authority and Tariq a mere servant delivering a message. When he bowed to the Valide, it felt as though he was also bowing to the eunuch. This was not lost on Salmeo, of course, who wore a soft smirk along with the voluminous, brightly colored silks today.

"Well, the Grand Master Eunuch is here now. Vizier, what is it that you had to say to us?" Herezah asked from behind her veil, her tone conveying her annoyance at being interrupted.

"I do apologize, Valide Zara, for disrupting your day."

"Tariq," she began again testily, "why *am* I being disrupted?"

No opportunity to string this conversation out, to make himself feel important. "The Spur is here, Valide. He insists on being permitted an audience with you. I requested that the Chief Master Eunuch be present only because the Spur asked." He allowed a brief smile to touch his own lips, glad that he had made it clear that he did not consider Salmeo important enough to be called into meetings as a matter of course.

He was irritated to see a glance pass between the eunuch and the Valide. They knew something. They knew why Lazar was there!

Of course they do, Maliz breathed into his mind.

"And what does the Spur want, Vizier? Have you established that much?" Salmeo asked, all sweetness.

Tariq felt his gut twist. The eunuch was doing this deliberately to unsettle him. How could the Valide allow him to usurp her authority by speaking for her?

He ignored Salmeo and directed his answer to Herezah. "He asked me to be present too, Valide. This obviously concerns all of us."

"Not really you, Vizier, but I shall hear him out. Send him in."

Normally, Tariq would have bowed and turned to do Herezah's bidding but he had taken the precaution of bringing his secretary with him. Still bristling from her direct insult, he looked toward the man who lurked at the very end of the chamber and gave him a signal, intensely pleased that his foresight allowed him to not bow again.

Maliz's voice broke into his thoughts. *Why don't you ask them more about why the Spur is so insistent? As vizier it's important, you know,* Maliz suggested. *Or perhaps I shall tell you instead. This is about a girl; the one presented by the Spur, the one who caused such a fuss. She went missing last night after Salmeo had left her. It's the Grand Master Eunuch's fault.*

Tariq felt a sharp spike of pleasure course through him. Maliz had his advantages. "Valide, may I ask if this has anything to do with the girl Ana? I hear she went missing last night, slipped past the Elim and mocked the Grand Master Eunuch . . ." He watched the rope of a scar twitch on Salmeo's face and his eyes become hooded with suppressed outrage.

Ah, the fat one didn't like that, Maliz cackled. *Hurt him more. Go on!*

"If the Grand Master Eunuch needs assistance in policing these children, I'm more than happy to organize a higher level of guard around the harem, Valide," Tariq offered, infusing his tone with innocence.

Maliz laughed. *Good.*

Salmeo didn't wait for the Valide to answer. His voice came sharp, each word a dagger. "That will not be necessary, Vizier. It was a momentary lapse and it will never occur again."

Tariq raised an eyebrow. "If a mere child can slip through your net—"

"Zarab strike you—"

"Stop!" Herezah admonished. "Perhaps it is a good idea to intensify the Elim guard around the harem. The girls these days are far too assured."

Tariq bowed to her authority, feeling smug. Salmeo uttered nothing, but his body language said more than enough.

Oh, he's going to make you pay for that, Maliz observed, full of glee.

He can try, Tariq replied, charged with confidence from the barbed discussion.

That's the spirit, Vizier, and with my help and presence, you will prevail over the fat eunuch. Think about it. I shall expect your answer by this evening. Then, without warning, the voice was gone.

Herezah had moved to sit on a simple bench, her regal bearing suggesting she was on a throne. "Where have you planned the flogging to take place, Salmeo?"

"Since we agreed to keep it private, I thought it best to conduct Ana's punishment in the Courtyard of Sorrows."

"Very good."

Although Tariq did not understand what they were talking about, he asked for no explanation. He could work this out for himself.

The Spur was shown in. "Valide," he said, bowing briefly. "Thank you for seeing me."

"You are head of Percheron's guard and of her security, Spur. Why should I refuse you?" Herezah smoothly replied, then added: "Ever."

Lazar pretended not to hear her couched invitation. "I am here today about Ana, the girl I brought to Percheron."

"The girl you sold to the harem," Salmeo qualified.

Ignoring the interruption, Lazar continued: "Valide, as you know, I returned her to the harem after her escape last night. Frankly, I'm as horrified as anyone else by the fact of her escape but I'd like to know what terrified her so." He glared at Salmeo.

"Lazar," Herezah began softly, naming him to ensure she gave the impression that they were friends, "Ana may be remarkable in looks and spirit but she cannot be treated any differently from the other odalisques, not until she can claim status as favorite or wife." Then in a more condescending manner, but still laced with gentle concern: "You do understand, don't you, Spur?"

Lazar felt his limbs stiffen at being so belittled but he forced himself to appear at ease. "Of course, Valide. I would not suggest otherwise. It's just that—"

"You see," she interrupted, "the Test of Virtue is never a pleasant event for any girl, but we must all face it during our lives. It was simply Ana's turn last night."

"I am aware of that, Valide. I came here today not to argue that case but to find out what your plan is for Ana."

"My plan?" Herezah repeated, a hint of derision creeping into her voice.

Sensing the turn of her mood, Lazar humbled himself. "Yes, Valide. You see, as I never took any gold in exchange for Ana, I feel I do still have a small claim as her owner."

"Do you indeed?" Herezah was angry now. "Is this correct?" she asked Salmeo.

"Valide, I have no such knowledge. I can check, of course, but even if the Spur did turn down the gold, that hardly required the harem to renege. We offered payment; it is the Spur's decision whether he wants to accept it."

"That's right," Lazar chimed in. "I am not making any claim on Ana; I am simply making an inquiry as to your position on her lack of foresight last night. Her immaturity, the newness of her surroundings, the strangeness of Percheron—and let's not forget the cutting of the slave—would have heightened her emotions, made her unstable. She is, after all, still young."

"I was far younger than Ana when I had to face the test, Spur, and I did not flee."

"Perhaps it did not occur to you, Valide. Perhaps the oppor-

218 • FIONA McINTOSH

tunity to do such a thing was not available. Presumably the Grand Master Eunuch failed in his supervision of this child. I am assuming she was left alone with access to her disguise?" Lazar watched the huge eunuch bristle. "Perhaps it is the Master of the Eunuchs who deserves the reprimand here, Valide, not the girl."

Herezah did not so much as blink. "You could be right, Spur. And I will consider such a measure, but Ana must bear the consequences of her own actions. As you say, she is young, but of an age when we can all be responsible—you might consider that my own son rules Percheron at fifteen. I was already a wife at this same age—a mother, in fact. It may be a tender age but it is not an immature one, Spur. Ana made a very unwise decision and one, I'm sure, given her intelligence, she understood would have repercussions."

Lazar knew he had lost this argument. He could not talk Ana free of punishment. It was obvious that Herezah and Salmeo intended to press ahead, that they were meeting with him purely for diplomatic reasons. He took a steadying breath, knowing what he was about to put in place would cost him dearly. As Herezah finished her speech, he felt a tingling sensation near his hip. He reached into the pocket of his loose robe and felt the warmth of Iridor. It gave him courage. "May I ask what her punishment is to be?"

"I suppose it is of no consequence to tell you." Herezah looked toward Salmeo to do the honors—a small crumb of revenge for him after the Spur's cutting words.

"It is the decision of the harem, which will always mete out punishment to its own, that the odalisque Ana will be flogged— thirty lashes."

Lazar blanched. "Valide! She is a child, she cannot withstand such a thing." He saw with disgust how his plea sent a shiver of delight through the veiled woman.

"And if she flags during her punishment," Salmeo continued firmly, "she will be permitted a day's recovery before completing the remaining lashes."

Lazar barely heard the eunuch's final words. His gaze was locked on Herezah's. Her dark eyes sparkled with triumph. She knew she had him right where she wanted him.

"In that case, Valide," Lazar said, bowing low, "I must invoke the Right of Protectorship."

The words hung in the air amid a shocked silence. Such a thing had not been claimed in living memory, though they all knew full well what it meant. The rule of protectorship was enmeshed in the tapestry of the harem's existence, even though a lowly odalisque could rarely win the notice of someone powerful enough to offer her protection, which is why the women within the harem schemed and made alliances. In its history, an odalisque had won right of protectorship only twice, and on both occasions the girl had had the backing of a compassionate Zar. To have someone beyond the harem or not of royal stature make such a request was a novelty and something of a challenge to the palace hierarchy.

"I'm sorry, do you know what that involves?" Lazar asked, infusing his tone with condescension.

"We know," Tariq said brusquely. "You will take the punishment on behalf of the girl."

"That's right. Valide, the law says—"

"I know what the law states, Spur," Herezah snapped. "But you forget that you need the sanction of the Zar first."

"He has it," Boaz announced, entering the room theatrically. Lazar felt his insides loosen with relief as he dropped a bow to their ruler along with everyone else in the chamber.

"Mother, quite frankly, I cannot condone the lashing of one so young. I find it, well . . . distasteful, to say the least."

"Mighty One," Salmeo began, bowing again for good measure, "the harem has a right to punish its own without the Zar's . . . interceding."

"I understand that, Grand Master Eunuch." Boaz's tone was measured. "But the Spur here has the right to make the claim. The girl was his find. This is also the law of the harem, is it not?"

"It is, Zar," Salmeo admitted grudgingly.

"And I for one would rather a man be flogged than a young woman. I'm sure Lazar can handle thirty lashes of the Sparrow's Tongue."

Herezah smirked coldly behind her veil. "Except, my son, the method of flogging is purely the choice of the harem." Her tone was so icy the very atmosphere in the chamber became brittle.

"What do you mean?" Boaz queried, faltering for the first time.

"She means that the Elim will choose what to whip me with," Lazar said, a bitter smile turning up the corners of his mouth. His eyes were locked with Herezah's, both dueling, both determined to hurt the other.

"Is this right?" Boaz demanded, looking at the Vizier.

Tariq replied, "Yes. The Elim alone make the choice of weapon."

Boaz's face fell. Lazar felt a rush of sympathy for the youngster. He shouldn't have been crushed like this, not when he was just beginning to flex his authoritative muscle.

"Your High One," he said, bowing, "I accept. Thank you for giving me your sanction to claim the Right of Protectorship."

"Zarab be merciful upon you," Boaz replied, knowing it was the best he could do. "Where is this Ana? I would speak with her."

"She is not yet ready, son," Herezah said.

"She's ready enough to take your punishments, Mother," Boaz said firmly, knowing she would despise being spoken to with such disdain in front of these men, particularly Lazar. "She's therefore more than ready enough to meet her Zar. Have her readied for a meeting with me, Salmeo." When Salmeo looked toward Herezah, Boaz snapped, "Is there a problem, Grand Master Eunuch, in taking an order from your Zar? Do you need sanction from the Valide as well?"

"Of course not, High One," the huge man replied, admonished. "I shall see to it immediately. What about the Spur?"

"I'm not going anywhere." Lazar's voice was caustic. "Just tell me where you want me to be."

"The Courtyard of Sorrows," Herezah said, wresting back some authority as Boaz stalked away. "And Ana must be present. She must understand what her actions have caused. "She nodded to Salmeo. "See to it."

THE ELIM HAD BEEN given strict instructions. Ana was to be bathed and dressed in a particular white robe that could be slipped off her shoulders to reveal her back for the flogging, but new orders arrived as the slaves were hurriedly tying up her hair. She could not hear what was being said but she could tell that the eunuch in charge of proceedings was filled with consternation. Stepping into the small bathing chamber after the Elim had left, he whispered to the senior slave. Then he too departed, leaving Ana alone with the two women who were preparing her.

"What's happening?" Ana asked.

"You are to be dressed in a different robe. Step out of that one, please, Miss Ana."

"Why?"

"You are not to be flogged."

Relief flooded through her, although she couldn't imagine why the harem had changed its usual course of punishment. "Tell me, please, what has occurred?" she begged the middle-aged slave who was pulling the white gown from her shoulders.

"I have no information, Miss Ana, other than to dress you in more formal clothes."

She got nothing further from the woman. Ana cooperated meekly, climbing into soft silk trousers and allowing a long silk jamoosh of pale blue to be draped over her until only her eyes showed.

"You must wait now, my lady, in the adjoining chamber. The Elim will come for you."

The slave led Ana next door. And then departed. She had not been in the same room twice since arriving at the palace and could only wonder at how many hallways and palatial rooms the harem contained. She sat alone on a divan, her head bowed and the doors guarded. Ana felt alone and confused. The notion of what had occurred to prevent her punishment kept nagging; something or someone important must have interfered, for she felt sure neither Herezah nor Salmeo would permit her to escape the harem's disciplinary action. There was no one those two schemers answered to save the Zar himself. Did this mean Zar Boaz had stepped in? It seemed impossible. He didn't even know her, had not laid eyes upon her. Suddenly the comfort of escaping retribution for her daring actions turned sour, crystallizing into something more sinister. Although frightening, the thought of the flogging was preferable to the unknown. Butterflies fluttered in her belly, and as if on cue, there was a sudden activity at the main doors and the dwarf came bounding through.

"Pez!" she cried, never so relieved to see anyone in her life.

He was pulling silk handkerchiefs from his sleeves, his nose, his mouth, and his ears. "I wish I were a fish who could fly through the ocean," he cackled, jumping and singing his nonsense tune. Suddenly he threw himself to the floor and stared up at the painted ceiling. "Are they watching?" he whispered.

Ana glanced toward the guards and shook her head. "How did you get past them?"

"I'm mad, remember. No one cares about me."

"Do you know what's happening?"

"It's Lazar. He's claimed the Right of Protectorship for you."

"What does that mean? They've told me I won't be whipped today." From the divan where she sat looking down upon the dwarf, she sensed that something grave had occurred.

"That is because Lazar will take the flogging on your behalf."

"Oh no!" she cried, standing up abruptly. The guards looked

around but without much interest. They'd seen dozens of girls get easily upset, especially around the dwarf. Smirking, they turned away again.

Pez hurried to reassure her. "Ana, hush. Lazar will be fine. He is a toughened soldier."

"How was he allowed to do this?"

Pez sat up but turned his back on the men so they could not see his lips moving. Ana took his hint and did the same as Pez explained. "The Right of Protectorship stretches back centuries and it was only because of an ancient yet infamous instance of it being invoked that it remains in the history books today. A wife of the Zar had made him cuckold to a eunuch."

"How can that be?" she interrupted.

"The eunuch's cutting had not been done properly and he had hidden this fact, managing to continue carnal relations whilst living among the eunuch community. He would have gotten away with his sexual activities if not for falling in love with one of the wives. She became pregnant and the Grand Master Eunuch knew it was not possible that she was pregnant by the Zar. The girl refused to reveal her lover, such was her devotion to him, and so the Zar, incensed, ordered her death. The smitten eunuch stepped forward and claimed the right to be executed on her behalf, invoking one of the oldest laws of Percheron: that a person can escape punishment if another accepts it instead."

"Oh, so this is custom?"

"In Percheron, yes. I don't know of anywhere else where such a law exists. The eunuch was immediately ganched, a hideously slow and painful death that involves being thrown onto hooks. Wherever on the body those cruel hooks snag is where the victim is suspended, eventually to die."

Ana flinched. "And my punishment is a mere whipping," she muttered.

"You have not cuckolded the Zar. There is no greater treachery within the harem."

"Do they still ganche people today?"

"Oh yes. Though there hasn't been one in a long time—I suspect we're due."

"How is Lazar?"

"Determined, aloof, angry as always."

"How can I thank him? How do I repay him?"

"By staying out of trouble, Ana. They have you marked now as rebellious. You must conform as best you can if you are to survive. I imagine Salmeo has been deeply humiliated by this event—even more so now that you're escaping his punishment."

"You think he'll want revenge?"

"I do, so you must not make it easy for him to take it. Stay out of his sight, Ana. Blend into the harem with the other girls and be dutiful. Learn all that they ask of you and perform your tasks diligently. Survive."

Thoughtfully, the girl nodded. "Can you take a message to Lazar for me?"

"Of course."

"Will you tell him that he is free of me? He is no longer beholden in any way. I am alone now and I accept this. I will be a dutiful odalisque, as you suggest. I bear no ill will toward him and I am"—she hesitated—"happier for knowing him."

Pez said nothing. He didn't have to. They sat in sad silence for a few minutes until the Elim arrived.

"It is time, Miss Ana," one said. "Be off with you, Pez," he added, pulling a face of disgust as the dwarf picked his nose, humming tunelessly. "You will have to get used to the dwarf, Miss Ana," the man said more kindly. "He has the run of the harem. We cannot stop him from being here."

"He doesn't trouble me," she answered, feigning indifference. "He doesn't even talk to me—he just seems to murmur nonsense all the time."

"He's been like this for years but he belongs to the Zar and, as such, is untouchable. Now, if you'll come with us."

Pez pushed himself to his feet and groped his crotch, then pointed to Ana. "This one will please the Zar," he said, giggling maniacally before running out the door.

16

S almeo's heart was pumping hard and it was not only pushing blood around his body. Anger throbbed in tandem. The eunuch hated to reveal when his emotions were being stirred; he preferred that no one know what he was thinking or how he was reacting to a situation. But the peacock Vizier and the arrogant Spur had belittled him before the Valide—just when he had begun to win her trust and complicity.

He banged the marble wall with his fist, in a rage. Even though his eyes were open, he saw nothing, for his thoughts and boiling blood blurred everything. He wanted revenge—and the Valide had given him the means.

A knock at the door brought him out of his angry thoughts. "Enter," he boomed.

His trusted and most senior Elim stepped inside and bowed low. "Master," he said, not straightening until his superior gave him permission to do so.

"Horz. You have heard what we do today in the Courtyard of Sorrows?"

The man stood up. "Yes, Master. I have been informed that we do not punish the odalisque but rather the Spur."

"Indeed we do. Who had you earmarked to perform the whipping on the girl?"

"Someone very experienced, Master, who knows how to lash softly and without marking."

"Change him. I want one of the apprentices to do this one."

"Master?" Horz asked in confusion. "An apprentice means it will almost certainly be badly done."

"The Spur is to be hurt, Horz. Must I say it more plainly for you? The Spur has called the Elim into question today. He mocked me in front of the Valide. He believes it will be a simple case of taking the child's punishment. I choose otherwise."

Horz could feel the hate emanating from the Grand Master Eunuch. The words of his master sounded chilling. Whatever was coming was clearly going to be dangerous.

Salmeo spoke quietly and forcefully. "I want the Viper's Nest to be used on him."

Horz blanched. The whip Salmeo spoke of was traditionally used only to kill or as a preamble to death by other means. "Master, please—"

"Do as I command you, Horz. The Viper's Nest it is and make sure whoever wields it has no idea how to use it. I repeat: I do not want the Spur softened; I want him hurt. And should he die . . ."

Die? Horz, in his horror, could barely speak. "Yes, Master?" he managed to choke out.

"We shall not be held responsible. I will see to it."

Silently and shakily, Horz bowed, expecting to be dismissed.

"I am not finished yet," Salmeo said, a slyness in his tone that told Horz he had yet to hear the worst of his master's plan. "I want the tongue of each viper to be dipped in drezden."

The Elim could not speak. His lips had gone numb.

"Have I made myself perfectly clear, Horz?" Salmeo asked, a threat in his question.

"Yes, Master," came the strained reply.

"Good, because it's your life and the lives of your brother and his family in the foothills if my orders are not followed to the letter. I suggest you apply the drezden yourself. Oh, and Horz—no one knows of this but the two of us . . . I suggest we keep it that way."

LAZAR HAD BEEN STARING into space, his mind empty of thoughts for the first time he could remember. He wasn't sure whether it was the dulling sense of anxious anticipation or the fear of what he planned to do beyond today. He had discussed the latter with no one yet, not even Jumo. It seemed to be the only decision he could take to rid himself of this asphyxiating sense of dread—that he was somehow connected to something far bigger than his own tightly kept world of Percheron. For some reason, his thoughts kept returning to the statue of Lyana in the tiny temple. Something in her gaze called to him—no, implored him—to do what, he didn't know. The effect had not waned over the days since he had first seen her. In fact, if he was truthful, he would admit it had only intensified.

Was this feeling of unsettlement the power of the statue? Or a result of the surge of Herezah into such a position of authority and her relentless intention to make him dance to her chosen tune? But his irritation with Herezah paled in comparison with the frightening sense of loss he felt for Ana. And why did he feel strongly for the young odalisque? He had told himself that she was merely a naive girl, but the truth was that though she might be young, her soul was old. He had accused her of being cunning, deliberately pulling at his heartstrings, but he had failed there too; there was nothing conniving in Ana. She was true: true to herself, true to him, and true to those she dealt with. He had even tried to convince himself that she would not remember his name after a year in the harem, that she was like all women in that brood—simply trying to better themselves.

Finally he had had to accept that Ana had so profoundly affected him that he could no longer think in the neat, straight way he was used to. Life felt suddenly disordered, routine was smashed, his secure, private existence in Percheron over. And still he could not target precisely what it was about this youngster that could have such an effect. He was reacting to her as if she were of a similar age to himself and, heaven forbid, eligible. He did not want his heart touched, yet she had done just that with a single look.

Lazar knew he would never be able to stomach being so close to Ana and yet so far away. That was why he was planning on leaving Percheron. He had only to get through today and then he would be gone—fleeing from all that had suddenly become so unsettling.

Sighing heavily, Lazar laid his head back against the cool marble of the wall and closed his eyes. He was sure Jumo would find him prior to the flogging.

He was right. Jumo had arrived at the palace and with Pez's

guidance had discovered where his friend had been asked to wait. Granite-faced members of the Elim greeted the former slave and would not have permitted him access but for the presence of Pez.

"We're here to see the Protector!" the dwarf had repeated over and again, spinning in frantic circles.

When the Elim began suggesting that they would allow Pez in but not Jumo, the dwarf had stamped his feet and grabbed Jumo's hand. "He's my friend," he howled, then growled and bared his teeth at the Elim. The guards, more than used to the small man's antics and capricious ways, looked at one another uncomfortably, and finally, one sighed and said, "What would it hurt?"

Once inside the chamber, the dwarf became serious. "They obviously agreed to it," he said to Lazar.

The Spur nodded. "They could hardly refuse. Thank you for suggesting it."

"I don't think you'll be thanking me soon, Lazar," Pez answered. He sighed, his expression begging their indulgence as he began to jump around, screeching loudly so that the Elim outside would not wonder why he had gone quiet.

Lazar and Jumo shared a look, each thinking the same thing. Salmeo would make the Spur pay a heavy price for this humiliation. Indeed, and ominously, though Lazar originally had been taken in the direction of the barracks, the Elim had taken a sudden and unexpected turn, bringing him to a wing of the palace he had never explored.

"This is not part of the harem," Jumo muttered.

"No. This is the Hall of Sorrows," Pez answered, becoming still again. "It's where prisoners of the royals are brought to wait before they face their punishment."

"I've only seen it from the other side," Lazar commented absently. "It's a very pretty courtyard, with birds as sentries, I think, around the edge of the walls."

"Yes, ravens," Pez replied. "The bird of sorrows."

Lazar nodded. "Fitting."

Jumo knew that Lazar had made a decision and would never go back on his word but one thing continued to trouble him. "Master, I doubt very much that they will use the same whip on you as they would have used on the child."

Pez nodded sagely. "The Elim confer with the Inflictors to choose, as I understand it."

"Yes, so I've been informed," Lazar confirmed. "I think we can stake our lives on the assumption that Salmeo will select something vicious."

"Are you frightened?" Jumo asked tentatively.

"My only worry is for Ana," Lazar said. "I have a feeling they'll make her watch."

"I think you can count on it," Pez answered. "But she's an incredibly assured young woman, my friend. I don't think you should fret too much about her. She will survive this. Just consider yourself now."

Lazar shrugged. "There is little to consider. They'll do what they will and I must bear it."

Jumo felt his stomach roll at the thought. His grim thoughts were silenced by the sudden movement of Pez doing a handstand against the wall and beginning what was known affectionately among the ranks of soldiers as his jibber-jabber.

The dwarf had sensitive hearing; within moments, four of the Elim had opened the door, stepping inside the courtyard. Another two guards remained outside.

"Spur, if you please," the most senior man, Horz, said courteously.

Jumo couldn't imagine that anyone among the Elim was too happy about his role today. The Elim were subject to the whims of their commander, the Grand Master Eunuch, and they were fearsome fighters, all of them. It was an unwise foe who imagined that because the Elim had been rendered sexless by the blade, they lacked the passion or courage that went with manhood. Far from it, in fact; most of the Elim proved their bravery by entering the service of the eunuchs as adults. The other eunuchs of the harem, those never permitted to wear the red robe, were mostly cut when they were still in childhood and unable to understand, beyond the pain and fear, what they were giving up.

The Elim expected to be rewarded in heaven for their sacrifices to the Zar, as promised by Zarab, whom they worshipped vigorously. In spite of their spiritual connection to their ruler, they still admired and respected his Spur, a fellow warrior and man of no excesses. To them, Lazar was just short of kin as he too followed a code of conduct based on honor, not dissimilar to their own.

Jumo stepped in front of Lazar. "I am his second."

Horz nodded. "As tradition allows," he said, speaking above the increasing din Pez was creating. Horz turned and bowed to Lazar. "I'm sorry, Spur, about the dwarf's interference but the Zar rules . . ."

"I know," Lazar replied. "I take no notice of him at the best of times."

"Can you tell me how this is all to be handled?" Jumo asked.

Again the senior Elim nodded calmly. "The Spur is to be flogged."

Jumo kept his face expressionless. "By whom?"

"I do not know the Inflictor."

"You mean you don't know the man himself or you don't know which of the Inflictors has been chosen?" Jumo persisted.

The Elim's hesitation was telling. As he opened his mouth to answer, Lazar cut him off. "Leave it, Jumo. It's going to be done, and frankly I don't care by whom."

Pez began chanting: "Don't hurt him, Horz, or he'll get angry." No one took any notice.

"If you'll follow us, Spur," Horz said, glancing briefly at Jumo. Something in that single look made Jumo's heart sink further. There was some layer to this scheme beyond what they were being told. He was sure of it.

"Thank you, Horz," Lazar muttered. The Elim were ruthless enough when required but he understood that none would be looking forward to today's event. He grudgingly accepted that they would probably have preferred to whip the girl than to humiliate, probably injure, a fellow warrior who was clearly innocent. That said, he could also sense their quiet admiration that he had offered himself up instead. He fell into step between the six Elim, each as tall as he was, and decided as he did so that he would not let himself down during his punishment. He would give Herezah no satisfaction this day.

THE SIX MEN and the victim stepped out into the sharp afternoon sunlight. Jumo unhappily followed, slinking into the shadow cast by the minaret outside the walls. His presence here was permitted merely as a servant available to carry, if necessary, Lazar's body from this place. Pez came behind Jumo, all but catapulting himself from the doorway into the Courtyard of Sorrows and tumbling into a series of manic somersaults aimed purely to irritate Herezah and her sycophants. He succeeded brilliantly by rolling to a halt atop a man's foot. Only one he knew wore jeweled slippers during the day and outside—he couldn't have planned it better.

"Curse you, Pez!" the Vizier exclaimed, kicking at the dwarf with his free foot.

Pez rolled away in mock agony, ensuring he made a loud to-do. Two of the Elim, one of whom was Horz, hurried up to help him.

"Vizier!" the senior Elim admonished. "Pez has the highest sanction in all of Percheron. You must—"

"I know, thank you, Horz," Tariq interrupted testily. He was angry with himself for such a blatant error but how he detested the dwarf! He especially despised that Pez had such free rein throughout the palace and especially in the harem.

Given his anger, he half expected the demon to speak but Maliz had been strangely silent since the meeting this morning. Tariq watched Horz pick up the still-writhing dwarf, carrying him to the edge of the courtyard, and he noticed Pez grinning back, mocking him. Oh, how he hated that fool. Today had been trying and now the dwarf's antics, which never failed to embarrass the Vizier, had allowed the tension he was feeling to boil over.

He made his final decision. Yes! He would accept Maliz's offer. He wanted power, he wanted riches, he wanted freedom from the shackles of people who were less than himself. He would no longer answer to any of these pitiful folk, least of all a deranged dwarf. Tariq grimaced with pleasure at the thought. It would only be a temporary arrangement after all, and what did it matter if the demon had use of his body for a short period? The rewards more than outweighed the brief inconvenience.

Tariq suddenly realized he was grinning fiercely, filled with joy at reaching a decision, but his elation was interrupted by a short fanfare heralding the arrival of the Zar, looking tall and suddenly proud.

BOAZ WAS ACCOMPANIED by his mother. Herezah was fully veiled but nevertheless dazzling in robes of deep blue. Mother and son stepped out onto the balcony that overlooked the Courtyard of Sorrows. At their appearance, the entire group within the courtyard bowed.

And then another door opened and Ana was escorted by two burly Elim to the center of the Courtyard of Sorrows. She too was fully veiled; Lazar hated that her expressive face was covered. Nevertheless the softest of smiles seemed to touch her eyes and he knew it was just for him. His heart felt as though it had been shattering into countless pieces and with that deeply despairing pain came understanding. He had decided to take her punishment not for honor, or for protection, but for the oldest, most simple of reasons that drove men and women to do courageous, often ridiculously dangerous things.

He loved Ana.

At this moment of realization he felt the warmth of Iridor burning next to his leg. Placing his hand against the tiny statue, Lazar felt its comforting heat, and with that warmth came a sense of peace. He had made the right decision; Iridor was telling him as much. It was best he leave Ana to her new life. And as for himself: he must not punish himself further by remaining in Percheron and being reminded constantly of her, of roaming the palace and knowing she was separated from him by only a few walls and yet might as well be on the other side of the world. No, he would not suffer that pain easily. Instead he would return to his homeland and face the consequences, start his life anew as Ana built hers among the halls of the harem. If Pez was right and Boaz's interest had already been triggered by the girl, then she had a future.

Salmeo's voice broke into his thoughts as the eunuch began explaining the events leading up to Lazar's punishment. None of it needed explanation, of course, for everyone was well aware of what had transpired, but Salmeo took pleasure in following protocol.

". . . and so it is with respect that we now inflict the punishment on Spur Lazar who has claimed Right of Protectorship over Odalisque Ana, property of Zar Boaz. The slave's transgression is considered extremely grave and by no higher authority than the Zar himself . . ."

Lazar returned to his reverie, considering his prospects upon returning to where he was born and what sort of welcome might await him. It wouldn't be warm, that was for sure. He noticed Salmeo turn toward him and speak, dragging his attention back to the eunuch's words.

". . . it is out of veneration to our Zar and to our way of life in the harem that we insist this punishment be taken seriously."

Lazar felt a stone hit the pit of his stomach. Salmeo clearly had something special in store for him. Lazar tore his gaze from Ana to stare at the timber to which he would be tied. He had seen many floggings, knew what to expect, grasped that Ana's punishment would be symbolic, whereas his on her behalf would be more stringent. He expected that some days of healing would be required before he would be able to move with ease. But now that the moment was upon him, the post and cross-timbers looked intensely sinister.

". . . It has been decided that the Spur will be given thirty lashes from the Viper's Nest." A murmur buzzed across the balcony as Boaz turned to his mother, concern apparent in his expression. Herezah whispered a brief response, hardly long enough to resemble anything close to a discussion. Lazar grimaced in sympathy. Poor Boaz—he was in for a harsh lesson this afternoon.

Lazar glanced toward Jumo and saw fear written across his friend's face. How he wished he could spare his companion this trial. A quick movement caught his eye and Lazar noticed Pez, his face ashen, skipping unhappily around the courtyard, apparently accidentally treading on the toes of the silent Vizier before careening through the door and away from the Courtyard of Sorrows. Lazar knew that wherever he was headed, the dwarf would be putting things in place to help when the flogging was done.

"Let us proceed," Salmeo proclaimed.

Before any move could be made, Ana, no doubt gathering that the Viper's Nest was no simple whip, began to struggle against her minders. "No, this is my punishment," she cried, tears overflowing her wide green eyes.

"Hush the girl!" Salmeo ordered.

"I demand to take my own punishment!" she yelled, cutting Salmeo off and looking directly at the Zar. "Your Majesty, overturn this decision, I beg you."

Boaz stepped forward and placed his hands on the balcony's

stone railing. Everyone fell silent. Salmeo closed his eyes, beseeching Zarab that the Zar would not acquiesce to the girl's plea. They saw the Valide lean slightly toward the boy—no doubt she had whispered something to him from behind that veil, for Tariq noticed how the Zar's body tensed. There was anger in the boy, he mused. They would not have him under their collective thumb for much longer if they all did not give him more credit. He and Herezah—and yes, Salmeo, too— would need to occupy the new Zar, shower him with diversions, pander to his whims, and free him from all responsibility if they were going to take complete control of Percheron.

Boaz took a calming breath. "Odalisque Ana," he called into the courtyard. "You have brought this despair upon yourself by your flouting of the harem's strictest law—the law of discipline. Did you know that crimes of this nature are sometimes punishable by death?"

At his words, Ana stopped struggling. She shook her head, dumbfounded.

"It is I who will not permit such a thing. It is I who have also permitted that your brave protector, our own revered Spur of Percheron, might take a commuted sentence on your behalf. Please do not beseech my generosity further, Odalisque Ana, for I fear my kindness to the women in my harem is being tested today. I am a friend of the Spur's"—Boaz looked around the courtyard, speaking to everyone now—"and I abhor what he is about to endure. But I admire him and respect him only more than I already did for his courage in protecting someone whom I should have protected from herself." He looked back to Ana. "You may be excused if you prefer not to witness the infliction of your own punishment."

Lazar bit back a smile, proud of and impressed by the boy.

Reprimanding Ana so publicly would save her further torment from her superiors. Now that the Zar had spoken, no one would be permitted to add to his censure. Ana could not yet know that not even the Zar himself could overturn certain rulings within the harem. Boaz's personal admonishment was a form of protection and now he was offering Ana a chance to escape the trauma of watching the flogging take place. The young man was becoming more canny by the day.

Everyone within the courtyard waited for Ana's response. She bowed to her Zar and then eyed him defiantly. "I will bear witness, Your Majesty, so I never again have any misunderstanding of the barbaric dwelling in which I'm forced to live."

Salmeo, Tariq, and Herezah gasped at her brazenness. Lazar prayed that Boaz's personal fire had indeed been lit by Ana, for he was all that stood between her and a life of misery; the three most powerful people in Percheron save the Zar were furious with her.

Boaz spoke again. "I shall have a private audience with Odalisque Ana in my chambers once she is rested. Await my instructions." His tone was harsh and Herezah, Salmeo, and Tariq breathed a collective sigh of relief; not only was Boaz taking charge over such insult but it appeared that he would be seeking his own private retribution later.

Tariq secretly thought Boaz should rape the girl, viciously breaking that precious hymen. Then kill her, even. What was the life of one slave girl, and a difficult one at that?

Good, Tariq. It's fascinating to hear your angry thoughts. Tariq started as Maliz's voice eased into his mind.

I thought you'd deserted me.

How touching. I like to be missed. Someone will need to take control of the Zar, for I fear he is taking full control himself. I trust you've reached your decision, Vizier.

I have made my decision.

And?

I have conditions.

I make no further bargains.

This is just a temporary arrangement. Will you confirm that?

I will leave your body the moment I'm done with it.

Tariq's pause was barely noticeable. *Then I accept.*

There was a moment's silence in his head and then deep laughter. *I shall see you tonight. Go to the bazaar—pass the slaughterhouse—I shall give you directions from there. Now I truly go. Preparations must be made.*

Maliz—

No! Not now. Come tonight, late. I shall explain all.

And the demon was gone. Tariq, as if snapped from a sleep, focused again as the famously handsome Spur of Percheron was led to the scaffold where, if the Vizier had his way, the man would be flogged to death.

17

A heavy silence fell upon the crowded courtyard. Yet another door opened and a young man, looking painfully unsure of himself, stepped into the arena. Behind him came an even younger bearer, carrying a white linen cloth upon which lay the fierce Viper's Nest. The whip comprised six leather thongs, which currently curled around one another harmlessly but when unleashed could snap against a man's back fast and viciously—akin to the movement of a viper. The cruel instrument was nicknamed the Snake, for each thong forked into two, like a serpent's tongue, and on the tip of each tongue was a tiny silver bead, sharp-edged and crafted deliberately to break skin.

Lazar swallowed hard, but to the onlookers he seemed unmoved by the arrival of the weapon. He had never seen the Snake used but he had heard of the intense injuries it could inflict. No wonder Salmeo was all but shivering in anticipation. Well, he would put on a good show for them and he would bleed hard—but he would not cry out for mercy. He would sooner bite out his own tongue than vent a plea to these mongers of pain. He raised his head to look around the rim of the courtyard at the birds of sorrow that lined the high wall. They seemed to mock him but he cared not.

"Welcome, Inflictor," Salmeo said. He bowed to Boaz again. "Your High One, may I present Shaz."

"This man looks young to be an Inflictor," Boaz said, estimating Shaz to be no more than a summer or two older than he was.

Salmeo dipped his head in mock humility. "Yes, Great One. Our Inflictor is away in the far north. I'm sorry to say his deputy is indisposed today—very unwell in fact—with a high fever."

"So who is Shaz?" the Zar persisted, sensing a ruse. He glanced toward his mother, wondering if any of this might have been her idea. Herezah gave nothing away in her dark gaze but shook her head slightly, as if this was all news to her. Boaz knew his mother well enough to ascertain when she had been taken by surprise. Shaz had nothing to do with her, then.

"He is an apprentice, Your Majesty," the Grand Master Eunuch replied.

"An apprentice!"

Salmeo shrugged innocently. "Your High One, what can I do? The sentence has been proclaimed. The rules of the harem demand that the flogging be carried out immediately. We had no idea that the Spur would choose this path or perhaps better arrangements could have been made. I would have insisted, in fact. But my understanding was that a member of the harem was to be whipped. Shaz is more than capable of lashing the odalisque Ana expertly," he offered up obliquely, not saying that the young Inflictor was incapable of using the Viper's Nest, and could wield only the harmless Swallow's Tongue with any precision.

"And the Spur?" Boaz demanded.

"Shaz's superior has indicated that he is the most talented apprentice in years," Salmeo lied.

Boaz bristled. Growing up in the harem had prepared him for the Grand Master Eunuch's subtleties. "Then because of the harem's incompetence and inability to provide a senior Inflictor, I am using my authority to commute this sentence."

Salmeo trembled with anger. "Zar Boaz, I must pro—"

"No, Grand Master Eunuch, it is I who protest. This is being handled badly. I accept that the odalisque Ana has committed a serious crime and I accept that she must be punished. We all accept, because it is written in our laws, that the Spur can claim the Right of Protectorship and take the flogging on her behalf. Finally, we all understand the law of the harem according to which the Grand Elim alone decides on the method of punishment. But, Salmeo, my word is the law of our land and I have the power to reduce this sentence, if not the way it is carried out." Even without the fully deepened voice of manhood, Boaz's tone brooked no argument. "Spur Lazar will receive ten less than the proposed number of lashes because of the bumbling manner in which this serious event is unfolding." He took a deep breath. "If I could, Salmeo . . ."—and Boaz deliberately used the eunuch's name rather than his title in order to reinforce his personal authority over the man—"I would postpone it until someone experienced could deal the blows. I know I cannot." He didn't wait for a response from the Grand Master Eunuch, looking instead to the uncertain young man awaiting the order to proceed. "Shaz."

"Yes, Your Majesty," the Inflictor replied quickly, confused and startled.

"Twenty lashes only. Do you understand?"

Shaz bowed low. "Yes, High One." He hesitated as if to add something, but caught the sharp shake of the head from Horz. So did Lazar.

This was all planned, then, Lazar realized. Salmeo must have contrived all of this over the past few hours. Impressive. Poor Shaz. He was being set up to make a complete mess of a man's body and Lazar understood he would have to steel himself against not just the lick of metal against skin but also the certainty of incompetence.

There was nothing he could do. Horz was already indicating that his robes were to be removed. As Shaz unrolled the Snake, Lazar quietly undressed, wishing this could have been a private debacle instead of a public event. He stripped down until he stood only in his white trousers and boots, his dark hair shining against his bronzed body.

On the balcony, behind her veil, Herezah took a long, steadying breath. She had pictured Lazar naked many times in her life; she had dreamed of him moving rhythmically above her, his expression filled with the ecstasy of riding her body. But no imagination could compare to the reality that was Lazar. He was, to her despair, infinitely more desirable in life than he had been in her dreams. He stood boldly before them, his broad chest visibly moving now with the deep breaths of anticipation. She took in the sight of his strong arms, shaped by hard muscle, which he usually hid beneath floaty robes. His light-eyed gaze was distant. He had left everyone here, she realized, and he was disappearing to a new place where perhaps he might escape the shock of what was coming. She felt vague pity that his beautiful body would be damaged before she could enjoy it, and squinted at the weapon in the young Inflictor's hand. From the distance of the balcony where she and Boaz stood, it appeared to all intents and purposes to be no more than a normal whip.

There was nothing she could do to help Lazar—even for cynical reasons of her own pleasure. All she could do was relish this opportunity to see him bared and humbled. After all, what were a few lashes to a strong man? She hoped he would groan from the pain and give her satisfaction for all the years of private groaning she had done on his behalf.

Herezah felt a soft shiver of pleasure ripple through her body as Lazar lifted his eyes and looked at her. Oh, the exquisite defiance in that glower. She wished she could drag him off and bed him now—nothing would give her greater release than to take him when he was so flagrantly thumbing his nose at those around him.

Was he scared? Surely just a little, for the whip looked suddenly fearsome as the young man, Shaz, unfurled it and cracked it in a couple of practice lashes. Zarab's Breath! But it was more complex than she had imagined—so many whips within the one weapon. It snapped loudly around the courtyard and she noticed Ana flinch. Good! She wanted to ensure Ana knew what she was responsible for. And Lazar, poor fool, blinded by honor, would shed blood today for a girl who would forget his very existence within a few months.

Herezah was dragged from her musings by Lazar's movement toward the post. She looked at his broad back now as his arms were raised and tied firmly to the crossbeam. The muscles that striped his body stood out in sharp relief as they tensed in readiness and Herezah held her breath, awaiting the sound of the Snake's first bite.

PEZ WAS RUNNING as hard as his stumpy legs could carry him. Though people laughed and some who knew him called out to the dwarf, he heeded no one. As he ran he felt a burning sensation. Though at first he thought he was getting warm from his exertion, as the feeling grew he realized it was not that sort of heat. It was not on his skin but in his mind and deep within his body. He felt suddenly connected to . . . what? Whatever it was, it was calling him. Compelling him. Where to? He reached out for the answer as he careened closer to the waterfront.

SHAZ NERVOUSLY FLICKED the Snake. He had not understood why the Deputy Inflictor had suddenly summoned him to his chamber barely an hour ago and given him instructions that made his hair stand on end.

"You will be inflicting a flogging today," Rah had said flatly.

"Sir? Is this a practice on the dummies?"

"No, Shaz. This will be on a real man."

Shaz had been understandably shocked. "I am not ready, sir. Only yesterday you said—"

Rah's eyes had appeared shrouded. He had sounded awkward and his tone had been angry. "I know what I said. I have been given orders."

"Sir, have I offended?"

"No. Just follow your orders."

Shaz had risked his superior's ire still further. "You cannot leave me to this, sir, when I can't—"

Again he had been interrupted. "We have no say in this! It comes from the highest authority. You have been chosen to do the whipping. Do your best. Remember all that we have taught you. If anyone asks, I have been taken unwell. Do not let your own down."

Shaz had felt his stomach turn over. "But I am not ready."

"No. But you also have no choice. This is what you've trained for—it's simply happening earlier than we or you would like."

"But I know I will injure him. He may not recover."

"Take a deep breath between lashes. See the place where you intend the whip to hit, visualize the tip on the spot of skin you are looking at, take aim, and snap the whip cleanly, as you've been taught. You know what to do—do the best with the skills you have, Shaz."

"What if I hurt him too much?"

And then Shaz's superior had looked down, beaten himself. "That is their intention, I imagine."

It had all fallen into place. Shaz understood that he was merely a pawn in a much bigger game, a game played by far more important people who did not respect the work he and his superiors did, the pride they took in doing it properly. "They're sending you away deliberately so that your apprentice makes a fool of himself and a mess of some victim's back?" he had asked, stunned.

Rah had remained silent for a long while, then said, simply and quietly, "You are instructed to use the Snake."

At this Shaz had quailed. "No sir, I cannot do it. I have never yet touched the Viper's Nest. I am not ready to wield it."

"That's what they're looking forward to, son."

"Who is the victim?" Shaz had asked, unable to imagine which poor soul had so offended the Grand Master Eunuch.

"The Spur of Percheron. I am sorry for you, Shaz. Zarab guide your fist."

And so here he now stood, trembling, terrified, the Snake lying limp in his clenched, sweaty hand, waiting to be fully awakened and unleashed mercilessly. Shaz had always admired the Spur, had watched his long stride around the palace grounds, been impressed by the way his loyal men had leaped to his bidding, had even gladly taken advice once when Lazar had caught him practicing his craft on the dummies.

"Remember that's a man, Shaz," the Spur had cautioned. "You must respect his body as you would your own. Keep mindful that he needs to be able to walk away from this post with a little bit of his pride intact. If you whip him too low too often, he won't be able to walk, and if you concentrate the lashes too high, he won't be able to lift his arms. Men have work, families, lives. They must be able to return to them. Whippings are punishment only for a transgression—you are not trying to maim or kill the man."

Shaz had never forgotten that guidance. It echoed in his mind now as he stared at the broad, unblemished torso of the very man who had given it.

"Spur." Salmeo addressed Lazar. "Are you ready?"

"Get on with it, curse you!" Lazar snarled.

"I am obliged to ask whether you would like something to bite on," Salmeo offered politely, keen to prolong the high drama of this moment.

"No!" Lazar spat.

"Very well. Horz, please position the odalisque Ana behind the flogging post."

"What?" Lazar roared, pulling against his bonds as Horz led Ana to stand in front of the Spur, saw the Elim whisper something briefly to her, although she did not respond.

"Forgive us, Spur, but this is part of the tradition when protectorship is claimed," Salmeo replied. "The true victim must share the pain of the protector."

"You barbarian, Salmeo."

The eunuch could not help a small smile but he said merely, "Shaz, you may proceed."

As the young Inflictor took a deep breath and flicked the Snake back in preparation for his first lash, Boaz turned to his mother. "I shall never forgive those involved in this."

"It is the Spur's choice," Herezah replied, her voice hard and as sparkling as a diamond. "You can only admire him for it. I do."

As she turned away from Boaz, the Snake struck for the first time.

18

Lazar had thought about closing his eyes to Ana but they seemed to have a will of their own. He saw her eyes water and he shook his head softly, willing her to be strong. Ana twisted her shoulder free of Horz's curiously protective hand and wiped at her tears quickly, mouthing something to Lazar that he would never see, for the veil covered her mouth.

It was just as well, for it would have undone him.

The first bite of the Snake struck wildly across his shoulders and Ana watched Lazar open his mouth in a wide grimace, but no sound came out. She would never admit to the smiling eunuch, who was watching her and not the Spur, that she would rather be here focused on Lazar's face than having to confront the damage at his back. Ana glanced toward Jumo, whose expression was blank, but she could read beneath it to the horror and the fear. He blinked as the whip was flicked back again for the second strike and she returned her attention to Lazar, who was breathing hard, his only way of steeling himself against the burning pain. The Snake bit again, and this time Ana saw its forked tongues curling around Lazar's chest, ripping savagely through flesh as blood rushed to the open wounds and ran down his body.

She heard a sound of awe mixed with horror. She was not sure who made it and hoped it was Herezah.

Lazar closed his eyes now, squeezing them tightly, but still no sound issued from his mouth. Ana felt her heart racing— eighteen more to go—and this time she risked a glance up at Herezah. Ana saw only hunger in those dark, cruel eyes.

The third strike was clearly off target, some of the beads, with their sharply jagged edges, raking through Lazar's hair, tearing the flesh of his scalp as Shaz inexpertly flicked the whip back. Ana noticed how horrified the young Inflictor looked. She could not see any of the damage, bar the wounds on Lazar's side, but she could see the lifeblood coursing from the injuries and could imagine how ugly it must already appear. Shaz faltered as he drew a shaking hand to wipe the sweat from his face. And still Lazar gave no sound.

The fourth stroke whipped cruelly around to Lazar's belly as Shaz desperately tried to adjust the height of his lashing to avoid the victim's head. Again skin tore and yielded bright blood, drenching Lazar's white cotton trousers. Blood was running down his face too, joining with the sweat that had been caused by pain. Lazar's freshly washed hair, once shiny in the afternoon sun, was now damp and clumped.

The fifth lash of the Snake won a groan, short and guttural. Salmeo smiled—he had obviously been waiting for Lazar's breaking point. The Vizier was less obvious, merely glancing toward his bejeweled sandals, but there was satisfaction apparent in his face, Ana noticed. After the next five strokes, Lazar's body gave little resistance, and although he made no further sound, he began to slump against the pull of the bonds that had once held him upright.

Halfway.

Ana saw that Shaz was panting, perspiration sheening his body. He cracked the whip again, his expression anguished. And as he dragged it back, his assistant handed him a cup of water, which he gratefully drained with a shaking hand.

No one offered Lazar anything but silent love or hate, depending on whom Ana looked at.

HE HAD COUNTED each shocking bite of the Snake, and with the mounting toll, he felt his strength being leached away with the blood that ran so freely now. By the eleventh, Lazar was losing the will to fight. He could no longer open his eyes and his throat was parched, his lips dry and cracked. Though he knew Ana was still in front of him, willing him to stay strong, urging him silently to prevail, he could no longer see her through the blur of the blood.

At first the pain had been searing and intense, the kind he knew how to withstand, if more vicious than anything he'd previously experienced. But now a numbness was coming over him—the body's own weapon against the shock. It felt like a death creeping through him, as if his very veins were running with a killing liquid rather than life itself. Lights, incandescent and of all colors, were flashing behind his eyelids . . . was this death beckoning? It would be so easy to give in to it. Should he?

Was that the fourteenth lash? He could no longer tell, could no longer count, could no longer hear anything around him. He wasn't sure he could even open his eyes to bid her farewell. Sweet Ana. He had not meant to give his life, but if he had to, he was glad it was for her. He knew she was too young to be loved the way his treacherous mind tormented him with, but he knew, deep within his fractured heart, that she loved him too. He did not care that hers was a childish love, for a first love is always the sweetest, the most intense and pure.

How odd that he could remember his so well. Lazar thought he had buried the memory of Shara too deep to lift it free again. Loving Shara had been so easy—youth made it easy and carefree and filled with such brightness that he never imagined it could be tarnished. But life had taught him that even the most radiant of treasures could be dulled. And now, just when he had allowed himself to believe otherwise, life was teaching him that same harsh lesson once again.

He envisaged his legs giving way, but unsure whether this had in fact occurred. He no longer felt connected to his body. Had he called out? He had no idea. Lazar wanted to believe he was still standing rigidly against the post, taking the punishment, but he suspected his stance was not nearly so proud as it had been. The sense of weakness he felt frightened him.

He began to tremble, became aware of it because his teeth were chattering, jarring him into a sense of wakefulness that served only to reinforce his belief—now a certainty—that he was dying. A rush of anger blazed through him at the notion that his death would give Salmeo and, no doubt, Tariq, great satisfaction—and that anger brought a measure of clarity to Lazar's dulled mind, allowing him to hear Shaz counting his seventeenth stroke. Seventeen! He had almost made it. But death was whispering gleefully to him. The Valide would not be so smug about his passing. She might be enjoying his suffering but she would not be smiling when he died, for who then, would protect Percheron?

Lazar felt himself withdraw fully. He suddenly felt himself tiny, retracting into his soul, which he must now relinquish to the gods.

It was time. *Give in, Lazar,* he heard himself beg inwardly. *Let go.*

And then a new voice, cutting shrilly through the pain and despair. *Lazar! You must live. Fight it. For her . . . for Ana, if not for yourself. Live, damn you.* In his agony, Lazar could not tell whether the voice belonged to a man or a woman.

Who? was all he could muster in response.

"Last stroke!" he heard, the voice sounding very far away. Was that the Inflictor? What had been the boy's name?

I am Iridor, said the intruder. *You are done, Lazar. They have finished with you—but we have not. We need you. Promise me you will live. Swear on Ana's life!*

I swear it, Lazar thought he might have replied as he slipped into the void of unconsciousness.

JUMO HAD WATCHED, traitorous tears betraying his usual stoicism, as his master sagged so deeply that only the bonds around his wrists prevented him from slumping fully to the ground. He had watched as Lazar's knees buckled at the thirteenth vicious stroke and heard as Lazar called out Ana's name on the sixteenth lash. Jumo saw all tension leave Lazar's body at the final bite of the Snake. His great friend had surely just yielded his life.

Jumo looked deliberately toward Salmeo, who sought permission from the Zar to end the proceedings. Boaz, white-lipped, nodded and then stomped away, acknowledging no one, leaving his mother in his wake. Herezah barely noticed her son's departure, Jumo noted, for she could not tear her eyes from the ruin of the blood-soaked man.

Jumo slanted a glance at Ana. The terror in her eyes pained him but there was nothing more he could do for her as she was hurried away from the carnage, blood spattering the veil she wore.

"You may remove the Spur," Salmeo said carefully. "Thank you, Inflictor," he added, tossing a purse at the feet of the trembling Shaz.

Everyone retreated from the courtyard in silence, leaving Jumo to look upon the mess with only Shaz and his younger, equally shocked assistant.

"Have I killed him?" Shaz choked out.

"He breathes," Jumo said with an intense relief that lasted only a moment. The Spur's breaths were slow and weak; he was very near death. "Water!" Jumo commanded, and the younger boy rushed away as Shaz approached, crouching and then falling to his knees beside the man whose flesh he had flayed. Bright bone shone through the bloody mess.

"Will he survive?" Shaz begged Jumo.

Jumo shook his head. "I cannot see how." He spoke in a monotone, not wanting to share the depth of his hurt with anyone.

Shaz began to wail softly, rocking backward and forward on his knees. "I told them I wasn't ready. I begged them not to force me do it but Rah made me."

"Rah?"

"The Deputy Inflictor. He was told to claim illness."

"What? When?"

"This morning, after he told me of this flogging. Felz, our superior, is away."

"Ah," Jumo replied, nodding as everything fell into place. "Salmeo suggested Rah be sick, you mean?" Shaz nodded through his haze of tears. "Help me cut him down," Jumo said, suppressing his fury. None of this was the young fellow's fault.

Before they could cut Lazar free, the assistant returned with a bowl of water and rags. Using his fingers, Jumo dripped water through the cracked lips of his unconscious friend, praying silently to his god that this life would be spared. Lazar coughed weakly but it was the gladdest sound Jumo had ever heard.

"Lay those wet rags against his back," Jumo directed, checking again that Lazar breathed. "There is nothing we can do for him here. He will need a physic's attention." The two young men set to. "Do it gently," Jumo cautioned unnecessarily.

As Shaz carefully placed a linen against Lazar's wounds, his eyes widened. "Sir, look," he said, nodding toward the Spur's back.

Jumo, who had been focused on checking Lazar's pulse, glanced at his friend's injuries. "What? I know they're bad."

"No, look," Shaz said, more fear in his voice now. "There," he said, pointing and gently wiping blood from the back of Lazar's neck. Strange bright streaks traversed the Spur's unbroken skin. "What could it be?" Shaz asked.

Jumo blinked slowly with resignation. So the palace had not intended for the Spur to survive. "There is only one thing that leaves livid marks like that," he whispered, his voice filled with rage. He looked up at Shaz. "Poison."

The young man shook his head in desperate denial. "No, sir, not me. There was no poison on the Snake."

Jumo's eyes narrowed. "Are you certain, Shaz?"

Again the youngster balked. "I don't know, sir. I swear it. I was given no instructions to poison the whip. To my knowledge no one tampered with it."

Jumo saw a new shiver overtake Lazar's body. The evening was warm but his body felt cool. The Spur was past shock; he was dying. There was no time for recriminations. "Pick him up," Jumo ordered, and both youngsters obeyed wordlessly, carefully lifting the Spur by his arms. "Lay him over my back!" Jumo commanded, bending slightly.

Shaz hesitated. "How will you manage?"

"Don't worry about me, Inflictor. Worry about yourself and whether your head will still be connected to your body after the Zar hears of this," Jumo growled. Without a farewell, he left the Courtyard of Sorrows and its stench of blood and betrayal.

For a thin man, Jumo was deceptively strong. He was all hard muscle and tough sinew and this was not the first time he had carried his master in this fashion. That previous mercy dash had saved Lazar's life. Let it be so again, he prayed. He hoped his legs would stay loyal and not buckle as he began to run with his heavy burden.

At first he hardly recognized that it was Pez shouting to him. Jumo was so focused on moving his feet forward that he didn't hear his own name being called. The dwarf had to grab him, drawing him to a halt.

"Quick! I have a cart," Pez said. "We must take him to the Sea Temple."

Jumo wore the expression of a man in deep shock. "He's been poisoned," he declared.

Pez nodded gravely. "I figured as much. Come, time is against us."

Jumo carefully laid Lazar on his belly in the back of the cart. "He breathes," he noted in a faraway voice.

Pez squeezed the loyal man's arm. "He's strong of heart, mind, body. If anyone can survive this, he can."

Jumo nodded, his throat closing on a dry sob. Odd questions roamed through his mind as they traveled; who was responsible for the poisoning, why did someone want the Spur dead, would he recover, and if he recovered, would Lazar remain at the palace? Would he want to find the perpetrator or would he simply leave Percheron, return to the nation that truly claimed him as its own? Jumo guided the donkey as if from memory, for he was certainly not concentrating, while Pez, in an effort to clear a path, ran ahead of the car, squealing and throwing nuts at the people they passed.

Jumo finally found his voice. "Why do you suggest the Sea Temple?" he called.

"We'll have help there. Hurry, Jumo."

They said nothing else as they weaved an exasperatingly slow path through the afternoon crowds. Though they had covered Lazar to hide his identity, many passersby still glanced into the back of the cart, raising their eyebrows as they saw the shape of a man beneath the light linen. Pez began to whistle tunelessly, pulling rude faces at the onlookers; Jumo ignored everything but the hammering of his heart, willing the donkey to go faster through the throng. Finally they were out into more open pathways and the beast could make quicker progress.

Standing on the steps of the Sea Temple was the priestess he had seen on the first occasion Lazar had visited the temple. She was shading her eyes against the glare of the sun, waiting for them anxiously.

"Quickly," she urged. "Lay him down by the altar just inside. Let Lyana look upon him."

Jumo grimaced. How many more gods would they call upon today to save Lazar? He hefted his friend once again over his shoulders and felt intense relief to hear the man groan softly. The flight of steps up to the temple entrance felt like a mountain with Lazar's weight on his body and the suffocating crush of fear within himself. Inside the sanctuary it was cool and serene, the silence and darkness calming Jumo slightly as Zafira fretted, pointing to the altar.

"Over there, please," she insisted.

"You have a bed, surely?" Jumo suggested, angry at her.

"Do as Zafira says," Pez said gently.

Jumo knelt and rolled Lazar as carefully as he could off his shoulders. Pez and Zafira guided Lazar onto his belly once again. The linen covering fell away and Zafira's hands flew like startled birds to her mouth, covering a cry of appalled shock at the sight of the Spur's injuries.

"Oh, Mother," she wept. "Help this soul, guide us in this."

Jumo gritted his teeth, suddenly feeling helpless. "The poison will kill him before the wounds," he growled.

"Do we know what type of poison?" Pez's question snapped the priestess out of her stupefaction. Both Pez and Jumo heard her knees protest as she lowered herself beside Lazar. Fresh water and linens were already prepared and waiting. Zafira squeezed out the first linen and began her gentle toil.

Jumo shook his head. "I don't, but I think Shaz is innocent of treachery."

Pez sighed. "I think we can assume that Salmeo is behind this. I wonder who else."

"Not Herezah," Jumo offered somberly. "Are you aware of her fascination with Lazar?"

Pez knelt too. "I'd have to be blind and deaf as well as daft not to be. You're right, she would not have sanctioned this. Lazar's too important to the realm, anyway. Herezah might be ambitious and wicked but she's far from stupid."

"The Vizier?" Jumo offered as they watched Zafira gently cleanse Lazar's back.

"Give him this," Zafira said softly to Pez.

"What is it?"

"It will bring a small measure of comfort. I can't risk putting him to sleep until we know more about the drug used on him. Jumo, help me clean away the blood—I need to see him more clearly."

As Jumo knelt to help Zafira, Pez continued: "Tariq does not have access to the Inflictors or their weapons. No, if this hasn't come from Herezah, and I think you're right in that, then it is all Salmeo's work. He alone can give such a command."

"Shaz seemed to know nothing of it."

Pez shrugged as he dribbled the concoction into Lazar's barely parted lips, grimacing as most of it ran down the side of the Spur's mouth. "Why would he? He is simply the unfortunate one who will take the blame. I imagine even his superiors are pawns in this."

Jumo cleaned the last of the old blood from Lazar's back. Now the Spur's wounds seeped bright, fresh lifeblood from the gentle new attention.

"Most would perish from this alone," Zafira muttered. She

gently traced the livid tracks of the poison. "It moves very slowly. I have no idea what it is."

"So what do we do?" Jumo asked, frightened all over again. Why had he thought an old priestess and a dwarf could save Lazar's life? He should have brought his friend to a city physic, he berated himself. Helplessly, he hung his head just as a shadow darkened the entrance of the temple.

"I'm sorry," Zafira said from the ground where she knelt. "You've come at a trying time, as you can see."

"I do see." The new visitor was a woman. She was soft-spoken and her voice had a musical quality as she asked, "May I come in? Perhaps I might help?"

Jumo watched the hooded figure step out of the doorway, where she was encircled by the light of the sun, into the shadows. Although she was petite, her presence seemed to pulse with an aura of authority. Somehow none of them could deny her access to Lazar.

She knelt beside him, making a soft sound of concern. She pushed back her hood and Jumo noticed first her pale hair, which he assumed must have been golden when she was young. As she turned to face him, he saw that the woman was indeed older, skin like beautiful ivory parchment, unblemished except for the handsome lines of time. Somehow she seemed familiar, though Jumo could not determine from where. The deep kindness she conveyed as she looked at him eased his despair even though her words did not. "He will slip beyond us within hours," she said gravely.

Jumo felt his heart sink. "Can you help him?"

"He is very close to death. I should have seen something like this coming." This last she said beneath her breath but Pez's sharp hearing caught it, and he frowned, puzzled. He glanced toward Zafira, who wore a similar expression of bafflement. They both snatched a look at Jumo but Lazar's friend was concentrating deeply, his entire focus given over to the old woman.

"There is poison," he confirmed, and she nodded, leaning close to Lazar's back and sniffing. Then she nodded again, deep in thought. "I think this is drezden. A nasty, debilitating concoction. Normally, it's administered orally to a healthy person— death follows within hours. It has a distinctive spicy smell, reminiscent of clove . . . can you detect it?" All three shook their heads dumbly. "You've all been a bit preoccupied," she offered kindly. "In this instance the drezden has been administered topically via the weapon used to flog him. It is not an effective way to deliver the poison, but as you can see by the tracks, it is working, albeit slowly. This is our single hope."

"He can beat it?" Jumo asked hopefully.

The old woman paused. "Unlikely, and his horrific injuries will probably kill him first." She gave him a look of genuine sorrow. "I'm sorry, Jumo. We will try to save him, but you should know we will probably fail."

Pez noticed that she used Jumo's name, making a friend of him, and yet they had not been introduced. "Do we know you?"

"In a way," she said, indicating that they should lay the wet linens back in place. "Those will need to be kept constantly damp."

"I have never met you before," Pez said, a soft challenge in his tone.

"Ah, but you have, friend Pez. Remember a red silk ribbon?"

His initial curiozity curdled to shock. The Bundle Woman! She looked different and yet, now that he thought about it, somehow the same. She was not as old as she had originally appeared to him.

"How do you know my name?" Jumo suddenly asked.

"I know all of your names. You are Jumo, this is Pez, and"—she bowed her head slightly—"here we have a sister, Zafira."

"You are a priestess?" Zafira exclaimed, obvious delight in her voice.

The old woman smiled but said nothing until she looked down upon their patient. "And this is Lazar, whom we shall probably lose but not without a fight." Her words reassured Jumo, even though he could almost hear the death knell for the man he loved.

"What have you given him?" the woman continued.

"The root of calzen," Zafira answered, "to ease his pain, not that it can really deaden this sort of pain. I couldn't risk a soporific."

"The right decision," the woman assured her. "I cannot do anything here. We have to move him."

"Is it safe to?" Pez inquired.

"Lazar is dying, Pez. Nothing we do can make much of a difference unless I can get him to the Isle of Stars."

"The leper colony?" Jumo exclaimed, voicing the shock Pez and Zafira also felt.

The stranger shrugged. "It's safe and no one will find him there."

"Is it not dangerous to risk the leper colony?" Zafira asked, unable to mask her incredulity.

"I doubt it. There are only a few inhabitants and none that will trouble us."

"Who are you?" Pez demanded.

"Questions, questions!" The woman smiled and the warmth made their hearts feel instantly lighter. "I will answer them all but I have a precious man's life in the balance. Please, help me get him to the island, although I suspect, Pez, that you should return to the palace."

Pez knew he would be missed at the palace and that was courting danger. "Yes but—"

"Go, brother Pez. You cannot help Lazar any more than you have. I promise we shall get word to you, and besides, I gather I have some questions to answer for you." Again her gentle smile prevented Pez from pushing further.

He touched Lazar gently on his blood-streaked face and then was moved to bend close and kiss his forehead.

"I shall see you again, my friend," he whispered, and with one sad glance toward the others, he left the temple.

As he wended his way back to the palace, Pez pondered— among the many confusing aspects of today—the few moments when he was sure he had lost consciousness. It had happened during Lazar's flogging. Pez realized that one moment he had been dashing at high speed from the temple to find Jumo again, and the next he was out cold on the roadside. No one had bothered with him and the dwarf had regained his wits slowly, uninterrupted by curious passersby. He could not account for the fainting spell, or what might have occurred during it. The sudden weakness made him uncomfortable.

And now the Bundle Woman returning to his life. Could she save Lazar? She'd convinced Jumo she could not, even though their friend still breathed, still clung to life. But she had soothed them all too. What skill, to comfort in the face of certain suffering.

Although Pez returned to the palace counting loudly in Merlinean, he was deeply confused and anxious, but no one noticed. It was what they were used to.

19

Ana was hurried away from the Courtyard of Sorrows and taken directly to a sleeping chamber, which, she realized, she must be sharing with three other girls. The four beds being tidied by a slave suggested as much. The Elim passed Ana into the care of an older woman who had presumably been waiting for her.

"She's in shock," the woman commented, looking at her.

Horz, who had accompanied Ana and tried to soothe her, had been ignored by the odalisque, blamed by him, in fact, for what had befallen Lazar. He spoke quietly to the slave. "She will need your care—perhaps something gentle to help her rest. As you know, she has been out all night and this afternoon she witnessed something no child should see. It has been difficult for her."

The slave nodded. "Come, child, Elza will take care of you

now." She held out her hand to Ana. "You are safe, my girl. It will be just the two of us."

Ana gratefully obeyed, glad to rid herself of the eunuch escort. "Does he live?" she demanded of the Elim before they left.

"I doubt it," Horz said softly, and again Ana refused the sympathy she saw in his unhappy eyes. "No one could survive that."

"Please, leave us now," Elza said, and turned back to Ana. "Let me take that bloodied veil off you," the woman said kindly.

"My name is Ana," she replied, glaring again at the head of the Elim, who still remained, looking surprisingly awkward.

Horz's presence seemed to distress Ana, and Elza glanced sharply at him. "You should leave her alone with me now, please." He and the other Elim did so silently.

Ana relaxed slightly once they had departed. "I want to keep this," she said suddenly, rolling the veil into a ball, as if by doing so, she could stifle the pain of Lazar's potential death within it. She could not think about such a grievous outcome right now.

"What?" the woman exclaimed. "This messy thing? Whatever for?"

Ana had no desire to let anyone know that Lazar's blood— her only physical connection with him—meant more to her than anything else. To cast the veil away would feel like casting him away. Keeping the droplets of his blood was ghoulish, she knew, but they were all she had. She would shed no more tears over this man. Though she hardly understood her feelings, she believed she loved Lazar—would never love anyone with the same intensity she felt for him.

Ana had chided herself the previous night, telling herself

that her heart was deceiving her. She was so young and she guessed Lazar was a man of almost thirty, maybe older. It was a ludicrous situation, but she could not control the rapid thumping of her heart every time the man was near. Although they had not spent much time together, she could re-create the feel of her hand in his, the smile she worked so hard to win on his face, the softening of his expression when their eyes met. She could bring to life in her mind the rich timbre of his voice with its foreign lilt. And the warmth of his body standing next to her the night before in the Choosing Room—it had felt to her as if a furnace had burned between them. She had risked leaning closer to him—in front of Herezah—just to feel the hardness of his body.

She had wondered long and deep, as she prayed to Lyana in the temple, whether it was wrong of her to desire Lazar. But she felt powerless in his presence. Where Salmeo's touch caused her entire being to clamp shut, just a glance from Lazar achieved the opposite effect. She felt overwhelmed by the flood of desire, tempted to act upon it, though she knew not how.

Lazar, she appreciated, had not once in their brief encounters behaved in anything other than an entirely appropriate manner. Even when he had let his guard down in the bazaar, his treatment of her had remained dignified. In Ana's moments of reflection, she had wondered if she was reading far too much into their few interactions. And yet this afternoon, in the Courtyard of Sorrows, she had felt their bond as a tangible link and she had known that she was right. She was not lying to herself. As he had borne her punishment, she heard him whisper her name. He had spoken to her alone *and* he had been prepared to give his life for her—it was too much, more than she deserved. And now, because of her, he might be dead. She forced herself to believe otherwise, cast a prayer to Lyana, made a bargain with the Goddess: *Let him survive and I will make no further claim on him. I will not pursue him and I will not encourage him. I will remain steadfast to my duty and cold to any entreaties I should be fortunate to win from him.*

Looking at the veil, Ana realized that Elza was still waiting for an answer. Pez's warning to trust no one resonated loudly in her thoughts. "This was part of my first formal occasion in the harem. It's a special keepsake for me."

"How grim of you, child. Very well—put it away and don't frighten the other girls with it. That's your bed over there."

"By the window?" Ana was surprised. "I would have thought that one would be taken already."

"Pez—the Zar's mad jester—came and slept on it last night. He refused to leave it until the girls got tired of asking."

"Oh?"

"And then he said he'd put a curse on the bed and the others got so frightened I had to shoo that terrible dwarf away. Have you seen him yet?" Elza didn't wait for Ana to answer, continuing, "He's such a fool. But the young Zar loves him as much as his father before him did. I don't see the charm, myself. I think Pez is a nuisance and I'm sorry you're left with a cursed bed."

"I have seen him," Ana replied carefully. "How did the women before us like him?"

"Oh, well enough. He entertained them. He's harmless, I suppose, but he disrupted those children so much they could hardly settle."

Ana had to suppress a smile. She knew Pez had chosen that bed just for her. It was easily in the best position in the whole chamber. "Well, I'm not afraid of any curse."

"That's the spirit," Elza said, though she wasn't paying

much attention to Ana's words, mostly glad the girl seemed unscathed by the afternoon's ordeal. "You've had your Test of Virtue, haven't you?" At Ana's nod, she continued briskly, "Good. Let's get you into a warm bath. Put this robe on and come with me. You're in for a special experience."

Ana slipped into the silken robe, feeling the soft touch of it against her skin, and then begged a moment to tuck Lazar's Veil—as she thought of it—beneath her pillow. He would always sleep close to her now.

THEY HAD ROWED in silence through the late afternoon. Jumo worked the oars while Zafira fussed over the unconscious Spur; the stranger sat with her back to the rest of them, chanting beneath her breath as if in prayer.

She spoke suddenly, interrupting their thoughts. "Can you row close to Beloch?"

"The waves might dash us against the giant," Jumo warned. The sea wasn't rough, but he was put out by her odd request when time was so against them.

"Beloch will not hurt us."

Jumo mumbled a protest but steered them closer to the giant, who loomed, massive, over their tiny boat. "Why must you do this?"

"I want to speak to him," she answered, and she did just that, balancing herself precariously as the boat rocked perilously. None of her companions understood what she said to the giant, for she murmured her words beneath her breath.

Jumo scowled. "We'll all drown."

The old woman smiled serenely at him. "Thank you. It meant a lot to me that I could do this."

"Do you speak to the giant each time you go to the island?" he asked.

"No," she said, her voice suddenly detached, as if her thoughts were far away from them. "I have never rowed to the island before."

Jumo, annoyed and confused, wisely held his tongue.

"WE REQUIRE NO REFRESHMENT," Zar Boaz said to Bin, dismissing the servant but also, to his frustration, revealing that none of his wrath had dissipated. He knew he must learn to disguise his emotions if he was to emulate his father. Frowning, he looked at Salmeo and Tariq, who stood before him. Immediately the two bowed.

Boaz did not acknowledge their courtesy. He reined in his anger and steadied his voice. "Have we heard any more?"

The Grand Master Eunuch adopted a look of concern. "No, Majesty. I dealt with the pig Inflictor," he lied, "who had no skill at all for his chosen career."

Boaz nodded. "Where were the senior Inflictors—Shaz cannot be all that we have in the palace?"

Salmeo shook his head, his frown deepening. "No, Great One, that's right, but the two senior Inflictors were unavailable. The Head Inflictor was not in the city itself and his deputy was sick; we had no option but to use Shaz. Would you like me to have him punished?"

"Not especially. I would prefer that you punish his seniors who were not present. We cannot have the head and his deputy both unavailable. It is unforgivable!"

Boaz instantly regretted calling this meeting while his emotions were still raw. Seeing his friend so broken had sickened him sufficiently that when he had strode from the balcony, he had actually lost his morning's meal into the bushes not far from his chambers. Mercifully, with no guards on the balcony with them, no one but his mother had been privy to this show of weakness and she had sensibly said nothing, simply offered him a linen to wipe his mouth.

"I'm retiring for the day, Boaz" were her only words, and hearing the slight quaver in her voice, he knew that Herezah was as sickened as he. She had learned to control her physical reactions and he vowed to do the same. Once again he privately acknowledged that no matter how much she frustrated him, she still had plenty to teach him, and his father had been politically astute to choose her as his favorite. In response to her words, he had nodded but also risked taking and squeezing her hand in thanks. He knew she would share with no one his embarrassing show of distress.

Salmeo cleared his throat and Boaz was returned from his thoughts. "Shall I punish them, High One?"

"What would you suggest?" Boaz privately admonished himself as he watched Salmeo's eyes narrow, and knew he was being tested by the Grand Master Eunuch.

"There are a few different options, depending on how far you feel this punishment should extend, Majesty," Salmeo replied carefully, deliberately being evasive while cornering the Zar into ordering someone's demise. "Are you calling for death?"

Boaz took a deep breath. "If the Spur does not survive the flogging, Grand Master Eunuch, then one of the Inflictors must pay for their collective failing with his own life."

"The choice is mine—is that what you're saying, High One?"

Boaz hated Salmeo in that moment. He fixed him with a stare he'd seen the old Zar give many times when his ire was up—and used the moment to decide whether or not he could back down; there was a man's life at stake but he was still privately enraged at the suffering of his friend the Spur, when his flogging, as a protector, was meant to be more symbolic than anything as sinister as it had become. No, he could not turn back now. His tone was cutting when he spoke again. "We're both speaking Percherese, Grand Master Eunuch. I'm sure you understand my order."

Salmeo bowed, disturbed by the Zar's sudden confidence. "As you command, Majesty."

"Where has the Spur been taken? Tariq, I wish my personal doctors to attend him."

Tariq's jewels glinted on the ends of his quivering beard. Really, this sort of task was below him but he supposed he ought to ingratiate himself with the Zar. "Of course, High One, I will seek that information for you. Is there anything else I can do, Your Majesty?" Tariq all but felt Salmeo's sneer.

"That will be sufficient. Where is Odalisque Ana?"

Salmeo answered. "The Elim escorted her to her chambers to bathe and rest after her night's adventures. Her clothes were bloodied, you know."

Boaz privately felt the girl should rest. "Bring her to my private study. Immediately."

"Yes, High One." Salmeo bowed to avoid revealing his expression of surprise. "Should I inform the Valide of—"

"My mother," Boaz began, unable to control his rising temper now, "has absolutely nothing to do with this. You would be well advised, Grand Master Eunuch, to learn to do my bidding without questioning it. I will not warn you again. I might be young, Salmeo, but I am the highest authority in this realm. Or are you already placing your loyalty in the wrong place?"

The huge man's flabby face wobbled with the effort of holding back his own rage. "No, my Zar. I just thought it right to caution against—"

Boaz laced his next words with contempt. "Don't think, Salmeo. When the command comes from me, just do it! And don't ever caution me again. Is that clear?"

Salmeo bowed to hide his own disgust at being spoken to publicly in this manner. "Yes, Majesty," he managed.

Tariq stifled a sneer.

"I'M AFRAID I CAN'T give you the treat I promised, Odalisque Ana," Elza said, returning to her after taking a whispered message at the door. "We have to bathe you quickly in a tub."

"Why?"

"The Zar wishes to see you."

"Boaz?"

The slave looked at her, aghast. "Hush, child! Never speak his name unless he alone gives you the authority. Haven't they taught you anything yet?"

"I've spent only a few hours in the palace. How could they?" Ana replied tartly.

"You'll do well to curb that defiance in your tone, Miss Ana. Take my advice, for your haughtiness will not be tolerated. Rule number one," the slave began, leading Ana to a small chamber filled with single cubicles, "is you never speak the Zar's name. He is Your Majesty, High One, Mightiest of the Mighties, or similar."

Ana nodded, listening carefully and remembering Pez's warning that she must blend into the community of the harem or risk Salmeo's attention.

"Rule number two: bathing daily is part of harem life." Elza pointed toward the cubicle. "We use these rarely. From now on, you will use the main pavilion and spend the entire morning there on your grooming."

"What a waste," Ana murmured.

Elza smirked. "You'd better start getting used to boredom, Miss Ana, for you'll spend your whole life getting ready and hoping the Zar will wish to share even a few words with you."

"Looks like I haven't very long to wait, doesn't it?" Ana replied wearily.

"Oh, child, you are in for a very rough time of it if you keep that attitude much longer." Elza sighed. "Now hurry, slip out of your robe. I have to get you washed and dressed."

So much for a rest, Ana thought, dreading what the Zar would want with her after his public admonishment.

JUMO INSISTED ON CARRYING Lazar on his back again. Their host led the way surprisingly briskly up broad, mercifully shallow steps cut into the cliff face. Zafira climbed slowly next to Jumo.

"What are we doing here?" Jumo muttered to her.

"I don't know but it feels right, don't you think? It's too much of a coincidence that she came along just when we needed help. She said she'd answer our questions—we must be patient."

At the top of their climb they saw a cottage set back from the cliff edge, a small copse encircling its back.

"Here we are," the old woman said. "The lepers are housed a long way from here. There are only six of them left anyway, and I rarely see them. Jumo, can you manage?"

"Yes, let's just hurry. He's struggling to breathe."

Once inside, the stranger took command again. "Lay him on the pallet and light some candles from that lantern, Jumo. We shall be busy and the sun will set without us knowing. Zafira, perhaps you would make us some quishtar?" The priestess, happy to busy her hands, immediately set to finding the utensils and materials she needed.

Their host returned her attention to the man on the bed and his anxious friend, who was placing lit candles nearby. "Are you afraid of snakes, Jumo?" Lazar's friend shook his head absently, focused on the gray pallor of Lazar's complexion and the rapid heaving of his chest. "Good. In the cellar is a heavy-lidded jar. Inside are two snakes. The yellow-bellied one is harmless. The one with the striped back is deadly. He is the one we need. Have you handled a snake before?"

"I have," Jumo replied. "What does this have to do with Lazar?"

"Drezden is made from the poison of the drezia snake. It's favored by assassins who want to be gone well before the death occurs. If not given orally, drezia venom is deadly but slow. On its passage to the heart, it simply numbs. Once it reaches the heart, however, it paralyzes and death is instant."

"You want me to milk the snake?" Jumo asked, deliberately rushing her.

"Precisely," she replied. "Here, straight into this," she added, pointing Jumo to a small porcelain cup.

And at last he heard through her mild manner to the concern she had worked to disguise. "Be careful," she cautioned. "If the snake bites you, I have no medicine that will stop the poison killing you."

"Very reassuring," he muttered as he began to descend and the stranger returned her attention to Lazar.

"His breathing sounds very shallow," Zafira noted.

"Not a good sign," their host replied. "But that's to be expected. My name is Ellyana. Forgive my poor manners."

Zafira nodded, accepting the woman's unnecessary apology. "Shall I take off the linens?" she asked, pointing.

"Yes, please." They heard a small scuffle from below. "Jumo?" Ellyana called, an element of fright in her tone.

"I'm all right," came a muffled voice. The two women glanced at each other with relief.

Jumo emerged a few moments later with a clear liquid—barely enough to cover the bottom of the cup.

"It is enough," Ellyana said, answering his look of worry. "Now, let me explain. I promise to be brief. I have seen this sort of poisoning before and delivered in a similar style. It can be beaten. However, if Lazar survives, you need to know that he will never be whole again." She paused, and when neither listener spoke she continued: "Jumo, your master will always need the poison of the drezia snake close. He and it are now bound together, forever, like lovers—even though they are enemies."

"What occurs?" Zafira asked for Jumo's sake; the man was so stunned by the news that he seemed unable to speak for himself.

"There will be no warning when it afflicts him again. A trembling, wasting fever will strike. Very debilitating. The only temporary cure is more of the venom in its purest form and in tiny quantities . . . far less than we have here. Right now, though, we have to flush the poison from his body. We need lots of quishtar and my own brew. There will be pain—severe—and you will both need to be strong for him. He is going to suffer badly if he is to recover."

"Will he recover?" Jumo dared to ask.

"If I'm frank—and I fear I should be with you—then I would say he will most likely perish. Too much time has elapsed, and his wounds are frighteningly dangerous. The poison aside, those injuries alone have the capacity to kill him," Ellyana said gently. "We will try but I think you must be prepared to lose him, Jumo."

"He is strong," Jumo countered.

Her tone was even more tender when she risked closing a hand over his arm. "I know. And you will be equally strong for your friend."

Jumo ferociously blinked back the tears rushing to betray him. "What about his wounds?"

"We will need to clean them thoroughly and then sew the deeper ones to close them against infection. For the rest we shall have to rely on this salve," she said, indicating a stone jar. "Could someone help me with that, it's very heavy." Jumo obliged, grimacing at its weight, and slid off the lid at her nod. "It smells bad but it is a wonder ointment," she continued. "Perhaps you wouldn't mind smearing that onto some of the less vicious wounds right now. It will seal them from the air, from disease."

"They're all vicious," Jumo said, shaking his head at the state of Lazar's body.

"Zafira, do you have steady hands?"

"I suppose, why?"

"You will need to do the sewing, my sister." Ellyana held up her own shaking fingers. "Part of growing old," and her sad smile was only for the priestess, who understood the afflictions of age.

Zafira looked worried. "I'm not sure I can—"

"I will help you," Ellyana assured, not giving the priestess another chance to protest. "We must all wash our fingers with this soap paste," she warned, pointing to a pot. "It will burn your skin but it will ensure your fingers are very clean and we will not infect Lazar's wounds as we treat them." At their nods, she continued briskly, "Right, let's clean our hands and then we begin. We have a long night ahead of us."

As if in response, Lazar groaned weakly.

"WHAT DO YOU MEAN, you can't find any trace of him?" Boaz demanded.

Tariq's lips pursed, evidencing his frustration at having failed the Zar in the first task assigned him. "Forgive me, High One. I have sent runners to the Spur's house, to the barracks, even to the city temples, where I thought he might be laid out by the priests for medical help. No one has any information to give us."

"Well, someone must have seen him depart. Where is Shaz? Perhaps he has some notion."

"No, High One. Apparently Shaz and his assistant handed the Spur's body to that fellow called Jumo, Lazar's second, and the man departed the Courtyard of Sorrows. One would assume he'd take him straight back to the Spur's house for care from a physic, but apparently not."

Boaz frowned. "Send out word into the city. Someone must have seen something. I want information from you and your spies by the end of the day, Vizier."

Tariq bowed, wondering at Boaz's new confidence. It was as though the boy had aged five years since the afternoon flogging. The Vizier felt he was being ordered around like a slave by a lad whose voice had barely broken. "Immediately, Your Majesty," he said through clenched teeth hidden by his beard. A soft gong sounded, saving him further conversation with the young Zar.

"Go about your business, Vizier. I'll await your news," Boaz said wearily. "Enter!" he called over Tariq's head. Bin emerged into the chamber as the Vizier departed. "Yes?"

"High One, the Grand Master Eunuch and Odalisque Ana await you in the antechamber of your study."

"Ah, good. I wish to change. Send in my dresser."

"Of course. I will bring your visitor into the study when you are ready."

Boaz returned to his bedchamber and within moments the servant arrived. After changing into loose linens, he asked the man to order refreshments. "Some frozen sherbets and a flask of chirro," he suggested. The man bowed and departed.

Boaz stepped from his chamber into a small reception room that led to his private study, which was smaller and more intimate than the one in which he normally received visitors. He was paying Ana a high compliment in permitting her to visit him in this room. He knew he was risking the wrath of all those vying for his loyalty, a fact that pleased him greatly. Once inside, he took a deep breath before reaching to pull a cord, sounding a bell outside.

The double doors were opened and Bin ushered in a slim, veiled figure dwarfed by a sour-looking Grand Master Eunuch. Boaz realized he was actually holding his breath in anticipation. He let it out slowly as the oddly matched pair stepped into the middle of the room, and Ana, well prepared by Salmeo, immediately sank to her knees and then prostrated herself as was required. Bin closed the doors.

Salmeo took the lead. "Your High One, this is most unusual, and breaks harem protocol. The girls are not yet acquainted with all of the rules and we haven't even enjoyed the ceremony of the handkerchiefs." Although the words were polite enough, the tone was acid. "Perhaps I should remain here with the odalisque Ana whilst—"

"That will not be necessary." Boaz was going to add *thank you* and stopped himself at the last instant. It was time he got used to giving commands. "I am changing some rules, Salmeo." He did not allow Salmeo a chance to suggest caution at such an idea. "The first is that it is to be my choice as to when and how I meet with the members of the harem. I think the handkerchief ceremony is romantic but trite for these modern days. If I'm old enough to rule, I'm certainly old enough to be in the company of a female my own age, in the middle of the afternoon and without a chaperone, and certainly without all the trials and innuendo that had to be plowed through in my father's day."

Salmeo's feelings, normally so well disguised, were plainly written over his aghast expression. "But, Your High One, this totally contravenes the way of the harem, I must—"

Boaz feigned dismay. "I trust you're not about to caution me?" he said, amazed that his voice was so steady, the tone so condescending. It felt suddenly wonderful to wield a power that could have a man such as this gabbling before him. He pressed his point. "I'm not bedding her, Grand Master Eunuch—not yet—I simply wish to talk with her. You're very welcome to remain whilst we speak." He paused only briefly to take a breath before adding: "So long as you remain outside. I desire a private conversation with Odalisque Ana."

The huge black man again opened his mouth to speak but nothing came out. He glared into the Zar's simmering expression. He could not win this one but he knew who could. "I shall do that, High One," he answered as humbly as he could manage. Then he bowed and left, hurrying to seek an audience with the Valide.

Boaz looked at the figure on the ground. "Please, Odalisque Ana, rise." When she was standing before him, her eyes still cast to the floor as presumably she'd been instructed, he gestured toward some comfortable divans by the grand windows. "Join me."

"I thought you were angry with me, Zar Boaz."

He sighed softly. "I am. Lazar has suffered pointlessly today because of your headstrong ways. But I made my rebuke public for entirely different reasons than you think. I think the Spur will have understood, so be assured I haven't asked you here to make you suffer more. I'm sure you're suffering enough."

She bit her lip hard in order to force back the tears. "I have never felt more lost than I do right now . . . or bereft. If I could change what happened today, if I could take back my actions, I hope you know I would, Zar Boaz."

Sincerely done, he thought approvingly. *Enough chastizing; she feels guilty enough.* "You'll have to forgive the decor," he said brightly. "This is my father's choice. I haven't the heart to change it, even though the Valide suggests I impose my own style."

"You loved your father." She spoke from behind the gauzy pale blue veil, eyes still downcast.

"You may remove your veil, Odalisque Ana. It is not required in my private presence, and I allow you to look upon me." She raised her eyes and he was pleased to see the directness with which she held his gaze now that permission was hers. She took off her veil slowly, careful not to disturb her hair, which had been brushed carefully with a hundred strokes, Elza counting each and smearing an oil into it to make it shine even more brightly. As her face was revealed to him once again, and this time at such close range, Boaz felt his breath catch. He had thought her beautiful from a distance, but he now discovered she was infinitely more fetching this close. Her skin was smooth and unblemished but slightly burnished from the sun. He remembered how his father's women had worked hard to keep their complexions pale but on Ana this golden coloring was like a glow from within.

"I did love my father very much. I miss him," he said in response to her earlier comment.

"I love my father too, Zar Boaz. I miss him as deeply as you miss yours."

"Please, sit down with me." He watched her glide to the divans and carefully seat herself opposite him. "Where is your family from?"

"West. The foothills. My father is a goatherd."

"Is he proud that his daughter now lives in the palace? It must be a far cry from what he is used to." He had considered this a fair question, one designed to encourage her to talk about the family she had left behind. He was not ready for the quiet rebuke.

"My father is a simple man, Your High One. He has no concept of palace life. He also had no say in my being brought here. If it were left to him, I think he would be proud for me to have remained as a goatherd's daughter." She lifted her chin, and as her eyes met his he instantly recognized a kindred spirit: both of them too young to be on the paths they were on, both wishing they could be pursuing the lives they wanted rather than the ones they were being forced to follow.

"Forgive me, Ana, I meant no insult."

"None taken, Majesty," she returned smoothly.

Boaz was already fascinated by her, did not know what to say next. He was relieved by a gentle knock at the door. "Come," he answered. A servant entered bearing a tray. "Ah, I took the liberty of organizing some refreshments," he explained as the man laid out the food and wine. "I hope you won't say you don't eat sherbet."

And Boaz heard the girl in her for the first time "Oh no, I do," she gushed, "I tasted it in the bazaar."

Boaz grinned. "I heard about your adventure. It's why I wanted to meet you."

Instantly her green eyes, brilliant as gems, clouded. "I've seen the error of my ways, High One."

"Ana, I wasn't going to reprimand you. I was going to congratulate you." She held his gaze, unsure of what she'd heard. "Zarab knows I yearn for some freedom myself."

"But surely you have that as Zar?"

"I think I am as much a prisoner of my own palace as you are. I wish I had your reckless spirit. Truly. It must have taken real courage to spit in the eye of Salmeo. I know I shouldn't say this to you but I felt elated when I heard." He all but whispered his words for fear the fat man could hear through the walls.

"Do you mean that?" Her eyes glittered again.

He touched his hand to his forehead and then his lips in the region's manner of communicating that he spoke the truth. "Our secret, though."

It was her first reason to smile since she had hugged Jumo the previous day—and at the memory, her smile was wiped from her face. "You were there this morning," she said flatly. "I can't derive any pleasure from my courage—as you call it— after what the Spur went through on my behalf."

"He must think very highly of you, Ana."

He watched her face darken, tried to imagine what thoughts she hid. "I think he feels responsible because it was he who bartered for me."

Boaz heard a hesitation in her voice, and wondered why. "He took no gold in exchange for you, I hear."

She nodded sadly. "I have not been given any information as to how he is."

Boaz knew he shouldn't be sharing so much information but it felt so long since he'd been around someone he wanted to call friend. "I have been trying to find out more. Rumor has it that he won't live past this day." He watched shock hit that lovely face as effectively as if he'd leaned over and slapped it.

"That can't be so, High One!"

"But you saw the pitiful state he was left in. Even from my more distant spot I could see his back opened to the bone. None of us should be surprised if he's already dead . . . but we should all be ashamed."

"I couldn't see the damage. I could only see his honorable face and what it cost him to bear his injuries without sharing his pain with all of us."

Boaz whistled low under his breath. "I don't think anyone there would have thought less of him if he'd screamed with each lash."

"I suspect screaming is not Lazar's way," she said softly. "He would consider it an intolerable weakness in himself."

"You seem to understand him intimately despite the short term of your relationship." Boaz saw her frown at his words.

"Er, I mean that you seem to know him very well." She did not respond and the young Zar struggled, feeling awkward. "I have sent runners out all over the city. We shall have news of the Spur soon." Her eyes rose again to regard him and he could see the hope reflected within. "I shall get word to you, I promise."

Ana studied him a moment longer. "You know Salmeo will be telling your mother about this meeting."

Boaz bristled. "I am the Zar, Ana, or do you, like the Grand Master Eunuch, forget that?"

"No, High One. It is my turn to apologize. I meant no offense. I am only concerned that I have been marked as a troublemaker and do not wish you to get into any bother on my account."

Boaz laughed. "I am the Zar," he repeated. "No one has any authority over me." Standing, he felt taller, stronger suddenly. "Thank you for making me remind myself of that."

"I beg your pardon, High One?"

"Well, I think I too had overlooked just how powerful a person I am now. My father tried to tell me on his deathbed. He urged me to remember that I was the Chosen One. He selected me above all of his other sons to rule after him. Rule I will and I will not be cowed by an ambitious eunuch . . . or my mother."

She appreciated his fighting words and heard a kindred spirit, but also knew how helpless she was by comparison. "I hardly know more than your name and age, Your Majesty, but I hope you don't feel it is forward of me to say how proud you make me feel. You speak to my own heart. Slave I might be considered but I too will not be humbled by Salmeo . . . or—" She stopped, realizing she might be about to make a grave mistake.

"My mother . . . you may say it," Boaz encouraged. He reached for his goblet of wine and drank, moving to sit by her. The sherbets had melted into a fusion of color in their silver dishes, untouched on the tray. "You may speak of her before me."

He saw how carefully she watched him and guessed she had been warned, probably by Lazar, to trust few, if any, in the harem. "Ana, I am not your enemy. You may speak freely."

"I think not, High One," she said finally, disappointing him further. "I must not speak out of turn. It is probably wise if I keep my thoughts to myself."

"You don't understand. I thought we might be friends."

"You have many new friends now, Zar. There are forty-one other girls, as I understand it. All pretty, all picked carefully to suit your needs."

"And I'll bet none of them is as spirited as you, Ana. I should like to spend some time with you. Perhaps I can teach you about life in the palace and you can teach me about life beyond it."

"A Zar teaching a slave." It wasn't a question and he could hear the note of disdain in her tone as if she couldn't conceive of such a thing.

"Why not? How do you think my mother rose to her station, Ana? Don't be fooled by all of the grandeur. Every Zar ever born is the product of a slave. My father and his father before him, and his father before that, mated with slaves and sired the next Mightiest of the Mighty."

She nodded, frowning as if seriously considering his words before she replied. "Your High One, may I ask a boon of you?"

"So soon, Odalisque Ana?" She looked back at him, chastened.

"A jest," he added quickly. "Ask me."

Her words came out in a rush. "Please don't single me out, Majesty."

"What do you mean by that?"

"I have been warned to keep my head down. I have been marked as trouble by powerful people. I have no choice but to live this life of an odalisque, but perhaps I can live quietly and not create more ripples that reach the Valide or the Grand Master Eunuch."

He nodded, understanding perfectly. "You forget that although they rule the harem, I rule them. If I choose to see you because you interest me, they cannot stop me."

"No, I suppose not, but that doesn't stop them making my life miserable as punishment."

"That's because you yet don't understand the ways of the harem. Your role is to interest me. You can hardly be punished for pleasing the Zar. Will you trust me, even though I suspect you've been warned to do the opposite?" He watched her blush and saw that he had guessed rightly. "Trust that I wish you no harm and that I would appreciate your friendship for now, nothing more."

"Of course—I can hardly refuse you, Zar Boaz."

He smiled sadly. She had been cautioned well. "I shall not allow anyone to object when I seek out your company."

"Will you be fair to everyone?" she implored.

"If I enjoy some of the others, yes, I will spend time with them. I cannot guarantee it. My father once told me that a beautiful woman can be just as vapid or dull as a plain one. Beauty is no guarantee of intelligence or charming company. I am only now beginning to grasp what he meant and I understand why he chose my mother. She was always ambitious but she was also quick of mind and wit—and that appealed to him."

"Is that why you pursue me, High One?"

Boaz laughed. "I think you're wonderfully daring. Something I'm not. If I didn't like you so much already, Ana, I'd urge you to keep following your feisty path and do everything you can to irritate and exasperate Salmeo."

"You will keep your promise and let me know what you might discover about the Spur?"

"I shall, for it gives me an excuse to see you again," he said brightly.

"The Grand Master Eunuch said it is not usual to—"

Boaz was quick to interrupt her. "Salmeo can say what he wishes, Ana. He is not the Zar. Things are going to change. My father chose me because he believed in me."

"And your mother?" she risked.

"Is Valide only because of me." As he repeated Pez's words, Boaz realized he hadn't seen the dwarf since the flogging. He returned his attention to Ana. "She will not give me too much grief. The first thing I shall do is introduce a picnic at each full moon."

Her eyes brightened. "Outside the palace?"

At seeing her pleasure, a jolt of desire coursed through him, startling him. "Of course. I too feel cooped up here. I know when I was younger and lived amongst the harem women, they always complained about how dull their lives were. For all the luxuriousness of their existence, each day was the same for them. Well, I can change that."

"You are wonderful, Your Majesty. I know I thank you for it and I feel sure the other girls will too."

He beamed, enjoying her praise, wanting to see that glitter in her eyes often and feel that spark of desire surge.

"I'm sorry about the sherbet," he said, eyeing the rainbow-colored mess on the tray.

"You're the Zar, I presume you can order it again?" she suggested airily, clearly emboldened by his words of power.

Boaz laughed. "You're good for me, Odalisque Ana. I'm certainly going to enjoy seeing you often."

20

Pez fretted that he should not have left Lazar to the ministrations of a stranger. He should have stayed, kept vigil, urged his friend to hold on to life. Why did he have such a sense of doom? The only reassurance he could derive was that Jumo was present. Jumo would sooner die himself than lose Lazar. Pez knew Lazar's companion would send news shortly whether the fight had been won or lost.

Lost? He couldn't imagine Percheron without Lazar striding around it. Man and city belonged to each other. Surely he couldn't die as a result of the city's own punishment system?

These troubling thoughts put Pez into a bleak state of mind. Instead of feigning his normal ridiculous moods, he plunged into a somber one. He began counting backward in Haslin— any scholar would recognize the language but it sounded strange to the lay ear, and that's what Pez needed. So long as he maintained an air of distraction, even of disturbance, no one at the palace would bat an eyelid over his not cavorting as usual. The numbers he muttered managed to keep him focused as he plunged deeper into the halls toward the harem. He intended to find Ana, but as he approached the forbidden entrance, he turned away. Suddenly the thought of seeing Ana made him feel even more guilty. She would look at him with her large, trusting eyes and hope to hear good news. He had none to give—no news at all, in fact, other than the grave observation that most likely Lazar would not survive.

Instead, he waddled down a different series of corridors that took him toward the eunuchs' chambers, an area half encircled by the harem so that the eunuch slaves had easy access to the women they served.

Deliberately Pez began to mutter. "Where is Kett, must find Kett, how is Kett, our new pet?"

A passing slave heard him. "Hello, Pez."

"Kett?" Pez asked, forcing a dazed expression onto his face and picking his nose.

The slave nodded in recognition. "Is that the new boy?"

Pez hopped around, not answering. "Poor Kett. Lost his flesh. The knifers took it."

The slave nodded. "He's being attended to now. They're going to remove the stent early, I think. You'll find them—"

Pez didn't linger; everyone was used to the dwarf doing everything except observing good manners. He belched instead and skipped backward down the corridor. After the man had gone by, shaking his head, Pez doubled back. He didn't need to be told that the priest and his knifers would be in the Hall of the Precious, a large, airy chamber with a glass-domed roof and a central table upon which the victim was laid for the unraveling of his bandages. It seemed to Pez to be premature for Kett to be unbound but he was no physic, and knew that sometimes it was necessary to remove the bandages early.

In the hall, he found Kett upon the table, supine and groaning. The marble table was slightly tilted and had grooved sides with a drain at the bottom. It had been used for centuries during this procedure.

Salmeo, of course, presided over the event. "Ah, Pez," he lisped. "We wondered where you'd got to. Proceed," he directed the priest.

Pez hummed distractedly but focused on Kett, who seemed to have lost much weight though his belly was bulging obscenely. The dwarf began to giggle, pointing at the boy's enlarged abdomen.

"Have respect, dwarf!" Salmeo hissed, then turning back to the priest, he inquired, "Are you sure about this?"

"Do you care?" the man responded testily.

Salmeo leaned forward, the air between the priest and himself suffused with the scent of violet. "I don't. But I think the Valide would prefer to know that her old friend's child and the former playmate to her son survives."

"In that case, I think this is our only choice," the priest said unflinchingly, directing the careful unwrapping of the bandages. "See how he perspires and trembles. His body is being poisoned by itself. We must release the fluid and hope he is strong enough. Normally, I would only do this after three whole days had passed, but the swelling of his body is a dangerous sign."

The Grand Master Eunuch nodded. "Do it."

"If no liquid is passed when we remove the stent, then he is as good as dead." Lowering his voice, the priest spoke in a whisper. "It would be best to help him along should that occur."

"I understand."

As the final bandages were removed, the horrific wound inflicted by the sharp curved blade was revealed, the pewter tube looking insanely odd as it poked upward from the mess of the boy's groin. The men attending to him became silent and still, Pez was sure they were all remembering their own similarly traumatic experiences.

"He is young," Salmeo muttered softly as if to reassure himself as the priest, reciting a prayer, reached for the pewter stick.

As the man pulled on the stent, Kett screamed.

"Pah! It is stuck," the priest admitted. "Quick, warm water and oil to ease the flesh back. Hurry!" His attendants bathed the area, and although Pez presumed they were trying to be gentle, it did not sound that way. Kett continued to writhe pathetically against the strong arms that pinned him to the cool marble. They were not able to soften his protest, though, and he sang it loudly, cursing the very mothers who bore them, losing vital strength with each insult.

The priest pulled again sharply on the tube and it gave. Behind it gushed a torrent of bloodied water and the relief in Kett's anguished sighs was obvious. The flow continued with force for several seconds and then dwindled, but didn't stop for a long time, and Pez noted now how well designed that marble table was as it drained the waste efficiently, allowing the slightly fevered body to cool.

Salmeo looked expectantly at the priest, who nodded. "He will live," he pronounced. "The water is running clear."

"I shall tell the Valide," Salmeo said, his shoulders relaxing as he departed, ignoring Pez, who danced away from beneath the approaching bulk.

Pez approached the table. "Can he hear me if I sing?"

"He is conscious," the priest answered patiently.

"And what if I whispered?" He grinned insanely.

The priest rolled his eyes in exasperation. "Don't upset him, Pez," he warned.

That was the last thing Pez intended but he smiled indolently all the same, knowing that no one present could deny him anything he chose to do. Leaning close to Kett's head, he whispered, "Kett, it's Pez. You've made it."

The boy said nothing, although his groans continued. "I'm going to make a suggestion for your work and you're going to accept it the moment it's offered. Understand? Don't say anything; just take my hand," the dwarf urged, his hand already hovering nonchalantly over Kett's. He felt a soft squeeze. "Good boy," he whispered. "Just trust me now. You get stronger—work hard to heal. Now cry out as if I've antagonized you."

Kett gave a weak yell, and Pez giggled in response.

"Begone, Pez," the priest said wearily. "Isn't it enough that this boy nearly lost his life?"

Pez began to sing nonsense, dancing his way to the door. Kett was safe. Now he had to find Boaz.

LAZAR WAS SEMICONSCIOUS now and raging. The very mild sedative, which was all Ellyana could risk, had worn off and it was taking all of Jumo's strength to hold him still while Zafira finished dressing his wounds.

"His back looks like a bad piece of child's practice sewing," she commented, embarrassed by her work.

"Such beautiful skin he has too," Ellyana said softly from behind.

"Lazar! Hush!" Jumo cried. "We are tending to you."

"He can't help it, Jumo, and he cannot hear you, I suspect," Ellyana advised in her quiet manner. "It's the poison. It makes him angry." At Jumo's quirked eyebrows she asked, "You are amused?"

"He's always angry," Jumo replied drily. "But I presume this is a good omen, him being disturbed enough to fight us?"

Once again his hopes were dashed. "The opposite. It means the poison is winning."

"I'm finished," Zafira interrupted wearily, stretching. "His wounds are sewn—as best I can—the salve is on and I've dressed his entire back."

As if the demons within had suddenly lost energy upon hearing her words, Lazar slumped against the mattress, still silent. In fact he became so still that Jumo had to look carefully to convince himself that his friend still breathed.

"They will need to be changed twice daily," Ellyana warned.

Both listeners nodded, exhausted by their labors and concerned about the days ahead.

"Are we losing him?" Jumo asked.

Ellyana stared into his earnest expression. "I won't tell untruths for comfort's sake. He's dying, Jumo. This is the final stage before the venom works on the heart. I think perhaps we were too late."

"No!" At his exclamation she laid a hand on his arm but he shook it away. "We have to save him. You brought us here, you made him make that journey across the water and up the cliff side." His voice broke. "You save him," he demanded. He glanced toward Zafira through a mist of tears he refused to spill and he could see the hopelessness in her gaze. So she too understood that Lazar was as good as lost, even after all her work.

"Jumo," Ellyana began.

"Don't placate me," he warned. "You wouldn't have come here if you didn't have a vested interest in him. I don't know what that interest is, and to be honest, I don't care. I just want you to try, even if you think you're wasting your time."

"It would be no waste to save this man's life," she uttered softly. "I want him to live too but I want you to understand that it's not within my power to give him life."

"But you can try!"

"Yes." She nodded, resignation in the soft sigh that followed. "I will try for you." She picked up the pot of liquid that they'd made and been forced to wait while it cooled. "This special tea we've brewed is made from the rare circad. It is the only thing I've discovered that can act aggressively against snake poison and it is especially effective against drezden . . . if administered quickly enough."

"How often do we give him the tea?" Jumo asked.

"As often as he will tolerate it. It is unpleasantly bitter. The more we get into him, the better his chances of healing. He will bring it back up but we will have to persevere."

"Then I will persevere," he echoed firmly.

Ellyana smiled sadly. "Jumo, leave this to the women. You have done all you can."

"What?" Jumo scowled—surely she couldn't be suggesting he leave Lazar in such a perilous state.

"Go back to the city," she replied calmly. "Wait for news."

"But why not—" he began, only to be stilled by the sad smile on the face of the old woman and the way she calmly lifted a finger to quiet him.

"Jumo, we now know that Lazar has enemies within the palace who feel sufficiently threatened by him to make a very determined attempt on his life. We are presuming it is the Grand

Master Eunuch at work but we are not certain. The Vizier could be involved, the Valide might have a hand in it, even the Zar, if he's been compromised in some way."

"Never," Jumo whispered, further angered by the suggestion, for Lazar had such faith in Boaz.

"We cannot be sure. And we shouldn't risk our tiny chance at reviving him by letting anyone know where he is."

Bitterness laced Jumo's tone as he asked warily, "What do you want me to do?"

"Return to Lazar's house and await our message. If he lives, you can spread the good news and be our eyes. Watch for who reacts positively but mostly for who does not. Pez will be a great help in this, as regards the palace, but you can keep your ear to the ground around the city and listen to what the people are saying. We need to know that Salmeo and his cohorts aren't spreading rumors about the Spur. We must be informed of Lazar's position before he sets foot back in the city."

"You speak as if you believe he will live," Jumo observed.

"If he dies, Jumo, then you and Pez can still be of more use to Lazar in Percheron proper than here. You can see who relishes the news of his death and get word to the Zar. Either way you are serving your master best by being close to the palace."

Jumo shook his head. "I would prefer to be with him . . . to the end if necessary. I don't want this man dying alone."

"He won't be alone," Ellyana countered firmly. "Zafira and I will be at his side for every minute that he breathes."

"I can't leave him," he beseeched. "I couldn't live with myself if anything should happen."

Ellyana took his hand in hers. "I will give every bit of myself toward saving him, and so will Zafira. It doesn't need three of us and Lazar can benefit from your presence elsewhere."

Jumo closed his eyes in frustration. "But the very moment I return to his home, I will be besieged with inquiries. What am I to tell them?"

"You will lie. Our aim is to keep Lazar's antagonists well away from him until we know he's strong enough again." Ellyana shrugged. "So, without knowing who his enemies are, we must treat everyone as foe. You will tell anyone who asks after Lazar that following your arrival at the Sea Temple, where he requested you take him, he fell deathly ill. The priestess said she would do what she could for him and suggested you leave him with her for a while until she could assess the extent of his injuries."

"No one will believe that," he said.

"You can say you were so shocked by Lazar's condition that you weren't thinking straight. The priestess gave you a drink and you had no idea that it was drugged with a sedative. When you woke, Lazar was gone and you've been searching ever since but have found no sign of him."

Jumo's incredulity deepened. "You think they'll accept any of that story?"

"Yes, because there is no word of him. There is no sign of him. No one saw us leave with him, and no one must see you return. You will have to go in disguise."

"And how do I explain my absence for so long?"

Zafira spoke up quietly. "You could legitimately claim that you were so overcome with grief that you found the nearest drinking hole and drank yourself into oblivion. You'd need to buy off the silence of the mosha-man, of course, but that won't be hard."

"I don't drink in mosha houses," Jumo complained, knowing it was a hollow attempt to thwart the idea.

"Then throw the liquor over yourself. You only have to smell of it to convince anyone listening to your torrid tale."

"She's right," Ellyana agreed. "It's a good plan."

"It makes Zafira out to be a villain, though."

Zafira snorted gently. "As if that frightens me, dear Jumo. We who worship the Goddess have lived as outcasts and villains for the entirety of my lifetime and well before that. I have my faith, and that is all I need. What people think of me in my dotage is of no concern."

"Jumo, can't you see that we are helping Lazar, not punishing you?" Ellyana pushed.

"Yes, of course I can," he snapped. "But you don't understand how much we've been through together." He looked at the face of the man he loved. It was devoid of expression, the lips a pale smudge on the once-bronzed skin that now looked leached of all color.

"It is best that you leave now—getting this tea down him is going to be ugly," Ellyana warned.

Jumo turned to her again. "What do you mean?"

"He'll rail against it with the little strength he has left and that exertion alone could cost him his life. It will be a gentle balance between forcing him to drink whilst not making him fight us as well as the poison. Leave us now, Jumo. Use the boat and row yourself back to the harbor. I promise we'll get word to you within the next day or so."

Jumo turned helplessly to Zafira for support but her expression was implacable. She agreed with Ellyana, that much was clear. He raised a finger in warning. "Be sure you do and be sure you save him, or so help me, Ellyana, I shall come looking for you."

21

It was humid in Percheron, the air stifling within the confines of the city. Despite the heat, the bazaar hummed with its usual activity as traders encouraged the evening's stream of humanity to buy everything from freshly baked honey puffs to painted tiles.

As usual, Gold Alley was the most congested area; the Percherese did not rush into the purchase of gold but loved to roam the small corridors of glittering stalls at leisure. Many would pay close attention to the changing prices over days, often weeks, before investing. Others just liked to sit down with the traders and touch the seductive metal long before they were ready to pay good cash. There was never any hurry. The merchants gave each customer time, often sending their subordinates to fetch tea that arrived in colorful glasses on small trays. Tea meant hospitality and fellowship. It prompted conversation and ultimately sales.

Tariq saw none of this, however, as he hurried through the sloping streets. The color and ritual of Gold Alley were lost on him, his eyes fixed ahead on the next corner, his mind enmeshed in visions of power and wealth. He didn't stop to help or even apologize to the youngster whose elbow he clipped, sending a tray of dark golden tea clattering to the ground as the cranberry-colored glass, edged in gold, smashed in a hail of tinkling shards. No one recognized him, for although the Vizier's forked and bejeweled beard alone normally marked him for who he was, on this night Tariq had taken measures to disguise himself. The tea boy would later blame an ignorant woman, tall and fully veiled in a jamoosh.

Tariq pressed on, his mind a whirl of possibilities mingled with fear. Was he doing the right thing? It was only temporary, he reminded himself, and then he'd be unimaginably wealthy for the rest of his life. He wasn't too old to enjoy riches, and if he was fully honest, it was the riches that attracted him more than the power. Power was for a younger man, he now realized. If Maliz had visited him ten or fifteen years earlier, Tariq might have bartered for influence with the Zar, but since this afternoon he had decided he was tired of the palace, wearied of the political maneuverings, unhappy that he now served a Zar who was still too young to grow a beard.

He'd never had a good relationship with Joreb—that much was clear, or he would already be Grand Vizier. But to be back at the beginning, having to prime and grow a new relationship with someone already so untrusting of him, was draining. Joreb had not cared much for Tariq but they had forged a working relationship; Tariq suspected Boaz was not interested in such a relationship. So perhaps in the end Maliz's offer of extraordinary wealth was the sole reason for agreeing to his terms. Tariq could see himself retiring and living the decadent life he'd always dreamed of. That kind of wealth was power in itself anyway. He would no longer be a servant to the royals but one of the people they entertained.

You will never regret it, Maliz had assured Tariq, his tone slightly mocking. He had given the Vizier directions and disappeared swiftly from the Vizier's mind.

And so Tariq had disguised himself as a woman beneath the veil, the only way he could think of to hide his instantly recognizable beard. Now he was hurrying through the streets, the spilled tea long forgotten as he made his way toward the harbor and an area known as the Ditch.

There were fewer lanterns here, so the shadows were deeper, and the salty tang in the air became stronger. People were dressed more roughly but nobody gave the tall woman a second glance. A new smell permeated Tariq's nostrils—fragrant and strong, layering itself across the almost permanently fishy odor that hung predictably around the foreshore. His nose told him he was close to the main spice market as the mix of seeds and powders, fresh herbs and spices, clamored for his attention.

Tariq felt safer in the bazaar, not only because there was so much more activity beneath the lanes of brightly colored wares but also because the lanes were crowded with women. Fewer were veiling themselves, he noticed with interest—it had been a long time since he'd wandered the streets of the common people. Full veiling of women had once been a national tradition but it had begun to die out over the last century as more liberal attitudes prevailed. Now only high-caste families insisted that their women remain veiled outside their homes. And royalty, of course.

Tariq forced himself to stop at several stalls, pretending to consider the wares on display. He figured it was more natural for him to weave his way west if he looked like a genuine shopper. Attention was the last thing he needed.

With a forced casualness, he dawdled by a stall selling hot spices, picking up cloves and cardamom seeds and smelling them, turning over chilies to check color and freshness before moving on, pausing briefly by a store selling only variations of pepper, feigning fascination in the colors and choice being offered. Finally he strolled down the middle of the main thoroughfare, turning toward the western gate and maintaining his casual meander, pretending to be absorbed in the produce until his eye caught the sign that read BELOCH'S TABLE.

It was every bit as vulgar as he'd imagined. A fat man with a dirty apron grinned at him, a calon hanging from one lip and smoking itself, it seemed, by the length of ash still clinging to it. "My sister, can we serve you today? Quishtar perhaps or a plate of yemshi?" he offered, oblivious to the cockroach crawling across his foot.

The cheek of it, the Vizier thought, simmering beneath the veil, *using the name of one of the city's great icons to herald this tawdry little eatery.* He passed over the karel he had readied. "I've been told to give you this. You have no memory of my being here," he said. If the grubby owner was surprised to hear a man's voice from behind the jamoosh, he gave no outward sign. "I wish to use your back door."

"Be my guest, er . . . sister," the man welcomed him, pocketing the karel as expertly as a master thief. No one had seen the coin change hands and the tall woman was instantly forgotten as the owner began soliciting new customers.

The Vizier moved quickly to the back of the eatery, pushing past servers and the two cooks until he spotted the open door and the lane beyond. He turned as instructed and could just make out, courtesy of a single lantern. the small green doorway at the end of the alley. It was dim, deserted, the noise from the bazaar muffled. A rat scurried by, leaping over Tariq's foot and causing him to let out a small shriek of disgust. He could feel his heart pounding. Was this such a good idea after all? He told himself that he could still back out. Maliz would be angry but what could the demon do to him? He was only a voice.

Tariq paused, now only a dozen steps from the door. This was it. If he was going to flee, it would have to be now. As if on cue, an amused voice filled his head.

Welcome to my abode, Tariq. Please, come in.

Too late, he thought, there was no choice anymore. "Where are you?" he called tentatively.

Step inside. There are a few of us but you'll know me soon enough.

Tariq reached for the handle of the green door, taking a deep breath. He had never been so scared in his entire life.

PEZ TURNED ON his usual antics for the men before knocking theatrically on the Zar's door. At night Boaz was waited on by guards on both sides of the door to his sleeping chamber, so Pez was greeted by a grim-faced man who obviously didn't appreciate the late-night arrival.

"Oh, it's you," he said, a hint of disgust in his voice. "We're to permit you even if he's sleeping, so I suppose you'd better come in."

"Do you like custard?" Pez asked earnestly.

"Not particularly," the guard replied. "Nor am I keen to wake His Majesty."

"Oh, His Majesty loves custard. I prefer dolphins. What about slugs, do you like them? They sing rather oddly."

The man raised his eyes in frustration. The hour was late enough without this nonsense. He turned on his heel and left Pez standing by the door.

Pez hesitated. He had made a curious decision to be not altogether truthful with Boaz. He couldn't say exactly why he had decided as he had, he only knew that it felt somehow right.

He knocked gently at the bedchamber door, wondering what in Lyana's name he was going to say to the boy about his whereabouts these past hours. From behind the door he heard mumbling and risked opening it.

"Purple flowers smell strange," Pez muttered.

The door was pulled back fully. "Where have you been?" Boaz demanded. Pez was taken aback by the vehemence in the youngster's voice. He looked around to see where the guards were, an excuse rushing to form itself when Boaz continued, "I've been worried sick about you."

Pez turned back, relieved. "I'm sorry, High One," he replied. "I can explain."

"Come on in. I couldn't sleep anyway. There's hardly a breath of air."

"It's worse in the city."

"Is that where you've been?"

"Yes," the dwarf lied.

"Good. I figured you'd been with Lazar. Now tell me where he is and that he's recovering. I shall send my own physics immediately. He must have the best attention." The Zar shook his head. "I haven't been able to think straight all evening. I——" He closed his mouth at his friend's grave expression.

"I can't help, High One," Pez replied solemnly. "I have no idea where he is."

"What? Not even you?"

"Not even me."

"Pez, no one can tell me where the Spur is. I've had the city combed and there's no word on the street of his whereabouts. How can a man who looked half dead and yet so recognizable just disappear?"

Pez's voice was hard. "He didn't only *look* half dead, Majesty. He was dying."

Boaz was silent a long moment. Then he said quietly, "Please tell me you're jesting."

"I lie not. It's true that I accompanied Lazar and Jumo to the Sea Temple. If they're not there now, I have no idea where they are," Pez replied, hating himself for the fabrication.

The boy studied him. "But you and Lazar are such good friends. Surely you would have stayed with him?"

"I don't care to be abroad in the city too often or for long periods, my Zar. I was no help anyway. Lazar was unconscious and his wounds were so horrific that both Jumo and I were helpless."

He watched Boaz force control over himself. The boy was close to falling apart but Pez felt a gentle pride in noting that the young Zar was rising to his station.

"Why the Sea Temple? No one goes there," Boaz queried.

Pez shrugged. "Jumo tells me it is a place Lazar discovered very recently. He liked its peace and the fact that it is deserted, save for an old priestess."

"So he asked to go there?"

"I don't know, Your Majesty," Pez lied again. "I imagine

not, for he was unconscious, as I said. I think in his panic Jumo took him to the quietest place he could think of."

"But there's no care there," Boaz groaned. "It doesn't make sense. Even from my distant vantage, it was obvious he was seriously injured."

"You have no idea of the extent of it," Pez murmured.

Boaz strode to the door, opened it, and waited, presumably for a guard. The Zar muttered some angry orders before slamming the door. "I've sent some runners down to the Sea Temple."

Pez nodded. He knew they would find it empty. "It was a shocking outcome, Great One," he risked. "Though you know Salmeo designed it to turn out the way it did."

"Of course I do! When it comes to the harem, however, I don't have as much say as everyone seems to think. Salmeo and the Valide *are* the King and Queen of the harem. I am merely he whom it services." He grimaced.

"How did your mother react?"

"To be honest, I believe it was as much a shock for her as it was for myself."

"Really?" Pez didn't sound convinced.

"I asked her directly whether she had any involvement and she denied it. I know my mother well enough, Pez."

The dwarf remained silent, duly reprimanded. So far the Zar had not mentioned the use of poison. "Tariq?"

Boaz shook his head. "No, this is all Salmeo's work. It has his cruelty stamped all over it. As for the Inflictors, someone will swing for this if I don't have news of Lazar soon."

"It was not the boy's fault, High One. He looked more terrified than anyone."

"I don't care," Boaz snapped. "Woe betide him if I receive

bad news about Lazar. I think you all forget that he was my friend—one of so few I have in this place." He slumped down on a sofa and stared out his window. "I met with the odalisque Ana today," he said, as if he wanted to change the subject.

"Oh? That's unusual. Must have delighted Salmeo."

Boaz managed a small but wicked smile. "He hated it. Went rushing off to my mother, who apparently told him to obey his Zar and not run to her with complaints. No doubt she has come to the same conclusion as us, that this was Salmeo's doing. She is not pleased."

"How was Ana?"

"Devastated, although I think my company was good for her, and I would be lying if I said the outcome wasn't mutual."

"So you like her?"

Boaz turned his gaze from the window to the dwarf. "You knew I would. That's why you risked so much that night of her presentation to the Valide. What are you up to, Pez?"

Pez leaped onto a seat. "Nothing, High One. I had seen her beauty and heard from Lazar of her intelligence," he lied. "I thought she might be someone who could offer you honest friendship as much as pleasant company. I'm just glad you liked her." He hesitated briefly, then asked quietly. "May I ask a boon?"

"You will whether I give permission or not," Boaz said, not unkindly.

"I sense Ana is about to be elevated to a status beyond simple slave and I'm wondering if you would be generous enough to appoint a single slave solely to serve her."

"What? She's only been here a few days. My mother would object fiercely." Boaz shook his head. "Though I'll admit that the whims of my mother are beyond me."

Pez didn't hesitate. "No, she'll be quite firm, I imagine, so you have to order that Ana has her own slave. Your mother already dislikes Ana, I'd suggest, because of Lazar. His obvious sense of commitment to Ana, so brilliantly and rather sadly displayed by today's bit of theater, has piqued your mother's curiosity. You and I both know how he fascinates her. She wants to know what's behind his interest in Ana, what drives it . . ." His voice trailed away as a knock sounded at the door.

"Come," Boaz answered.

It was the head guard. "Your High One." He bowed low and long.

"Do you have news of the Spur?"

The man straightened. "Majesty, the Sea Temple is deserted, although we did find bloodstains in front of the altar."

"And no one knows of the Spur's whereabouts?" Boaz persisted, knowing it was a pointless query.

"I had men ranging throughout the harbor for any news. A child thought she saw a man being loaded into a boat but the mother was scared of us asking questions and the little one clammed up. When we tried again she denied it and claimed she had dreamed it."

"What sort of boat?"

"A rowboat, she said," the man replied doubtfully, "but there is nowhere, Majesty, that is close enough to row to where help can be sought."

"What's that island not so far away?"

Pez held his breath as the guard frowned and then brightened. "There is the Isle of Stars, High One, but that's a leper colony."

Pez belched. "And who'd go there?" he murmured.

Boaz sighed. "All right, Briz, keep trying with your men. He must be found."

"There's fifteen of them still hunting down anything they can."

"Wake me if you hear anything at all."

"Yes, High One." The guard touched hand to heart and took his leave.

"Take some rest, Boaz," Pez suggested.

"What were you going to ask me about Ana?"

Pez sighed. "The newly made eunuch," he began.

"Kett."

"Yes. He would make a good servant for Ana."

Boaz nodded. "I share your guilt, Pez. But now is not the time to be singling Ana out for special status. She has begged me to treat her the same as the other odalisques, and because of my mother's interest, I'm inclined to acquiesce."

"We should help him," Pez persisted, unsure why he felt so strongly but somehow certain that Kett was important—though whether to him, Ana, Boaz, or someone else he could not say.

"Leave it with me," Boaz compromised. "I will not see him badly done by—he could begin by being directly on hand in the harem to assist her and perhaps in time we can consider the position you have suggested."

Pez nodded. It would have to be enough for now.

"You never did tell me where you've been all this time," Boaz urged, and Pez realized he was not going to be let off the hook that lightly.

TARIQ STEPPED GINGERLY through the doorway, only to be confronted by several people in various stages of decomposition. Most were old—or at least that's how they appeared—and each was filthy, dressed in rags. All were ravaged by starvation. He knew these to be members of the city's lost, which was how people with a conscience referred to them. Most called them the Sewer Rats. These were people wholly forgotten and ignored by all but the Vizier and his council, who wanted them "removed." Tariq himself meant "removed from the earth" and would have gladly signed their death warrants, but more conservative council members were still arguing as to whether the Isle of Stars—already designated as a place for the unwanted—could be used as a convenient spot where these undesirables could waste away. Tariq was fearful that Boaz would demand that Percheron take better care of its lost people. The Vizier wanted no drain on the city's budget for these fools, who were, in his opinion, too lazy or useless to lead a productive life. The city was far better off without them.

He grimaced as one toothless hag staggered toward him; fortunately for Tariq, the woman was almost blind with cataracts and he pushed her aside, kicking at another body in front of him. "Maliz!" he called, emboldened by his power over the wretches around him. He avoided a third of the damned, dropping his shoulder and callously shoving the helpless man into a wall, sending him spinning into the shadows. Tariq sneered. "Demon! I seek you."

And I hear you, came a familiar voice in his head.

I can't see you.

Come closer, Vizier.

Suddenly Tariq felt the spike of fear he had held at bay take full hold. Perspiration broke out beneath his robes and he threw off the jamoosh as much to see more easily as to cool himself. "Where?" he whispered into the darkness.

Not far.

The voice might be coming from behind him, he thought. He swung around wildly, leaping back at the same time, but no one was there, save the same pathetic souls he'd already dealt with.

"I . . . I have no idea where you are," he called, far less confidently. "Show me." He smelled rather than heard or saw the tiny figure that crept out of the darkness to stand before him.

"Do you see me now?" asked a frail voice.

"You?" Tariq asked, incredulous.

The feeble old man, barely able to stand and seemingly ravaged by disease, nodded. "Don't be fooled, Tariq," the man said in a wispy voice. "I am he who you feared meeting."

Tariq stepped back. His arrogance returned. "Who could be scared of you?"

"Are you testing me?" Maliz asked evenly, his fetid breath making Tariq wince. "I'd advise against it. You are beguiled by appearance alone, Vizier, and that is a mistake. You should keep in mind that I choose to walk in this form."

"Why?" Tariq asked, trying to avoid breathing through his nose.

"It suits my purposes," replied the frail man. "Who would think to find the demon Maliz here amid Percheron's unfortunates?"

"Who indeed?" echoed Tariq, lacing his voice with sarcasm.

Suddenly the more familiar voice boomed in his head. *You are the one who is pathetic, Vizier. You look at me as if you could snap me in half and be done with it. Why bother? Go back to your life, Tariq. Return to the palace and be abused by Herezah and upstaged by Salmeo and treated like a filthy servant by the Zar. You*

*are nothing to them. Nothing! An inferior, aging politician with
nothing to contribute to any of their goals, save being a useful
punching bag . . .*

Maliz continued the stream of insults but Tariq didn't hear
any more. His anger was roused as the truth of the demon's
words exploded in his mind. He *was* nothing. They *did* all treat
him as though he were dirt on their shoes. "Enough!" he
roared.

The old man gave a black-toothed, diseased smile. "Does
the truth hurt, Vizier? I can make it all so different for you."

"Prove it! Show me your powers, show me riches, give me
unequivocal proof that you are who you say you are."

The old man sighed as Maliz's deep and ancient voice spoke
in Tariq's mind. *If I'm to show you such things, you will need to
leave your body here.*

Tariq baulked. "No!"

*Fret not, you will still own it, still belong to it, but I can take
you to places you have seen only in your dreams.*

"And I will not die by leaving my body?"

No.

"Will you steal it?" Tariq persisted suspiciously.

Maliz laughed but there was no humor in it. *I can't. I am not
permitted by Zarab. You must offer me your body before I'm permitted to enter it as anything other than a voice.*

Tariq heard the truth in Maliz's confession. "Do it, then.
Show me all you can to convince me to utter the invitation you
so desire."

The Vizier closed his eyes instinctively and felt a mighty
push, as though all the breath were being squeezed out of him.

See for yourself, said Maliz.

Tariq knew he was trembling with fear—or was it anticipation?—yet could not feel himself shaking. And similarly, though he told himself to open his eyes, he sensed that there was no physical movement but he could suddenly simply see.

Herezah? he exclaimed.

I thought you'd like to look in on the person whose attention you crave most.

I'm in the harem!

Not physically, Tariq.

Herezah was taking a late-night tea infusion alone but Tariq could see she wasn't sipping from her cup. She looked maudlin and disinterested. Sadly she was clothed—he would like to have seen her naked.

I can give you that too, Maliz breathed into his mind.

Tariq ignored the way the demon read his mind. *Why is she so moody tonight?*

Think! You want to be Grand Vizier yet you ask the simplest of questions, which perhaps even that fool, Pez, could work out. The Vizier felt the sting of criticism. *You are aware of why she is angry, depressed tonight, I promise you. Work it out. There is rarely more than this reason for any woman to be so low of mood.*

A man.

Which one?

Tariq paused, nervous. *Boaz?*

Maliz growled his disappointment. *Don't be naive, Tariq. Herezah plays her game better than any other. Try again.*

Lazar.

Yes! Of course Lazar. There is no other man that interests her sexually.

She's depressed because of his flogging?

Because of his apparent death, I should think. It isn't looking good for the Spur.

Do you know everything, Maliz?

Sadly, no. I know only what I see or eavesdrop on, and everything I see or hear is open to interpretation. Fortunately I am sharp enough to get it right most times. Herezah is not so shortsighted, by the way. A lot more is at stake than her own desires.

She's worried about Percheron's security.

Correct.

I see. I hate Lazar. I hope he is dead.

I know. I know everything about you, Tariq.

Tariq uncomfortably brushed aside Maliz's assertion. *Show me more.*

What do you want to see now?

The harem proper. The girls.

Tsk-tsk, Vizier, Maliz admonished. *Then look,* he said. And Tariq was moving through the empty halls of the harem.

It's beautiful, he gushed.

Always the best is hidden, Maliz said, laughing. *The girls are asleep.*

Except one, Tariq replied as he spotted Odalisque Ana sitting on the bench of a window. *Can you eavesdrop on her thoughts?*

I have not tried. I can if you wish, but not everyone is as open to me as you have been.

No, show me the Zar instead, Tariq demanded.

He was instantly aware of Boaz, also slumped at a window in his suite. Nearby sat the dwarf.

Another person I hate is Pez.

He is no one, not worthy of your hatred, the demon reassured Tariq. They watched Pez suddenly cock his large head to one side.

Tariq gave a sound of disgust. *As usual, he's not paying attention. The Zar is talking to him. This is so typical of the ingrate.*

Now they watched Pez stand, his body tensed.

"Now what's wrong?" the Zar asked.

The dwarf began to leap around the furniture, singing madly.

"Pez, stop," Boaz urged. "No one is—"

Pez's sudden high-pitched squeal shocked the young Zar into silence.

"Must write, must write!" Pez began to moan.

"Write what?"

Boaz and his two invisible visitors watched the dwarf scrawl something onto a tablet of paper. Then he coughed at it, repeatedly. He sat on it and farted.

Tariq groaned. *I truly despise Joreb for bringing this troll into our lives.*

He's harmless but I take your point. It's a pity that the son thinks so highly of him. Maliz watched Pez suddenly rise again, lift the crumpled sheet of paper, and fling it at the astounded Zar.

"The birds are pecking me," he shrieked at Boaz. "My flesh is burning," he howled, running out the door.

I just hope he has a seizure and dies sometime soon, Tariq said caustically.

Maliz said nothing, watched Boaz read the note absently, and then, curiously, set it alight from a nearby candle. The parchment burned, the Zar watching it disintegrate to ash. Both Tariq and Maliz observed how Boaz suddenly looked angry. Striding to the door, the young Zar demanded one of his guards to enter.

"Yes, High One?" the man said, bowing and straightening with a concerned frown.

"You tell Pez that if he ever writes such obscenity to me again, I will bar him from entering my rooms. Make it clear to him, will you?"

The man nodded, stunned by the outburst. "He never takes any notice, Great One."

"Tell him anyway," Boaz ordered, flinging the door closed behind the retreating guard.

Oh, that's interesting, Tariq said. *Perhaps a falling-out between our Zar and the fool. Maybe the half-wit went too far this time.*

It appears so, Maliz admitted. *I'd love to know what he wrote that so upset the Zar.*

Finally, show me riches, Maliz, Tariq said, no longer interested in eavesdropping on the royal apartments.

As you wish. Is this our final journey?

Yes. You have convinced me of your magical power. All I need now is to see some of the treasures you've promised and we will seal our bargain.

BOAZ FOUND PEZ, as instructed, in the Golden Garden, a private courtyard to which no one but the Zar himself had access. Sometimes it was used to entertain one of his favorites or to impress a new odalisque, but mainly it was a place for peace and reflection away from the palace life.

"What was that all about?" Boaz hissed.

"Forgive me, Boaz," Pez said, sounding unusually rattled. "I had to get us away from there."

"What in Zarab's name happened?"

The dwarf shook his large head. "I don't really know, in truth, but something chilled me."

"I don't understand."

"No, neither do I. I think something or someone was with us in your chamber."

"You jest."

"Do I look like I'm trying to entertain?" Pez snarled.

"No, you look frightened. I've never seen you like this. You think someone was eavesdropping? But where? There aren't many places to hide in that particular room."

"No, I don't mean like that. I mean someone was with us in spirit."

Boaz raised his eyebrows in mock defeat. "Oh, I see. An invisible eavesdropper."

"Don't mock me, Boaz. I did what I did for our own protection. Someone was listening, I tell you. I don't know who it was or why or even how they were doing it, but my Lore skills picked it up instantly."

Boaz looked chastened. "Sorry, Pez. I don't mean to make fun. It's just so hard to believe."

"Zar Boaz, you witnessed and experienced firsthand the power of the Lore. You must trust me when I use it as protection for us."

"I do trust you."

"Then know that whoever was listening to our conversation was not friendly. There was something dark and malevolent in its presence."

"I can't believe this," Boaz said, standing from the fountain edge he'd been sitting on. "What do you expect me to do?"

"Nothing! Just don't ignore my warnings or devalue them by not taking them seriously. Someone who is not your friend visited you today, Boaz, and it was done using magic. From now on, we must be on our guard."

"Well, if I can't see or hear this person, how will I know when I must be careful?"

"You won't but I will. If I should behave as I did tonight, you'll know I am warning you."

"All right . . . are we safe here now?"

"If I'm discovered—"

"What would it matter, in truth, to anyone in the palace?" Boaz asked quietly but not aggressively. "What could anyone do if it was revealed that you have your wits about you, that this has been a trick you've pulled for years?"

"It's not the people of the palace I worry about, my Zar," Pez replied cryptically. "Come, the feeling of being observed is gone. You can return to your chambers to sleep."

Boaz sighed. "I won't be doing much sleeping until I hear about Lazar." But he followed Pez anyway as the dwarf crawled out of the Golden Garden braying like a donkey.

"ALL RIGHT, HOW?" Tariq demanded, his mind still reeling from the riches he had seen. Maliz had shown him the hidden treasure of the legendary Zar Fasha, who had insisted on his corpse being entombed in the desert along with his fabulous wealth and entire harem. The people of the harem, unlike their Zar, had been very much alive when entombed; their twisted skeletons, jaws open in agony, were testimony to the desperate way in which they'd perished, screaming to be let free of their deep prison beneath the sands. Tariq had barely noticed the people, however—all he could focus on was the treasure itself, imagining the decadent way he would soon be living. "Although I've never understood how it is that you mean to share my body," he added carefully.

Maliz was back in his wizened guise of the near-toothless man. "I have explained everything. You want what I can give you. Now either you take what I'm offering or you leave and never come back. I can find another."

Another what? Tariq wondered, his mind racing. *Another fool?*

Another host, came the deep-voiced reply in his mind. *Let me be your guest,* he offered, more gently now. *And I will teach you and show you all that you have desired these years gone. I will keep my promise.*

Have you always used another?

Yes. When I am dormant I deliberately seek old, unremarkable bodies to live within. They don't require much effort from me and they can move around without drawing too much attention to themselves. This one is my favorite so far. The demon laughed nastily.

"What do you mean, dormant?"

Maliz gave a despairing sigh and spoke in the old man's voice again. "Must I explain everything? Surely you know your history. I rise when Iridor does."

"Iridor?" Tariq asked, clearly baffled.

"The Messenger."

"Whose Messenger?"

"Hers! The Goddess . . . Lyana!"

Tariq couldn't stop the nervous laugh that escaped. "Lyana? Are you mad? I know Maliz was a great sorcerer once—legend says he made some terrible bargain with Zarab—but Lyana is just someone the priestesses of old fabricated to win favor."

"You are the one fooled. Lyana is as real as I am! I sense her coming and I know Iridor has returned. He is cunning; he can hide himself better than she can. I must find them and destroy them."

"Is that your bargain with Zarab? Everlasting life?"

The old man nodded, his vile grin wide on the ravaged face. "Life everlasting has its advantages, Vizier. You can be part of it."

"What do you mean?"

A weak groan issued from the darkness of the building. Both Vizier and demon ignored it. "Youth. I can provide you with it along with all the other promises I've made."

"You mean my body can actually become younger as well as looking younger?" Tariq asked, astonished.

"You can be anything I want you to be. You just have to tell me," Maliz answered, his tone seductive. "We are a partnership. You lend me your body—for a while. I bring all your dreams to life. I am not interested in your pursuits, Tariq. I have my own mission and the two don't have to conflict. We just help each other achieve our desires."

"As simple as that," Tariq said flatly.

"It need not be any more complicated."

"And then you will leave my body . . . when you have achieved your dreams?"

"Of course," Maliz assured him. "I have no need of it beyond such time."

Tariq hesitated, tempted but still wary. "Why don't you just enter a young man's body, then?"

Maliz's patience was running out. "You can only make a bargain with someone who wants what you're offering. You were an easy choice. I need someone with intelligence, with some wisdom of years, and with a desire to help me as much as I can help him." Tariq nodded, close to giving in now. "I find the young too selfish, self-absorbed. They don't aim high enough these days. They want everything given to them. They are lazy. Not like you, Vizier. You've worked hard to make something of yourself and it's fitting that your efforts be recognized. You are everything I have searched for. Will you not invite me in, brother?"

"All right, Maliz. I give you permission." Tariq capitulated, hardly daring to breathe now that he'd uttered the words.

The demon was silent a moment, then said, triumph in his voice, "You must say this: Maliz, come into me. Take my soul."

Had Tariq thought through the careful phrasing, he might have sensed the trap, but his thoughts were swollen with notions of power and grandeur. Without thinking, he repeated the phrase dutifully.

And felt the spine-tingling entry of Maliz into his being and heard the cold, malevolent laugh of the demon as he gleefully betrayed Tariq. In the end, the person who had been the Vizier didn't even have the strength to make a fight of it. It was probably the shock of discovering Maliz's treachery, and all the lies that had been spun simply to have the Vizier's body for his own, that left him unable to do anything but capitulate to the mighty force that was the demon Maliz. He gave a sad scream of impotent rage as his soul was shredded and spat out through his own mouth in a red mist of surrender.

Maliz smiled, Tariq's mouth stretching wide. The demon had risen.

22

Pez had spent most of the night talking with the Zar, who was clearly too fretful to sleep. And when the young ruler had drifted off in the early hours, Pez had been too anxious to take any rest himself. The previous evening's intrusion had frightened him—it still did. Pez had never experienced anything like it before, and as much as he tried to convince himself that the visitor had been somehow spying on the Zar, he could not shake off the notion that the intruder was watching him, not Boaz.

By sunrise, none of the sense of dread had dissipated; worse, Pez had convinced himself that the invisible watcher had meant only harm. From now on, he would have to be intensely careful about how he conducted himself. Conversations with Boaz could no longer be open and honest. He would have to use his Lore skills to set up a special ring of protection around the two of them—and although that would prevent any spiritual being eavesdropping, it was also a clear sign of magic and it would sap his own strength.

Dawn shone brightly into Boaz's bedroom, threatening another hot day, and the Zar had risen immediately and taken a bath in his private chamber. After his first meal he began reading through some of the day's duties. But Pez could tell the Zar was restless, eager for news of Lazar and keen to think about something other than his council's advice regarding the city's homeless, the need to finance a new cistern, celebrations for the holy month . . . the list seemed endless. Under the dwarf's distracting influence Boaz was soon dispensing with Bin's notes and instead discussing his idea of a picnic for all the new odalisques. Pez thought it was a charming notion and nodded excitedly as the young Zar outlined his plans.

"You'll need at least eight barges, High One, to carry that number of people."

"At least they're all young and slim. If my father had done something like this, he'd have needed twice as many barges for the same number of women."

Pez muttered a gentle sound of admonishment. "Shame on you, Boaz," he said, though he grinned to soften the sting of the words. "The women couldn't help their size. They had nothing to do but indulge themselves."

"I know," Boaz admitted. "I understand that now and it won't happen in my harem. I'll see to it that the women have plenty to occupy themselves of a more physical nature."

"Ooh," Pez said, pulling a face of mock embarrassment.

Boaz looked momentarily mortified but composed himself quickly. "I didn't mean that," he replied archly. "I meant—"

He was interrupted by a knock at the door. "Come," he called as the dwarf began rolling around the room wildly like a ball, yelling "kick me!" and bumping up against the Zar's foot.

"What is it, Bin?" Boaz asked, ignoring the tempting invitation.

"Forgive my interruption, Zar Boaz," the young man said, bowing low. "But you asked for any information about Spur Lazar to be delivered immediately."

"What news?" Boaz demanded. Even Pez rolled to a stop.

"A runner has been sent from the Spur's house, my Zar. His manservant has returned, we're told, and he's blind drunk."

"Jumo, you mean?"

The youngster nodded. "I think that is his name, yes, High One." He inclined his head, waiting for orders.

"Is the runner still here?"

"No, we have sent him away, my Zar. I presumed you would want to speak directly with the Spur's manservant."

"You presumed correctly. Send our own men from the palace to escort him back."

"Should we give him some time to sober up, Zar Boaz?"

"I want to see him as fast as they can bring him here. No excuses—I don't care how drunk he is. And I mean our men, Bin, not the Spur's soldiers."

"I understand, Zar." Bin bowed once more before disappearing.

"Jumo drunk? It's hard to imagine," Pez commented.

"Perhaps he's celebrating Lazar's well-being," Boaz said hopefully.

"Then why didn't the runner mention the Spur's presence? No, this doesn't sound good." Pez felt a fresh sense of dread grip him.

Boaz gave a moue of disdain. "Don't put the jahash on it before we know the situation."

"I'm not cursing it. I'm telling you what I think."

"Then keep your baleful thoughts to yourself, Pez. I'm taking this as positive news. If anyone knows where Lazar is, Jumo will."

Pez kept his own counsel but the feeling of trepidation simply got stronger.

JUMO WAS BROUGHT to one of the Zar's receiving chambers. This particular room overlooked a vast courtyard with an ornamental pool and had no windows, only open archways, so that on hot days cooling breezes could blow through the less formal meeting room. Pez loved this chamber for its beautiful tiled ceiling of blue and white. The first time he had walked into the room he had instantly recognized the work of the Yaznuks, painters who had been captured and brought from the far east along with their exquisitely delicate work, most notably floral designs, that looked almost abstract from this distance. These days those designs, the paints they used, and all of their techniques were a closely guarded secret held within three families who, over history, had assumed the role of keepers of the art. They alone had royal sanction to produce the Yaznuk style and marked their work with a distinctive dragon emblem.

Pez was so mesmerized by the beauty of the room that he registered Jumo's arrival by the man's smell rather than by sight. A stench of liquor hit his nostrils and his attention was instantly dragged from the ceiling to the doorway where the spry man, normally so contained and correct, hung limply between the grip of two of Boaz's private guards. Pez was taken aback; as stunned, in fact, as Boaz looked, for this was more than the merry stupor of a man intoxicated. Though Pez managed to keep up his pretense of disinterest by circling the room and humming to himself, his focus was riveted on Lazar's manservant. Jumo appeared ashen, unfocused, and, if Pez was right, filled with grief.

"Let him go," Boaz commanded, slightly embarrassed for Jumo, and they all watched Lazar's closest companion in life slump and then fall hard on his knees. The guards grabbed for him to keep him upright.

"Is this how you found him?" the Zar asked, dismayed. He had always known Lazar's quiet, foreign friend to be entirely in control of himself.

"No, Great One. When we arrived at the Spur's house, he smelled as highly as he does now but curiously he seemed sober." The man hesitated briefly.

"So what is this? An act for my benefit?" Boaz demanded, irritated more by the look of uncertainty in the man's eyes than by any notion of guile on Jumo's part.

The head guard arrived. Bowing low, he ordered, "Briz, explain what has occurred."

Pez felt a fluttering about his heart and suddenly was breathless with tension. There was something dangerous about this situation, something not right. He watched the head guard pause, considering his words carefully before delivering them.

"O Mighty One, moments after my men arrived at the Spur's house, so did another messenger."

"Yes, and . . . ?"

Pez felt himself freeze with anticipation. His humming grew softer and less manic; no one was paying him any mind anyway.

Briz was noticeably reluctant, tripping over his words. "That messenger brought the gravest of tidings, High One. This is Zafira, Majesty, of the Sea Temple." He nodded to a tiny figure who now stepped out from behind the guards. She tiptoed closer and bent herself in half to bow with great care to the young ruler.

"Zar Boaz," she whispered.

Pez tried to breathe in and found his lungs would not obey. If Zafira was here, everything had surely gone wrong.

Briz noted the Zar's rising frustration and hurried on. "When she arrived at the Spur's house, the priestess Zafira informed Jumo of his master's death, which occurred last night."

Jumo let out a heartbreaking groan. The anguished sound gave voice to Boaz's silent, tightly held reaction and to Pez's feeling of utter despair. "She said she would do everything to save his life," the distraught man wailed softly.

"The Spur is dead?" Boaz queried, uncomprehending, his throat tight with emotion.

"Sadly it is so, Great One," Zafira confirmed, glancing briefly toward Pez. The dwarf was so shocked he closed his eyes, hoping no one would notice how still he was.

"What happened?" Boaz growled, too stunned to make even a pretense at civility toward the old woman.

Zafira, trembling beneath her azure robes, stepped farther into the room and bowed once more before clearing her throat. "I tell this tale—as I told Jumo—with the heaviest of hearts." They all saw her steady herself and blink away a mist of tears. "Spur Lazar took his last breath as a great cloud obliterated the moon during the small hours of this night gone. It was an omen, Highest One, for the darkness that reigned for several minutes signaled death for the Spur from the hideous injuries he sustained at the hands of those who punished him for protecting an innocent."

It was a cleverly couched yet nonetheless direct insult to the Zar and he knew it, as did everyone in that chamber. Boaz stared at the old woman, took in the defiant lift of her chin despite the pallor of her skin and her frailty, and wondered at the long night she had spent battling to save a man's life. He let the insult pass, almost felt he deserved it. As he glanced toward the once-proud Jumo, a surge of pity welled up in him. He registered the shock on the face of the dwarf. And realized they all needed time to digest this tragedy. "Leave us!" he said to the men.

"Zar Boaz, I think——" Briz began, but Boaz raised a hand, silencing him.

"I wish to speak to the priestess in private. You may wait outside if you insist, although I can't imagine I will come to any harm from an old woman and a clearly incapacitated man, both of whom I presume have already been thoroughly searched. Send messengers to the Valide and the Vizier. Have them wait in the antechamber until I summon them. I will give the news to them myself. No one is to discuss anything of what has gone on here. Is that clear, Briz?"

"It is, Mighty One."

"Good. See to it your men obey my command. And help Jumo into a seat before you depart."

With the men dismissed, the young Zar returned his attention to the old woman, who had seated herself—with a nod from Boaz—next to Jumo, who was looking steadfastly at his feet.

As soon as the door had closed on the last man, Pez opened his eyes. "Zafira! I pray this is a ruse."

Boaz noticed that she did not look him in the eye but shook

her head sadly, and began to weep softly. "We tried everything, but in the end the poison killed him."

"Poison?" Boaz interrupted. "What are you talking about?" Then as he realized what the dwarf had said: "Pez, do you know this priestess?"

Pez nodded gravely. "I know Zafira and she knows of my sanity. We took the injured Spur to her at his instructions." He didn't want to say too much more about his connection to the priestess, and he knew Boaz was too filled with despair to ask why the dying Lazar would wish to go to her. "The whip was laced with poison, High One. We only discovered this at the temple and knew it was a race against time that we would probably lose."

"Why didn't you tell me?" Boaz yelled, suddenly losing control. "So that's where you were yesterday!"

Shocked by the outburst, everyone sat in frozen silence. Finally Pez spoke. "It never occurred to me that Lazar would not live. In hindsight, not telling you was wrong, Highness. Forgive me, but I presumed the Spur would make his own decision about where to lay blame once he recovered. I didn't feel it was my place."

"Not your place to tell me when you know of an intrigue that not only affects my realm but kills my head of security?" Boaz roared. And then, as suddenly as it had arrived, the anger went out of him. "But who would do such a thing? The flogging was accepted by everyone as appropriate punishment for Odalisque Ana's indiscretion."

"I'm sure the Snake would not have been used on one of your concubines, Zar Boaz," Jumo said, raising his head defiantly and surprising them all with the vehemence in his voice. "This was far more deliberate than you are giving credit for."

"You're forgiven your insolent tone, Jumo, because of your grief," Boaz replied mildly, surprising Pez with his maturity. "Explain the poison," he demanded to the room at large.

Pez signaled to Zafira, and the priestess spoke up. "We discovered it was drezden, Zar Boaz."

"What is drezden?"

"Snake poison," Pez answered dully. "The chosen brew of assassins."

"And you know how to deal with it?" Boaz asked, looking between the woman and the dwarf.

"I have some experience with healing snakebite," Zafira lied. "Lazar needed the special tea known as drezia, which is formed from the venom itself. He also needed sewing, for the wounds were savage."

Boaz shook his head in wonder. "And you did all this?"

The gray-haired woman nodded. "And anything else I could think of, but we lost him all the same. The wounds were too deep, the poison had had too long to work."

"He was rallying," Jumo countered angrily. "She said if I left he would likely pull through."

Boaz frowned at Jumo's rudeness, but Zafira squeezed Lazar's friend's hand and responded immediately. "I did think Jumo could be more help back in Percheron, Highness. It occurred to me that his network of contacts might yield more information and be of more assistance in the long run than to have him fretting by Lazar's side. The Spur was all but unconscious by that time anyway. He was in a delirium before he slipped into a coma and succumbed to the full paralysis of the poison. It was probably best his close ones did not have to witness his end."

Pez looked sharply at the priestess. Zafira was hiding Elly-ana. Why? What were they so afraid of?

"Who are you suggesting brought this about?" Boaz de-manded.

At this, all three pairs of eyes looked wary. Pez shrugged. It would not be politic to say the name. Zafira's expression turned blank.

"There are those who were jealous of the Spur," Jumo an-swered.

"Name them!" Boaz ordered, once again ignoring the man's inappropriate lack of protocol.

"It is not for me to say. I have no proof."

"Then I'll say it for you, shall I?" Boaz threatened, his ire up again. "There are only three suspects—my mother, Vizier Tariq, or the Grand Master Eunuch." He paused, and when a careful silence confirmed his assertion, he continued: "I do not need to defend her but you should all understand that this is not my mother's way. She loves Percheron, its security, and above all, her own. She knew who gave us this security." He glanced to Pez, who was nodding in agreement. "Vizier Tariq has no spine. He is sly and he has ambitions, but he would not dare risk such a death finding its way back to his hands. Salmeo is the most capable of this cunning and despicable act but I can't imagine why he would do such a thing." No one answered him. Even Jumo had realized he was negotiating dangerous territory. The accusation would not come from his lips.

The Zar continued. "No doubt if it was Salmeo who poi-soned the whip, it is because he felt humiliated by the Spur un-dermining his authority. I imagine he wanted retribution for Odalisque Ana's snubbing of harem rules. Except resorting to murder seems an overreaction, wouldn't you say? And from my perspective, unlikely. There is more to this surely than a simple act of revenge. And I will get to the bottom of it."

Although none agreed with his reasoning, not one of them said so, each knowing that pointing fingers and throwing around blame would not bring Lazar back to them.

"Where is the corpse?" Boaz asked Zafira, ignoring Jumo's wince at the harsh word.

"The Spur rallied momentarily before he slipped into his coma. He begged me through his delirium to give him to the sea, my Zar. It was his last wish and we could not argue it, for he lost consciousness."

"Gone?" Jumo was astonished. "His body is gone? He asked for this?"

The priestess nodded. "He was determined. I had no choice but to agree—it was a dying man's request. He said nothing else. He knew he was close to death."

"Where did he die?" Boaz asked, almost as an afterthought. "No one could find him."

Zafira sighed. She had not taken her hand from Jumo's. "He died at the temple. I had his body removed and taken to Z'alotny."

Pez was surprised by the lie, but he did not question it. Perhaps Ellyana did not want it known that Lazar had died in her home. In any case, he had no reason to doubt Zafira. "The burial ground of the priestesses?"

She shrugged defensively. "It is peaceful there and I am familiar with it. In fact it is precisely the sort of place a troubled man *should* take his last rest on this plane. I washed his body and dressed it in fresh robes before I had him rowed out to Beloch. I dropped him out of the boat beneath the giant." Only now did she sound unsure. "I thought it fitting it was done there."

Jumo's anger held him as rigid as the statue Zafira mentioned. "I should have been there," he protested.

"I couldn't find you, Jumo. I sent a messenger," Zafira said softly. "I'm so sorry about all of this, but I have few resources. And the Spur won my promise about giving him to the sea. He murmured something about it carrying him back to his homeland as he slipped away from me."

Jumo's expression softened immediately. Gone was the anger, replaced by something new, akin to fresh pain. "He was considering leaving Percheron for a while," he admitted softly.

His pronouncement seemed to rattle Boaz. "Was Lazar unhappy?" the Zar asked sharply.

"Not unhappy, Highness," Jumo replied, choosing his words with care. "He struck me as . . . wistful in the days after we found Odalisque Ana. He was not pleased about being given that task by the Valide, it's true, but when you're out in the desert, Your Majesty, you often reflect about life and its possibilities."

"So he was planning to leave us?"

"No, Zar Boaz. I believe he was simply wondering about his homeland, his family probably."

"I never asked him about his childhood or life before Percheron," Boaz replied, genuine regret in his voice. "I wish I had now." Sighing, he straightened, his face suddenly resolute. "I will inform those who need to know about this tragedy and then I will declare three days of public mourning. Although sadly we will not have a body to commemorate the passing of the spirit, we will send him off nonetheless."

"And the perpetrator?" Pez prompted.

"And after that," Boaz declared, iron in his voice, "I will have someone ride the needle for this untimely death, so help me."

Zafira blanched and even Jumo could not hold back a grimace. Pez felt his stomach roll over. "Oh Highness, I'm not sure—"

"I *am* sure, Pez. You have all, in not so many words, accused someone connected to the palace with murder. That in itself is abhorrent to me. The fact that the victim was a close friend of mine, someone I admired and respected—loved even—for most of my life, makes me more determined to see his murderer pay. I will leave no stone unturned until I uncover the treacherous wretch. And when I do I will visit the penalty of a traitor onto his cursed body and leave him for the birds and insects to devour. He will have no burning ritual from Percheron, for he has desecrated my reign with this act."

Pez dropped his head, acquiescing. He had never seen Boaz like this, never heard his tone so terrible or commanding.

"What about the Spur's family?" Jumo asked.

"Yes, we must send a courier, but to where? We don't know anything about Lazar."

"I will go, Highness," Jumo said, his tone resolute. "I have no reason to remain here and I would welcome the diversion of tracking down his family."

Boaz nodded. "I understand. Organize what you need at the palace's expense. Now, the Valide Zara and Vizier Tariq will be waiting. I imagine both of you would prefer not to meet them." He nodded to Jumo and Zafira, who both looked grateful, if ruefully so. "Pez will show you how to leave here without using this entrance. May Zarab guide you across the waters, Jumo, and bring you back to us unharmed."

"Thank you, Highness," the man from the north replied, meaning it and bowing low in honor of the young Zar. Boaz, he knew, had treated him with courtesy and respect when he probably had not deserved it.

Boaz turned to Zafira. "I'm not sure how to offer an appropriate blessing to you, Priestess, except may your goddess keep you safe. You have my personal thanks for doing all you could to save the life of a man I called friend. I know he didn't die alone or without care and for that I am grateful. A donation will be made to the Sea Temple to acknowledge your commitment to Lazar."

"It is not necessary, Zar Boaz," the priestess replied gently, "and I fear the Vizier will not take kindly to the city donating a single karel to any temple of Lyana."

"You misunderstand me. The donation will be made from my personal coffers. I understand that he died beneath the altar of your goddess. Consider it a private thank-you to Lyana for watching over him in his hour of need."

Zafira nodded. She had not expected such grace or composure in one so young, or such tolerance. He was wise beyond his years to understand how dangerous it could be for her to become visible to those in power. No one had any time for the remnants of a bygone era.

With Pez's subdued guidance, she and Jumo took their leave through a small archway that led into the beautiful but simple Mirror Courtyard, which had won its name from the reflection in the grand pool, and through a series of corridors.

Boaz waited for his visitors to be well and truly out of sight before he sat down on a divan and privately grieved. His tears fell silently but his despair at Lazar's loss was intensely felt. With his father and the Spur gone, he had no adult male he could confer with—unless one counted Pez, but the dwarf, Boaz understood now, had his own secrets. And apart from Pez, there was now no one left in the palace he could call friend . . . no one except Ana. His heart lightened slightly. He had promised to bring her news of Lazar as soon as he received it. How would he ever be able to deliver these grim tidings without her hating him—or worse, holding him responsible?

A soft knock interrupted his thoughts and Bin entered at the Zar's command.

"My Zar, the Valide is getting . . ." The young servant paused diplomatically.

"Testy?"

"You might say that, Mighty One. She insisted I remind you that she and the Vizier await your pleasure."

Boaz smiled sympathetically at his servant. "Please inform the Valide that my day has been interrupted with some urgent news, which I am dealing with. Ask both herself and the Vizier to find some patience. I shall see them as soon as my time permits."

Bin blanched. "Are they to wait in the antechamber, my Zar?"

"Yes. And pass on no further demands to me from my mother, Bin." Boaz smirked slightly, despite his upset. "Take a deep breath and give her my message. Then come back in here."

"OH, THIS IS RIDICULOUS. I'm not a servant to be kept waiting like this," Herezah snarled at Bin.

The personal attendant made a soft noise of apology. "The Zar begs your patience, Valide. He has urgent matters to attend to."

"More urgent than the one he summoned us here for?" Tariq asked, an uncharacteristic insolence creeping into his tone.

"Apologies, Vizier. Please excuse me. I must attend to the Zar's duties," Bin replied, backing away from his two indignant superiors.

But Tariq had not finished with him yet. "And what, pray tell, servant Bin, is keeping His Highness from his mother?"

Even Herezah was surprised at the Vizier's defiance. Bin was only a servant but he was the Zar's eyes and ears too, and she knew how Boaz was starting to flex his wings, to build a loyal group of men around him. Bin might not take kindly to such a pugnacious attitude from another servant, no matter how lofty.

"I am not at liberty to discuss this further," Bin said, again apologetically, albeit firmly, and retreated more hurriedly to escape further interrogation.

Herezah turned to her companion once Bin had disappeared. "My, my, Tariq, it's not like you to be so belligerent. Aren't you feeling yourself today?" She smiled and the Vizier saw how her amusement mocked him.

It no longer affected him, of course. "Now that you come to mention it, Valide, no, I haven't been feeling myself today." He laughed, just as mockingly but gently so no offense could be taken.

Herezah lifted an eyebrow in query and noticed, as she paid him a moment's genuine scrutiny, that the Vizier didn't have quite the same curve to his back as she recalled. She'd gotten so used to Tariq's stoop that it never occurred to her that he might have the capacity to straighten . . . and yet he certainly seemed to be sitting more upright. "What an odd thing. You seem to be your full height again," she said, unable to miss any opportunity to offer a couched insult.

"Thank you, Valide Zara." Tariq's eyes glittered beneath his bushy brows. "I've discovered a marvelous new tonic. It's doing wonders for my health."

"You must share your new potion with me. There's not a woman alive who doesn't want to know how to look younger," she replied, frowning slightly. Was it her imagination, or was there a new intensity in Tariq's manner?

"I certainly shall," he agreed.

"Does this remedy have a name?"

"Oh yes, but it's my secret for now," he replied, chuckling softly to himself.

Herezah didn't understand his amusement but determined she would look into it—if there was a newly discovered herb for youthfulness, her physic would surely know it.

"Why do you think we have been called by your son, Valide?" Tariq asked, abruptly changing the subject.

"I have no immediate idea. I thought it might be about a private meeting he had with one of the odalisques that terribly incensed Salmeo. But now that you're here, I have to assume the topic is of a more formal nature. Have you any notion?"

The Vizier nodded slyly. "I think the Grand Master Eunuch will have a lot more to worry about than an unscheduled rendezvous by the Zar with a concubine, Valide Zara."

Her attention was riveted on him now. Since when did the Vizier have the audacity to intimate he knew something about her son that she didn't? "What do you mean by that?"

He shrugged, self-assurance evident in the gesture. "You asked if I had a notion and I do." He replied playfully enough that she could not be entirely offended.

Nevertheless, Herezah didn't want to play. It was perplexing enough having Tariq behave with such confidence without him having information about her son that she did not already know. "Tell me," she ordered evenly, troubled but careful not to display her frustration. "If you're going to enjoy the patronage you've always desired from me, Tariq, you'd better start remembering your place. Don't toy with me, Vizier."

"Valide, I would never do such a thing," he said, feigning surprise at the suggestion. "I just don't want to spread rumors without evidence. It is not my place to comment on Salmeo's position."

"But you just did!" she hissed. "Now, what do you know?"

"I only suspect; I know nothing," he replied. This was true. Since claiming Tariq, Maliz no longer had his omniscient view of the world. It took all of his presence and energy now to be Tariq, to work his body, to think within him, to effect the mannerisms he had studied for so long. Being the ancient Sewer Rat had required little effort, particularly as the skeletal old man did nothing more than lie still, slowly rotting away. For two centuries Maliz had roamed from frail body to frail body, never giving himself entirely over to any of them, simply killing the soul and then hovering within the host, refusing to fully claim it. Although this lack of immersion meant he could barely move the bodies, the freedom did permit him to project himself outside the body for short periods—which was how he had communicated so effectively with Tariq's mind. Alas, no longer. He was the Vizier now—wholly. When the Vizier's body died, he would die with it, and then his spirit would have to lie dormant in another series of frail bodies until he felt the rising of Iridor again. So from now to the moment of his next death, Maliz had only Tariq's eyes to see with and his ears to hear with. He would definitely need to increase the network of spies the Vizier had already set up if he was to keep abreast of even half of the information he'd previously had access to.

Before becoming the Vizier, Maliz had witnessed the conversation between the Deputy Inflictor and the apprentice. It had been a chance occurrence—he had been hurrying back to the old man's body when he'd overheard the exchange. There had been no mention of Salmeo in the conversation, of course, but Maliz knew who they referred to as "the highest authority." He understood the blackness of the man's soul, admired him for it.

Herezah persisted. "I want you to tell me what you suspect, Vizier."

Maliz pasted an expression of capitulation on Tariq's face. "Valide Zara, I have no proof but I believe we have been called to hear about the fate of the Spur."

"Lazar?" Though she hid it well, he did not miss the tinge of hope in her voice. "I can't imagine why it's taken so long."

"Can you not?" He raised an eyebrow now. "I think the delay is because he has died."

Shock hit her eyes—the only part of her face he could see. "What?" she breathed.

"I'm sure his injuries weren't lost on you, Valide."

She was silent a moment. Her eyes continued to betray her alarm but she did her best to hide her true feelings. "What has Salmeo got to do with all of this?" she asked with disdain.

"Everything, Valide. I suspect he not only chose the weapon wielded against the Spur, but also who would wield it."

"You heard what had happened to the Inflictor, what he said."

"I heard only the excuses of a young man not ready to take on the role of delivering punishment, Valide."

"And you think this was deliberately contrived?"

He shrugged, annoying her once again with his secretiveness. Usually Tariq fell over himself to share his thoughts with her, desperate to impress her. "I am making a personal observation, Valide. I make no accusation."

"But Salmeo's absence suggests you might be very much on target."

He pulled a face of resignation. "We must be patient. I'm sure we'll learn soon enough."

He was right. A few moments later, Bin returned. "The Zar will see you now, Valide Zara, Vizier Tariq. If you'll follow me."

"About time, young man," the Vizier grumbled, winking at Herezah. "The Valide is being kept from the important business of the harem."

Herezah tried to keep the confusion from her face. She couldn't believe the audacity of the man. He had never winked at her before, never even acted playful before. What in Zarab's name was happening to the Vizier?

ONCE THEY WERE CLEAR of the Zar's rooms and well away from prying eyes, Pez, who had been singing and skipping since leaving Boaz, led Jumo and Zafira into his own chamber, where he became instantly serious.

"Tell us everything," he ordered the priestess.

"I told the Zar everything in front of you. I have nothing more to tell."

"Well, how about why you're hiding Ellyana?" Pez pressed.

"Or the fact that you said Lazar died in the Sea Temple when I know only too well he was taken to the Isle of Stars." Jumo's grief had hardened into anger but Pez was glad to see the little man had it under control.

Zafira dropped her gaze. "It is true that Ellyana requested that her presence not be spoken about. It is not necessary that anyone hear about her or the island."

"Why?" Jumo demanded. "I hope she hasn't forgotten my promise."

"That you'd come looking for her?" Zafira asked. When he nodded, she gave a sad smile. "You won't find her, Jumo. She is . . ." And here Zafira hesitated.

"She is what?" Pez asked, feeling the hairs on the back of his neck stand on end.

"I would have thought you of all people would know," she replied, looking at her dwarf friend.

He stared at her for moments, his thoughts in turmoil.

"What does she mean?" Jumo asked.

Pez had his secrets but the death of Lazar changed everything—he had thought the Spur would be part of Lyana's struggle for supremacy. Lazar was one of the critical supports Pez had hoped he could count on. Lazar's death felt so wrong and now Pez felt as though he were suddenly part of a covert group hiding facts about his death. Ellyana, Zafira, and he alone knew the truth about where Lazar had spent his final hours, and why the women hid this fact he didn't know. He had always trusted Zafira and there was no reason not to trust her now, yet she was confusing him.

Jumo was glaring at him, so Pez felt obliged to answer. This time he told only the truth. "Ellyana came to me once. It was a long while ago. I was in the harem and she came in with the Bundle Women. She looked different then. She was not interested in any of the odalisques or wives, not even the servants. She was interested only in me."

"But everyone thinks you're a dozen goats short of a herd," Jumo queried, "so why you?"

"That's my point," Pez answered. "She knew otherwise. And it terrified me."

"What did she say?"

Pez looked vaguely embarrassed. "Well, I don't really understand it, Jumo." He hesitated, scratched his large head. "She said I had to discover who I truly am."

"And what's that supposed to mean?"

"I don't know," he lied.

"Anything else?"

Again Pez hesitated, considering all the strange events that had occurred—most recently Lazar's death.

Jumo tired of the protracted pause. "Lazar is dead because of Ellyana—"

Zafira leaped in. "That's not fair, Jumo. Ellyana did everything within her power. There are other things afoot. Things I don't understand yet, but I know Ellyana is involved. We must trust her."

Jumo rounded on the priestess, relishing the opportunity to release some of his anger. "You're talking in riddles, Zafira. Let's speak plainly here. Ellyana is hiding something and you're helping her do it. And now Lazar is dead!" Though his voice cracked on the final word, it did not break, and Pez and Zafira could see how he was fighting his emotions. "He was rallying, I tell you. I could feel it, even if I'm no doctor. That moaning and groaning was Lazar fighting and don't try and tell me otherwise. Lazar and I have a bond that goes back a decade. You don't spend as much time together as we did and not know each other inside out. Lazar would not have given up the fight."

"He didn't," Zafira said, her voice suddenly cold. "His circumstances beat him."

But Jumo was not ready to let it go. "Pez, when I asked you if there was anything else about Ellyana, you hesitated. Do you want to tell me everything?"

"Why do you say that?" Pez asked.

"Because I'm sensing secrets all around me. I feel as though no one is being entirely honest. Lazar is dead, his body already disposed of, and Ellyana has gone. Is this not ringing any alarms in your mind, Pez . . . or is it just me who smells something rotten?"

Pez secretly agreed with Jumo but wasn't ready to declare it. "When Ellyana arrived with the Bundle Women, she was young, very beautiful, but she kept herself hidden. When we spoke I thought my eyes were playing tricks on me, for she seemed suddenly old. No, not old; ancient. It was most unsettling."

Jumo said nothing, simply held the dwarf in a stare that seemed to look right into his heart.

"I forgot about her," Pez lied, hating the deception but needing some time to sort his thoughts privately. "But then she reappeared at the Sea Temple when we all met her. I didn't recognize her at first."

"Yes, I remember your surprise," Jumo admitted, frowning. "So she has been deliberately following you, do you think?"

"I have no idea," Pez answered truthfully. "Have you met her previously, Zafira?"

"I met her for the first time when Jumo did," she replied,

"although ever since, I have felt strangely comforted by her. Do you remember our conversation upstairs in the Sea Temple, Pez, when I said I felt something was happening and that I was involved but I couldn't say what it was or why?"

"I do. You seemed unsettled, unsure."

"Well, I think Ellyana has some answers."

Jumo turned away, making a sound of disgust.

"Forgive us," Pez said, taking Jumo's hand, wanting to give him comfort. "You have a sad journey to make and are filled with grief. I will give you this promise. Whilst you are away I will find Ellyana and I will seek the answers you need."

Jumo fixed him with an unrelenting gaze. "I will rely on you," he said, his tone thick with emotion. "I would track her myself if not for my duty to my master."

"Lazar always trusted me. You can too."

Jumo turned to Zafira. "I can never forgive you, Priestess, for disposing of my master's body without my consent."

Zafira matched his somber tone. "I didn't need your consent, Jumo. I had his."

"Nevertheless. Nothing I've heard you say about Lazar rings true to the man I knew."

"I am sorry you do not believe me. Make your journey and after your return we shall talk again. Perhaps then you will be more able to understand my position."

Pez raised an eyebrow, noting Zafira's careful wording. Perhaps Jumo was right. Perhaps the priestess *was* hiding something. She was being so careful about how she spoke.

Jumo nodded, too angry to speak about it any further. "I go. Have either of you any idea where to begin?"

Pez sighed. "Yes, I do, although this was a secret Lazar shared only with me."

Jumo's eyes narrowed. There had never been secrets between him and the master. "Why would he tell you?"

Pez shrugged. "Perhaps so that in the event of this very situation of his death . . . that someone know."

"Why not me?" Jumo asked, the hurt evident in his voice.

"Because it would have affected your precious relationship with him, Jumo. Lazar loved you too much to compromise the friendship you shared."

"What do you know?" Jumo demanded, breathing hard.

Pez looked to the priestess. "If you'll forgive me, Zafira . . . I gave my word a long time ago that I would share this knowledge with no one but Jumo should the time arise."

She looked intrigued but put her hands in the air in mock defeat. "I understand. I shall wait outside and then we can return to the Sea Temple together," she said to Jumo.

He said nothing, and as she left, Pez fixed him with that strange yellow gaze of his and said, "You believe that Lazar is from a noble line in Merlinea. He liked to pretend he wasn't from an important family but you have always suspected otherwise . . . that he was running from them; perhaps he was a second or third son who hadn't reached his potential, or had been banished for having an affair with the wrong woman."

"Something like that," Jumo agreed guardedly.

Once again Pez sighed. "Lazar's real name is Lucien. Does that mean anything to you?"

The small man shook his head, although the news clearly startled him.

The dwarf gave Jumo his final shock for this day when he said, "Lucien is . . . was, not from Merlinea at all. He was King Falza's eldest son, and heir to the throne of Galinsea."

23

Boaz declared three official days of mourning for the death of the Spur of Percheron. He sent messengers to the various quarters of the city to make announcements of Lazar's passing. No actual details of how he had died were to be given, although the Zar knew rumors would become rife very quickly.

At the shocking news, Herezah had retired to her chambers and demanded that no one disturb her. Boaz privately reconfirmed simply from her reaction that his mother had had nothing to do with Lazar's punishment and subsequent death. The stillness of her body as she received the tidings, the horror she couldn't hide in her eyes, and the slight trembling of her voice when she asked a tentative question gave him more than enough proof that the Valide was as devastated as he was—although no doubt for different reasons.

The Vizier's reaction had been a surprise. Boaz had found

there to be something different about Tariq; something about the way he listened thoughtfully before offering comments when ordinarily he rushed to say anything in an attempt to impress, to be part of any royal conversation. Boaz even found himself appreciating his steadfastness when the Vizier cautioned against overreaction.

"May I humbly suggest you take your time, my Zar. This situation is grave indeed, and if our Spur has been hurried to his death, as you imply, it will not do to leap to conclusions. A proper inquiry should be made, formally appointed and delicately handled. Let it take as long as it must until the guilty party is hunted down. The Spur was too admired by too many for justice not be seen to be done . . . especially so early in your reign."

Boaz had not expected such levelheadedness. He knew of the acrimony that existed between the Vizier and the Grand Master Eunuch. It was based on years of jealousy, intensified since his father's passing, and the desire of each to win his mother's trust. Of course neither man had reckoned on the young Zar wanting to have any involvement in the running of the state. They thought of him as merely a boy, assumed that his mother would rule as Zara until he reached an age when he was ready for such responsibility. Boaz guessed they had counted on at least three or four years of autonomy, by which time it would be hard for the young Zar to wrest back full control of his realm. Well, they had been wrong. Boaz had every intention of taking full control now, before misconceptions about his right or fitness to rule could arise.

He had dismissed both his mother and the Vizier but not before he had made a point of thanking Tariq for his wise words. Boaz had waited for the Vizier's usual preening of feathers and plumping of chest; instead he had been surprised once again when the man had hardly blinked at the compliment. Instead he had bowed graciously and simply said, "My Zar, please call upon me whenever you need."

Boaz had watched the Vizier gently guide his mother—like Boaz, astonished by the man's graciousness—from the room, careful not to lay so much as a fingertip on her person. The Zar frowned, intrigued not just by the Vizier's behavior but also by his straighter bearing. The man's stoop had improved. He wanted to talk to Pez about this sudden metamorphosis, but first, he had to arrange for money to be given to Jumo, and then he would need to speak with Odalisque Ana, to break the news that would surely shatter her.

JUMO WALKED BACK with Zafira to the Sea Temple in a simmering silence. The priestess had the good sense not to try reasoning with him again but she felt her own heart fracture when she watched him finally kneel by Lyana's altar and kiss the dried smear of blood where only yesterday his master had lain dying. Taking a risk, she knelt by the softly keening manservant and put her arm around him, expecting a sharp rebuttal. None came. Jumo's anger was spent; he was now consumed by grief and despair, and in this, he knew he was not alone.

"I'm so sorry, Jumo," she whispered. "So sorry for doing this to you."

They remained kneeling in silence for several minutes before Zafira painfully pulled herself to her feet. "I shall leave you to your thoughts and private prayers," she said. "When you're ready, let me share quishtar with you before you leave."

Later, as she busied herself with her brew, she heard men's

voices. Soon enough she heard slow footsteps on the stairs and turned to see Jumo standing in her small room.

"Ready to go?" she asked, trying to infuse her tone with a gentle brightness.

Jumo nodded. "The Zar has sent money." She saw a heavy-looking pouch in his hand. "It is too much, far too generous. I came to ask you if I might leave some behind . . . here? Perhaps you can make better use of it in Lyana's work. Lazar was always impressed by those who serve the Goddess."

"That's because his people worshipped her more recently than the people of Percheron. It took longer to get rid of us priestesses in the west." Though her words were sharp, Zafira delivered them without malice.

"Lazar believed in no gods, Zafira. Not yours and not Percheron's."

"That's sad to learn. It probably means at some time in his life he had been badly let down. It is interesting to me, though, to see that he was drawn to Lyana that day before you all left to find the new girls for the harem. We spoke then about the Mother Goddess. He felt a special pull to her statue, said she gave him a sense of peace." She took a step toward him, her tone beseeching. "Jumo, this needs to be said. I understand the depth of your sadness but you must recognize it as grief, not hate. Lazar would not want you to hate me."

"I do not hate you, Zafira. It is Ellyana I despise for her treachery."

"Please, I beg you, allow some room in your heart for her. She had hard choices to make."

But Jumo shook his head. "She made choices beyond her authority. I should have stayed. Perhaps he might have lived if I had. And if not, at least I would have been with him as he died. I cannot forgive her. She has no place in my heart."

It hurt Zafira deeply to hear these words. She wanted to tell him more about Ellyana but fear stopped her. "Don't leave the money. The Zar is already donating some and you might need it—you have no idea what you're going into, or how long you'll be. I presume you now know how far you might need to travel to find Lazar's people?"

He said nothing in response to her mild prying, was still incapable of believing Pez's tale. For the time being, he had deliberately stopped thinking about it. Crossing the Faranel would give him plenty of time for dwelling on Lazar's great secret.

Zafira was far too sensitive to press him. "Keep the money, for safety's sake. You can always leave it later upon your return."

He tucked the pouch inside his robes. "Then I shall go. I thank you for the offer of quishtar, but another time perhaps when some wounds have healed. I have a ship to find."

Zafira nodded her gentle understanding. "Then go safely, Jumo. I shall look forward to sharing a healing quishtar with you on your return."

And he was gone, his footsteps retreating down the stairs and padding softly across the stone of the temple floor. She watched from the vantage of her window as he emerged into the quiet of the long peninsula and walked away until he was lost in the crowd and action of the busy harbor. She wondered if she would ever see him again. She wondered if Lyana herself would ever forgive her for hurting a good man so deeply.

Zafira steadied her thoughts. She had to find Pez again. She had forgotten to give him something important, something

Lazar had insisted upon him having. It frightened her to have it in her posession. Zafira knew the old stories—what this statue of gold signified chilled her to the marrow.

Iridor was rising. And she had been instructed to give the statue to the strange, mysterious dwarf she called friend but knew so little about.

BOAZ SUMMONED the Grand Master Eunuch, who was shown in, puffing from the exertion of meeting the urgent call to the Zar's chamber.

Boaz gave no time for polite preamble. As the hefty man completed his bow, the Zar was already talking. "Did you request that Odalisque Ana be readied for a conversation as instructed?"

"Yes, Majesty. She is being prepared now, although I would caution—"

"Salmeo, I am tired of everyone in this palace cautioning me. I shall make myself perfectly clear for the last time to you and to those who would question my authority. I will make my own decisions, good or bad, and should I ever require your counsel, I shall seek it. Until then, just follow my instructions as I have already outlined to you!"

Salmeo seethed beneath the expressionless countenance he had mastered. "Of course, my Zar. We have only your best interests at heart."

"Then perhaps you can explain why I have no Spur of Percheron."

The eunuch looked around him, as if he thought the Zar was speaking to someone else. "Majesty?"

Boaz reined in his anger. He'd had years of experience

watching Salmeo in action. It would be a pity to waste that knowledge so early in their new relationship by allowing the eunuch to provoke him into explosions of anger or manipulate him in any way. "Lazar, our Spur," he reminded calmly. "I'm wondering if you have any thoughts on how serious it is that we no longer have Percheron's highest-ranking member of our security force available to us."

Salmeo appeared taken aback. "Well, Highness, I suspect he will have to heal considerably before he can sit a horse again or command the men." He struggled to say more, then added: "A few days perhaps?"

"A few days? You were standing quite close, Grand Master Eunuch. I'm sure the extent of his injuries was not lost on you."

Salmeo affected an innocent shrug. He closed his eyes, as if sympathetic to the Zar's observations. "Yes, Shaz made a bad job of it, my Zar. I have confined him to his quarters since, not that he's up to much. He himself admits he botched it."

"And yet you had felt confident he could carry out the sentence," Boaz reminded him.

"Zar, I didn't have much to choose from. Someone had to do this task. Shaz's superior assured me that he was the best available. He is apparently adept with the whip."

"Yes, the whip, for flogging servants and other dissidents within the palace. Perhaps even for striping a wayward odalisque who needed reminding of her place. He had never even been allowed to touch the Snake before. I'm sure you were aware of this."

"I am afraid I was not, Highness. Time was short and Shaz's superiors were not available for lengthy discussion."

"Did you know that Shaz had never flogged anyone before, only dummies in the practice courtyard?"

Salmeo shook his head slowly. "My Zar, this is the first I've heard such a thing. How do you know this?"

Boaz knew when he was being fed an untruth. Silently seething, he ignored Salmeo's question. "Have you heard any news about the well-being of the Spur?"

"No, Zar. But I gather the Vizier was going to send out parties of runners. Has he failed you in this?"

"News has arrived, Grand Master Eunuch, but perhaps you've been too busy with harem matters to hear it."

Salmeo had not, in fact, heard the news. He disguised his wrath; he would personally deal with the Elim spies who had apparently failed him. "Oh, Zarab be praised. I'm pleased, High One. I did hear that a party of messengers was sent out a few hours ago and I hoped that was to deliver news of the Spur. All good, I hope?"

Boaz fixed the fat eunuch with his best stare, one he'd learned from his father. "News, yes, but none of it good, Grand Master Eunuch. New messengers have been sent at my behest to spread news of the Spur's death."

"His death," Salmeo repeated softly, his hand across his heart.

"Are you surprised?"

"I'm shocked, Zar Boaz. The injuries were bad, I'll grant you, but the Spur was strong, still a young man. If he had had the right care, the healing might have taken a while but . . ." His voice trailed off. "Dead," he echoed, still seemingly unable to accept it.

Boaz was confused now, although he worked hard to keep his expression hard. He had hoped to push Salmeo into some sort of confession, hoped that Salmeo would at the very least let slip some information that might indicate he was behind the murder. Perhaps the Grand Master Eunuch really was innocent and aspersions had been cast without proof.

"It's all my fault, Zar Boaz. If I hadn't insisted upon such tradition, the Spur would have been spared. I have killed him." The man, deeply upset, struggled down to his knees. "I have inadvertently killed him through my actions. Oh my Zar, I was only trying to do the right thing. You are young and we all want to support you, make the transition as easy as we can. I thought that by making an example of Odalisque Ana, we could prevent any further embarrassment to the royal family. Who would have thought Spur Lazar would take her punishment himself?"

Boaz was taken aback. He suddenly felt out of his depth, wishing for once that his mother was nearby to offer advice. Was the eunuch weeping? Yes, he was. Boaz wanted to look away but knew he mustn't. "You might have spared the Spur the Viper's Nest, Salmeo. That in itself was unnecessarily cruel and, in my opinion, a punishment that did not fit the crime."

Salmeo opened his arms wide in a plea. "Oh, Zar Boaz, I would have. It was never my idea to use the Snake. You must believe me. I have never called for its use before. I believe it should be reserved solely for traitorous acts."

"If you did not order its use, then who did?"

"No, Zar Boaz. I take full responsibility. I cannot blame anyone else for this. I permitted it, after all. But I promise you from my heart, Mighty One, I was only trying to do the right thing."

"Salmeo, there is yet one more layer to this dark deed," Boaz warned. He watched the eunuch grow still. Salmeo's face was already slick with tears and perspiration but somehow it seemed to darken as his eyes widened.

"What do you mean by that, Great One?"

"Please stand," Boaz commanded, discomfited by the huge

bulk of the Grand Master Eunuch imploring him from his knees. The man took several seconds—and the support of a conveniently placed divan—to heave himself back to his feet. Once again he towered tall and Boaz was relieved that he had himself chosen to stand on a raised part of the chamber. He cleared his throat. "Lazar's injuries were horrific but we know this was mainly the result of an amateur's work."

Salmeo nodded. "He should not have died from them."

"Well, we shall never know. What sped Lazar to his death, however, was the use of poison."

"Poison?" Salmeo uttered in apparent disbelief.

Boaz nodded. "Drezden. Have you heard of it?"

"Yes, of course. It was used by Zars long ago."

"Do you mean to tell me that you are aware of having this poison in the palace?" Boaz said, aghast.

Salmeo looked mortified. "Great One, this is my fault, and my fault alone. Your father asked me to dispose of the small amount remaining in the palace. It was safely under lock and key and I had forgotten about it until now."

"Really," Boaz said drily.

Salmeo feigned confusion. "But when did the Spur drink it, Great One? If he consumed it before he was taken to the Court-yard of Sorrows, then the perpetrator could be anyone outside of the palace."

"That is true. Except one presumes that if it had been administered orally, Lazar would never have made it to the flogging. He would have died then and there."

"Not necessarily, High One. Drezden, as I understand it, is a very slow killer. That's the point of it. It gives the murderer time to retreat."

"I see. Either way, drezden was not swallowed by the Spur."

"Oh?"

"From what I can gather, the tips of the Snake were dipped in the lethal potion. It then entered his body via the wounds from the flogging."

Salmeo's shock appeared complete. "No" was all he could say, vehemently shaking his head, flesh wobbling tremulously beneath the sober-colored robes he had chosen this day.

"Who chose the Viper's Nest if not you, Salmeo?" Boaz urged.

"I can't—" Salmeo groaned.

"You must, Grand Master Eunuch, or the full blame of the Spur's death will rest on your shoulders. I will not lie to the people about this. Answers are required. Someone must pay for the murder of this man."

The eunuch wept harder. It was disconcerting enough to watch this normally arrogant man humbled, but to hear him cry was the most uncomfortable moment Boaz had known in his life. "It was Horz, my Zar," the Grand Master Eunuch suddenly blurted out. "Horz, the head of my Elim guard. He said he was going to take revenge on the Spur but I didn't believe it. I kept hoping that in his drunkenness he was just talking rubbish."

"Horz?" Boaz repeated skeptically. The head of the Elim was one of the most trustworthy and sober people he knew.

"Horz had a grudge against Lazar," Salmeo explained.

"What are you talking about? What grudge?"

"Horz is related to Odalisque Ana, Great One. He is brother to her father. He resented that she had been brought into the harem to be made a concubine. Perhaps her father is furious— she did say that he did not sanction the sale."

"Ana's uncle?" Boaz's mind was reeling. "She never mentioned it."

"Why would she? Ana is secretive by nature. But I make a point of knowing all I can about our odalisques, Majesty."

"And he used the drezden? Are you sure?"

"Who else could it be, Zar Boaz? Horz has access to it. Only he and I have keys to the dispensary. And once we had heard about Spur Lazar's intentions, it was to Horz I turned to help me set up the flogging. I briefed him and left it to him, my Zar. It was Horz who chose the Viper's Nest. Believe me when I say it was a shock to me too, to see that vicious weapon being brought out. But by then it was too late—what could I do?"

"Intervene?" Boaz snapped, angry.

"With all due respect, High One, I could not. I have invested my faith in Horz, Great One, as you invest yours in those who serve you well. He has been a model Elim, and has been an exemplary guard. I trust him completely; I would never have compromised his position by undermining his authority at the flogging. As I said, I was surprised, but having been told that Shaz was the best new Inflictor, I felt it would be handled with caution. Furthermore, once you commuted the sentence—"

"Which you didn't seem to agree with," Boaz interrupted.

"That is true, Mighty One. I believe in upholding tradition and forgive me if my expression reflected a reluctance to stray from that path." Salmeo stopped talking, breathing hard from his urgency to explain.

"So Horz had the motive and the opportunity, you say?"

"That's right. I thought it was mere talk—the talk of the liquor—it never entered my mind that he would actually carry out his wish for revenge."

Boaz sighed, deeply disturbed by all that he had heard. "Family honor is a powerful motivation."

Salmeo nodded sadly. "I take full responsibility, my Zar. I appointed Horz. He is my man."

"Don't be ridiculous, Salmeo. You didn't ask him to do such a thing, nor did you guide his hand. This is murder—a calculated killing, and I will not tolerate it in my palace."

"What will happen to Horz?" Salmeo asked, a new and plaintive tone in his voice.

"He must pay for his crime. I will require a full confession from him by sundown. Bring him to me just before the feast gong. I would prefer not to handle this on a full belly."

"Yes, my Zar."

"Salmeo, for the time being, this is between us. If I discover that anyone has learned of Horz's actions—or our discussion—your head will roll with his. I want to know the truth from his lips before I make my decision."

"I understand, Zar Boaz. I will prepare him."

"Will he be honest?"

"He is an honorable man, Great One."

Boaz nodded. "I wish to be alone now to consider all that I've heard. I shall see you in an hour. Please have Odalisque Ana brought to me then," he said, sadness creeping into his tone.

Salmeo bowed low and turned to leave. The Zar could not see the way the scar on the Grand Master Eunuch's face lifted with the man's sly grin.

24

The man looked sickened. "Lie to the Zar? Admit to a terrible sin I did not commit?"

"Unless you want your family slain, Horz," Salmeo agreed conversationally. At the Elim's stunned expression, his chief continued slyly: "Or did you think I didn't know about them? I know everything, Horz. I know that you were once married and have three children—two boys and a girl, if I recall correctly. I know that your wife died—your error in making her travel during an illness—and that your brother's family has raised your children whilst you, as a penance of sorts, offered yourself to the Elim."

Horz's face had drained of all color. He stood before the Grand Master Eunuch pale and rigidly still.

Salmeo looked at his nails, made a mental note to have a slave neaten them again this evening. "I know that your children live with your eldest brother. Your other brother is a goatherd in the foothills. His marriage is less than perfect but he has five children—one of them not his. The middle girl is an orphan, adopted by your brother. Her name is Ana and she was found by Spur Lazar, purchased fairly and brought to the palace. Except the negotiations were with the shrewish wife, not your brother, and he is hurting and you are angry that one of your own has been given to the harem. Odalisque Ana recognized you but did not give you away—she's a clever girl. She'll cost me more grief than I deserve, I'm sure, but she protected you, Horz. It was you who gave yourself away. I knew nothing about your brother in the foothills until I began to make inquiries after your reaction at the presentation of the girls. You were protective toward her, and I became suspicious. And now it's simple, Horz. I need a scapegoat and you're the perfect solution. I can't possibly take the blame myself."

The Elim said nothing, presumably understanding all too clearly now that he was staring into two pits—both dark, both horrible. One meant death to the family he loved; the other meant death to him. There was no choice, really.

"Now, if you go along with my suggestion," Salmeo said softly, his lisp more noticeable as a result, "I will give you my assurance—a blood assurance, if you insist—that I will take care of your children. Your sons will have money and some land or a shop if they wish and a house each of their own in the city. You may choose. Your daughter I will help find a good man for . . . someone she likes, I promise, someone who will treat her kindly. A rich man. She will want for nothing. Your brothers and their families will receive an annuity each year in gold and camels. Even in your most vivid dreams, you couldn't have hoped for this much."

Horz shook his head sadly but said nothing.

"It's how much I value what you will do for me. I pledge it. All this will occur if you'll lie for me . . . and die for me. You are Elim, after all."

Still the man stayed silent.

"And if you will not lie, Horz, then your family will die. Not just your children but both of your brothers, their wives, and all their children between them. I hear the youngest is just a summer old. Pity. There is nothing you can do, there is nowhere they can hide. You should know," Salmeo said to the proud man who now gazed fearfully at the ground, trembling, "that I have already sent men to encircle your people."

Horz looked up sharply, hate radiating from his dark eyes.

"Oh, come now, did you expect anything less? Of course I've already dispatched men—killers too—but they will not act until they've heard from me. Does your family live or die, Horz?"

ANA WAS LED IN by two senior eunuchs and she immediately sensed that the Zar was not in the playful, chatty mood of the previous day. When she stood before him, he signaled the escort to remain. This was a formal meeting, then.

She eyed him through the slit of the charcoal veil she wore tonight over creamy loose pantaloons and a billowing chemise. Ana was glad that the veil hid her fear. The Zar's grave countenance could mean only one thing: he had bad news for her. It was obvious Lazar was not coming back in a hurry.

Why she had held such hope that he would be striding through the marble corridors within days was beyond her. One didn't have to be wise to see that Lazar's injuries were so horrific that he would need months to recover. And this was all her fault. Her selfish attitude had brought about his suffering. Remembering how he had looked at her before the flogging, she knew in her heart that Lazar had already forgiven her. But could she ever forgive herself? She doubted it.

Ana swallowed hard and reminded herself that this soul-searching was yet more self-centeredness. She was already wondering how she would cope without a glimpse of Lazar or a chance to hear his voice. She loved him, and wanted to tell him that she had mouthed the words behind her veil, but of course he would not have understood; she could only hope her eyes had conveyed her feelings truly. She knew she was a child in his eyes, but he had sold her into the harem for an adult's role. If she could make love to the Zar, she could make love to the Spur.

Oh shame on you, Ana, she chided silently. *Your wicked thoughts will dismantle you.* Ana watched Boaz approach and then fell to her knees, flattening herself as she had been taught, arms spread wide in supplication.

"Please stand, Ana," Boaz commanded graciously.

She did so, straightening her robes but not offering him eye contact until she was given permission. From now on, she would do everything the right way, and then she would earn the palace's affection and hopefully Lazar's respect.

"I wish to talk with you privately but I've asked the Elim to remain. Let us move here so we may not be overheard."

She nodded, wondering both at the secretiveness and at the reason Boaz had requested the Elim's presence.

"You may look at me, Ana. It would please me."

She heard the struggle in his voice and decided to help him.

"My Zar, I believe that you have called me here this afternoon to give me news of the man who so generously offered his own skin to save mine. Thank you for keeping your promise."

To her surprise, Boaz didn't look any happier for the aid. "Your intuition serves you well, Odalisque Ana. Yes, this is about Spur Lazar, but first I must ask you something."

"I'll answer whatever you wish to ask, Highness."

"I want your truth," he counseled seriously. "The man called Horz, do you know him?"

"He is the head of the Elim, Highness," she answered immediately but carefully.

Boaz's serious expression did not waver. "I know. I want to know if you know him outside of that role."

Ana blinked. "He is my uncle," she said softly. "I hardly know him but I have seen him once prior to the palace, when he came to visit my father and our family. It was a long time ago but I don't forget faces, Highness."

"I see," Boaz replied, and she could sense a swell of disappointment overcome him. Why was he upset? Was he angry with her for not saying something sooner?

"My Zar," she began, leaping to the wrong conclusion, "he has shown me no special treatment. I have hardly seen him since my arrival, other than in the Choosing Room when I was to be presented with the other odalisques. He also was in charge of me at the flogging but we did not exchange so much as a word. He pretends not to know me and I him."

Boaz sighed. "I thank you for your honesty."

"You look so unhappy, my Zar. Please unburden yourself and give me the tidings of the Spur—the pain is mine, for the fault is mine. I know he was badly hurt and I suspect you are disappointed that he will be out of service for a long while."

She saw Boaz's eyes widen slightly. There was deep grief hidden in that startled expression and there was pain in the way his mouth twisted, urged itself to say the words. "Ana, it is my sad duty to tell you that Spur Lazar will not be returning to the service of Percheron."

She heard him clearly but the words made no sense to her. "Has he gone away?" she asked, feeling injured that Lazar had not sent word of farewell.

"He has gone away for good, you could say," Boaz said gently. "He has gone to his gods, Ana."

She cocked her head slightly as if listening to an inner voice. She couldn't seem to grasp his meaning.

"Spur Lazar died in the early hours of this morning, Ana. It was confirmed by an old priestess from the Sea Temple."

"Zafira?" she whispered, hardly knowing she uttered it.

"Yes. He died in her arms. She has disposed of his body as he requested."

Ana was trembling. Boaz signaled to the Elim, who were at her side in moments, preventing her from falling.

"He died from his wounds?" She began to wail softly. "How can this be?"

"I'm afraid I know nothing further," Boaz lied.

"He can't be dead," she groaned. "He can't. Have you checked with Jumo, my Zar?"

"Jumo was here with me this morning, Ana. He is as upset as you and has agreed to find Lazar's family and pass on the news with my deepest regrets."

"Jumo's gone to Merlinea?" she stammered, no longer thinking straight, just talking, saying anything to keep the horror at bay.

"Yes. Ana, you need to lie down. You are in shock. The Elim

will take you back to your chambers and will give you something to help you sleep. We shall talk again soon."

"Boaz, no!" she shrieked, ignoring all protocol. The Elim gripped her hard, angry at her manner with their Zar.

"Stop," he ordered them. "Be gentle with her. Carry her back to the harem, and if I hear of a strand of her hair so much as pulled from her head, you will both regret it. Ana," he said, gently, wishing he could cup her face or hold her hand but unwilling to touch her in front of the Elim, "go now. We will know more soon. Be brave; Lazar would want you to be as brave as he was." Looking to one of the men, he ordered, "Ask her maid to give her a soporific immediately. She must sleep off her shock and someone must be with her the whole time. Pez will do." He saw their puzzlement. "He's mad, yes, but he's also company and he can soon alert the harem when she wakes or if she needs anything. Do as I command. Find him and tell him I said he's to stay with her."

He looked away as the baffled men, unsure of how to order Pez to do anything, ushered the silent, grief-stricken figure away.

PEZ TOOK ONE LOOK at the tearstained face and understood immediately that Ana had learned the shocking news.

". . . and you're to remain here with her, dwarf, do you understand, you fool? Zar's orders," an Elim was saying.

He ignored the man, humming to himself, but as the Elim bent down to make his point, he sneezed into the man's face. And then kept sneezing, much to the man's horror and disgust. Pez could see the man's fingers twitching into a fist, desperate to make the dwarf pay for such insult.

"Don't," the Elim's mate cautioned. "It's not worth your own skin. He's mad, you know."

"Sometimes I feel as though he knows exactly what he's doing," the first man grumbled, wiping his face. "Come on, let's go."

Mercifully, they left and Pez was finally able to turn and lay his hand on the slightly feverish forehead of the restless young woman. Ana moaned softly, caught in a drug-induced sleep. As before, as soon as he touched her, Pez felt a strange sensation tingling through his palm and traveling up his arm until it entered his body proper and warmed him throughout. It was unsettling—as though her fever had passed into his body—and yet it was also somehow comforting. As long as he kept his hand on her body, the sense of glowing within remained.

She stirred. Her eyelids fluttered open but her eyes remained unfocused, her pupils dilated. The warmth running through Pez intensified. He half expected Ana to sit up and then walk in her sleeping state—he had seen others do this—but she began to murmur instead, incoherently. He leaned in close to hear better and realized that she was speaking a language he did not understand but recognized as an ancient one.

Suddenly she gripped his hand with such force he winced. Her body had become rigid although her eyes continue to stare blankly. "Pez."

Her voice sounded distant, odd. A trickle of fear crawled up his spine. "I'm here, Ana."

"Tell Lazar I'm sorry."

He did not want to lie but did anyway. "I will, although he needs no apology."

Seemingly at his words, the warmth through his body increased.

"The owl is yours."

"What?"

"Get the owl, Pez."

A sudden chill shivered through him. "The owl?"

"Zafira has it. Get it now!"

"I will, I promise," he replied, baffled.

And then Ana's grip relaxed from his wrist, her body became limp again, and she slumped into deep sleep, her lips slightly parted, her expression no longer troubled but serene. "The owl," he said quietly to himself, not understanding any of it. What should he do? He had orders to remain, but if he sneaked away, the Elim would just think he was being his usual contrary self. However, these orders came from Boaz, and Pez didn't want to disappoint his friend. And yet somehow Ana's need felt more desperate, and that searing heat through his body had been too strange and frightening to ignore. And besides, he had good reason to visit Zafira. She was going to tell him one way or another how he would find Ellyana. He had an oath to keep to Jumo.

BOAZ HAD SPENT the last hour steeling himself for this confrontation. It hurt him to think that he might have to deal severely with a man he admired while ignoring the one he despised. Boaz couldn't fully believe Salmeo and yet he could not disbelieve him outright. The fact of the matter was that if Horz admitted to this shocking deed, Boaz would have no choice but to bring the full weight of his crown behind the punishment. It was treachery of the highest order—not just the slaying of a man of rank but a man close to the Zar—the Zar's absolute protector, in fact. The people would demand no less than death and nothing honorable about it either. More serious than all of this, of course, was the betrayal from within. That Boaz could be treated so traitorously by one of his own, especially one in the prestigious Elim, demanded the most punitive retaliation. If he did not act with the utmost severity, it would set a poor tone for his reign.

Bin somberly announced the arrival of the Grand Master Eunuch and the head of the Elim.

"Bring them in," Boaz ordered.

Bin disappeared momentarily to the study and returned with the two visitors. Salmeo bowed low but Horz fully prostrated himself.

"Stand," Boaz ordered. The head of the Elim returned only to his knees, head bowed. "Horz," he began, glad his voice was free of all the tremors he had feared, "the Grand Master Eunuch has shared—most reluctantly, I might add—some information that has devastated my feelings about the Elim. I gather you know to what I refer?"

"I do, my Zar. I beg you not to blame the Elim for this deed. Its honor is intact, for the act you refer to is all my own doing."

"So you admit it?"

"I admit that it was my sole doing, High One."

"What exactly are you admitting to, Horz?" Boaz asked quietly.

The man swallowed hard and Boaz could see his hand trembling. "I killed Spur Lazar with poison that I stole from the apothecary. Without the Inflictors' knowledge, I dipped the tips of the Viper's Nest into the lethal potion known as drezden." He fell silent. Salmeo nudged Horz with his toe and the man began speaking again. His voice was detached, as if he were reciting from a prepared script. "I had already blackmailed the head Inflictor into leaving his post on a pretend excuse; the deputy, Rah, was ill. That left only the apprentice, Shaz, who I was sure would botch the flogging, particularly using the snake whip which I insisted he use."

"Stop!" Boaz commanded. "Grand Master Eunuch, would you leave us for a short while. I wish to speak with Horz alone."

Salmeo gave a soft, bouncing bow and departed. Boaz did not miss the glare he threw toward the Elim on his way out.

"Look at me, Horz," Boaz said gently, and the man reluctantly lifted his head. Boaz looked at the angry eyes and defiant set of the mouth that belied the humble tone and willing confession. It didn't take much to put the scenario together and he regretted deeply not sending a runner to fetch Horz far earlier and confronting him with Salmeo's claims as he stood before the Grand Master Eunuch. He felt suddenly empty. "I thought as much," he said sadly. "What has he got over you, Horz, that you would lie for him? It can't be loyalty, for what you're admitting to surely goes against everything you stand for, have always stood for."

Horz took a moment to compose himself, and when he spoke his voice was even, no wrath flavoring his words. "I am not lying, Highness. I am honorable in this confession." His eyes silently said something different.

It broke Boaz's heart but he was helpless. It was obvious that Horz had somehow been compromised but the man was openly and determinedly confessing to a murder and it was he alone who must take the full blame. Boaz called for Bin and asked him to readmit Salmeo. The eunuch flounced in confidently but was careful to keep his expression somber as he bowed yet again.

"Is everything all right, my Zar?"

"Yes, everything is exactly as you described it, Grand Master Eunuch," Boaz replied smoothly.

Salmeo inclined his head in thanks and Boaz had no choice but to allow the head of the Elim to continue to weave his sad lies.

IT WAS DONE. Boaz imagined Salmeo was inwardly gloating, although his expression betrayed nothing but intense sympathy for the kneeling figure.

"We will require a formal witness from my council for sentencing," Boaz said. "Bin?"

The manservant stepped forward from the recesses of the chamber. "My Zar?"

"Fetch the Vizier, and I suppose you had better fetch the Valide Zara too."

The servant bowed and left the room, urgently calling for runners. Boaz excused himself without much courtesy. He could no longer bear to look at Horz or the smug Grand Master Eunuch.

But, as his father had constantly counseled, information is power. Boaz knew only too well how Salmeo's mind worked and the eunuch no doubt understood this. Salmeo's eloquent presentation of the role of Horz in this murder was plausible, and given the circumstances of the Elim's hollow-sounding confession, he could hardly accuse both men of lying. Why Horz might go along with such a grave untruth he couldn't imagine, but Boaz was sure Salmeo understood that his Zar suspected the lies. It gave Boaz some satisfaction to know that the fat man might never again feel comfortable in the Zar's presence.

BIN WAS SURPRISINGLY SWIFT in rounding up the Vizier and the Valide prior to supper, and Boaz returned to the study quickly. Horz had not moved from his kneeling position, although Salmeo had deliberately distanced himself from the criminal. Boaz felt the flutters of anger again at the chief eunuch's audacity but he damped them down, knowing them to be a useless waste of energy.

"Mother, Tariq," he acknowledged. As both bowed, Boaz was once again struck by the new posture of the Vizier. His eyes must be deceiving him, for the man seemed ever straighter, taller than he had just a few hours before—even his complexion looked less pasty. His mother, by comparison, looked deeply unhappy. Dressed in dark garments with no adornments whatsoever, she looked almost as though she were in mourning.

Boaz wasted no further time on courtesies. "You are here to witness the sentencing of Horz, head of the Elim, who has confessed to the premeditated murder of Spur Lazar." Herezah uttered a soft sound of shock. Not much surprised the Valide but this statement had. Tariq, Boaz noted, said nothing and in fact barely flinched at the news, suggesting either that he didn't care or, more likely, that the man knew more than he was sharing. "Grand Master Eunuch has assisted in winning this confession," Boaz continued, his words couching a silent threat to Salmeo.

"And what reason, my Zar—if you don't mind my inquiry—has Salmeo wrung from Horz for wanting to murder our Spur?" It was said innocently enough but Boaz looked sharply at the Vizier. It seemed Tariq too had already discounted Horz's involvement in Lazar's death.

The eunuch demurred. "It is not my place. I shall leave that to our Zar to explain."

Boaz briefly explained the connection between Horz and Ana to his mother and Tariq.

"Because of that girl!" Herezah exclaimed, angry now. "She is more trouble than she's worth—first the escape, then the Spur's flogging, and now we learn he's been slain because of a father's anger on the girl's behalf."

"Mother, please," Boaz soothed.

But Herezah would not be appeased. Her anguish at the realization that she would never again look upon the Spur had crystallized her feelings during the past couple of hours and her sense of self-pity at losing him had turned to anger. She could not forget Joreb's counsel to her to keep Lazar close to their son. Now she was fearful for her young lion—and for her position and the power she had worked so long and so hard to attain. Her emotions spilled over. "She's a goatherd's daughter, a peasant! We've lost Lazar because of her."

Boaz knew his mother was grieving for Lazar, but he also felt the many underlying agendas in the room. The intense feelings emanating from the various people he now faced had very little to do with sorrow that a good and senior man had lost his life to deceit. "Silence!" Boaz snapped, more harshly than he intended. "Bin, you will record this and name the Valide Zara, Vizier Tariq, and the Grand Master Eunuch, Salmeo, as witnesses. Horz, please stand."

As the tall man finally stood, Boaz declared, his anger rising at being forced to punish what he deeply believed was an innocent man, "You have confessed to the murder of Spur Lazar and thus you will be taken from here to the Palace Pit, where you will await execution. You are hereby denounced as a traitor to Percheron and will be accorded the appropriate punishment." Boaz no longer minced his words. "Horz, you will ride the needle at the bell of midday tomorrow. Until then you will be given no food, water, or companionship. You will not address the Elim, and you will not be permitted to speak with any family members. You have betrayed your Zar and your country, and therefore your corpse will rot on the needle as a warning to all who choose to betray me."

Boaz could hardly believe the vehemence in his own voice, although the pain reflected in Horz's face almost undid him.

The Zar hoped he might privately make retribution on behalf of the head of the Elim, but sadly not while the man lived. Horz would have to enjoy his satisfaction in Zarab's Kingdom. "Begone from me," Boaz added. "May Zarab offer you the sanctuary that your Zar cannot." His one consolation was that he knew Horz understood his careful words of regret.

25

S he turned at the sound, rising from her chair. "Oh, it's you."

"You knew I would come, Zafira."

"Can I offer you something?"

"Information only this visit. I can't be away long."

"Then sit, Pez. You're making me nervous."

"Have you reason to be?"

He noticed how she rubbed her hands against her robe. "Why would you ask such a thing?"

"Because you're uncomfortable and I've never known you to be anything but entirely relaxed in my presence."

"Sit, Pez." The priestess sighed. "This has been a difficult few days."

"I know," he replied, seating himself on the only comfortable chair in the room.

Zafira lowered herself into one of the harder, upright chairs at her table. "You want to know where Ellyana is," she said, reading him accurately.

"I gave my word to Jumo."

"Please, Pez, I can't answer any more questions."

"Why, Zafira? What are you scared of?"

"You would be scared too," she groaned, turning to face him now.

"If I knew what?" he demanded.

"Why I have been told to give you this," she replied quietly, reaching into her robe and bringing out a small gold sculpture. Her hand trembled as she held it out to him.

Pez frowned. "An owl? It doesn't belong to me."

"It does. It always has. It just has to find you each time."

Pez shook his head. "I don't understand you, Zafira."

"This statue was given to Ana in the bazaar before she was formally taken into the palace. She asked Lazar to look after it for her because she knew she would not be permitted to keep it in the harem. Ana told Lazar that it was to remind him of her. She did not expect to see him again."

"She was wrong." He didn't mean to sound so petulant but he was feeling frustrated and scared.

Zafira nodded. "Lazar kept the owl. He planned to keep it close as Ana had begged, but at the island—" she faltered slightly, suddenly pausing.

"Yes?" Pez prompted.

"He tried to give it to Ellyana."

"Because he knew he was dying?"

Zafira shrugged.

Pez tried not to show his frustration at her evasiveness. "You're going to tell me she refused," he guessed.

"She did. Ellyana said the owl makes its own journey to

whomever it seeks. She told Lazar that Ana had made her choice who to pass it to and Lazar must now make his choice. She cautioned that it must pass forward, never backward."

"I see. How was Lazar to know who was the next recipient?"

"Ellyana said his heart would tell him—he must follow his instincts."

"Lazar chose me," he said flatly.

She nodded slowly, her eyes locking now with his.

"I have no idea why," Pez said airily. "I've never seen it before and I'd prefer not to keep something so obviously valuable about me."

"Pez," she urged, her voice hard. "Do you know in whose image this statue has been crafted?"

He knew he didn't want to hear what she was going to say. He heard the warning bells in his mind, felt the beat of his heart warning him to flee, but he was trapped in the chair as if the weight of the world was pressing him down into its cushions. He also knew who the owl was.

"This is Iridor. And he belongs to you."

As if mesmerized, or under some sort of hypnotic spell he'd witnessed Yozem practice against gullible folk, Pez reached out his hand. Everything inside him screamed at him to refuse it but he watched in dread awe as the red jewels of the eyes sparkled with what seemed to be their own fire.

Accept me, Pez, it urged in his mind, and whether he thought he was imagining that voice or not, he answered its call, taking the owl into his palm and closing his fingers around its searing warmth.

Then he vanished.

———

HE WAS IN THE DESERT, could hear his own panicked breathing, but he could not see anything. It was night, dark and starless, and it felt as though the Samazen was whipping up about him. He didn't feel frightened, though; strangely enough, he felt comforted by the warmth burning within him.

What just happened? Feeling stupid, Pez called out Zafira's name but his voice was fractured and carried away on the shifting sands that seemed to swirl about him.

He wasn't sure whether he was still sitting or whether he stood. He couldn't move but somehow he felt oddly safe here. Slowly the noise of the sand and wind died away. The moon appeared, a great silver orb hung low and beautiful in the night sky, while millions of stars winked at him. Pez sighed out a long breath of pleasure. Wherever he was, he wished he could remain here.

Pez.

He replied instinctively. *Iridor?*

Thank you for knowing me.

Why am I here?

To fight her battle once again.

The Goddess's?

He imagined whoever owned that voice nodding. *Lyana must prepare for her war but the Messenger must rise first.*

And I am the Messenger?

Yes.

I don't understand.

You have been chosen, Pez, as others have been chosen before you.

What is my role as Messenger?

You are wise counsel to those who protect and nurture Lyana.

*You are their friend. You are eyes and ears for them, for her. You tell
her what she needs to know.*

But that is you, Iridor, not me.

We are one.

How can that be?

*Because you are chosen. Release me from the statue. Let our
spirits combine.*

How?

*You have already opened your mind to me. Now open your heart.
I am friend, not foe. I will never hurt you or those you love, but we
together are warriors for the battle.*

Against Maliz?

Yes.

Has he begun remaking himself? Pez asked, astounded, remembering the old story.

Yes. It is done.

How will we know who he is?

You will discover him, as he will discover you.

Pez felt suddenly overwhelmed. *Are you sure you want me?
You can see me, can't you? An ugly dwarf, a supposed imbecile?
What can I possibly do, how can I—*

Hush, Pez, the voice soothed. *You were born this way in order
to be Iridor. You learned early how to hide your true self. You have
known your abilities since you were very young . . . and you have
hidden them well. Accept me fully, Pez.*

Is that even my name?

*Your earthly name, yes. Your heavenly name has always been Iri-
dor and all of us who worship the Mother see nothing but your beauty.*

At this Pez thought he might have wept, though he couldn't
be sure. The voice talking to him was gentle. It demanded noth-

ing. It simply asked him to join the fight, make use of the powers he had been gifted.

Do I belong to Lyana?

Of course. You always have.

The calming words, the gentle voice, the warmth throughout his being, all told him to accept this special task.

I won't let her down.

You never have. When you awake, we shall be one but you cannot come into your full power yet, though you will have to soon. Until then you will still have questions. Listen closely to those who can help you.

And the desert night blazed into a silvery fire.

HE SUCKED IN a huge breath and realized that Zafira was standing over him, her face a mask of worry.

"Pez!"

"What was that?" he asked, shocked by her nearness and concern.

"You tell me. One minute we were talking and the next you became silent and rigid in the chair. I couldn't reach you. I was talking to you and pulling at you but you were like the statue you grasped so hard in your fist."

He relaxed the white-knuckled grip, his hand opening slowly to reveal a silver owl with jeweled eyes that were no longer red. They glittered yellow now, as if all the gold from the body had been absorbed into its eyes. He realized they were exactly the color of his own eyes, his strange yellowish eyes that had always fascinated and repulsed people.

Zafira gave a sound of exclamation. "What's happened to you, to it?"

"I don't know how this happened," he claimed truthfully. "I . . . I felt like I was traveling."

"When? Just now, when you were like stone?"

He nodded. "I can't remember what occurred," he added, deciding to lie now. He was not ready to share his secrets with Zafira and his mind was suddenly aware that an ancient knowledge lay within him. He couldn't touch it yet, for it sat dormant as the spirit had promised. He wondered when he would be called to rise.

Zafira was still talking anxiously. "You called my name but then I felt as though I'd lost you."

Pez was silent. He knew he was shaking. "I can't remember anything," he reiterated, wondering why Zafira looked as shocked as he was feeling. "I do remember what you told me, though. I have some questions."

"Ask them," she said, no sign of her concern dissipating.

"The old woman in the bazaar who gave the owl to Ana—"

She anticipated his question. "Yes, it was Ellyana."

"She was also my Bundle Woman."

"I know."

"So she deliberately sought me out and then with the same intent went after Ana and Lazar. Why not just give me the owl when we first met?"

"Pez, I don't know as much as you think I do but I gather that Ellyana was drawn to all of you as she was to me. She was compelled, you could say. The owl finds its own, as I have explained. And when Ana approached her, Ellyana realized she was the young woman she was seeking. Lazar I'm not sure about. He could have simply been a bystander."

"Then why would she try and save his life?" he persisted. "It doesn't make sense."

"Compassion?"

He snorted. "Don't play me for a fool, Zafira. I'm not suggesting that Ellyana's cruel but her mind is set on one thing—whatever it is—and it involves me and Ana and I'd suggest Lazar as well as yourself. There was nothing coincidental about her arrival at the temple and there was nothing casual about her decision to aid Lazar. She wanted to save his life, needed to save his life. He is as involved as the rest of us. But now she's lost him—that's where it all falls apart. How did she react to his death? It must have been a shock."

Zafira shrugged, looked uncharacteristically awkward. "I was too upset to take much notice."

"Yes, but you recall she was so calm at the temple. She even mentioned that she should have guessed something like this would happen. She was perturbed but not terrified for his life as the rest of us were. It was as though she knew something we didn't. And still he died." He shook his head. "It just doesn't make sense. Didn't you talk to her? Hasn't it struck you as odd that she's turned up now?"

"Yes, of course. But, more importantly, since she arrived at the temple my feeling of being unsettled has disappeared. She is a fellow priestess and her quiet presence has calmed me."

"What did she say to ease your anxiety?"

Zafira hesitated. "She said that we are sisters and that I have already contributed to the Mother."

"That's it?" Pez pushed.

She hesitated again.

"You must tell me," he urged.

"She said that Lyana was coming again. She knew because Iridor was rising. Ellyana assured me that my work was just beginning and I would be instrumental in aiding Lyana for the battle ahead."

Pez fell silent. It was as disturbing to him to hear Zafira's words as it was for her to repeat them. Awed and overwhelmed, they stared at each other, helpless.

"And I'm Iridor," he said finally. He still didn't want to believe it. Still couldn't, in truth.

"Yes, that's what I think Ellyana must have wanted you to understand, why she gave the statue to Ana, hoping it would find its way to you in the harem. But Ana gave it to Lazar . . ." Her voice trailed off.

"And still it found its way to me." He finished her thought for them both. Sitting forward, Pez took Zafira's hand, a plea in his voice. "But how do we know this is truth? What do we know about Iridor? How can we possibly accept that I am this . . . this—" He couldn't bring himself to say it.

"Demigod?"

He nodded.

"Tell me what you do know of Iridor."

He sat back, despondent. "Very little. He's an owl."

She looked suddenly intrigued. "Iridor is known for hiding himself from others, listening, gathering information. He is able to take the form of a silvery-white owl at will."

Pez forced a smile. "Well, I fit the bill on the first three but that last item surely counts me out. I ask you, Zafira, do I look like a bird?" His voice was filled with amusement.

"As a matter of fact, you do," she surprised him.

He snorted his derision. "A silvery-white bird?"

"Come with me, Pez," she said softly.

"Where?"

"Over here," she said, standing and walking toward a small bureau that held her comb and brush, her chain with the Cross of Life pendant, and a few other possessions, including a pretty ornamental hand mirror worked in silver. She picked up the mirror and offered it to Pez. "Look at yourself."

And Pez did, taking the mirror from her hand and staring into it, aghast. He had never cared much for his reflection at the best of times but now he was stunned.

Staring back at him, he saw his face, pale with shock, surrounded by hair of the purest white.

When Ana woke the following morning, Pez was back at her side. He was wearing a madly colored knitted cap that hugged his squarish head and made him look even more ridiculous than usual.

"Do you like my new garb?" he asked.

She gave a wan smile. "No one will miss you in it."

They looked sadly at each other for a few moments and Pez reached to take her hand.

She looked earnestly into his strangely yellow eyes. "Is it true? Not just a bad dream?"

"Lazar is dead," he said as gently as he could, although the words still caught in his throat. "Jumo sailed yesterday to find his family. And Horz will pay with his life today for murder of the Spur."

"Horz?" she exclaimed, fully awake now. She sat up. "He did not do such a thing."

Pez gave a small shrug. "No one knows the truth, child. He has admitted it to the Zar in front of witnesses."

"Then he has been forced into speaking a lie."

"I'm sure that notion has been explored but there is nothing to be done about it. And it should not be something that affects you anyway."

"The death of an uncle?" she said, her voice hard and flat. "No wonder Boaz asked me to confirm it."

"Call him the Zar, Ana. It's important you keep your head very low now. Are you telling me Horz was kin to you?"

She nodded, glad for the admonishing reminder. "I promise you I will be careful." Her eyes filled with tears. "Yes, Horz is my father's brother. We kept it secret. Neither of us said anything about it when we first saw each other in the Choosing Room and we kept it that way. Pez, I'm not sure I want to live. My life is stretching out before me. It looks long and pointless in the harem. And now with Lazar dead because of me . . ." She couldn't finish.

He pulled out a spotted silk square. "Dry those eyes, Ana, and bury that hurt, I beg you. You will never have a pointless life and I will protect you as I promised Lazar. Lazar is gone, though, Ana, and he would have been gone for you anyway. You would not have been permitted to see anyone other than the harem members or the Zar. You must accept that. Put Lazar from your mind."

She looked at him as though he spoke in a different language. "Put him out of my mind? How can you ask that of me? I loved him," she said fiercely.

If she expected him to be shocked by her admission, she was disappointed. Pez glanced around, making a hushing sound. "So did I, child. I will miss him, as will Boaz, as will

Jumo, but we must all get on somehow. You must rise above your pain and forge a new life, for you would never have been permitted to love him except as a distant memory. I hear you've already caught the Zar's eye—that in itself should give you hope."

"To be his concubine, you mean? At his beck and call, to service his sexual needs?"

Pez gave a tutting sound. "You do view it dimly. Give the young Zar a chance. You may be surprised. He is not obsessed with carnal pleasure. He is actually something of a scholar, and charming company. I was thinking of something far beyond concubine for you, Odalisque Ana. I see no reason why you will not be a wife, if not Absolute Favorite."

"It doesn't change anything, Pez," she said morosely. "I'm still a prisoner."

"Only of your own mind. The Zar is talking about change. He's planning a picnic for the girls—and that's just the beginning."

She looked at him. "Perhaps I could effect change through him."

The dwarf grinned. "Good girl. Look ahead, Ana. Pretend Lazar is not dead. Tell yourself you simply can't see him anymore; it's what they would have done to you anyway. Time will heal that pain in your heart, I promise. Make your own destiny, child."

His words roused in her a new sense of hope. "Has anyone ever told you that you look like a bird?" she asked suddenly, and regained a small sense of amusement at the look of surprise that claimed his face.

———

AFTER THE PREVIOUS DAY'S unpleasantness, Boaz was taking his first meal late, slumped in a small alcove off his main study. It was an eating chamber that his father had built a few years prior so that he could take a private meal during a working day. The chamber was fully tiled—every last inch of wall was covered in beautifully glazed squares, each bearing a fruit. It had been quite a daring design for its time, and in fact still was, and it was one of Boaz's favorite chambers in the whole palace. He loved that it was his, even though he was not currently regarding it with his usual sense of wonder.

The Zar munched absently on the meal that Bin had personally laid out for him, the intuitive servant deciding that the last thing the Zar wanted was a team of fussing attendants putting out food and waiting on his every whim.

Bin had assumed correctly and once again Boaz was grateful for his servant's ability to anticipate his needs. He was replaying Horz's confession over in his mind as he chewed on some roasted lamb smeared with a pungent garlic and yogurt sauce. It was delicious, cooked specifically for the Zar much earlier this morning in the private kitchens of the royals, but he tasted none of it, not even the fat ripe figs also picked that morning. Bin let the Zar's dining staff know that the food had been enjoyed. They worked hard, striving to satisfy the youngster who needed to develop a sophisticated palate so he could entertain and be entertained in style.

The kitchens never stopped. Their fires fanned every hour of every day to prepare hundreds of dishes for the countless people in the palace who needed to be fed. They took up one entire wing, a dozen huge chimneys billowing smoke all day and all night in separate units that were linked by short corridors. The harem was normally serviced by three of these units, one devoted exclusively to the Valide Zara and the wives. Another eight were given over to dignitaries, soldiers, the Elim, and all the other people attached to the palace. The final chimney stood alone in a closed unit. This was for the Zar's food. He had his own vegetable and herb gardens. He even had his own orchard. No food ever crossed from any of the other units into this one. The kitchen staff was handpicked and trained rigorously, not just in cooking, but in discretion as well as security. Bin was aware that a good relationship with the kitchen team meant they would always go to extraordinary lengths to please their Zar. It also meant they would be vigilant and never permit strangers any access to his food. This last point was of paramount importance. Bin mentioned it now to the young Zar as he entered to refill Boaz's glass. "My Zar, the Vizier has made a suggestion that I think has merit. Perhaps you'll permit me to mention it?"

"Oh yes? What does he suggest for me?"

"Well, my Zar, Vizier Tariq is mindful that without the Spur, our security is compromised. Until we find a worthy replacement—"

"There is no worthy replacement," Boaz cut in. "There is no replacement at all in fact. I am not ready to accept his death and so I have no intention of putting another man into that position."

"Of course, Great One. But in the absence of anyone to fill that position, Vizier Tariq wants to place a permanent guard around your kitchen. He thinks it's a fundamental aspect of palace security that everything connected with the Zar be checked, double-checked, and triple-checked and nowhere is more vulnerable than where your food is prepared."

Boaz was surprised. Tariq showing concern? Tariq had

treated him with not-very-well-hidden disdain when he was nothing but a prince and even at his father's death the man had been condescending. "When did he suggest this?"

"Last night, my Zar."

"Who does he think should do this?"

"He believes there is no one more trustworthy than the Elim. He thinks the Valide should select the team. She knows all of the more senior members of the Elim."

"He says this even though one of the Elim has proven to be a traitor?"

Bin said nothing, but when Boaz glanced at the man's face, he could see that Bin—and presumably the Vizier—believed the story of Horz's treachery almost as much as they had believed Pez when he had once told them all he could fly.

"I should like to see the Vizier."

"I shall summon him immediately."

AFTER VIZIER TARIQ was announced, he entered with none of the usual flouncing bows Boaz expected. "My Zar," he said softly, touching his hand to his lips and heart as he bowed graciously.

Boaz immediately noticed how somberly the Vizier was dressed—this in itself was unusual. But even more surprising was the absence of the tinkling bells and sparkling jewels in his beard. In fact, the Vizier's beard was no longer forked. It ended in a neat plait. The normally ostentatious affectations were vanishing before Boaz's eyes, and he couldn't help himself from asking, "Vizier Tariq, are you well?"

"I am, thank you, High One," the man said, straightening.

"No, I mean, you don't seem quite . . . er, yourself."

"How odd, my Zar. Your mother suggested the same thing only yesterday."

"Nothing's wrong?" Boaz inquired.

"Not at all. In fact, I don't believe I've ever felt better."

"Good," the Zar replied, still feeling unsettled by the Vizier but thinking it would be imprudent to press further at this point. "Please, join me," he added, gesturing toward a long cushion on the floor opposite him.

"This is a wonderful chamber," Tariq said. "Your father had such fine taste in art forms."

"Yes. I wish he hadn't worked so hard to hide it."

"I'm not sure he did. Just look at this room," Tariq said, sweeping a hand gently around him. "It is so advanced for the age. And consider all the additions he made to the palace—each has superbly enhanced its beauty by paving a way for its future rather than looking to past glory. Your father's wives, especially your mother, were chosen with an eye not just for their exquisite looks, but for their intelligence. Whatever his own desires were in terms of whom he spent his time with, he was again looking to the future. He wanted heirs with nimble, shrewd minds."

Boaz had never heard the Vizier make such an observation in all the years he had known him. Tariq usually contented himself with agreeing with the powers that be.

But Tariq was not finished. "And his faith in his own judgment has been borne out in you, my Zar, if I may say so. From what I know of you, you maintain a very good blend of the finer qualities of both of your parents."

"Oh yes?" Boaz replied, amused now. "What have I won from my mother?" He expected the Vizier to lavish him with praise.

"Her looks obviously," the man replied matter-of-factly. "But from what I can see, since you've assumed your new role, you also have her intuitiveness. And that is a quality to be admired."

Concise, direct, brief. Boaz was amazed. "And from my father?"

"Well, your father was shrewd indeed. I'll admit his interest in life around him lapsed toward the end of his reign but he will be remembered for his incisive decisions. Joreb—may Zarab keep him—was never one to shirk making a stand. Right or wrong, he made decisions swiftly. You showed that same courage yesterday, my Zar, if you don't mind my mentioning it. That was a very difficult situation—and not one any of us would like to have faced. No one who was present could be anything but impressed by your composure and ability to render that toughest of all judgments. Sending a man to his death is easy if you have little conscience."

Boaz swallowed hard. The Vizier had clearly, yet carefully, couched the suggestion that Horz was lying and taking the blame for a dark deed he had played no part in.

"It weighs heavily on my mind nonetheless," Boaz responded, equally careful not to commit himself one way or the other.

He saw recognition of this flash briefly in the Vizier's eyes before it was shrouded, and was certain the man was applauding him. "It was the right decision to make, my Zar, if that helps."

"I've been struggling with it ever since," Boaz admitted.

"As you should. It would only be curious if you didn't. Of course, the whole business of the Spur's death is a curiosity, wouldn't you say, my Zar?"

Tariq cut deep into the pain Boaz had been trying to hide. He felt powerless to hide his own feelings when the Vizier was being so honest. "I will not rest easy until I have the truth," Boaz confirmed.

"So you doubt Horz?"

"How can I? The man has confessed."

The Vizier said nothing but his searching look spoke volumes.

"I suspect there is far more to the truth than we have learned," Boaz answered more fully. "That is what I will search for in my own way and over time. For now the people must be satisfied that justice has been seen to be done."

"Bravo, my Zar. You are thinking like a pragmatist."

For the first time ever, Boaz felt proud to be complimented by the Vizier. "May I offer you some zerra, Tariq?"

Inwardly, Maliz smiled. "I would be delighted, High One. Thank you."

Bin, who had been quietly attending from the shadows of the room, emerged from his dark corner to pour out a glass for the Vizier.

"Thank you, my Zar." Tariq sipped and his expression of pleasure said enough about the quality of the zerra. "I have some changes I'd like to effect. If you would permit, I would like your kitchen to be permanently observed by the Elim."

"Bin mentioned that. Is it really necessary?"

"I wouldn't say it if I didn't think it was important, my Zar," Maliz said, belatedly realizing what a contradiction that was for anyone who had known the old Vizier. This was confirmed by the grin that the Zar could not force back. "Do I amuse?" the demon asked, knowing full well that he did.

"Forgive me, Tariq. Whatever this change is that has come

over you, I just want you to know that I appreciate our conversation. Are you aware of how different you sound?"

"My Zar, may I be candid?"

"Please."

Boaz watched as Tariq sipped again. "I respected your father enormously but it served my purposes to behave the way I did in the past. I can't put it any more plainly. Your father came to his throne a grown man, quite set in his ways and with a lot of experience under his belt. I was newly appointed and I had to quietly assume my role, ingratiate myself with the right people to win their trust. That has taken years."

Boaz couldn't help himself. "Tariq, my father didn't respect you very much. I know he didn't like you," he said, more bluntly than he had intended.

"Do you think I didn't know that?"

"I must say I have to wonder when I consider some of your . . . affectations," Boaz admitted. He was confused by Tariq. He'd spent a lifetime ignoring the man, disliking him even, but now found himself impressed by his calm counsel and insightful comments.

"That's all they were, High One. Affectations. It helped me to disappear . . . don't you see?"

"No, frankly, I don't."

"Sometimes, Zar Boaz, people will portray themselves a specific way with the deliberate intent to shield others from their true selves."

"Why?"

"Defense. Invisibility. The peacock you saw was all that you saw. You never knew that behind that facade worked a shrewd mind."

"A modest one too," Boaz countered.

Tariq shrugged and sipped again, a smile at his lips. "I'm merely explaining it for you."

"So it's all been an act?"

"That's perhaps exaggerating it. I have always done my work diligently—I'm sure your father never complained about that."

"No, not at all. In fact, I heard him say on countless occasions that as much as he disliked your presence, he couldn't fault your efforts."

"And that's the reason I climbed to the position I have," Tariq replied.

"Wouldn't it have been easier to be yourself and earn respect along the way?"

"Perhaps, but then I wouldn't have learned as much as I have."

"What do you mean?"

"Zar Boaz, my presence at the palace is only part of what I do. My real job is to listen in on the streets, to hear what your people are grumbling about, their needs. I have a network of contacts to run and it has suited me to appear flamboyant and shallow because people never took me seriously. They talked around me, over me. They thought my appointment as Vizier a jest but figured I was someone who could be easily compromised."

"And can you be?"

At this, Tariq smiled. "Zar Boaz, I am revealing the true Tariq to you so that we start out truthfully in your reign. You are young—I don't mean that as insult—and you need sound counsel. Your father never needed someone like me in quite the same way you do. I am offering myself up honestly to you. I hope that we can work closely and that you'll trust my judgment, hear my advice, include me in your decision making."

Boaz took several moments to consider the Vizier's request. He wanted to be sure he chose his words carefully. "Vizier Tariq, until yesterday I intended to begin distancing myself entirely from you. I disliked you even more than my father did, for I didn't even respect the role you played." He watched the man nod in humble acceptance of his harsh words. "But you have surprised me. I would be lying if I didn't admit that I feel as though I am sitting here tonight with an entirely different man."

"Does that mean we have a future together, Zar Boaz?"

"That's precisely what it means. It will not happen overnight, of course, Vizier. You must earn my trust and respect. But what I want most is for you to understand that it is me who sits the throne of Percheron and not my mother."

"You have made yourself perfectly clear, Zar Boaz. Perhaps I might begin our new relationship by organizing for the guard around your kitchen?" At Boaz's nod, the Vizier smiled and continued: "Is there anything else I can do?"

"Keep me informed."

"My Zar?"

"I want to know everything you do. All that you learn from the streets I want shared with me. You are the one promoting this partnership, so prove it. Show me that I can trust you."

"And what's in this for me, Zar Boaz?"

Boaz's eyes flashed darkly. "That's the old Vizier talking!"

"No, Highness. The old Vizier would not have had the nerve. You've proven yourself to be pragmatic, so continue in that vein. Nothing in life is free, my Zar."

"What do you want? Riches?"

Tariq laughed. "No. I want the title of Grand Vizier."

Boaz nodded slowly, suddenly understanding. "Equal status to Salmeo."

"Yes, my Zar. Too long I have been treated as his inferior. I want the same privileges and freedoms he enjoys."

Boaz nodded. If Tariq continued to impress, he would not find it difficult to agree to such a request. "We have a bargain, then, Vizier. Earn my trust and my respect and you will earn yourself a promotion."

"Thank you, Zar Boaz." The Vizier raised his zerra. "To your reign, High One. I will work diligently and unrelentingly toward achieving your goals."

"You do not know them yet," Boaz replied mischievously.

"Oh, but I intend to learn them, my Zar. I shall begin by learning more about the last hours of the Spur. Is that a good beginning?"

Boaz raised his cup to the newly reinvented Vizier and the curious alliance they had made tonight. "To new beginnings," he replied, draining his wine.

27

Salmeo brooded in his chamber. Horz had been immovable but he had been able to sense the anger and suspicion emanating from the young Zar nonetheless. This meant he was not free from the Spur's blood smears just yet. "I am an impetuous fool," he murmured to himself, regretting for the umpteenth time his rage that had led to the poor decision to bring drezden into the Spur's punishment. As it was, Shaz had done a far uglier job than even Salmeo could have imagined and it was highly likely that the Spur would have died from his injuries alone.

It was not at all like Salmeo to act so recklessly. Now, in the calm after the storm of the proceedings, he could see how careless he had been—how close he had come to ruining his life. He had thought drezden undetectable—damn the interfering priestess! How she could have identified it was beyond him.

He needed to cover his tracks. The Head Inflictor was still away in the far north, which was convenient. His deputy had been compromised with similar threats to his family and a small parcel of land. He had been easier to manipulate than Horz, who had no need for land or wealth, but of course everyone could be bought if you threatened those they loved. That's why no one could ever compromise the Grand Master Eunuch— he loved none but himself. With Horz taking the blame, the deputy could be kept quiet. That left only the youngster, Shaz, who might possibly know something. Presumably the lad had quailed at the job, which meant he must have asked questions of his superior. Salmeo's agile mind thought it through. The deputy had to tell him something and most likely would have ordered him to do as he was told, would have said that they had no say in this. Shaz was young but not mindless—he could work out that the only person capable of giving an order that could not be questioned was the Grand Master Eunuch himself.

Salmeo pulled a grape from the glistening bunch of black fruit one of his attendants had delivered. He bit down on the grape, enjoying the explosion of juice, letting it trickle down his throat as he considered his position. He spat the seeds out. Yes, he knew what he had to do now.

BOAZ WAS FEELING UPLIFTED by the Vizier's visit. It was such an odd sensation to actually like the man and yet he couldn't help it.

Just then Bin emerged, looking slightly uncomfortable. "It's the Grand Master Eunuch, my Zar. He seems very agitated."

"Important, you think?" Boaz asked.

The man nodded. "I believe it is."

"Show him into my study. I don't want to see him here." Bin turned to leave. "And he is not to know that I've been with the

Vizier," Boaz added as an afterthought, and regretted it when he saw the crestfallen look on his servant's face. Boaz knew Bin was far too discreet to let such a thing slip but Salmeo had a way of finding out anything and everything.

Bin exited and reappeared a few moments later. "He awaits you, my Zar."

Boaz nodded and made the eunuch wait another three minutes before he stepped into the study. "You asked to see me, Chief Eunuch," he said, knowing how Salmeo preferred to be addressed by his grander title.

"Forgive me for the interruption, my Zar," the huge man replied, bowing.

"I imagine it must be important."

"It's about the Spur."

"I thought we'd settled that. I want to put it from my mind. It is not easy passing sentence on a man's life, especially one as seemingly loyal as Horz."

Salmeo fixed a chastened expression onto his face. "I can only imagine. But my conscience weighs heavily upon me, my Zar."

"Explain why."

"Thank you, High One. I've been wondering how Horz would have been able to dip the thongs of the Viper's Nest into the drezden without an accomplice. You see, my Zar, although the head of the Elim would have access to the dispensary—and thus the poison—he would not have had such ready access to the whips. These particular instruments are looked after by the Inflictors alone."

"Well, we've established that the head of the Inflictors was away, correct?"

"Yes, my Zar, he still is."

"So that negates his involvement. And his deputy was unwell?"

"That's right, Zar Boaz. Rah was running a high fever. I sent my own physic to care for him," Salmeo lied. "The physic can corroborate how sick the Deputy Inflictor was."

Yes, I'm sure he can, Boaz thought viciously. "Is he feeling better?"

"The fever has run its course, Zar Boaz, but he is still unable to work. At the time of the Spur's flogging, he was unable to hold himself upright."

"So that leaves us with who?" Boaz asked, knowing with a deep sense of pity whose name was about to be announced.

"There is only one other person, my Zar, who could open the weapons bureau. That's Shaz."

"Now, why do you think a young man like Shaz would want to murder the Spur?"

"There is only one thing that propels most men into committing dark deeds, my Zar." Salmeo's lisp was pronounced now as he spoke softly.

Boaz smelled a vague breath of violets wafting over him. "And what is that?"

"Money, Zar Boaz. Money alone galvanizes most men—young or old—into action."

"What about love? Respect? Loyalty?"

"Powerful indeed, but riches are compelling, especially for a man who barely sees more than a few karels a month, Zar Boaz. What if he was promised what sounded like a small fortune?"

Boaz had heard enough. "Take me to the Inflictors' quarters."

"Now, my Zar?"

"Immediately."

"They will probably be resting after practice sessions," Salmeo risked.

Boaz fixed the eunuch with a look that was hard enough to crush rocks. "You disturbed my rest, Chief Eunuch, because you felt it was too important to leave until later. Let's sort this out now. If we're going to have another execution on our hands, I want them done together and I want this whole matter put behind us."

Salmeo bowed obsequiously. "Of course, my Zar," he said, straightening. "Let us go now."

Boaz had very little to say to the eunuch as they made their way to the Inflictors' quarters. Instead he spoke quietly to Bin, whom he'd asked to accompany them, using the time to brief his secretary on what had transpired.

The few people they met were daunted by the trio and either bowed low as they swept through corridors or flattened themselves against the walls to bow in their wake, muttering words of joy to the Mightiest of the Mighties. Boaz ignored them. He was in no mood to be generous of spirit and he noted, not for the first time, that it didn't matter anyway. The truth was he could do what he liked, act how he felt. He could slap passersby if he so wished, and he knew, with a terrible sense of destiny, that they would probably thank him for acknowledging them. It was easier to pretend they meant nothing and ignore their cringing good wishes.

After crossing several courtyards, Salmeo finally pushed open a timber door that led into a small wing of the palace that housed the Inflictors' quarters. Inside, people at their work dropped to their knees as though suddenly stricken by a sickness. It was most unusual for any royal, least of all the Zar himself, to visit these humble accommodations. Boaz fixed a tight smile at his mouth, moving swiftly behind the bulk of Salmeo to step inside the main chamber.

The Deputy Inflictor sat inside. At Salmeo's entrance, he visibly paled. "Grand Master Eunuch, this is—" He cut off his words as he saw who accompanied Salmeo. It took moments to register that the Zar was, in fact, standing before him. He fell to his knees. "Oh Great One!"

Boaz winced. "Please stand. You are?"

The man trembled. Boaz could appreciate that his arrival might make the deputy nervous but the man seemed unnecessarily terrified. Did he have something to hide? "I am Rah, Great One, the Deputy Inflictor."

"Ah, good. Are you alone?"

"My wife and son are inside, my Zar. Is anything wrong?" Rah stammered, glancing toward Salmeo, who pursed his lips. The sign was enough to alert the Deputy Inflictor that this was official business and it didn't take him more than a moment's consideration to realize what it must be about.

"Can we talk somewhere privately?" Boaz suggested.

"Er, you're welcome to come into my humble quarters, my Zar," Rah offered uncertainly.

Boaz nodded. "Send your wife and son outside—this is not for their ears."

The family was hurried away and Rah returned, embarrassed, awkward, and betraying his nervousness through twitching hands and a voice far from steady. "May I offer some refreshment, my Zar, I—"

"No, that won't be necessary. I'm here to clarify something with you, Rah, and I insist that you converse with me in all honesty, without fear of reprisals."

The man nodded dumbly, again glancing at Salmeo.

Boaz was tired of Salmeo's imposing presence. "Grand Master Eunuch," he said, "you may wait outside."

Salmeo bristled but bowed nonetheless and departed. Boaz watched him carefully for any sign of threat to Rah but the eunuch's face remained blank.

As he had done with Horz, Boaz turned now to the deputy. "Do you know why I'm here?"

"No, High One," the man spluttered, terrified.

"Be calm, man. I am here only to ask you a question." Rah nodded, wide-eyed. "I want to know if anyone, bar the Inflictors, has access to your instruments."

Rah shook his head immediately. Boaz, already suspicious, felt his reaction was too swift. Most people, he was certain, would show some consternation at being asked such an odd question without preamble. "No, my Zar," Rah continued, his voice laced with horror. "Absolutely no one has access to the canes, whips, or any of our implements of punishment. Why do you ask?"

"Because a man has died. You've heard about the Spur?"

Rah looked thunderstruck. "He died? Forgive me, my Zar, I have only just recovered from my illness."

It was either a superbly rehearsed act or the man was telling the truth. "How did you learn about the Spur claiming the Right of Protectorship?"

"The Grand Master Eunuch came to see me. He was shocked that I was sick, my Zar, and incapable of doing the job. He already knew that our Inflictor Felz was not even in Percheron city. He was at a loss as to what to do."

Boaz knew better. Salmeo was rarely at a loss when it came to intrigue. "So he asked your advice?"

The man nodded fearfully. "I didn't have much to give. If I

could have stood unaided, I would have done it myself, my Zar. Forgive me. It was I who suggested Shaz—when the Grand Master Eunuch explained that the job had to be done immediately—he was our only option. Shaz has been well trained and is our best apprentice. He knew what he had to do—I believe the tension of the moment and the celebrity of the Spur must have unraveled him. I had high hopes he would do all right."

"Well, he didn't. He was perspiring, nervous, and trembling. He was incapable of handling this task. I could see as much and I was the farthest person from him."

"I can't imagine he killed the Spur, though, Mighty One."

"No, I don't believe he did. I think the poison might have had something to do with it."

The man's head snapped back in shock. "Poison," he whispered. "You jest," he urged, forgetting his manners and all protocol.

"I would never jest about something as grave as this. The Spur of Percheron is dead because someone dipped the whip in poison before it was used on his back."

The man blanched. There was no way, in Boaz's estimation, that his reaction could have been contrived.

"Who chose the snake?"

Rah could barely talk, so great was his shock. Finally he stammered, "I can't imagine why he would do such a foolish thing, my Zar, but Shaz would have made that choice. The Elim and Grand Master Salmeo have never involved themselves in such a decision. They have always left weapon choice to the Inflictors."

"What could possibly have made him choose the hardest weapon to wield on his first living victim?"

Rah shrugged lightly. "Maybe the lad got excited. Shaz knows he's the best apprentice by far, so it's possible that arrogance could have gotten in the way of good sense—you know how youngsters like to show off." And then he caught himself, suddenly realizing that he was talking to someone not far from Shaz's own age. "Perhaps the boy is in debt to someone and he was bribed?" he offered softly. "I didn't know any of this, my Zar, until now."

Boaz felt light-headed. Surely he would not have to order the execution of Shaz as well as Horz? In his heart he knew Horz was not guilty, nor could he imagine the man paying a boy to do his dirty work. The Elim were too proud for that. And yet Boaz had no proof of innocence for either Shaz or Horz, only evidence of guilt. He felt a blood rage threatening. "I have found what I came for," he said tightly, and turned, angry and distraught.

He stomped out of the small dwelling and strode past Salmeo, who stood a little distance from the main door, looking grave. As the Zar disappeared, Salmeo turned to Rah, who had appeared at the doorway, still trembling.

"Did he believe your story? Did you tell it precisely as I instructed?"

All Rah could do was nod and mutter, "Zarab help me." It was obvious he was feeling sickened to his soul. Not only had he lied to his Zar but he had also incriminated innocent Shaz, whose only flaw might be that he strove too hard to please those he worked for.

"You have done well. Your family will live . . . and they will thank you for your steadfastness."

Rah began to weep. "What will happen to Shaz?"

"Who cares?" Salmeo replied, smiling cruelly. "Don't worry about him—collect a purse from me tomorrow after it's done. That will ease your troubled conscience, Deputy."

SHAZ WAS ONLY JUST beginning to recover from the previous day's trauma. He had not yet heard the news that the Spur had died and he lived in hope that the man he had admired and cut so badly would forgive him. He planned to be one of the first to visit the Spur—if he would be permitted to do so—so that he could beg forgiveness in person. He'd even changed his mind about his profession. He no longer wanted to be an Inflictor. Flogging a man was nothing like flogging the practice dummies. Felz had said all he had to do was remove his emotion and pretend the man tied to the post was just a dummy. But Shaz had been unable to distance himself from the emotion or the reality. Had he not been in front of the Zar, whom he also admired, he would have refused to continue after his first few botched lashes, no matter the harsh consequences. It would have been hard enough to complete the punishment with a single whip. Putting the Snake into his hands had been a ludicrous order.

He was taking a rest after a practice session when the soldiers came for him. They were angry too. News that their leader was dead had flared around the barracks as fast as a raging fire— killed by the ineptness of an apprentice Inflictor who was deep in a conspiracy led by debt and greed. Salmeo would be pleased at how quickly his fabricated tale was being embellished by gossip.

Shaz was dragged from his bed, slapped and punched, kicked and shoved, as the four men moved him, without explanation, from his tiny room to the Pit, where he joined Horz. The older man, saddened by the young man's cries, figured out what had transpired and gave a nod of appreciation at Salmeo's cunning.

He and Shaz would die tomorrow for a crime they were innocent of commiting, but Horz knew he would die proudly and calmly. He was ready, had accepted his fate from the moment Salmeo began his threats. The Elim were trained to accept their destiny; this was his. He was regretful only that his death was not enough for Salmeo. It was a pity the boy had to die too. Poor Shaz. In the darkness of his stone cell, Horz sent a prayer to Zarab that the ending of their lives would be swift, if not for him, then certainly for the young man.

28

Pez sat alone in the marble coolness of the palace infirmary with Kett and watched the slave hobble back and forth unaided. "Is it working properly?" he asked carefully.

"With the help of the tube," the boy answered, turning away so the dwarf would not have to share his troubles.

"It's all right, Kett. I won't say I understand—how can I? But I do understand your grief. I think it is important to weep and mourn your loss."

The boy cleared his throat nervously. "The Grand Master Eunuch came to see me."

"And?"

"He wants me to present myself for duty tomorrow."

"Has he given you a role yet?"

"No. I'll just be one of his slaves, in the harem. My dream of working for Spur Lazar must be buried," Kett answered, the pain of his shattered hopes evident in his voice.

Pez realized he had found yet another person whose life had been touched by Lazar. The boy would grieve when he learned of the Spur's fate. "Kett, be patient. Wheels are turning that I can't explain just yet. I'm optimistic you will have a position to your liking."

"Oh?"

The hope in the boy's voice was gut-wrenching. "I will tell you more when I am more certain."

"Pez, may I be plain with you?"

"Of course. I am with you."

"Yes, that's what troubles me. You are sane."

Pez smiled. "I am. You must keep it our secret."

"The Zar knows too, doesn't he?"

"He lied to you only to protect me. He has known since he was old enough to talk," Pez said. "And now you know as well."

The boy's grim countenance was brightened briefly with a grin. "I am privileged to share such information with you and my Zar."

"So you will keep my secret." It was a statement, not a question.

But Kett nodded solemnly, his hand touching his forehead before settling over his heart. "I shall take it to my grave."

Pez knew he could not keep Lazar's death from the boy any longer. "I have some news," he said solemnly. "You have been recuperating, so I presume no one has told you yet what has happened to Spur Lazar."

The boy shook his head. "What do you mean *happened*? Is he hurt?"

"Worse," Pez answered grimly, and he proceeded to tell Kett the entire sordid tale.

When Pez had finished, Kett remained silent for long moments. He stared at the ground, clearly deeply upset. Finally he spoke. "He tried to have me spared," he said, his voice trembling.

"Yes, Lazar would not tolerate anyone's suffering. He would have thought your punishment grossly out of kilter with the sin."

"As was his own. At least I'm alive."

Pez swallowed his own sadness. "Good, Kett. That's the spirit, child. You are alive. The gods have spared you; perhaps there is good reason for this."

"I have a purpose?" the boy asked with bitter disdain in his voice. "I'll grow fat and act like a woman."

"I don't notice any fat Elim, and none of them could be accused of acting in any way other than fearsomely and loyally."

"Not their leader, it seems," the boy countered angrily.

Pez's own temper flared at the boy's quick presumption. "Don't be so sure, Kett. There are things in motion here that you cannot understand. If you believe that Horz is guilty of murder, then I feel disappointed by your judgment and thus more sorry for you than I already do. You did know Horz, I gather?"

The boy, duly reprimanded, nodded. "He is as worthy of death as I was to be gelded."

"That's right. He is taking the blame for someone else's dark deeds."

"Do you know that for a fact? Why don't you say something?"

"Do you suppose that people haven't already guessed as much? Horz has admitted his own guilt—that's impossible to counter. And anyway, no one would listen to the ravings of a lunatic."

"But you're not mad!"

"Very few know that, Kett. As I said before, it is our secret, one I need you to keep for me."

"Why do you trust me?"

Pez shook his head. "In all honesty, I can't really say. I feel compelled. I think we were meant to meet, though I wish it had been under different circumstances."

"Will you be honest with me, now that we share this secret?"

Pez nodded slowly. "I promise."

"How is it that the guards saw me but neither you nor our Zar?"

The dwarf had been expecting this question. "That's another secret. Can I trust you with it?"

"You can, Pez."

"I have the Lore."

The boy's eyes widened. "The Lore," he repeated, slowly and carefully, as if the very word itself were precious. "Why didn't you hide me then too?"

Pez grimaced sadly. "I couldn't. Sustaining the invisibility for two was hard enough and I knew it would only last for a few moments. The guards knew someone was behind that screen and I couldn't risk them lingering to search. I couldn't risk the Zar being found. I'm sure you understand."

"So I was sacrificed," Kett said sadly.

"You shouldn't have been there," Pez answered mildly.

"Neither should you. I know you're allowed, but you were still spying, Pez."

"I had the Zar to consider. It was my fault he was present in the first place."

Kett frowned. Then he locked eyes with Pez, a serious expression on his face. "What are you here for?"

"I honestly don't know," Pez replied. It was partly true, which was more candid than he'd been with many others as of late.

"Who else knows about your sanity?"

"Oh you're part of a very elite few. I can list them on one hand," Pez said, counting off on his fingers. "Lazar knew, of course. And his servant Jumo, Zar Boaz, Odalisque Ana, and a priestess called Zafira."

"And now me."

"Yes."

"Why do you keep your sanity a secret?"

"Each who knows of it has asked this same question. I answer the same way every time: I don't know. I have acted this way since the moment I entered Percheron as a prisoner. My antics caught the attention of the men who buy slaves for the palace, and I was fortunate that the old Zar happened to be traveling through the slave market one afternoon. He saw me, laughed, and had someone buy me for him. I've been at the palace ever since. That was two decades ago."

Kett's eyes widened with surprise. "How old are you?"

"Ancient," Pez replied wryly, knowing he spoke more truthfully than Kett would know.

"I will not betray you," promised Kett.

"And that faith will be rewarded."

"How?"

"You will see."

———

"YOU ARE NOT REQUIRED to be present, Boaz," Pez advised.

"But I must be, don't you see. Horz is lying—and he knows I know."

"I still don't understand."

"Yes you do. This is about honor. I will honor Horz for his noble sacrifice. What the Elim don't realize is how loyal he is. He is giving his life to protect his leader."

"So you accept this is Salmeo's doing?"

"I never doubted it, Pez. I just can't prove it."

"And now Shaz is to die as well. Must it be so?"

"If I don't act harshly, Salmeo will spread word throughout Percheron—as cunningly as we know he can—that I did not punish the co-conspirator. He has hatched this plan to cover his tracks; now he has rid himself of two of these people who might have revealed him. The third, Rah, has been coerced to the point where he would rather lie to me than risk whatever Salmeo has threatened him with."

"Justice must be seen to be done?"

"Precisely."

"Someone else somewhere will know something of the truth."

"I can't imagine who, but if you can find that someone, bring him to me." Boaz sighed. "What if I let myself down?"

"You won't, child."

"How can you be sure?" Boaz paused, then whispered, "The Lore?" At Pez's nod, he took a long, slow breath. "I thought you said you never wanted to use it."

"I didn't. I don't. But you've had so much on your shoulders, I wanted to make sure you'd remain strong," Pez lied.

"All for me?" Boaz asked, still obviously fascinated with Pez's skill.

"All for you. But now I must beg a favor in return."

The Zar gave his friend a look of gentle warning. "What?"

"We've talked about it before. I want you to give Ana her own servant when the time is right."

"Kett, you mean?"

Pez nodded. "Salmeo's told him to report to duty tomorrow. I'm not sure how much he's capable of just yet but the Chief Eunuch insists he be given his tasks."

"And you want him trained in the harem? What's your interest in Kett?"

"I feel responsible for him," Pez answered, not altogether untruthfully.

"As you should," Boaz grumbled. "I hear you've been visiting him while he's been recovering."

"Yes. I've shown myself to him."

"Zarab save us, soon you'll be sharing it over quishtar with my mother and I'll no longer have the worst-kept secret in Percheron! All right. I shall see what can be done for him—I too feel responsible for his unhappy situation."

Pez gave a brief bow. "Thank you, my Zar."

"It cannot happen immediately," Boaz warned. "Give it some time. You must let him fully heal. Let all of us fully heal from these recent tragic events. Give me up to three moons."

Pez nodded. It was longer than he had hoped but he was not in a position to argue. "Until autumn, then."

"You have my word."

"Thank you, my Zar."

"Just stay close today, will you? I'm filled with dread and you're the only one I can admit it to."

"I will protect you."

THE ZAR WAS TRANSPORTED to the executions in the curtained, slave-carried karak. He wasn't traveling far but his journey passed through countless manicured gardens and various gateways—six in all—that took him at last to the main courtyard that accessed the city itself. He would not leave the palace grounds proper but rather stop in the Moon Courtyard, where, for centuries, Zars had climbed a special royal stairway that led to the parapet from which they could view public exhibitions, processions, entertainments, and executions.

Boaz did not like traveling in the karak, having never quite outgrown the childish nausea that resulted from the swaying sensation. It niggled at him now like an unwelcome but familiar visitor as he sat unhappily on silk cushions. Next to him sat Pez, dressed in silks identical to the Zar's.

"Bit scratchy, aren't they?" the dwarf commented in an effort to divert his Zar from the ordeal ahead.

"Wardrobe thought it fitting that you be seen fully as the fool."

Pez spoke softly so he could not be overheard. "Is that so? You should be cautious that they don't inadvertently make you look the fool, my Zar."

Boaz found a small grin—what felt like his first in an age. Then his expression darkened again. "How bad is it going to be, Pez? Tell me honestly."

Pez pursed his thick lips. Honesty was probably the last thing Boaz needed right now but it was also necessary. "Worse than you can possibly imagine. You know about Riding the Needle but, Boaz, you have no conception of how truly shocking a death it is. And Shaz is to be ganched—is this right?" Boaz nodded mournfully. "Have you ever seen that occur?"

"No. My father maintained there was more than enough time for me to see sights of this magnitude."

"Joreb was right to protect you. He no doubt hoped you wouldn't have to deal with such things until much later in life. Spiking is cruel beyond belief, Boaz. They haul the victim up on pulleys on a special scaffolding from which are hung terrible, sharpened hooks. The victim is dropped without warning and the fun of the spectacle for the crowd is to see where on his body the vicious hooks snag. If he's lucky, it's across an artery, then death is relatively swift."

"And if not?" Boaz asked, his feeling of nausea suddenly much worse.

"If it's through his belly or chest, he takes a long time to die."

"I'm not going to be able to watch this," Boaz moaned, dropping his head into his hands.

"You have no choice."

"What if I can't help but close my eyes or look away?"

"I won't let you. My magic can compel as skillfully as it hides, my Zar." The swaying karak halted. The sound of the people's excited murmuring from the other side of the thick walls was loud enough to tell them that a large crowd had gathered for the executions.

"Why do they want to watch this?" Boaz murmured.

"Morbid curiosity, dark fascination, macabre entertainment."

"Then I make myself a promise to provide new entertainment for my people. We are a nation that prides itself on culture, Pez, why—" Boaz cut off his words, gulping air and trying to compose himself.

"Boaz," Pez said firmly, "I applaud your sentiment. But public execution has its place. It is a valuable reminder, if nothing else, that life—no matter who you are or what your situation might be—is precious. Any potential lawbreakers watching will know after today that you will not tolerate anyone who thinks they are above your laws."

Boaz nodded but Pez hadn't finished. "Your subjects will know after today, High One, that whilst you could so easily have covered up the crime within your own palace, you have been ruthless with one of your own. Your point will have been made, and everyone will take note."

Boaz hardly heard his friend's words, so intent was he on holding back his vomit. Pez fixed him with a fierce stare, which somehow gave Boaz strength, and then the dwarf rolled out of the karak squealing.

Boaz fought back his fear and emerged sedately, squinting slightly at the harsh light of the hot morning. The sky was a bright canvas for the sun to splash its golden rays across, interrupted briefly by a few scudding clouds, leftovers from the previous days of overcast skies. Today there would be no rain to wash away the blood or the stench of death.

Boaz was already sweating into his formal robes, and the wrapped silk about his head made him feel even hotter, but this had little to do with the weather. Pez rolled back to him and took his hand, acting like one of the monkeys Boaz used to be so amused by in his father's zoo. Rolling his eyes comically and tugging Boaz toward the steps in an exaggerated manner, the dwarf whispered, "Beware, my Zar. Salmeo has plotted another surprise."

ANA AND A FEW of the girls had been assembled in a large airy chamber that enjoyed a sweet breeze that blew in off the Faranel. Most of the young women were enjoying sitting around the grand stone fountain in the adjoining courtyards. But Ana remained in the chamber itself, admiring the exquisitely pretty tiles depicting the Tree of Life. She was feeling sorry for the youngest odalisque, Eishar, who stood apart from the other girls. She was only nine summers and looked permanently terrified—and with good reason, Ana thought, knowing full well that Salmeo would not have spared the youngster his special private exploration of her body.

"Did you sleep well, Eishar?" Ana asked, trying to ease the child's fear.

"No, I'm frightened they'll come for me at any time," the girl half sobbed.

"They?"

"The Zar's people." Eishar's voice was small and frightened.

"You must stop worrying," Ana reassured her. "I've met the Zar and he's really a very gentle man. He's quite young . . . about my age, and he will not be looking to call you—not yet, not for a while anyway."

She hoped she was telling the truth; she had no real idea about the Zar's tastes or desires, but if her judgment was sound, Boaz was not interested in children. Eishar reminded Ana of her smallest sister and she wondered how her family was getting on. The Samazen could come at any time, and when that happened, her father would have to bring his two small herds closer to their dwelling. He wouldn't have her help this year and that saddened her deeply. She loved to spend time alone with her father, especially when he would relate the tale of how he found her—"the prettiest of babies," he would say—in the scrub of the farther reaches of the foothills, just before they yielded to the desert proper. A pain knifed through her as she understood that she would never again see her beloved father. That sense of emptiness reminded her of the only other man she'd loved. He too would never look upon her again. At least her father was alive, she comforted herself, but Lazar had died for her, because of her selfishness.

All the girls turned at the sound of the Elim arriving. Most of the older girls were excited at the prospect of being taken to the main bathing pavilion, while Ana suspected Eishar would have liked nothing better than to be allowed to play beneath the cypress trees.

But the two Elim who arrived did not offer the usual greetings, and the subsequent entrance of the Grand Master Eunuch set off a palpable tremor of fear among the girls.

"Sisters," Salmeo lisped.

Everyone watching the huge man became deathly still.

Ana glanced at Eishar. The youngster looked ready to wail.

"Welcome to your first proper day in the harem of Zar Boaz. It was my intention that you begin your formal training today, but I regret to inform you that those activities will have to be postponed. Something rather important has arisen that involves one of your number." He let that statement sink in, pausing dramatically before he continued. "We've come to collect Odalisque Ana," he finally said softly, sounding almost apologetic. "Where are you, Ana?"

Ana had suspected that Salmeo would call her name, though for once she had no idea why.

"I'm here," she said. "Have you come to collect me for another of your spectacularly unpleasant shows?"

"Careful, Ana," Salmeo warned. "I have been tolerant because these are still early days. But once your formal training begins, I will be forced to employ a more stringent discipline." Raising his voice, he spoke to the wider audience now. "You should all be warned. Odalisque Ana is being shown some leniency today because she must face something . . . well"—he searched theatrically for the right word—"shall we say unsavory."

A murmur passed through the girls. "Fret not, my lovelies, Ana will be returned to you shortly, unharmed." He smiled, one last time, his tongue flicking briefly through the gap in his teeth. "Come, Ana," he added, firmly this time, and she knew not to disobey.

After being dressed and appropriately hidden behind a long dark veil, Ana was led by the same two Elim beyond the main entrance. They assisted her into a tiny curtained karak and carried her swiftly through the beautiful series of manicured gardens. She chanced pulling back the curtains a mere crack and realized they were taking her toward the Moon Courtyard. It felt as if a lifetime had passed since she had last been here, though it was in fact mere days. In a moment of crystal clarity, it came to her that taking her life might be easier than facing the dullness that stretched out before her: no Lazar, no friendships with the girls who would soon see her as enemy rather than friend as the jostling for the Zar's attention began. Thinking about Boaz gave her some hope—his intelligence, his youth, his desire not to imprison the girls of the harem but to find new ways to entertain and educate them. And dear Pez . . . perhaps her lifeline.

The karak was settled on the ground and Ana became aware of a loud murmur of voices outside. One of the Elim opened the curtain. "You must accompany us now."

"Why are we here?" she asked, keeping her voice light and playful, although she suspected the Elim had seen every approach over the years. This one, however, was young and perhaps not as jaded because he did respond.

"There's to be a public execution today, Miss Ana. You are required to bear witness."

Ana gasped, shrinking back into the karak. She hadn't learned anything from Pez's careful warning—Salmeo was going to ensure that she paid many times over for her challenge of him—and she had even baited the fat eunuch again today, impressing the younger girls and enjoying the shocked glances from the older ones. It had been stupid of her and it had served only to intensify Salmeo's power over her. He enjoyed it too— enjoyed it especially because he knew she could never win. No amount of defiance would ever diminish his authority over her. She was his to command.

"I can't," she implored the waiting Elim.

Now his companion, an older man, looked in, irritated by the delay. "Hurry," he snapped, "the Grand Master Eunuch awaits."

"You must come now, Miss Ana," the young guard repeated with sympathy.

She shook her head but the older Elim reached in, all but pulling her from the karak. "You will behave, Odalisque Ana. I am answerable to the Grand Master Eunuch, and if you give us any trouble today, I will personally make your life as unpleasant as I can."

And so Ana understood now that the chain of misery passed down the line of command from Salmeo to his Elim. "It can't get any worse," she said.

"Be very sure that it can, Odalisque Ana. Now hold yourself erect and do not let the harem down."

BOAZ FELT HIS THROAT close tighter still at Pez's warning. He looked up at the great wall that surrounded the Stone Palace and its grounds and he instantly recognized the enormous bulk of Salmeo standing next to a petite figure in dark somber robes. The second figure was too small to be his mother, and no servant of hers would be permitted to leave the harem for the purposes of a public execution. There was only one other person who would be forced to witness this event—it had to be Odalisque Ana. Salmeo obviously intended to crush Ana's spirit well before she acquired any delusions that she might survive the harem with her integrity and personality intact. Even his mother had learned to play by Salmeo's rules and it would be no different for Ana—unless he himself made it different.

Boaz turned to face the special steps cut into the wall. Every Zar had mounted them at one time or another, whether it be to make some proclamation or simply to observe his people going about their daily lives. Today these steps would afford him the best possible view of suffering. He wished with all of his heart he didn't have to be there, but he knew there would be no escaping his duty today. He could see Pez waiting at the top for him, going about his silly antics and raising guffaws from the crowd.

The Zar of Percheron took a deep breath and began the long climb, his steps matching the rhythm of the single haunting drum that announced his impending arrival.

IN THE THRONG awaiting the two barbaric executions stood a person in a dark gray jamoosh, holding the hand of a lad no more than ten. The youngster looked fearful, glancing up every few moments toward his companion, who had eyes only for the top of the palace walls and the various figures that stood upon them.

"That's her, that's Odalisque Ana, standing next to the Grand Master Eunuch," whispered the boy.

"So I gathered," came the reply.

"And the Valide Zara is here today as well. She stands near the Vizier. Can you see him?"

"I can, although I would not have recognized him without his garish silks and showy beard."

"That drum is sounding the arrival of the Zar."

"Thank you, Teril," the man said, and in the tone was a gentle admonishment that suggested this was not news.

The youngster was not deterred. "Should we get closer?"

"No. I think you'll regret being here soon."

"I've attended many floggings," the boy boasted unconvincingly.

"I know," his companion said a little sadly. "But this time you know the prisoner. Have you ever seen someone die slowly in excruciating pain?"

The boy shook his head.

"Well, that's what's ahead for young Shaz. Perhaps we shouldn't stay."

"But you asked me to bring you," the boy protested, confused.

"I did. But I have entirely different reasons for being here, which have nothing to do with an execution."

"Because of her?" the boy asked, nodding at Ana.

"Yes."

"You cannot speak to an odalisque. That privilege belongs to the Zar alone."

"I don't intend to speak to her. I simply needed to see her for myself. Do you see the dwarf prancing around?"

"Yes. That's Pez."

"I want you to get a note to him from me. It's very important, very urgent. Can you do that? I will pay you."

"I will not accept money. I owe you this." The person nodded and the boy read thanks in the intense look from beneath the jamoosh. "Where is the note?"

"Here." The figure pressed a small folded parchment into the boy's hand.

"Now?"

"As soon as you can, Teril."

"I may have to wait until the dwarf comes back down those stairs."

"I can never thank you enough for helping me in this way."

"Then our debt is settled, Spur Lazar?" the boy asked in a whisper.

"Fully," Lazar replied, his voice scratchy from the bitter tea concoction that Ellyana and Zafira had been forcing down his throat every hour but mostly from the drop of drezden that had numbed him. "And now I must leave." He placed a hand on the youngster's head, ruffled the boy's curly hair. "Be careful. No one must read this but the Zar's jester."

"I understand. But how will you walk? You needed my help before."

"I shall manage" came the brusque reply.

The lad nodded unhappily. He gave a brief farewell wave before melting into the crowd.

Lazar pulled the jamoosh hood farther over his face before glancing up at Ana, trying to imprint her features onto his mind. Finally he turned unsteadily, the pain of his exertion hidden beneath the veiling garments, and then hobbled away on two gnarled walking sticks. Lazar knew he should not have come today, knew it would cost him dearly in terms of his health. The two priestesses had saved his life, that much was sure, but oh, how Zafira had railed at him when he had begun this slow, debilitating journey down from the hut on Star Island into the boat, where Teril awaited him. Was it fate that the same child who had attended Shaz at Lazar's flogging also had a father with leprosy . . . or was this Lyana's work? He would never know. All he knew was the intense burst of joy he'd felt at seeing the familiar face of Teril when the boy had come running by the hut. Lazar asked himself again as he slowly limped away from the mob whether it was by chance or design that he happened to be rugged up, sitting outside on the clifftop, taking some air, when Teril had come skipping by. They had recognized each other instantly.

"Spur Lazar?" Teril had choked. "Zarab save me, I thought we'd killed you."

"Zarab himself tried," Lazar had croaked, not expecting the boy to understand. "But I defied him."

"The whip was poisoned," the wide-eyed boy had beseeched, no preamble required.

Lazar had given a growl. "This has nothing to do with Shaz. He made a mess of my body—that's all he is guilty of."

"He had no choice, Spur. Rah made him do the whipping."

"I gathered as much. Tell me about yourself?"

"I am called Teril. My mother begged the palace to take me when my father became a leper. She had no income to take care of us children and she died not long after. I suspect she killed herself from a broken heart, Spur. She loved my father and all of us."

Lazar had nodded. "Who took you in?"

"Horz. He felt sorry for my family. He took my two brothers too but they work in the kitchens."

"He is the finest of the Elim."

"He will die shortly, alongside Shaz."

"Die today? What?" Lazar had roared, shocked, although his voice no longer had the power he was used to. The youngster had nodded, terrified. "What do you know?" The child's words had come out in a big rush. Lazar's fury had intensified as Teril had recounted how two men had been expertly framed for his death—all lies, he assumed. It had to be Salmeo behind the poisoning. "The odalisque . . . Ana?"

"I don't know, Spur. The business of the palace harem is not for the likes of me."

Lazar hadn't needed confirmation from the lad to know that Salmeo would insist upon Ana being in attendance for the execution. It was just another way to humiliate her, unravel the few threads of herself—pride, courage, determination—that she kept tightly bound. Lazar knew at that moment that he had to see her and he had to find a way to contact Pez. No longer would this charade be allowed to continue. "Help me up."

"Spur Lazar, if you'll forgive me, you don't look as though you can stand."

"With your help, Teril, I intend to stand, to walk somehow, and to get across to the palace before the execution."

Teril had shaken his head, looking worried. "I have to tell you, Spur, I'm not sure we can make it back in time." He had looked up toward the sun and marked the time of day. "They could already be dead," he had said sadly.

Before Lazar could respond, a cry had interrupted him. "What are you doing?" Zafira had called, limping out of the cottage, her expression one of intense worry. "Lazar! What is this?" She had looked at the boy who had lifted Lazar unsteadily to his feet. "Who are you?"

"This is Teril, Zafira. He was present at the flogging. He tells me that Horz of the Elim and Shaz, the junior Inflictor, will die today as a result of my sentence."

Zafira's worry had turned to fear. It had ghosted across her face, making her seem all the more frail. It had seemed to him she'd already heard the news. "Lazar, my son, you cannot go, you cannot help those two men. This is not your doing. This is the palace tying up loose ends . . . surely you know this?" She had looked at the scared boy standing next to Lazar, who was nodding without knowing it. "All the more reason to keep your life a secret."

He had looked at her, pained, knowing she spoke the truth. "Not from everyone, Zafira. Not from Pez, not from Jumo."

"And Ana? You cannot inflict any more suffering onto that girl. She has to learn to survive in the palace . . . without you, Lazar."

He had looked momentarily beaten, swaying on his legs. "I know," he had croaked. "I am not going to make contact with

Ana. I already know I probably cannot save Horz, although nothing would give me greater pleasure than to declare myself alive, show them."

"You cannot!" she had spat, angry. "Someone wants you dead, Lazar, and they almost got their wish. I beg you, do not reveal yourself yet."

"Innocent people will die," he had persisted.

"They always do," she had countered. "In any struggle, the innocent perish. We fight for something far bigger than two lives, Lazar. I beg you, Lazar, you must let your body heal."

Lazar had been torn but he had to do something. "I must get word to Pez," he had groaned. "I need him to do some things for me."

"I can do that for you," she had insisted. "Stay here whilst—"

"No! I trust only myself," he had lied. He knew he probably couldn't get close to Pez without revealing himself to others. And he simply had to lay eyes on Ana once more. Just one more time and then he would let her go.

"Lazar, please, you are not well enough—"

"Be still, Zafira. Don't you think my own body tells me how sick I am? Give me pure drezden."

She had looked suddenly terrified. "I cannot—"

"You can! You will! Ellyana said it would revive me."

"Tempor—"

"Temporarily, yes! I know, I know. Let it revive me sufficiently—and temporarily—to make this journey. I understand I'm not ready, I already accept that I will pay a hefty price afterward. I am prepared for the relapse and I will fight it once again."

"The drezden revives only when the body is strong enough

to cope with another dose but, Lazar, not yet. It could kill you," she had pleaded, her eyes begging him to listen to her.

He had remained implacable. "Fetch the drezden, Zafira," he had said in a wintry tone. "A drop on my tongue, your companion told me." He had stared intently at the priestess. "I watched you both milking the snake. I know we have enough. Do this for me and I will return and rest, and heal," he had promised. Finally she had relented, resigned as she hobbled back into the hut.

He had turned back to Teril, who had been watching this interaction with huge, disbelieving eyes. "You have a boat, I presume?"

"Yes, Spur," the boy had stammered.

"Then you will row me across the harbor and help me up to the palace."

The boy had begun shaking his head, no doubt terrified that he was going to be accompanying a corpse by the afternoon. "I cannot—"

"Teril," Lazar had growled with effort, coughing and steadying himself against the boy's shoulder. "You owe me. It is the least you can do." He hadn't enjoyed blackmailing the youngster but he had had no choice. He had to win the child's help.

Teril had flinched at the hard words, but had finally nodded. "I will help you in payment of my debt," and Lazar had felt relief flood him. Frail or not, he would see Ana once again.

29

Boaz was given a tumultuous welcome by the city of Percheron. It was not often that the Percherese saw their ruler in person and the first formal glimpse of their new Zar prompted great cheering and excitement. Boaz stood, acknowledging their cries, tall, lean, and broad-shouldered, not at all like his stout father of later years. Although few had ever seen his mother, they knew her by reputation to be an incredible beauty and this young man's dark curly hair and altogether handsome appearance suggested a resemblance to the new Valide's famed looks. Many in the crowd had been surprised but also delighted to hear of the young Zar's proclamation of not one but two public executions so early in his reign. There had been rumors that the young man was studious, bordering on scholarly, and those rumors had gathered momentum, leading to suggestions that he was also squeamish in nature. Several of the more outspoken city leaders had tactfully queried among themselves whether this prince was cut out for the role of Zar and whether he could rule with a firm hand. Others had replied, quite rightly, that his father—so feared in his prime—would have chosen carefully from his many heirs. They argued that Joreb would not have selected a boy unable to summon the kind of strength needed to hold Percheron in his grip.

And now Boaz was seemingly proving his father correct. To onlookers, the young man seemed far from timid as he acknowledged the crowd's welcome.

"All right?" Pez whispered to his Zar, even though no one stood close enough on the parapet to overhear him.

"Yes, surprisingly. Are you using it on me?"

"Not yet," Pez lied. "You are handling yourself perfectly. I'm proud of you." Pez was channeling his magic so gently that Boaz could not feel it. Soon the Zar might be more conscious of the Lore but for now Pez wanted to instill confidence in the young man.

"Should I keep smiling at everyone?"

"Yes, you're giving them precisely what they want. Soon you should call for silence so that your executioners can proceed."

Boaz raised a hand and at his signal a hush washed across the crowd. He nodded gravely toward the fearsome-looking palace executioner. "He did this for my father for so many years," he uttered softly to his friend.

As the man began to announce the sentences, Boaz glanced surreptitiously toward Ana.

"It's not right that she's here," he whispered angrily.

"I don't know why you're surprised."

Boaz grimaced. "I thought that with Lazar's flogging and subsequent death, it was over between Salmeo and Ana."

Pez frowned. "Don't be naive, Boaz. It's only just begun."

They stopped talking as a small gate opened in the palace wall and the two victims were led out. Although one walked proudly, the other was jabbering and crying, needing to be all but carried between the two Elim who escorted him.

"Oh Zarab! Poor Shaz," Boaz whispered, his tone fraught with compassion, and Pez knew the time for gentle channeling was over with.

HEREZAH LEANED TOWARD TARIQ. "Is it really necessary for me to be here?"

"Forgive me for imposing upon your goodwill, Valide. I felt our young Zar needed your support today."

Herezah stared at the Vizier for a long time, long enough to make him frown. "Tariq," she finally said, "I don't know what to make of you anymore."

"What do you mean, Valide?" he asked softly, ignoring the executioner's drone below, the apprentice's hysterics, and the excited whisperings of the crowd.

"I mean that I cannot make you out. There is something about you that doesn't fit with my image of our Vizier." He chuckled deep in his throat. She liked the sound of his laugh, unlike anything she'd heard from Tariq in all the years she'd known him. "And there's that laugh. I've never heard you make such a genuine sound of amusement, Tariq."

"How have I been before, Valide?"

"Like a sycophant," Herezah answered directly. "I've watched you calculate your fake chortles for years. In fact, everything about the Tariq I recall is calculated and controlled." She shook her head. "Your amusement just now sounded utterly genuine."

"It was," he replied, glancing down to where Shaz, upon hearing his sentence, began wailing all the more forcefully.

Beneath her veil, the Valide bit her lip, in thought. "I've also never thought you cared much for Boaz."

"I didn't." He smiled at the obvious shock that registered in her eyes. "What I mean is, until a short while ago your son was simply another heir . . . another prince-in-waiting. Now he is our Zar, the Chosen One. I do care about our Zar, Valide, and I especially care because Boaz is still young enough to need guidance from those who have wisdom to share."

"You see, Tariq, this doesn't sound a bit like you," she whispered.

He smiled once again, flirtatiously, his eyes sparkling as they had never done before. "I can't imagine who I sound like, then."

She joined his mood, replying playfully, "It's as if there's an intruder. Someone has stolen Tariq's body."

Maliz had to temper his desire to throw back his head and laugh loudly. "Perhaps someone has. Would you prefer that I go by a different name?"

Herezah stared at the Vizier quizzically. "No, that will not be necessary. I can't say I'm not impressed, though. I like the curious metamorphosis you seem to be going through, I like it very much, and I can only put it down to the brew you said you are taking. I see your stoop is all but gone—it is clearly working."

"Thank you. I do feel stronger than I have in a long time."

"And I'm especially pleased that your concern is, for once, not selfishly shown," she added, ignoring his wry glance, knowing he found her hypocritical. "I do think Boaz has been especially brave in his decisions regarding these two traitors—his actions were necessary and he made the right choice, but I know it will take every ounce of his courage to stand here and bear witness."

The Vizier looked thoughtful. "Boaz will make a great Zar with the right people around him. He has his mother's extraordinary looks and poise, enabling him to charm people, as well as the warrior bearing of his father for intimidation. It's a prized mix."

"I would never have thought it but I think you're right— these last few days he has reminded me strongly of a young Joreb."

"We must remember, though, that he is still young enough to be influenced—and we really have no idea who is influencing him."

Herezah drew back in surprise. "What do you mean by that?"

"Nothing sinister. I may have taken little more than a cursory interest in him previously, but now that he is Zar, I will be taking a far more proprietorial approach on behalf of the Percherese. To whom does he defer? Where does he go for advice? I need to know more about him."

"You've known the boy since he was born, Tariq—you know as well as I that his two great friends are the hated dwarf and the Spur. Now Lazar is gone and my son is left with a half-wit for his closest companion."

Tariq turned and stared at Pez. The dwarf was standing on one leg, threatening to overbalance into the crowd beneath, clearly in his own world.

"I had Yozem, my crone, do a blood reading on him, you know," Herezah added casually.

"And?"

"Nothing. Pez is blank to her. She is unable to read him at all."

"Is that common?"

Herezah snorted. "Yozem has never failed me before."

"I see," Tariq muttered, distracted, a vague sense of gentle magic swirling about him. He tried to follow it, lock onto it, but he couldn't. It was as though it knew it was being hunted. He had no idea where it was coming from. Frustrated, he turned his thoughts to the dwarf. *I must take more interest in you too, Pez,* he pondered. *Perhaps there's more to you than meets the eye.*

On the wall, still dancing, Pez prayed that the Goddess would protect him from discovery as he carefully channeled his magic.

ALL THE FORMAL pronouncements had been made. Above Shaz's pitiful moans, the executioner turned to Boaz for the next bit of theater before they got down to the serious business of killing two men.

Boaz took a deep breath. He had one last hope of saving a life today while maintaining a firm ruling hand. "Good people of Percheron," he began, and the crowd below became silent, "the law of the Zar has been proclaimed. Shaz the Inflictor and Horz of the Elim have betrayed me and they are now under the shadow of death for their treachery. That said, I am mindful of the old traditions of our nation, too many of them lost in recent times. I am hopeful that together we might rekindle some of those rituals observed by our ancestors that have made us the wealthy, educated, and cultured people that we are today." Whistles and cheers rippled through the crowd.

Boaz raised a hand for silence. "To this end, and as Zar Bael-zeemen did three centuries ago, I hand over the power of the Crown to the people." This won more applause, even though no one in the mob understood what he was referring to.

But the Vizier did. Maliz had lived long enough to have known the reign of Zar Baelzeemen. The demon nodded, coolly impressed. "He's far cleverer than any of us have credited."

"What do you know?" Herezah demanded.

"My history—as does your son. The Zar he refers to al-lowed the crowd to show mercy when there were two or more executions planned for the same day."

Herezah opened her mouth to reply, then shut it as Boaz began speaking again.

"People of Percheron, if there is ever an occasion during my reign when more than one person is to be executed on the same day, I will allow you to overrule, if you so choose, and show mercy to the condemned. Zar Baelzeemen was a compas-sionate man and I intend to rule with the same sense of human-ity. I cannot forgive these two prisoners for what they have done—I must not, in fact—but you can reprieve one of the sentences if you so choose.

"Show me, my people, if you wish to see Horz of the Elim suffer the consequences of his dark actions," he shouted, emo-tion lacing his voice as he silently prayed that the older man might be spared. The crowd roared back its response, their arms raised in unison.

Horz would die today. Boaz swallowed his disappointment. It had been too much to ask for. Still, he continued: "Having heard his deeds, now show me if you wish to see Shaz the ap-prentice Inflictor pay the price I am exacting for his part in the Spur's demise."

There was an embarrassed murmur followed by an awkward silence as only a small number of arms shot into the air.

Pez began clapping from relief but he turned it into a joke, mugging for the audience, making whooping sounds as though he didn't really understand what his excitement was about. Boaz laid a hand on his companion's shoulder and the dwarf immediately became still.

"See how he can control him," Herezah whispered to the Vizier. "No one else can."

Tariq nodded, intrigued now by Pez. He stole a glance at Salmeo, who scowled in his direction. Tariq smiled back. He knew how much the Grand Master Eunuch would resent the Zar's overturning of Shaz's punishment, leaving a loose thread the eunuch would have to tie off later.

"My people have chosen to spare Shaz the apprentice," Boaz called, suppressing his delight with effort.

The crowd below was not so circumspect and the roar of approval was deafening. Shaz himself looked confused, unable to believe that he had cheated death as it knocked so loudly against his door. He looked at Horz, who nodded, a soft and sad smile about his lips as he silently congratulated the lad. Then the rough hands of the executioner's aides were pushing Shaz back into the Moon Courtyard. There he began hugging every soldier, every servant, even one of the executioner's team. Seeing a familiar face in the distance—Teril, one of the youngest apprentices of the Inflictors—Shaz waved, too ecstatic to speak. The lad returned the gesture, motioning that he would see Shaz in a few moments. When Shaz nodded, turning away to hug another bystander, Teril looked away, up to the top of the wall where Pez was doing one of his famous jigs.

"Hey, boy, you're not allowed here! Our Zar is up there," a

soldier commanded officiously, approaching hurriedly. "You'll get yourself knifed for less."

"I have a special note for the dwarf," the lad mumbled. "It's important."

The man laughed. "What? And you think the fool can read it?"

The youngster looked suddenly uncertain. "I don't know. I just promised one of the priests that I'd get it to him." The lie came easily to his lips. "I don't care if he understands it or not."

"Let me see it," the man said, slightly chagrined at the mention of Zarab's holy men.

"No, sir. I cannot," Teril said. "I cannot do that. This is a private note between the priest and the dwarf." Hurriedly moving on from his lie, he added, "I am wearing my palace uniform. You can see I am allowed to be on the grounds."

"Show me your mark," the man said, unwilling to take any chances with the Zar thirty feet above them.

The lad rolled back the loose sleeve of his shirt to reveal the special branding that all palace servants were forced to endure. The man nodded. "Who is your direct superior?"

"Rah," Teril answered. "I am returning to him once I pass on the note. You can watch me."

"I cannot let you go up there. No one but the royal party is permitted. But you also may not remain here, so near to the Zar, or it's my neck in a noose."

"Will you let me win the dwarf's attention, see if I can get him to accept the note?"

"The dwarf wouldn't have a clue—"

"I know, sir. But I gave my oath."

"All right," the man said, feeling a bit sorry for the lad. He had a son of a similar age and understood how important it was to instill a sense of duty into boys of that age. The lad was only trying to see a task to its proper end. Furthermore, all the soldiers were happy to hear of Shaz cheating death; none believed he'd had any part in the downfall of their Spur. It couldn't hurt to show a bit of the same generosity of spirit that their own Zar was promoting. "Go on, then, see if you can win his attention."

Teril whistled. As fate would have it, the noise outside the walls had dwindled almost to silence as the crowd waited quietly for Horz to ride the infamous needle. His sound pierced the air. Both figures above heard it and turned. "You've been magnificent. Don't ruin it now. Keep looking ahead," Pez cautioned his Zar, looking down with irritation to see the young lad beckoning him. "What's this?"

"Who is it?" Boaz hissed.

"I've no idea. I don't recognize him from here but he obviously belongs to the palace."

"What does he want?"

"Me, I think. I can't tell. Shall I find out?"

"No. Let him wait. I don't want you to leave."

"I won't. He's waving something at me. Let me just get it." Pez disappeared down the steps, pausing regularly to grab mindlessly at the air and mutter loudly about flying fruit.

"Well, you're in luck, lad. The fool has fallen for it," the soldier said as they watched the dwarf descending.

"I like Pez; he's funny."

"Funny, yes. He's also mad. I can't see what this Zar or the old one could see in having that thing ranting by their sides all day."

Pez was grinning when he finally arrived. "Is it dinner already? Are we eating the elephants from the zoo?"

"Go on," the soldier said, nudging the lad.

"Er, Pez, sir," Teril began, unsure how to appropriately address the court jester.

Pez stared at man and boy, scratching his crotch. "Did you see all those flying pomegranates just now? I had no idea they could sprout wings or talk."

"The, er, lad has a note for you, Pez," the soldier said, ignoring the dwarf's babblings.

Pez stared at the proffered scroll. "Is this my dinner?"

The man looked at the boy with sympathy. "Just put it in his hand. You can tell your priest that you fulfilled the duty that was asked of you. If the idiot eats it, that's his problem."

Teril did as he was told, pushing the scroll into the strangely oversize hands of the dwarf, trying not to gape at the huge knuckles and long fingers. "I was asked to give this to you," he explained tentatively.

Pez smelled the note and then began to drool from the side of his mouth, his eyes fixed vacantly on something beyond.

"Go now," the man urged the lad. Hesitating only briefly, Teril hurried away.

"And the elephants?" Pez asked, seemingly returning to himself.

"Soon," the soldier said, quickly taking his leave as well.

Pez clutched the scroll, feeling a chill crawl up his spine. No one had ever written to him—the only people who would were those who knew the truth about him. That meant someone on the outside of the palace had asked the lad to get this note to him. Was it Jumo? The servant couldn't write but he could have

had it scribed. Zafira perhaps? Or even Ellyana? Well, one thing
was for sure: he couldn't read it now—it would be too obvious.
Instead he sniffed it again, knowing others were watching him.
Then, after nibbling the edge and spitting the fragments straight
back out again, he tucked the note into his shirt and climbed the
steps. He had not allowed the Lore magic to wane while he was
occupied but he could feel Boaz's anxiety level increasing. It
seemed the executioner's team was ready to begin.

30

Boaz's complexion had turned so pale Pez wondered if the boy would pass out. The Zar was staring fixedly ahead, his eyes glazed. Pez increased the wave of magic and his friend seemed to recover some equilibrium.

"Pez," Boaz muttered, swaying slightly. "How can I let an innocent man die?"

The dwarf ignored the question and increased his channeling. Boaz was going to have to learn about situations of intolerable cruelty.

Pez looked down and felt his own gut twist at the sight below. Horz—naked except for a small piece of linen tied around his hips—was being laid out on the ground.

"I've read about this in the books in the library. Do you know it was invented by one of the Zars?" Boaz seemed mesmerized and repulsed at the same time.

Pez could feel the boy leaning into the magic, trying to take more because of his fear. "Boaz, you must teach yourself to let go," he cautioned. "I have you. You are safe. I can make you blind to it if you wish, but I think that would be cowardly. Think of Odalisque Ana standing over there alone, watching her uncle die hideously. She has nothing to help her, save whatever courage she can muster from within." It was the right thing to say. Boaz stood straighter, taller, at the mention of the girl's name. "Now let go as I say, and I will keep you safe. You will not disgrace yourself."

"What about Ana?" the Zar whispered, taking deep slow breaths.

Pez felt the greedy grip on his magic lessening. "Ana is strong. Her hatred for Salmeo will get her through this." Boaz nodded thoughtfully, and Pez felt further lessening on the hold. There was no more time. He had to move quickly. "Now, Boaz, I must go."

"Go?" Boaz exclaimed.

"Hush, child, I want to say good-bye to Horz."

Boaz looked chastened. "He's a good man. I had hoped they would pardon him. Can your magic not help him too?"

"No, I won't use magic," Pez replied, keen to be gone. "You stand there and focus on me. I'll be near Horz so it will look as if you're watching the condemned man. The Lore will not fail you, Boaz. Trust it."

The Zar nodded miserably. "Tell him I'm sorry."

"I think he already knows."

FOUR MEN TOOK HOLD of the bindings around Horz's wrists and ankles and pulled, tightening the straps, so that the Elim was now spread-eagled on the ground. The executioner looked up to his Zar, who sadly lowered his head as the signal to proceed.

The hush in the crowd was so thick it was oppressive as Pez emerged from one of the gates, snarling and running at the onlookers, who backed away, unsure. Was this part of the entertainment? Or was it just the oddity of the infamous dwarf? It was not often that they got this close to the Zar's famed jester but his reputation preceded him; he was known to be contrary, one moment happier than the birds at dawn and the next dark and angry like a gathering storm. And it looked to them as though dawn had come and gone—the storm was surely brewing. Pez was hissing at everyone, including the executioner. "I want to kiss him good-bye," he suddenly moaned, breaking into sobs. He kept repeating it, furious, like a child determined to have his way.

The executioner had been handed a thick, vicious pole, sturdy and fearsome. It had been sharpened to a savage point and the executioner positioned the sharp end between Horz's spread legs, just moments away from impaling the trembling yet silent man of the Elim.

Pez increased his volume until he was shrieking.

The executioner, unusually rattled by the dwarf's behavior, turned once again to his Zar for approval. The young man, standing alone, trembling in tandem with the man about to die, nodded and the executioner stepped back, allowing Pez his request. Everyone near the front of the mob and those on high watched the dwarf change instantly from hysterically angry to smiling and serene. He bowed to his Zar, then to the executioner, before waddling over to kneel by Horz and whisper close to his ear.

"You are the bravest man the Zar knows," Pez said. "Go to

your god with a clean conscience, friend." Pez silenced any reply by placing his mouth on the lips of the innocent man.

When he lifted away Horz stared back at him in shock. The dwarf had tricked them all these years! He was as sane as Horz—the Elim heard it in the words, could see it in the intense yellow gaze of the man.

"Shh," was all Pez would say, a finger to his lips, and then he was cavorting away, grinning and clapping. "I kissed him," he boasted, and his bemused audience could only shake their heads as they watched his short figure cartwheeling and skipping back to the small palace gate, finally disappearing through it.

Their attention diverted by the dwarf's madness, no one saw Horz die as he bit down on the pellet Pez had passed into his mouth. The poison was swift; his heart stopped in a matter of seconds and he sighed softly to his death with his eyes open and not so much as a twitch of his bound limbs. It was a peaceful, painless end—and cheated the executioner of Salmeo's victory.

Everyone marveled as the brave Elim didn't even struggle when his torment began. Their awe at his courage when he didn't scream as the pole was rammed into him was so palpable it was like a living, breathing entity of its own. A few people were violently sick as the executioner used a huge mallet to ease the pole's passage through Horz's body, and even two of the men stretching his limbs looked away when the tip of the pole burst through flesh and bone, emerging at Horz's shoulder. The shrieks of disgust in the crowd quieted, at last, to reverence. Condemned as a murderer, Horz would live on in the history books as the Elim's most famed warrior, almost godlike in his stoicism.

"Raise him," the executioner called, as taken aback as any member of the crowd by Horz's lack of protest or struggle.

Horz was raised, impaled on the pole, which was now set into the ground. He would remain there for three days until the smell of his corpse offended the palace and then he would be removed to a special mound on the fringe of the city where he would rot fully, reminding the Percherese for a long time of their Zar's intolerance of any treachery.

ANA HAD CLOSED her eyes to the terrifying scene below and refused to open them even when the fragrance of violets told her that Salmeo was leaning close.

"Your uncle is a stunningly brave man," he lisped. "Not even a sound. I must say that impresses even me and I've seen the bravery of the Elim over the years."

"I hope his spirit never lets you rest easily again," Ana replied.

Salmeo laughed, although he was infuriated by the proceedings. Not only had Horz died courageously but Shaz had been released. The boy now posed a very real threat to the eunuch, knowing what he did. Fortunately Salmeo knew just what would make him feel better. He licked his lips. "Come, Ana, you will learn that I am not threatened by spirits. Now let us really begin your training as a slave. I have so much in store for you."

IN THE KARAK, on the way back to his wing of the palace, Boaz felt what was a mild headache gaining in strength.

"It's the after-effects of the Lore," Pez said matter-of-factly. "You should tell your aides that you wish to be left in peace."

Boaz shook his aching head. "I am humbled by Horz's bravery." He stared absently into the silk screen that hid him from the view of palace passersby.

"We all should be. I told him what you said," Pez lied.

"And?" Boaz asked eagerly, desperate for some relief from his guilt.

Pez took pity on the boy. "He offered thanks."

There was a difficult silence between them as Boaz thought about the brave Elim. "I am going to see more of this in my life, aren't I?" he asked eventually.

"You will see suffering, yes."

"Next time I will be as brave as the Elim. I will emulate Horz and not call upon the Lore."

Pez nodded in approval. "I am proud of you for that."

Boaz sighed. "It's over, then."

"What is?"

"The business with Lazar."

"Not for me," Pez muttered bitterly, quietly enough that Boaz could not hear. He called for the Elim to stop, tumbling out of the karak before the men could fully halt. Laughing maniacally, he stuck his head back through the curtains.

"What was that for?" Boaz whispered.

"You need time alone. Rest. I shall take supper with you later if you wish."

The Zar nodded absently. "Can you get a message to Odalisque Ana for me?"

Pez nodded, the mention of a message reminding him of the folded note pressed against his chest. "Of course."

"Tell her I'm sorry she had to witness that. Tell her I will keep my promise about the picnic."

"I'll go and find her for you now."

Boaz touched the little man's gnarled, clawlike hand. "Thank you, Pez."

31

Before he went to find Ana, Pez returned to his own chamber, the parchment scratching against his skin as he closed his door on the day's events. For no reason he could explain, he felt all of his skin itch in anticipation; every inch of his being was prickling with expectation.

Checking first through the windows to make sure that no one was around outside, he took the extra precaution of sitting on the floor next to a huge painted chest of drawers that held his silks. It completely covered him from view should someone suddenly decide to look through those windows. He remembered now as he unfolded the note why the youngster who had brought it was familiar to him. He had been present in the Courtyard of Sorrows, as Shaz's assistant, who had carried the Viper's Nest behind the apprentice. A fresh wave of foreboding washed over the dwarf. Pez opened the note, recognized with a chill the handwriting despite the scrawl, and finally, hardly daring to breathe, read its terrifying contents.

HE COULDN'T KNOW how long he had stared at the note. Many minutes had passed, he was sure, as he had read and reread in disbelief.

"The note tells no lie," said a familiar voice. Pez looked up to see a dazzling young woman standing before him.

"Why am I not surprised to see you?" he said, anger simmering not only for what he'd read but for her audaciousness in coming here again.

"I sense your distress," she answered levelly.

"Oh, I wouldn't call it anything so mild as distress. *Betrayal* is the word that leaps to mind, *treachery* perhaps. A good man died today."

"So I saw," she replied softly.

"And it had no effect on you, I see," he said darkly.

"What I noted most was that he didn't suffer. That was one of your best performances."

"Losing life before one's time is not suffering?"

"I won't debate this with you now, Pez," she said, suddenly losing interest. "There are more important things to discuss."

"More important . . ." His voice trailed off into silent rage. He pointed a gnarled finger, punctuating his remarks with furious jabs. "I'm not part of your intrigue, Ellyana. I will not be coerced as you have coerced others. "He paused, then added, "Neither, I'd wager, will Jumo."

The strange woman sighed. "Yes, I imagine he will be vengeful."

"Ready to kill, in fact. And with every right after what happened—the way you manipulated him and everything connected with Lazar's death."

"I understand your anger—"

He interrupted her with a sound of disgust. "Where?"

"You will know soon enough."

He nodded wearily. He had not been expecting such a straight answer. "Leave me. I want nothing more to do with you."

"Not before I finish what I came here to tell you. Hate me all you wish, Pez, but I am not your enemy."

"Who needs enemies?" he bit back.

"You have one. He is already hunting you—he senses you."

"I don't know what you're talking about," Pez asserted, though his tone was uncertain and he felt his stomach turn over unpleasantly.

"Yes, you do. You have the owl. It has marked you. I know you've lied that the whiteness of your hair was achieved with dye. That white is her permanent mark. You remember the dreamscape too—I can see in your eyes how it haunts you. You know who you are."

"I am Pez," he growled.

"You are hers! You are Iridor!" she hissed. Her beauty faded with her angry demeanor: her creamy complexion turned to translucent, parchmentlike skin; her eyes, originally a startling blue, turned milky and she shrank before him. Even in this guise, she blazed power but he was not cowed.

"Who are you, Ellyana?" he demanded.

"You know enough about yourself now to understand that the rising of Iridor is prompted by a visit from the crone."

"The Mother?"

"An embodiment of her, a Messenger for her, a servant. Call

me what you will," she said, suddenly gentle. "I repeat, I am not your enemy, Pez. We are allies in the same struggle."

"For the Goddess, you mean." He finally admitted to himself what had been troubling him since the frightening dream at the Sea Temple. It turned his blood to ice to say her name aloud because the whole notion that he was one of her disciples, her closest in fact, terrified him. "Go on, admit it," he pushed. Ellyana spoke such provocative words without ever explaining herself. That would stop—must stop—now.

"Yes, it's true. For the Mother Goddess. Iridor is almost fully risen, Pez, and he heralds her next coming."

"I don't understand any of it," he said, waving her away in a desperate bid to rid himself of this frightening new responsibility.

"You won't understand . . . not until you change."

"Change?"

"That's what I came to finish telling you. You must transform entirely now."

"Into what?" he asked, astounded.

"Iridor's true form."

And that's when it all fell into place. Pez sensed a click in his mind, as if a final jigsaw-puzzle piece had slotted into position. He knew. Had in fact known all his life. Her words felt as though they suddenly completed him. It was as if his previous life was simply a vessel and now that vessel, no longer required, lay shattered in hard, jagged bits about him. "The owl?" he whispered, still not wanting to believe.

"Look in the mirror. You're almost there."

Pez tried once again, adopting his more regular sarcastic tone. "I am a shrunken, deformed, mad dwarf, Ellyana, or hadn't you noticed?"

"You are Iridor for this battle," she said softly and with such affection it almost reduced him to tears. "You are also Pez, dear one. You don't have to give up who you have been but you must accept who you are. Don't be afraid—it is your destiny. You have been chosen, as have all of us."

Pez frowned as another dark thought struck. "And Maliz?"

She nodded grimly. "Has risen. He is amongst us."

"Already?" Pez felt his stomach knot with fear. "How will I know him?"

"You won't. Not yet. It's always the same. But by the same token, he doesn't know you either—not yet. He is looking for you, though, and when he knows you, you will lead him to her."

"Her?"

"Lyana."

He dared not say it as he frowned, repeating the beloved, revered name in his head. "Who is she?"

"I do not know. None of us do. The Mother works in mysterious ways, but Lyana will reveal herself in time and you must protect her. Be her eyes, her ears."

"How do I become Iridor?" he asked, running his short fingers through his whitened hair.

She nodded gently, approvingly, at his acceptance. "Go to the Sea Temple. There you will find answers."

"Can't you help me?"

"I am a merely a Messenger, like you. I know only what I'm told. We serve, you and I, that is all. Go now and don't be seen—may Lyana bless and keep you safe in the perils ahead." Ellyana touched his face with fingers that felt feathery against his skin, or was it the other way around? "I must go," she said.

"I'll show you a way out," he said, reaching for the door, keen to have her gone, to have some silence to think.

Ellyana smiled. "No one saw me come and no one will see me leave. You keep yourself safe. You are the critical link now. Trust no one in the palace, not even your friend the Zar. For all we know, Maliz could have taken him."

Pez grunted. "I would know, I think."

"Not necessarily," she warned. "Be suspicious of everyone. Now go. Lyana awaits."

PEZ MADE HIS WAY to the Sea Temple as if in a stupor. He had changed out of his normal comical clothes into a soft sand-colored jamoosh, beneath which he was naked save for his white linen wrap. Because Pez rarely wore the traditional clothes of Percheron, they afforded him the anonymity he needed. He required none of his art of guile as he ran, every fiber of his being tingling.

He arrived breathlessly at the Sea Temple and stood awhile dragging in deep lungfuls of air. As Pez looked up, sucking down the salty air, he noticed for the first time the tiny balcony that ran around the bright blue dome of the building.

How odd, he thought, *that I haven't seen that before.* Doves and the occasional seabird called from the balustrade where they were afforded a magnificent view of the harbor and the city. Pez's attention was diverted to the dark doorway; he knew that when he stepped through it, his life would change. Casting a single glance out to sea, his gaze fell across Beloch and Ezram, reminding him that he had been meaning to visit the giants of the harbor since he had first talked to Boaz about them. Whatever happened today, Pez promised himself, he would make that visit in the next few days.

And then he was climbing up the stairs into the cool darkness where Lyana awaited him. The soft smile at her lips seemed broader today. Was that a faint blush at the cheeks? He knew he was being fanciful but he suddenly felt very aware of being in the presence of the Mother Goddess.

He knelt, bent his head, and reached a short arm out to touch the folds of her robe, and suddenly he heard her voice in his mind.

32

There was no sign of Zafira. Pez couldn't understand why, for she had never been away when he had visited before, but as quickly as the surprise of her absence came, it left him, driven out by his shock that Lyana had spoken to him in his mind. At first he had thought he was imagining it but the sincerity of the beautiful voice and her obvious love and gratitude had been all too real. He had begun sobbing within moments of hearing her musical tone welcoming him and his emotions had grown only stronger when she had thanked him for the gift of his life.

Pez had hazy memories of childhood. He had blocked most of them out, but still—the echoes of torment and humiliation periodically called to him across time. He had learned at a very young age to act thick-skinned, to turn people's taunts back on themselves, and to use humor to make people enjoy him rather than detest him. He recalled joining a traveling circus. It was passing through his town to make camp at the big city of Merent. He sighed. He couldn't remember the last time he'd thought of Merent or his origins. The circus had paused in his village to water the animals at its fast-running stream and the performers had grabbed the opportunity to slake their own thirst at the local inn, glad to have the sudden and unexpected income. Pez had been an entertainer at the inn, singing bawdy songs, making up rhymes about the villages, and generally getting up to the tomfoolery that amused simple folk, especially those in their cups. He had been enchanted by the colorful, exotic people from the circus, and when the twins who shared a body walked through the inn door, arguing loudly with each other and silencing the patrons with their strangeness, he decided then and there that these circus folk were his soul mates. These were other people who were Mother Nature's accidents—just like he was—and could understand and sympathize with his sense of dislocation from his family and their friends. Among the circus folk Pez believed he would no longer feel so different or unique and within the circus world he could hide himself—and his Lore—fully. He had been right; it had not been hard for him to melt into their numbers looking the way he did, and once the ringmaster saw him perform some acrobatics and juggle as expertly as he could, he was welcomed. Pez never did say good-bye to his family—he regretted that now—he had simply left the village in one of the many carriages that formed the circus caravan and never returned. Most of the circus people performed acts of great daring or trickery; his job was simply to make people laugh, and it wasn't hard, considering his stature and looks.

Many years later, he had been part of a small breakaway group of the circus troupe who had set off on a roving journey through the less traveled but fabled lands of the Faranel to seek new acts, and it was there, in the Faranel, that he had been captured by slaver traders and brought to Percheron. Pez was not his true name. It was the name he had adopted for the circus and it had stuck. It suited him. He wanted no memories of what had come before the happiness and companionship of the troupe.

Life had been good ever since. He had enjoyed the royal patronage that gave him power through his freedom to roam every inch of the palace, insult whomever he chose, enjoy those he truly liked, without risk, as well as the safety such power afforded him—for no one dared touch the Zar's cherished jester and companion. He could hardly complain—especially with such genuine friends as Zar Joreb, Spur Lazar, and more lately, Zar Boaz, but Pez had never been truly loved by anyone—not his family, not Joreb, and if he was truthful, not even Boaz. And yet, a few minutes ago, as he had sunk onto his knees, crying like a baby, a goddess had told him how much she loved him—unconditionally and forever.

Pez walked as if in a trance to the top of the temple, past Zafira's tiny living area, through another small trapdoor, and out onto the roof, where a warm wind blew in off the Faranel, causing the small flotilla of boats in the harbor to rock at their moorings. In spite of the warmth, he shivered. He was terrified.

Trust me, my old friend, Lyana had beseeched. And when he had tentatively explained that what she asked of him was very frightening, she had filled his body with the comfort of her soft tinkling laugh. *We always have this conversation, Iridor. You are always fearful and yet we never let each other down. Trust me now as I trust you.*

And so he trusted her now, ignoring the nagging fear as he

looked out toward Beloch and Ezram, and beyond to Star Island. He was so unnerved by the height he felt dizzied, but despite being unsteady, he forced himself to undress on the rooftop to the sound of cooing doves. He did so carefully, taking the time to reestablish a fragile sense of peace—just enough, he hoped, to give him the courage to take the first step toward giving himself over completely to Lyana. Once he committed that first physical step on the rooftop, Pez knew there would be no going back. Unwrapping the linen from his hips, he laid it softly on the discarded jamoosh. His skin trembled slightly but he wasn't sure whether it was from the caress of the warm wind or the terror of what he was about to do.

Pez took a deep, long, and slow breath. He had learned many years ago how to listen to the rhythm of his heart. He did that now, and as always, he found some measure of calm. He opened his eyes and looked down upon the rooftops of Percheron, its twinkling lights and gently moving harbor. He looked out finally to the Stone Palace, the only item of architecture that he had to look up to see. It had never looked more beautiful, glowing softly in its lantern light, high on its hill.

There was nothing more to do or think about, other than Lyana's request. Summoning every last ounce of courage, he forced himself to move, and so, naked, Pez climbed onto the balustrade, disturbing a small flock of doves who flapped away. He balanced there, willing himself to find the courage. There was no longer any choice.

For me, Pez, she whispered into his mind, and he knew he could not ever let her down.

Pez, court jester to the Zar of Percheron, opened his short arms as if in supplication to the Goddess, took the deepest breath of his life, and then, like the doves before him, launched himself off the Sea Temple toward what felt like certain death.

He waited for the ground to meet him, imagined people gathering about his dying, mangled body, muttering to one another about the waste of life. But the ground never came; instead he became aware of a comforting sensation of buffeting warm air.

Pez opened his eyes and could feel nothing but elation as he saw the great white wings spread out on either side of him.

He was an owl. Silver white, majestic, beautiful. And he was flying.

Iridor had risen.

The Percheron Saga

continues in

EMISSARY

available now in trade paperback from Eos

Turn the page for a preview of the next chapter
in Fiona McIntosh's stunning epic fantasy.

The slave held a painted silk parasol above the woman's head as she glided along, her face turned out toward the glistening Faranel. It was still only early spring, but the women of the harem preferred to keep their complexions pale, unblemished by the harsh Percheron sun. This woman was slim, taller than she had been when the slave first remembered seeing her and much more curvy, but her hair—loosely plaited today—remained its familiar brightly golden color. The eunuch slave had gotten to know her well this past eleven moons and could sense her wistfulness this morning.

"Are you in good health today, Odalisque Ana?"

"I am, Kett. Thank you for escorting me."

"You seem sad. Is there anything I can do for you?"

She smiled. "Dear Kett. I have always felt that is the precise question I should be asking you. After all you—"

The memory of Kett's emasculation had always hung between them, an unspoken grief of an evening in which both had shared much despair. On the night that Kett had been made a eunuch, Ana had been sold into the care of the palace; both had become instant prisoners of the harem.

"Don't, please, that was nearly a year ago. I am recovered and almost fully resigned to my situation." The slave shrugged. "It was never your fault."

She knew as much, but it didn't stop her feeling connected to him, sad for him. She stopped walking, pausing to stare out toward an island that was beyond the harbor but still under the watchful protection of the giant statues, Beloch and Ezram. "Why is my gaze always drawn there?" she wondered aloud. "What is that place?"

Kett looked out to sea. "It is a leper colony, Miss Ana, and although I have never visited it, I hear that it is very beautiful. Perhaps you are drawn to handsome, rugged, windswept things?"

In spite of her mood, she giggled soft amusement at his words, and touched his arm briefly, feeling how his skin shivered at her small show of affection. "You make me smile. I'm fortunate to have you in the harem."

"But, Odalisque Ana," he exclaimed softly, "everyone loves you. You are the most popular of all the women."

"Not so popular with the Valide and the Grand Master Eunuch I fear—although, Kett, I am really trying to keep my word and fit into the harem. I have not raised either's ire in many a moon."

"And yet you stare out across the water, Miss Ana, searching to escape—in spirit perhaps, if not in body?"

"Ah, Kett, you know me better than anyone," she said sadly.

"Only because I feel the same as you do. It is why I am only *almost* resigned to my situation. We both wish we could escape this place—am I right?"

"Yes, although I could admit that to no one else. I have given my word to those who care about me and made an oath to myself that I must not attempt to leave the harem again. I have learned that the repercussions often stretch painfully to others."

"You refer to Spur Lazar, I think?"

She flinched at the mention of his name. "The Spur is dead because of my irresponsible actions. I can never forgive myself."

"He would never blame you, Miss Ana. He wanted to protect you, that's why he claimed Protectorship, took your punishment." The story of the Spur's self-sacrificing decision had spread like fanned flames through the harem, firing the hearts of the young women hoping for romance in their lives—who, sadly, would probably go to their graves unfulfilled. Love did not often blossom in the harem.

"I know, but still my actions killed him," Ana said, unable to mask her pain. She changed the subject though the former Spur was still very much alive in her mind . . . and her heart. "And you, Kett, how do you cope with being a member of the harem? I suppose at least you have some small measure of freedom."

"I run errands for Grand Master Salmeo on occasion, yes."

"Do you ever think of running and never coming back?" she asked, a yearning in her tone.

"Always." He looked back at her, his wide-eyed gaze intense. "But on each occasion I have returned."

Ana's expression told him that she was assuming it was a lack of courage that brought him back to the palace each time. She tried to hide her disappointment by returning her wistful gaze to Star Island. "I wonder why?" Ana replied, finally continuing her journey into another part of the palace again. She did not see the look on the eunuch slave's face, did not appreciate the subtle message of loyalty and love that he had tried to pass to her. "I'm sure if I had your opportunity I might be tempted to break my word and my oath, for despite my strong words, the faith behind them is hollow, dear Kett. I think I am a liar to those around me and to myself."

Her friend frowned. "Please, Miss Ana, do not utter such harsh rebuke against yourself."

"But it is true," she returned calmly, waving to one of the girls who stared out from behind the latticed windows of the Sherbet Rooms. "I want to believe I would keep my promise—really, I do—but as I consider a whole lifetime stretching before me here in the harem, I think I would take any chance that came my way to escape."

"And risk death?"

"Yes," she answered without hesitation, then added softly, "For this is a living death for me anyway."

"There is a story amongst the Elim about an odalisque who did escape from the harem once." Kett hadn't meant to share this apparent myth, but it had spilled from his mouth in an attempt to lift his friend's spirits.

Ana turned her head to stare gravely at her companion. "You jest, surely?"

Kett shook his head. "Only yesterday I saw the Grand Master Eunuch laughing at the idea—the story is so old that no one knows if it is true anymore—that she persuaded one of the bundle women to carry her out in the bundle itself, and so escaped to freedom."

Ana stopped in her tracks. "Forever?" she asked, her expression incredulous. "But—"

"Hush," he cautioned, eyes frightened, gaze searching for eavesdroppers. "Let us continue, Miss Ana." He guided her forward once again.

Ana obediently began moving, but persisted, "Do you mean she was never returned to the harem?"

"Apparently they never found her. Salmeo said such a thing would never happen under his keep."

"How did the odalisque do it?" Ana demanded in a tight whisper. "What did she offer the woman?"

"She stole something and used it to bribe the bundle woman. The older Elim didn't say what it was." At the look in Ana's eyes, Kett wondered whether he might live to regret sharing this tale of escape. "Come, Miss Ana, you cannot be late for His Majesty."

"Forgive me for dawdling," Ana apologized immediately, "but I am intrigued by your tale, Kett."

"Not too intrigued, I hope. It's far too dangerous and I would hate to lose you," the slave said sincerely, hastily adding: "So would all the girls of the harem."

Ana smiled. "You're very kind. Here comes the Zar's men," she said, noticing the two mutes approaching. "I would be lying if I said I didn't enjoy these meetings with Zar Boaz. He is a very good conversationalist. We even talk in different languages sometimes. I test him on his Galinsean."

"Are you better than him?" Kett asked, impressed.

"A little," Ana admitted, conspiratorially. "I'm told I have a natural tongue for language, although linguistic skills are of little use to me here."

"You never know," Kett said. "I imagine the Zar will choose you soon, Miss Ana. It is obvious how fond of you he is."

"Not too soon, I pray," Ana replied, before fixing her veil across her face. "Thank you for the story of the odalisque, Kett. I know you told it to me to cheer me and it has." She smiled reassuringly at his trusting eyes before she turned to address the mutes, who were upon them now, with a gentle nod of her head.

He grinned and handed the parasol to the mute Salazin, who would now escort the odalisque into the private chambers of the Zar.

As he watched her petite figure retreat, dwarfed by the warriors who formed an elite guard for the Zar, Kett wondered when his former childhood playmate would take Ana for his Favorite. He suspected it wouldn't be long now, for the Zar was nearing seventeen and Ana had grown from a beautiful child into an exquisite woman.

He sighed as he realized he would very soon be forced to love this woman not just from afar, as he had this past year, but also as another man's wife. And he would have to continue to lie to her and at times to himself about his true feelings for Odalisque Ana.

1

Three moons later . . .

It was Pez's idea but it was Zafira who had found him, had seen the potential; still she was shocked by his skill. She feared for the young man, but his uncannily calm manner and quiet confidence convinced her that he was right for this curious role. He asked for no money, which made it harder for her to ask him to do what she did. And when she pressed him for his reason for taking on such personal risk, he had staggered her by confiding that all he wanted to do was serve the Goddess. At his tender age what could he know about Lyana? And yet he had been firm in his claim that he had been called by the Goddess to this dangerous task.

Now Pez echoed all her anxieties. She had hoped he would ooze his usual confidence—needed him to—but it seemed he was as unnerved as she was by this youngster.

They sat in a small room stirred gently by a soft breath of

wind that although it had journeyed halfway up the hillside of Percheron, still carried the scent of the sea. They could see the harbor from here. The massive giant statues of Beloch and Ezram gazed out across the Faranel, ever watchful for the long-feared raid that hadn't come in centuries.

"How does an orphanage command such a view?" Pez wondered aloud.

"I gather the palace gave it over to widowed wives of the Percherese Guard. Down the decades those families were given better care—separate housing, a stipend from the royal coffers—and this building became defunct. Then one Zar gifted it to the orphans of Percheron. It's still known as the Widow's Enclave."

"It's wonderful."

"Yes, although there's talk of that magnanimous act being revoked now."

"Surely not?" Pez frowned, unable to imagine Boaz drafting such an ungenerous decree.

"So the sisters quietly claim."

"What would the Zar want it for?"

"Not the Zar. I think his newly intimate adviser has designs on it."

Pez pulled a face of disgust. "Tariq is certainly carving a new role for himself."

"Well, his role is to advise the Zar, of course. But according to what you've told me, it sounds as though our last Zar never chose to have his close counsel."

"And who could blame Joreb? The odd thing is that Boaz always despised the man as much as his father did."

Zafira nodded. "I saw Vizier Tariq the other day—"

"That's Grand Vizier Tariq, Zafira," Pez interrupted, grimacing. "It's amazing what nearly a year's worth of constant ingratiation can achieve," he added bitterly.

"What is it, Pez?" she inquired gently. "Has Boaz cast you aside?"

The dwarf shook his great head. "No, but he doesn't look to me for all of his companionship now."

"He's coming up toward seventeen. He had to grow up sometime, my friend. You've been his confidant for many years. He's just spreading his wings a little," the priestess reasoned. "He has a man's job to do—little wonder he had to cast off childhood so fast."

"True." Pez sighed. "I just wish it hadn't been Tariq's arms he walked into," he complained, adding, with a tone of frustration, "The man's undergone some sort of metamorphosis."

"Well, how odd that you say that," Zafira said, leaning forward eagerly. "When I saw him the other day, we passed each other around the main fountain in the market and I hardly recognized him."

Pez frowned. "Curious, isn't it?"

"Am I deceiving myself?"

Pez gave a derisive smirk. "No, I've noticed it, too. Younger, straighter, more ... what is it?" He paused, searching for the word. "More presence. The old Tariq was weak, and his greatest weakness was craving attention from the royals. This newly invented Tariq exudes absolute confidence. He needs no endorsement from anyone, it seems. I swear he all but treats the Valide Zara with disdain."

"Well, so do you," Zafira reminded him.

"But I'm supposed to be mad, remember ... and rude to everyone—especially Herezah, whenever I can find the opportunity. Tariq has all of his faculties intact and he openly does not suffer fools gladly."

"Are you saying the Valide is a fool?"

Pez gave some semblance of a rueful grin. "Far from it, but I sense she's as baffled as I am by this relationship that seems to deepen by the day."

"And you? How does he regard you?"

"Tariq? I sense that he's suspicious of me. He watches me carefully. He thinks I don't notice, but I am aware of his constant attention."

"What is he suspicious of?"

"I don't know. He can't know the truth of my sanity, I'm sure of it, but it's as if he suspects there's more to me than meets the eye and so he keeps watching for some sign."

"Iridor?" the priestess posed, her voice a whisper.

Pez shook his head. "Why would he suspect that?"

She shrugged. "If you have magic, why not others?" she suggested, keeping her voice low. "Or perhaps it's that Tariq's jealous of your relationship with Boaz."

"It could be—that would make sense. Yet I feel as though he is searching for any slip, any small sign that I am not what everyone believes me to be. It doesn't add up, but then neither does his behavior over the past year. I need to be more attentive." Pez moved restlessly to the window to watch the children playing a boisterous game of pigball in the courtyard.

"Are you sure about him?"

"He's astounding, Pez. He can do it. But can you do it to him?"

"There are bigger things at stake than individual lives, Zafira."

"Except, if you lose enough lives individually, you can lose a nation," she counseled softly.

"Don't preach at me," Pez said mildly.

"I just need to be sure that you understand the stakes. You're gambling with his life, not yours."

"I'm aware of that, Priestess, no need to remind me," Pez replied, a spike of irritation in his voice.

Zafira responded in kind, angry that Pez wasn't helping to diminish her own guilt, and if she was honest, angry at herself for agreeing to this madness. "And I suppose I don't need to remind you that he doesn't want your money either?"

"Pardon?" Pez said, swinging around to face her. "What does he want?"

"Nothing we can give. He told me he's doing it because he serves Lyana."

Pez's expression changed from confusion to incredulity. "And you accept this?"

Zafira shrugged helplessly. "He made it clear that she had called upon him."

"Do you believe him?"

"I believe he's true, yes. He told me she first spoke to him in a dream when he was very small. She has come to him frequently since, he says. He mentioned the name Iridor but didn't seem to know what it signifies."

Pez looked deeply troubled. "I'd prefer him to accept the money," he admitted.

"I imagine it would ease your conscience."

"Zafira—" Pez began, his tone exasperated.

She interrupted him, equally frustrated. "I'm sorry, Pez, but I am fearful for this boy. What he is prepared to shoulder is frightening. We both know that should our clever plan be discovered, he will not be given an easy death."

The dwarf's irritation dissipated. His head dropped in resignation. "I know it."

The priestess heard such a depth of emotion in those three words that she hurried to soothe her friend's troubled soul. "You have equipped him well, Pez. I would be lying if I told you that he's not ready."

"I hope so." He found a sad smile. "Tell Lazar I shall visit later today. We have things to discuss. How is he?"

"Oh, angry, distant, scowling, handsome, exasperating. Need I go on?"

Pez smiled genuinely for the first time during their meeting. "That sounds promising."

She nodded, reflecting his smile. "I think he is recovered physically, yes."

"Not emotionally, though."

"Ana has scarred his heart. There are times I wish the two had never met."

"Then none of this would have happened. No, Zafira. This is Lyana's work. She is manipulating all of us. Lazar and Ana were meant to meet, though I don't understand why. What's the purpose of such a brief meeting—and one marked by such pain and suffering on both sides?"

"The Goddess works in mysterious ways, Pez. Let that be a comfort." Zafira thought briefly of the mysterious stranger Ellyana, still found it unsettling that the woman had come into their lives at a time of such high drama and then left so soon, with no warning, no farewell, and no further instructions . . . except for a caution; she had told Zafira that Iridor, the demigod in his owl form, would rise, and once that occurred, then the battle of the gods, which she had spoken about, would have begun. She had counseled that Lazar was integral to the success of the Goddess but wouldn't, or perhaps couldn't, explain why.

Zafira hadn't really understood much of it at all, but Ellyana was not one to be pressed, and then she had disappeared. They hadn't seen or heard from her in almost a year. And though Zafira had suspected who Iridor might be, she had had no idea of what his rising meant for her, or any of those who served Lyana. She was none the wiser now, although her suspicions of who the Messenger of Lyana the Goddess was had been confirmed on the night after Horz of the Elim had died. It had come as no surprise in truth, but despite her easy acceptance, she nevertheless experienced an intense feeling of awe every time she saw the beautiful snowy owl.

Pez broke into her thoughts. "It's a cold comfort but I'm glad our man is back. Now we have to discover his purpose."

"He may have already served it. He nearly died, after all."

Pez shook his head. "No. Lyana has more in store for the former Spur. We just have to be patient."

Eos Books

Celebrating 10 Years of
Outstanding Science Fiction
and Fantasy Publishing
1998-2008

Interested in free downloads? Exclusive author podcasts? Click on **www.EosBooks10.com** to celebrate our 10th Anniversary with us all year long—you never know what we'll be giving away!

And while you're online, visit our daily blog at **www.OutofThisEos.com** and become our MySpace friend at **www.MySpace.com/EosBooks** for even more Eos exclusives.

Eos Books-The Next Chapter
An Imprint of HarperCollins*Publishers*

0108